MW00476437

PEACE
AND
TURMOIL

PEACE AND TURMOIL

THE DARK SHORES: BOOK ONE

ELLIOT BROOKS

ISBN 978-1-7336643-0-1 (Hardcover Edition)
ISBN 978-1-7336643-1-8 (e-book)

Book design by Jay S. Kennedy.
Cover art by Sarah Hodgson.
Creature illustrations by Madison Crawford.
Portrait illustrations by Elliot Brooks.

elliotbrooksnovels.com

Printed in the United States of America.

For my first book, I'd like to dedicate it

to the first person who knew me, held me,

and loved me:

My mom.

ACKNOWLEDGMENTS

First and foremost, a huge thank you to my parents. You've not only loved me more than any parents could love their child, but you've taught me the meaning of hard work. I will forever be in awe at how much you accomplish with graceful hands, humble hearts, and happy smiles.

Thank you to my husband. I'm sorry you had to reread this book so many times. I'm grateful for that, and for the love and patience you have for me. I love you.

Thank you to my editor Mollie for helping take this from the ramblings of an aspiring writer to the book it is now. You were the best editor I could've asked for.

Thank you to Maddison for the amazing artwork of the fiends. I honestly don't understand how you're so talented. The fact that you're so young makes it a little depressing.

I mean inspiring.

Thank you to Jay, who made the cover and formatted the book. You walked me through way more than you should've had to. I am both appreciative and very sorry.

Thank you to Cassandra and Karen. You were the first critique partners that really made me believe my story was worth telling.

Lastly, thank you to all of you: readers, subscribers, supporters, beta readers, friends. I wouldn't have been able to do this without you.

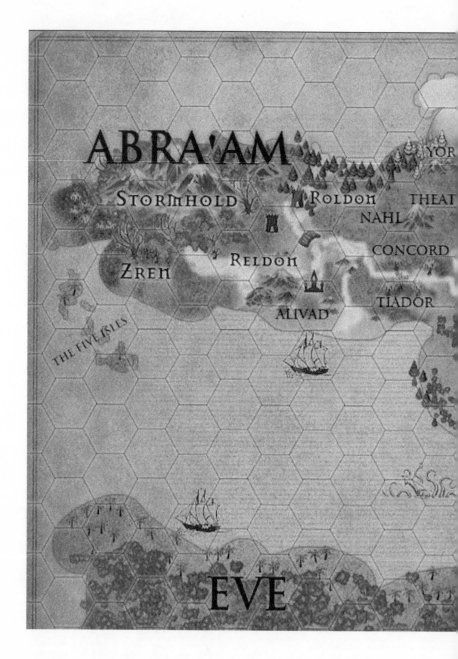

PART ONE

⚘ACROSS ABRA'AM⚘

It would be better to die than to continue living the way I live.
Not just for me and for my sanity, but for all of Abra'am.

Dietrich Haroldson

I've never seen the man aside from portraits of him as a boy. He hasn't been seen since then, so my depiction is based on my own imaginings.

From the sketchbook of Elizabeth al'Murtagh

PROLOGUE

DIETRICH

Night was coming.

Dietrich, son of Harold, son of Rorik, Cloaked Prince of Sadie, knew the night. He knew it better than most knew the voices of their loved ones. It was his. It was home.

Sovereignty, Sadie was ablaze as nightfall came. Dusk meant the yellows of the desert became orange, and the sky became purple and pink and red. Even the balcony Dietrich stood on seemed gold from the descending sun.

He watched the colors shift and change from beneath the hood of his cloak. Most of the colors sank into the clays of the capital's buildings, but some reflected from the glass domes of the hospitals and temples. If Dietrich weren't standing where he was, he'd see the coming night reflecting from the domes of his family's palace as well.

His family's, not his. It hadn't been his for years.

"Dietrich?" his mother whispered. Her voice was rasped from having just awoken. "Dietrich, is that you?"

He didn't respond. He continued to stand silent, motionless, with his back toward where she lay.

"Dietrich?"

She said his name with more urgency. He inhaled deeply and made to face her, bracing himself, but stopped.

There was blood on his shirt.

Hurriedly he wrapped his cloak around his torso. There was blood on it too, but not as much. He didn't think she'd notice it against the dark fabrics.

"It's me," he said, turning. He watched her release a breath and he released one too, grateful her eyes didn't flicker to the red on his clothes.

"It's been so long since I've seen you," she whispered. Her lips, cracked and dry, pulled into a smile.

Dietrich swallowed. From where he stood she looked so different, so weak and frail and weary. But her smile was familiar, and that pressed him forward. When he reached her bedside, he sat on his knees and embraced her.

Her smell struck him. It was foul, overwhelmingly so, and filled with the remnants of sweat from a fever and saliva from days asleep. It lay derisively against her skin and along her sheets, proving what he'd tried so hard to deny.

She was dying.

He made to hold his breath, to force the truth away, but whatever was plaguing her was tangible. He could feel it, or rather he could feel what it had done to her. Her shoulders were jutting and her collarbone dug into his chest. Her face, buried against his neck, was sharp from protruding cheekbones. Even her thick hair was thinning.

As he pulled away, the green eyes he'd looked into so many times seemed desperate to stay closed. Lenore managed to keep them open, but so many small lines of red lingered in the whites that it'd almost been easier to look at her when they were shut.

Dietrich held down the sorrow building in his chest. How could this be his mother? He understood aging, he understood wrinkling skin and graying hair, but how could he understand this? How could he fathom her deteriorating while she still lived?

He'd pulled away, but he hadn't stopped holding her. His hands still clutched firmly to her arms, afraid they'd vanish.

Perhaps this is my punishment, he thought, finally releasing her. *Perhaps this is the Creator's way of reminding me of everything I've done.*

"What troubles you?" she asked, as if knowing, as mothers always seemed to, that guilt had taken him. She lifted her hand and reached for the cloth hiding his face.

He flinched as she pulled it down. The bitter air of dusk stung against his nose and jaw.

"I like you much more like this," she insisted. She patted his cheek, then lowered herself back into her blankets. Instinctively he reached for the red and orange *auroras* in his mind, forcing them to bring heat to his palm. When he had them comfortably in his grasp, he put his hand on hers, hoping to halt her coming shivers.

"I know it's custom in Sadie to wear such a thing," she continued, eyeing the cloth she'd pulled down, "but that cloak is nothing but a facade on you. You're not the man it's made you out to be."

"I am that man," he said simply. The blood beneath his cloak, the blood he prayed she hadn't felt as he'd held her, seemed to dampen in agreement.

She sighed, then motioned for him to sit near her. He ground his teeth and complied.

She was wrong to think he was a better man than he was.

He knew that, but it would do him little good to try persuading her otherwise. He wanted her to think of him as her sweet son, remember him for the thoughtful boy he'd once been.

Better that than the killer he'd become.

"I'm sorry," she said, nestling her head against him. "I never wanted this life for you."

He bit back a swell of emotion and squeezed her hand. He thought to comfort her more, knowing her memories in that moment likely mirrored his own, but he didn't. Nothing he might say would make her feel renewed.

"Rest, Mother," he whispered, kissing her forehead. He released the fire element he'd been holding, pulled his hand from hers, and opened his mouth to ask if she wanted another blanket, but stopped when he noticed her closed eyes.

She'd already fallen back asleep.

Gwenivere is nothing likes us, Gerard. I fear for her future, because she is so strong-willed outwardly, yet compassionate inwardly. How do I raise a daughter with such a demeanor? I myself am so much the opposite.

How much longer until you're home?

From a letter between Rose and Gerard Verigrad

Chapter 1

GWENIVERE

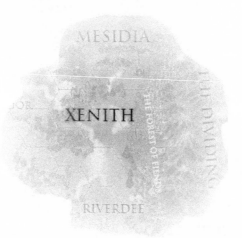

G wenivere fiddled with her Amulet and watched her brother Aden. Her eyes, strained and blurry from reading, were more occupied by the game he and his knight were playing than by her book. Their game was simple: remember where the card lay, then present its match whence found. Yet the mind always seemed to play tricks, the griffon that once appeared near the edge of the layout replaced by the icy, taunting eyes of a dragon. A simple game, truly, but so very, very frustrating.

Had it been Gwenivere and Aden playing, the number of pairs each discovered would likely be the same. He was young, five springs to her twenty, but he was a worthy opponent with a mind that rarely forgot. She waited with him as his knight Maximus turned over the first card.

A serpent, she thought, craning her neck around the knight's broad shoulders. Her eyes flickered to her own knight Garron, hopeful the statue of a man wouldn't notice the lack of attention she gave her book. Thankfully his stern gaze seemed entirely consumed with Aden and the fidgeting Maximus.

Gwenivere set her book *The Art of Calling* beside her and looked back at the cards. She rattled her brain and fingered her Amulet, knowing she'd seen the serpent's match earlier in their game.

Not in the first row, she thought, biting her lip. *Not in the second row, not in the third row, not in the fourth row . . . wait, yes! Fourth row, third in!*

She held her breath, hopeful for Maximus's pride that he would remember its location. How embarrassing it would be, a young knight of Xenith, to lose a simple game of cards to a child. A smart child, and a well-educated one, but a child nonetheless. If she were in his place, unable to best her own brother, she would order any and all taunts silent.

After surveying the card table, Maximus finally, hesitantly, reached out. He chanced a look at Aden, but the prince just smiled.

Maximus turned the card over and grunted, slapping his hand against the table. The card—not the third in from the fourth row—showed the painting of a fiend. Gwenivere thought it looked like a panther of sorts, with shadowy-black fur and tentacles for whiskers, the tips of which were painted a teal green. The tail, long and curved, looked the same, and the eyes shone a similar bluish hue.

Gwenivere scrunched her nose and tried to think through all the fiends Garron had demanded she read about. There were hundreds of them, thousands even, all with some ability to manipulate or absorb the same elements humans cast. She glanced at the tan leather of Garron's and Maximus's jackets, the stitching sewn together with the thread of were'ghul fur. Scarce, and expensive, but highly absorbent to any elements thrust their way. Even the stones of her modest crown and the bracelets along her wrists harbored such defenses, the pieces likely taken from the scales of some poor draconid. Neither though, in spite of their rarity, were made from anything like the panther creature in Maximus's hand.

"Damn game," Maximus muttered, shaking his head. He turned his mismatched cards back over, placing them where he'd found them, and slumped in his chair.

"Watch your tongue," a shaky voice called. "Such foul words around the heirs is shameful."

Gwenivere looked toward the room's entrance to find her father's knight Charles walking in. She snatched *The Art of Calling* back up, pretending to flip through its pages. He seemed not to notice, or not to care, the wrinkles around his eyes lifting as he scanned the room.

"Where's the king?" he asked. Aden, with a quiet, mocking snicker, snatched the panther card Maximus had discovered and paired it with its twin. Maximus crossed his arms and fumed.

Gwenivere thought about making some jab about how Charles of all people should know her father's whereabouts, but chose instead to bite her tongue. Despite being her father's personal knight, Charles was extremely, terribly old. Why her father insisted he continue to serve when the rest of the knights were practically half his age was beyond her. Still, her father was Gerard Verigrad, the mighty King of Peace. Whatever he commanded, she accepted.

"He retired to his chambers," she answered, tossing *The Art of Calling* aside. She stood up from her lounge chair—a gesture made more dramatic by the useless ruffles of her clothes—and tried to appear as regal as she could. The old man was always talking down to her, treating her as if she were a child. She wanted to look the authority figure she was, the princess of Xenith and the Guardian to the Amulet of Eve. The lace of her dress, though, still wrapped around the buttons of the chair, decided she should look otherwise.

Cursing under her breath, she yanked as discreetly at the fabric as she could.

Charles stared at her a moment, then as he always did, looked to Sir Garron instead.

"He's where the lady has told you," Garron answered. His voice was a low rumble as he narrowed his eyes at Gwenivere, likely noticing the incessant tugging she made at her chair. "He wasn't feeling well. If you wish to speak with him, it will have to wait."

"No!" Gwenivere finally pried herself free, annoyed as red locks of hair fell against her face. "Whatever you must speak of to my father, you can speak of to me. I hold just as much jurisdiction over Xenith as he—"

A loud banging sounded from the game table. Gwenivere flinched, let out a curse much fouler than Maximus's, and shot him a glare.

"If you're going to lose, lose with dignity!"

The knight rubbed his reddened palm and hung his head. Aden, continuing to grin, joined his new pair of cards to the stack beside him.

"I'm afraid King Gerard has asked that I deliver these messages to him directly," Charles answered. She turned back to face him, half expecting he would chastise her for her childish behavior. Instead, he shifted his hands from behind his back and revealed a pair of envelopes.

They were royal, the seals atop their covers too elegant to be from a commoner. A serpent shape lay on one, the symbol of the eastern kingdom Sadie across the Dividing Wall. Interesting, undoubtedly, but unimportant. The four-cleft leaf of the second envelope, shaped and dried from a dark-blue wax—that one had Gwenivere's attention.

She grabbed at the Amulet hanging from her neck. A chill crept down her spine when she touched the swirling jewel in its center.

"Very well then." She cleared her throat and gave Charles the warmest smile she could muster. "I shall accompany you to him."

She hoped her voice sounded as even as she intended. The letter had likely come from Roland, the prince and heir to Mesidia. He was her dearest friend, and if the term lover could be applied to a couple who had never made love, then her lover as well. But Charles had said her father ordered the letters passed directly to him. Why would he insist on such a thing? What was beneath the parchments' folds that her eyes needn't see?

She had an idea of what, she just hated admitting it. She swallowed the lump in her throat and fingered her Amulet again.

Charles stared at her before glancing back at Garron. Gwenivere frowned at him, then at Charles, then back at him again.

After a deep breath, Garron nodded.

"Your presence would be most welcome, Your Highness," Charles said. Gwenivere scoffed at the feigned reply and walked over to where Aden and Maximus sat. She grabbed two cards from their game and lay them down on the table.

"It was driving me mad," she said.

Aden and his knight looked at the cards—Behemoths, from the Age of Old—then immediately started arguing about who should get them. Gwenivere smirked and walked away, Garron and Charles following.

Paintings welcomed them as they crossed into the castle's hallway. The pieces of art were a flash of color amid the dreary place, the frames alone holding more vibrancy than the castle's grey stones. It hardly mattered what lay in the frames, the paintings themselves commonly replaced for newer or prettier ones from down another hall. By the time Gwenivere had time to notice one, to grow fond of the scene it depicted, it would be gone. Not completely gone, of course—her father would never be so wasteful. Just simply someplace else within the castle. So many of her mornings had been lost trying to find the paintings she fancied that she no longer fancied any at all.

Regardless, the paintings supplied a strange comfort. Her

mother had loved art, no matter the kind, and had spent their wealth extravagantly to support anyone with an easel and a brush. Musicians too, and poets and bards—anyone and everyone who considered themselves masters of finer things. Gwenivere wondered if that was the reason her father still kept the paintings everchanging, to keep thoughts of her mother alive. The Light knew his heart was a duller vessel without her presence.

The door to his chambers lay shut as she approached. He never used to hold his privacy so dear, but he seemed to value solitude much more as of late. Gwenivere lifted her fist, stopped to brush any loose strands of hair back behind her ears, then gave the door a heavy tap.

"Father, may I enter?" she asked. The pleasantness she forced tasted bitter as she glanced back at Charles and Garron. What senseless circles they insisted on spinning over a few letters.

"Yes," she heard through the door. The usual booming of her father's voice seemed muffled. "Come in."

The smell of burning wood hit Gwenivere as she entered, a fire crackling from the cutout near the room's bed. Wet wood smelled too, and the glass of a nearby window was open as small patters of rain fell against a desk. How odd of him to both warm and chill his chambers.

He's getting old and strange like Charles, she thought, noting the grey that streaked her father's hair. It had been nearly black, years ago, but not anymore. Not since her mother had passed and Aden was born.

"Gwenivere, to what do I owe the pleasure?" Gerard returned the portrait of her mother he held to the drawer of his dresser. Gwenivere knew she was likely mistaken, but she swore the tiniest drops of red were speckled against the portrait's face.

She clasped her Amulet as she tried to collect her thoughts.

Thankfully, Charles's sudden wheezing snapped her back into focus.

"We have letters!" She whirled around and reached to take the parchments from the knight, who stood with his free hand shielding his face. Garron, still a constant, looming presence, settled himself in the room's corner.

"Charles, if you please?" Gwenivere said, extending her hand out more. The knight concluded his fit of wheezing and furrowed his bushy brows, looking to the king.

"It's fine, Charles, thank you."

The old knight nodded and handed Gwenivere the parchments. She didn't bother hiding her annoyance as she snatched them from his bony hands and pointed toward the door.

"You've done your duty. Return to guard the hallway and allow us some privacy."

Charles's expression was blank. He merely stared at her a moment, glanced at her pointing finger, then looked toward the king.

Infuriating.

"Go on," Gerard said. His voice was sympathetic, but his dark-blue eyes, which stared straight at Gwenivere, were not. After twenty years, she still couldn't help but cower under his gaze.

Charles gave no indication of impatience or annoyance. He simply dragged his haggard feet along and left.

Thank the Light, Gwenivere thought. She brought her sunken shoulders back up and faced her father.

"Was that necessary?" he asked, cutting her off as she opened her mouth. She tried again to speak, then sealed her lips, knowing she needed to think through whatever rash, overzealous thing she was about to say. Her father was the King of Peace. Friendly manipulation was his forte.

"These letters." She lifted the parchments up for him to see. "Was there a reason you insisted I not be permitted to read them? You often insist I be ready to take Xenith's throne, but how might I accomplish such a deed when I'm so frequently ill informed?"

Her fingers went numb as she made her confrontation. Her father was known for being intimidating and evoking humility. He was a head taller than most and always dressed in black, the clothing he adorned never truly hiding his soldier's physique. The dark beard along his jaw, trimmed but thick, shadowed the face of a kind yet shrewd leader. What a contrast he had made to the slender, red-haired queen with the pale skin and pretty lips. What a contrast indeed.

He never scared Mother, though, Gwenivere thought, running her finger across the smooth blue wax of Mesidia's seal. Gerard was allowing the forwardness of her query to linger and die in the sound of the rain and the crackling fire. *He doesn't scare me . . .*

"Those are merely confirmation of our allies' attendance," he finally said. He crossed his arms over his barreled chest and leaned against his desk. It creaked beneath the strain of his weight.

"Xenith is to host a gathering and masquerade," he continued, "for the thirty years of peace since the War of Fire. All nations, friend or foe, are asked to attend, in hopes that we can convince the greedy to humble themselves, perhaps sway the bloodthirsty to drink from another cup."

He held his hand out to her. She shut the mouth she only just realized hung open and handed the parchments over.

As if to torture her, her father tossed the Mesidian letter onto his desk and began opening the one from Sadie. The raindrops from the open window soaked into the parchment as the thunder outside bellowed a hearty, mocking laugh.

Gwenivere clenched her fists and closed her eyes. In her mind, the bright colors of her *auroras* raged.

They beg for me to burn him, she thought, noting how

strongly the streaks of red flickered. She opened her eyes and felt her palms grow warm, tempted then to humor the elements and make her father's bottom burn. Not anything damaging, of course, just something to make him squirm a little.

A sudden glare from him, as if knowing her thoughts, shoved the fire away.

"Sadie will be sending someone," he said, looking back down at the letter. "Prince Dietrich, it says. How interesting." His attention seemed lost as he pursed his lips and nodded. "Is that not fascinating, Gwenivere? The Cloaked Prince himself. Perhaps the insurgence of the East has finally settled."

Gwenivere cared little for the affairs across the Dividing Wall. She only cared about Roland, and his letter, currently continuing to soak beneath the window. With hardly a thought, she felt the swell of her clear *auroras* just before the air in the room closed the window shut. She jumped at the sound and gasped as her father released a surprised, heavy breath. Beside them, Garron continued to stand in silence.

"I'm sorry," she stuttered. She was, truly, though her frequent temper made it difficult to seem sincere. The window shutting was not the first time her anger had released unintended elements. Aden, since the day he was born, carried the mark of a burn against his belly. Gwenivere had not possessed any aversion toward him then, nor had she meant to cause him harm, but she'd hated that her brother's life had stolen away their mother's. She hoped her father believed her apology now more than he'd believed it then.

"Will . . . will anyone from Mesidia be attending this gathering?"

Gerard's chest heaved as he tossed the Sadiyan envelope on the desk. He opened the window back up, cool air returning.

"Dorian," he answered. "And the al'Murtagh siblings. I've been told by the duke that Natalia will be attending as well."

But no Roland, Gwenivere thought. She hardly had a moment to think about anyone else, or wonder how her father knew without opening the letter.

"I see." Her fingers were running over the Amulet of Eve again, but she chose not to fight it. Somewhere, hopefully, Roland was holding the Dagger of Eve, loving it for its connection to her but loathing it for keeping them apart.

"If you expect me to choose a husband at this gathering, I . . . I cannot. I'm not ready." Gwenivere pulled her hand from her Amulet and returned it to her side. She opened her mouth to speak again, but her father's hand rose to silence her.

"It will not be long before Xenith is bestowed unto you." There was a graveness in his words, and a sadness, but the terse tone of his voice demanded she keep quiet.

"You are to ensure our prosperity, make certain we will not only flourish but aid our neighbors in the path to affluence. You are also to protect the Amulet of Eve as every Guardian in your lineage has before you. I have faith in you, faith that you will fulfill these roles, but I fear what terrors face you if you accept them on your own." Gerard reached forward and took Gwenivere's hands in his. His lips pulled into a defeated smile.

"You understand this, yes? You understand how I fear for you—my treasured daughter? Abra'am's kingdoms have kept peace for thirty years, but it was not always this way, and it will not be this way forever. I wish terribly to know you will have someone to rule alongside you when the time comes." He lifted his arm up and brushed away the red strand of hair that fell against her face.

Her lips tightened.

"I understand." She pulled away and looked to the floor, ashamed to face the man she knew only wished her protected.

"At least," she added, "do me the decency of admitting what my part in this gathering is. Please. I care little for being leashed like a hound." She looked back up, the fury of being forced to marry more refined then her blur of guilt. "You wish me to pick a husband, don't you?"

Gerard sighed, a frown visible beneath his beard. He pulled away and leaned further against his desk.

"I don't wish it, Gwenivere." He crossed his arms and stared down with conviction. "I command it."

I remember my grandfather telling me stories of when people thought called weapons evil. He said those were the better days, but he was a blacksmith. He likely just missed the profits of selling his touched blades so readily.

Mesidian merchant

CHAPTER 2

ROLAND

THE ARCTIC

MESIDIA

YENDOR

THEATIA

XENITH

R oland studied the elk and slowly lifted his bow. It felt almost weightless in his hands, as all *called* weapons and shields should, the black *auroras* perfect in balancing their creations. Even so, holding the arrow in his mind and keeping its path true was far more difficult than wielding a *called* blade. At least in close combat a blade was always attached, and the hilt was always present in the hand. The *auroras* were tangible as a sword, even if the sword had no weight at all.

Bows were vastly different. Disjointed from their arrows, they existed in different and unique parts. It took multiple threads in the mind to connect such parts, and the threads distanced further still when the *called* arrow was released. Thus the bowman had to imagine more than just his arrow. He had to imagine the arrow within the air, and the resistance the air would give. He had to know the angle the arrow would take and what it would feel like when the arrow pierced its target. And, once the arrow struck, the bowman had to know what it would feel like for the arrowhead to wedge itself in its target's flesh.

It took a master of manmade *touched* bows to know how to use a mind-made *called* one.

Roland grinned and took aim at the elk.

The right eye is dominant, he told himself. *Rely on it too much and you miss by half a yard. And there shall be no such mistake with Dorian watching.*

Roland breathed in, deeply but silently, the coolness of the forest air filling his lungs. They burned, his chest muscles stretched as he pulled the bowstring to its fullest. Such a distance was necessary, the massive animal having likely heard the wood of his *called* bow straining. He could see its ears twitching as it grazed.

He tilted his bow upward, only a degree or two, took one last breath, and released.

The arrow's path held true as it struck with a *thump*. Had it been a *touched* weapon—a manmade weapon—the animal likely would've fled, and he'd have needed to chase it down to where it eventually collapsed and died. *Called* weapons, which were crafted with the strength of the black *auroras*, were stronger than any weapon a blacksmith or bowyer made. Roland relaxed as the elk fell to the ground.

"Impressive!" Dorian said. Mesidia's ambassador sprung from where he sat, the dark mud of the forest clinging to the thick wool of his clothes. His black hair blended with the black of his wolf cloak, the pelt draping over his shoulders and down to his boots. He was like an elegant shadow, mud and all, the mud only seeming to give his regal look more demand. Roland might have been jealous, if he cared of such things, but at that moment he only cared about his kill. Humility existed in his silence, but not in his thoughts. He doubted the ambassador had ever made such a shot.

He exhaled slowly and *vanished* his weapon, his body instantly releasing the tension it held. All of his tutors told him black *auroras* used less energy than colored ones, that *called* weapons were better for hunts than elements. One could hold *called* weapons for longer, they claimed, than a vine trap or an arrow of ice. He hardly believed such insistencies in that moment, his every muscle grateful as the bow disappeared. Beneath his own wolf cloak, beads of sweat dripped.

"You said you hunted as a tyke, yes?" Roland asked.

Dorian shrugged indifferently and nodded.

"Aye, but only for small game. Rabbits, squirrels, anything I could skin and eat myself. That was over twenty years ago, before your parents took me in. Since then, I haven't hunted for anything."

Haven't hunted for anything? How strange a thing to hear in Mesidia. All men in their kingdom hunted. Light, most women in their kingdom hunted. Women were actually—usually—better at it. Roland's mother said it was because women were more patient. *Animals require time and focus to be killed,* she said, *and men have neither.*

Dorian was not truly Mesidian, though, but Yendorian. It wasn't a secret; his olive-tinted skin, gold eyes and black hair would certainly have made it a difficult secret to keep if it was. No Mesidian shared such a blend of features. Most, rather, looked a spitting image of Roland: blond, stocky, and blue eyed. And, according to the lovely Gwenivere Verigrad of Xenith, Roland was the least attractive of them all.

Blasted girl, he thought with a grin. He reached instinctively to the Dagger of Eve along his thigh and rested his fingers against its hilt. His grin quickly deepened to a frown.

"Your cousins told me you were good at hunting," Dorian said. "William especially. Peter tends to agree, but then insists he's better."

Roland chuckled, releasing the Dagger.

"I'm better than my father too, but he'll never admit it."

"Don't say that too loud," Dorian whispered jestingly. He crouched down and opened his gold eyes wide. "He's around somewhere!"

The sound of Roland's laugh seemed to pull King Pierre out of his place of hiding. His lids were thin as he peered toward them, the sharp, intense blue of his gaze marking him either upset or freshly awoken. Roland could certainly imagine his father had used the hunt for napping, as he was often weary and distressed from settling Mesidia's civil disputes. He was strong for his age, and still surprisingly lean, but no amount of muscle could fend off fatigue. The flecks of leaves in his hair proved as much.

"We shall feast tonight," Pierre said, the sound of his boots almost noiseless as he made his way to the fallen elk. Roland stood patient and said nothing as his father surveyed the animal. Even if it was the largest elk in all Mesidia, he knew his father would give him no praise.

They wasted little time skinning it. Both Roland and his father stood at a different point, *touched* hunting blades steady as they made incisions near the beast's joints. Dorian, not being either the king or the elk's killer, was forced to bear the burden of proving the elk a bull, as they had no means to carry back the antlers and killing a cow was illegal. He glanced displeasingly between the elk's legs and carried out his task with as much dignity as he could, then tied the small pouch to his horse.

It was tempting to tease him, deliver reprisal for all the taunts Dorian had given him as a boy, but Roland kept quiet. Mocking glances were amusement enough.

"Elk is Gwenivere's favorite, is it not?" Dorian asked, walking back to them. "Perhaps I shall bring her some when I depart for the celebration."

Pierre looked up with narrowed eyes, nostril's flaring. Roland noted the glare, surprised, but ignored it.

"Celebration?" he asked. The elk's shoulder ground loudly

as he broke it. "When do we leave?"

The ambassador grimaced, looking down. Not down, truly, but away.

"Not we," Pierre answered. The cold blue of his gaze turned remorseful as he faced Roland. The grip on his hunting knife tightened. "You and your mother and I are to stay in Mesidia. Dorian will travel without our company."

Roland squinted and looked searchingly between the two men. They were guilty—both of them—of harboring some secret, each tightening their jaws and gritting their teeth. Instantly Roland reached for the Dagger of Eve at his side, fearful suddenly that the celebration meant Gwenivere betrothed. It was perfectly plausible. She'd been writing to him for some time that Gerard was pressing her to marry. But she would have told him, would have written him the moment she chose a suitor. He had always assured her he would not begrudge her when she did. He would only begrudge the Dagger he currently held.

Cursed thing, he thought, glancing at his side. The jewel in the Dagger's hilt glowed slightly, the swirling colors shifting and shining through his clenched palm. It was so aggravatingly queer, the jewel dancing from green to blue to violet. He wanted to stab it into the elk and bury it deep in its flesh. At least then, maybe, he would be free of its incessant glow.

"Xenith is our greatest ally," he said, meeting his father's gaze. "Perhaps it would convey a false sense of abandonment if Mesidia's royal family were not in attendance."

Pierre shook his head and returned to skinning the elk. "It's an ambassador's duty to represent the royal family when our presence isn't needed." He carefully peeled the hide back. "Do you not trust Dorian to fulfill his role?"

Roland grunted and eyed the ambassador for answers. Dorian kept quiet, likely pulled between his loyalty to the king and his sympathy for the prince.

A bloody coward.

"What I don't trust," Roland said, looking back to his father, "is how you waltz about this." He released the Dagger and pulled another *touched* carving blade from his calf, plunging it into the animal's shoulder and ripping it apart. He could feel Pierre watch him as he rested the meat against the opened hide, careful even in his confrontation not to dirty it against the soil on the ground.

Pierre stabbed his own *touched* knife into the mud and brushed off his palms, then stroked the bit of stubble along his jaw. "Fine. You're right, you're a man now. I should be able to speak to you as such.

"King Gerard is hosting a masquerade, a Peace Gathering, to celebrate Abra'am's thirtieth year without war. He intends for Gwenivere to find a husband there and have her wed shortly after. You're not to attend, nor are you to see her again, until this has occurred."

The king stopped abruptly, his words returning with an echo from the forest. He looked down at the elk before him, then stared at his carving knife again before yanking it up and meeting it with the kill.

Roland ground his teeth but didn't reply, careful to mind each piece of the animal he tore apart.

The trek back to Stonewall Castle was a quiet and somber one. Dorian would occasionally open his mouth, likely in an attempt to say something jesting or uplifting, then close it when Roland gave him a scowl.

Pierre's rigid shoulders and squinting eyes were no help

either. The king hadn't always been a stubborn man, but the carefree nature of his youth had been stripped away by the trials kingship bestowed. Blood boiled in many Mesidians' hearts that he was their ruler, the Victorian rebels scattered across the land having gained in numbers despite his efforts. Civil dispute had long rooted itself in their history, the kingdom torn in two when the Dagger of Eve was forced into unworthy hands. Those hands had belonged to Roland's ancestors, and though generations had passed since the act had been done, time had yet to heal the wound the Victorian rebels felt.

Such pressing weight and expectations left the king unsympathetic toward many matters. Roland would receive no pity from him.

Up ahead, with sandy-blond hair and simple blue garb, the al'Murtagh family stood. They would be a welcomed deterrence. The coldness between Roland and his father and Dorian was almost colder than the Mesidian air itself.

It seemed the al'Murtaghs had just arrived, servants from within Stonewall Castle bustling about to tend to the five royals' horses. Catherine, Pierre's sister, beamed when she saw them, both Roland and his father temporarily abandoning their fury as they dismounted and feigned happy greetings. The short woman ran over to Roland and clutched his face, pinching his cheeks and kissing him smack on the lips.

"My goodness, Roland, look how handsome you are!" She gave a mocking glance at Pierre before shaking her head, then squinted and studied their faces. "You know, I think Rosalie may have had some other men around when you were off training your Elite soldiers, Brother. Roland has your hair—or what *used* to be your hair—but where he got that perfect jaw is beyond me!"

Roland's grin was halfhearted as his lips remained shut.

"Careful how loud you jest," Pierre warned. "The Victorians will hear jokes that Rosalie was adulterous and tell the rest of the kingdom it's true. You already know Yvaine has spread her fair share of rumors."

Roland watched Dorian grimace as Catherine's eyes turned toward him. The woman had never completely accepted Pierre's choice to bring Dorian into the family. He was a man who evoked whispers, a man who the Victorian rebels insisted was Pierre's bastard from a Yendorian whore. No matter how often they dispelled the lie, some still believed it fervently.

Thankfully Roland's cousins were all smiles and hugs as they embraced him and Pierre. William, the eldest of the three and the stockier of the brothers, smiled at Roland as an equal, never having been sheepish or shy. He made his way to Dorian as well, despite his mother's glare, and wrapped his arms around the ambassador.

"Who made the kill?" he asked, his head cocking to the meat the servants took away. His hooded eyes widened when Dorian and Pierre each pointed to Roland. It really wasn't a surprise. Roland was the best bowman among the three, but William acted jovial nonetheless. He smacked his rough hand proudly into Roland's chest and beamed.

"You'll have to tell us all about it when we dine. Or perhaps before. I'm not sure Elizabeth will want to hear about killing while she's eating."

The party all turned to Elizabeth, who blushed furiously. She was the most delicate thing in Mesidia, a little, simple bloom that refused to die away in the harshness of their land. She looked a spitting image of her mother, though perhaps a little more attractive, but Roland supposed it was youth that made it so. She was pale and rosy-cheeked, with light lashes and dull-colored hair. Even if her brothers didn't guard her so protectively, she would still not be the royal most men would eye. Nonetheless, her pleasant, docile nature made her pretty. Dorian exchanged a smile with her, and Catherine flashed another disapproving glare.

"I'll listen to your tale whenever you wish to tell it," Elizabeth insisted. She brushed aside the short strands that blew against her cheek before Peter shoved her aside.

"My pa and I killed one bigger!" The scrawny youth pointed back toward his father Joel, the quiet, long-nosed man standing beside his wife with a mischievous look in his eye. Peter's eyes held the same mischief.

"Really, though, you think I jest, but it was, oh, I don't know, maybe twice that size."

"My, that's really impressive, Peter," Dorian muttered. Roland stood silent as he watched the ambassador glance again at Elizabeth, her brows furrowed at her brother's outlandish remarks. The red in her cheeks deepened when she saw Dorian's smirk.

"Not to ruin this grand reunion," Pierre said, "but my feet ache, and I yearn for a bath." He gestured to his furred clothes, then back toward Roland's and Dorian's. "As you can see, we've had a long day of hunting. There's a considerable amount of blood under all this dirt."

The al'Murtagh family nodded in understanding, each filing in line as they followed behind Pierre. Roland listened absently as Peter continued to tell the tale of his and Joel's kill, Joel occasionally nodding impishly whenever Peter looked to him for confirmation. Catherine and William quickly abandoned listening to the exaggerated ramblings and chose instead to speak with Pierre and Elizabeth. Roland walked in the back beside Dorian, his feet trailing behind as he brushed his thumb against the Dagger.

"Whose horses are those?" Peter asked. The party turned toward the stables the royal pointed to and noted the white stallions standing beside the other mounts.

"Duke Bernard's, and Natalia's," Pierre answered. His weathered face hardened as he said the names. "The Duchess Yvaine has chosen not to join them, though."

An air of anger emerged from the group. None of them cared for the Barie family, the Duchess Yvaine most of all. Roland found himself relieved she hadn't accompanied her pig-faced husband and devious daughter, the invitation a political courtesy alone, but the idea that she was absent was reason for concern. She was the one who championed the Victorian rebels' claims and insisted the Dagger of Eve and Mesidian crown should be restored to her husband's family.

If she wasn't there, it likely meant she was busy with the rebels.

It hardly helped matters that Dorian had once been her daughter's betrothed.

"Will Bernard and Natalia be dining with us tonight?" Elizabeth asked, always first to break the silences. She shivered in the cold and chanced at a smile.

"Yes," Pierre answered grimly. "They will."

Roland ignored the rest of the conversation as he glanced back at Dorian, wondering how the ambassador was faring with his former betrothed nearby. Natalia was hardly any different than the deceitful Yvaine, only more beautiful and slightly less conniving. Not surprisingly, Dorian was no longer in sight.

"If you'll excuse me, I'm going to head to my chambers," Roland said. He realized it was the only thing he'd said to his family, and his words were laced with an unintended gruffness. Knowing it was too late to mend that, he gave them each a courteous nod, then quietly slipped away.

He hoped Dorian had simply retired to his rooms. It'd been a long morning, and a long ride's return. He supposed Pierre's mention of the baths had simply drawn Dorian off, or perhaps the constant, hateful glances from Catherine had set off Dorian's nerves. Either way, the ambassador's own chambers would be best. If he were in them, then Roland could head to his own.

Dorian's current rooms had once been the ones Roland

slept in as a boy. Before the Victorian rebels' uprising, when Dorian was still considered Pierre's son and next in line for the crown, the opulence of heir and eldest child were given to him. Roland didn't begrudge him for it. He'd never cared that the Laighless bloodline might be carried on through a man with no Laighless blood. The way he saw it, Dorian was his elder brother, and a perfectly suitable choice for king. The Laighless followers, devout and steadfast, thought so as well.

Now Dorian dwelled in the lesser of their chambers, and Roland was forced to guard the Dagger of Eve.

"Dorian," he called, tapping on the ambassador's door. He heard footsteps, but light, dainty ones. He knocked again. "Dorian!"

The door swung open, a full-chested servant staring flushed and wide-eyed. Her cheeks grew red as she curtsied.

"Milord," she said quickly. She opened her mouth to say more, but Roland held up a hand.

"Is Dorian with you?" he asked. It was an implying query, certainly, and her blushing deepened. It was hardly a secret between the two men that Dorian enjoyed the company of the castle's maids. "Has he come by here?"

The curls atop the maid's head bounced as she shook her head. "No, sire, Master Dorian hasn't returned yet. Shall I fetch him for you?"

Roland raised a brow. "Do you know where he is?"

Again, red cheeks. And an embarrassed frown.

"No, milord."

Roland nodded. He saved the servant any further humiliation and walked away.

If not in his own rooms, that likely meant Dorian was in Natalia's chambers. Though Roland wished to help the man, he had no desire to be anywhere near the duchess-heir.

No servants waited with plunging necklines as Roland walked into his bedchambers. Unlike the ambassador, Roland didn't mend his aching heart by burying himself in the arms of random women. He never saw the appeal. What good would a few moments of passion do him when it was Gwenivere he desired? What would seconds of fulfilled lust matter when the woman in his bed wasn't his beloved?

They would do nothing. His flask, though, filled with bitter, belly-warming liquid, would do him all sorts of good.

He grabbed it from his bedtable and took a swig. All sorts of good indeed.

He sat awhile in silence, dwelling on what his father had told him in the forest. He supposed he understood why Gwenivere hadn't spoken with him, why she hadn't written him for some time. Knowing Gerard, she was likely forbidden to communicate with him anyway. The bloody King of Peace was always protective of her.

Piss-petty whoreson, Roland thought, taking another drink. The liquid burned down his throat and into his stomach, easing away the chill in his weary bones. He shook his head and drank again. *Lightless bastard.*

Knowing it useless to sulk, he stood from where he leaned and headed to his bathing room. It was large, and nearly windowless, the giant, pool-like tub embedded in the ground making it more a bathhouse than a private chamber. It must have taken the servants half the day to warm the water, given how weak many of them were with *auroras*. Anyone could use their elements, but that didn't mean everyone was good with them. When one's profession consisted of menial tasks—washing clothes, tidying rooms, readying baths—there wasn't really a need to become proficient in *calling*. It took a great deal of time and effort to master, much like playing an instrument; everyone had the capability to learn, but few rarely got beyond the basics.

Without knowing how long he'd be hunting with his father and Dorian, Roland could only imagine how many times the servants had come back to reheat the water. Feeling guilty, he unstrapped the *touched* blades at his sides, along with the Dagger of Eve, then slowly removed his muddied cloak and clothes. He realized he should have brought a towel, or at least something to change into, but the temptation of the steam called. He walked in with flask in hand, welcoming the warmth of the water's embrace.

It didn't take long before the cold in his body began to fade. He leaned back and closed his eyes, his arms resting along either side of the bath's edge. Sweat dripped down his face and his chest, meshing perfectly with the clear waters, and the smell of musky soap filled his nose. Gwenivere had always said that smell made him seem like an old man, but he knew she was fond of it. As a jest, he would rub the occasional letter with it, see if she would mention it in her next response. She never did. She hated giving him the satisfaction.

He knew she noticed, though.

Light, I miss her, he thought, recalling the soft wave of her hair. It was red, the most stunning, subtle shade, and her eyes shone an alarming turquoise beneath frequently arched brows. She was not perfect, her nose almost too straight and her smile crooked, but Roland thought her the most beautiful thing he'd ever seen. He cursed the Dagger of Eve and her Amulet for keeping them apart. He opened his eyes to glare at it, make it feel his hatred, but it wasn't where he'd left it.

He sat upright. He'd placed the Dagger by his other knives with the hilt beneath his clothes to hide the glowing jewel. Panicked, he tossed his flask aside and grabbed at his clothes, hoping it was there.

It wasn't.

"Looking for something?"

Roland spun around. In the room's corner, wearing nothing but a thin silk shift, stood Natalia Barie. The Dagger twirled between her fingers.

"You really should be more careful as its Guardian," she said. "Wouldn't want someone *calling* on its immortality, would we?"

She stopped spinning it and held out its jewel.

Roland's jaw ached as he clenched his teeth.

"You seem quite stiff for someone bathing," she said. "Perhaps it might help loosen you up if I join."

She bit her lip and took a step forward. Slowly she emerged from the shadows, her silvery-gold hair falling to the center of her waist. Her body moved gracefully as she lowered herself into the other end of the pool, the clinging silk of her shift leaving no curve of her figure unnoticed. The Dagger stayed firm in her grasp.

That wasn't good. Never mind that she was Dorian's former betrothed—she was the daughter of his family's political rivals. He needed to get the Dagger back from her.

"Leave, Natalia," Roland commanded. His shoulders heaved and his breath escaped in loud bursts, but he managed to keep his words even. "Now."

A devilish laugh escaped Natalia's lips. "And miss this sight? Why, Roland, how dare you deprive me of such a thing."

She placed the Dagger tip against the stones beside her and twirled it between her fingers again. The glowing of its jewel danced off the water's surface.

"You've heard by now that Gwenivere is to find another, have you not?"

Roland said nothing.

"I'll assume yes. Perhaps now, knowing such a thing, you can move on from your obsession."

"And what, marry you?" He chuckled and sat back down. "You're quite the jester, Barie."

Natalia's smile widened. "As are you, Laighless. To lead on that poor, freckled wench for all these years when you knew Guardians were forbidden to marry. Quite the jester indeed."

Roland's temper flared, but he forced another smile. He'd repay that insult to Gwenivere, but not yet, not today. He could do nothing while Natalia still held the Dagger.

As if sensing his worries, Natalia halted the Dagger's spinning. She held it up and examined it, icy blue eyes shining as the jewel glowed against them.

"What do you imagine Dorian would think if he knew I was in here?" she asked. "What do you imagine, a man that's practically your brother, would think of you bathing with his former betrothed?"

Roland shrugged. "Nothing. At least, nothing of me. For you, well, he knows your ways."

Natalia let out a throaty laugh. Strangely enough, it sounded somewhat sincere.

"I shall see you at the feast tonight," she said. She tossed the Dagger aside and backed away. "Don't mind me if I borrow this." She picked up his wolf cloak and brushed off the dirt, then swung it over her shoulders and walked out of the chamber.

Roland knew she would smirk at every stable hand who noticed his cloak and nod at every servant that smelled his scent. Then, more than likely, she would torture Dorian, flaunt their obvious visit until she had all but convinced him she'd shared Roland's bed. Angered and helpless, Roland splashed the steaming water against his face and released the breath he held.

If there was one thing he could be grateful for, it was that she'd gone. And, appallingly, that she'd left the Dagger of Eve behind.

Roland's kill had been prepared for the evening's feast.

The Laighless, the Barie, and the al'Murtagh families all

convened for it. Pierre sat at the head of the table, Queen Rosalie removed from her seat across from him to give the illusion of power to Duke Bernard VII. There the two men sat, one at either end of the elegant wood, both exerting their dominance as a dog claims its ground. Natalia was to the left of her father, like Rosalie to the right of her husband, the queen's stature diminished to that of the duchess-heir. Between them were Elizabeth and her parents, and on the other side, drunk and jesting, sat Peter and William. Roland's place, unknown to him until he entered the hall, was between Natalia and Dorian. As the kitchen maids brought out the feast, only the al'Murtagh brothers seemed excited. Peter's hands brushed together as he looked at the food eagerly.

"Is this elk?" Rosalie asked. Pierre's eyes immediately found the ambassador's.

"Yes," Dorian replied, nodding to the queen. An amused smile lit his face. "I assure you, no laws were broken in its killing. A gift from our great hunt today was actually given to the duchess-heir. Or rather, left at her door. I'm afraid she wasn't present when I stopped by her chambers, but I'm sure she'll be happy to show you the gift later."

A gift? The only thing from their hunt Dorian had taken was the elk's . . .

Roland looked up from the wine glass he'd been about to bury himself in. Dorian, at his side, was wearing an extremely proud smile.

At the end of the table, Pierre's face paled.

"Perhaps it's better Natalia doesn't open it," Rosalie said, catching her husband's expression. "She should keep it, as a safe token for her trip with you to Xenith."

The loud clanging of cutlery sounded.

"*She's* coming with us?" Peter asked. Roland shook his head slightly as Duke Bernard scowled and Natalia smiled.

"Yes," Rosalie answered. "King Gerard's invitation was to

all of you. Now please, let us say thanks."

She took her husband's hand and her wine glass, lifting it up. The table joined in raising their own glasses, each taking a drink before beginning to eat.

Roland could feel Natalia watching him, her slender fingers refilling his cup each time it emptied. Any concerned glances from Elizabeth were met by Natalia's harsh gaze, which in turn made Elizabeth cower. Roland decided to pay it no mind. His ears and eyes caught bits and pieces of the conversations that carried on across the table.

"The fiend made me sit here," he heard Peter whisper to Dorian. Roland could see the ambassador hold his breath until Peter's statement was over, careful not to let the ill-smelling remark come too close to the air he took in.

"What?" he asked.

"My sister." Peter pointed his cutting knife toward Elizabeth. She'd likely heard, as Peter's whispers were hardly quieter than a normal man's speech, but she continued to keep her head down, eyes on her plate.

"I would've had her sit beside you," Peter continued. "I know she wanted to, but that former betrothed of yours wouldn't let me."

"Wouldn't let you?" Dorian asked. "Come now, Peter, you're a man. Are you really going to let an empty threat keep your sister and me from sitting by each other?"

"Please, no one thinks me a man."

The ambassador chuckled, his gold eyes looking across the table at Elizabeth. Her cheeks flushed when she caught his gaze. She took a sip of wine, followed immediately by a sip of water.

"Never, not even in your dreams, Ambassador," William whispered. He shook his head and poked Dorian with a knife from behind Peter's back. "You'd have to duel me first."

Dorian swatted the knife away and grinned. "Perhaps I might."

The conversation faded as another started. The party continued in their merriment, feigned and genuine, the emotions dependent solely on the person and the conversation at any particular time. Each reaction, excitable or irritable, was enhanced as the night carried on. All the elk the kitchen maids had prepared was cleared long after the first bottle of wine, and a course of the finest delicacies were brought out on Pierre's request.

Roland managed to keep his anger hidden, his usual carefree nature suppressed by the continual flow of liquid that met his lips. If not filled by Natalia, it was Peter filling his cup, a secondary but considerate gesture after filling his own. William filled it too as he challenged Roland to sparring matches in weapons both *called* and *touched*, each gamble confirmed by a pour and a clink of glasses. Even Dorian joined in the wine giving, which seemed more a gleeful gesture than a personal one.

Despite his now-blurred senses, Roland felt something resting against his leg. He looked down from his plate, noting Natalia's hand resting against his thigh. It was out of sight from watchful eyes, the table's surface covering it. With careful fingers, she took a key from beneath her dinner cloth and slid it under his.

"If you feel so inclined," she whispered.

Roland bit the inside of his cheek, grabbing the key angrily and hiding it in his palm. He didn't want to risk picking up the dinner cloth later and revealing it there, not with Dorian sitting just beside him.

"I'm guessing this is to the guest chambers my parents granted you?" he whispered tersely, leaning in close. Natalia's answer came in the form of a smile, one that seemed to ask if he was serious.

"I see. You're nothing if not persistent. You must know by now that I despise you."

He pulled away, not wanting to risk attention with his hushed remarks. Dropping the key intentionally on the floor, he reached out and grabbed his wine. Natalia's hand continued to travel, shifting between light and firm motions.

When her fingers brushed higher up, just along the inside of his thigh, the glass in his hand shattered.

Elizabeth gasped. Dorian took notice too, cursing on Roland's behalf. Roland hardly realized what he'd done. He looked at his hand, shards of glass stuck within it. Blood quickly began oozing. Natalia's hand now rested in her lap, motionless and innocent.

"Are you all right?" Elizabeth asked. She handed over her dinner cloth, then quickly took Peter's and handed it over too.

Roland accepted them, pressing them to his palm. "No," he answered, shaking his head. He exhaled slowly, meeting his cousin's eyes.

It was obvious by his tone that he wasn't referring to his hand. Elizabeth slunk back in her seat, eyeing him with concern.

"Is that so?" Pierre called across the table. Roland looked up, not having realized his and Elizabeth's exchange had been overheard.

"That's surprising," his father continued—"I can't imagine any son of mine would be upset over such a minor wound."

Roland ground his teeth, his uninjured hand squeezing into a fist. He was acutely aware of the rest of the people at the table, each now looking between him and his father.

"Really, Roland," Pierre said, stabbing his fork into his food and taking a bite. When he'd chewed it and swallowed, he leaned back in his seat and angled his fork in Roland's direction. "Have you something to say? Or do you wish to just sit there, dripping blood and wine all over the table?"

Roland shook his head.

"I've got nothing to say. It was an accident is all."

"Are you certain? Because you've hardly said a word all night. And I can understand if you're upset about something. Really, I can. But I can't understand you having so little tact and class toward our guests."

Roland shot his father a glare, silently cursing him. Why had he waited until now to provoke him? Why, with both their family and their political rivals at their table, did Pierre choose their feast to press him?

"I've got plenty to say," Roland answered finally, "but it doesn't concern anyone here."

"Care to tell us who you might be concerned with, then? Gerard perhaps. We did speak of him earlier today. I could understand if he were on your mind."

Roland laughed bitterly.

"Yes, Father, that's right. I've got Gerard Verigrad on my mind."

"Gerard's a good man. A man worthy of respect."

"He's a Lightless bastard."

At that, Pierre stopped. Roland's skin felt clammy, his breaths escaping sharply. Everyone around them sat perfectly still, no one offering a distracting word or gesture.

"His wife is dead," Pierre said quietly, leaning forward and holding out his palms. "His daughter's heart belongs to you, the one man he can't permit her to marry. And he's dying. Which he can't tell Gwenivere, of course, because he knows how faithful a daughter she is, and how quickly she'll wed a man if it means easing her dying father's troubled mind. She won't think the decision through. She won't pick the best suitor. She'll just wed herself off to the first person who asks. So tell us Roland, tell us all your reasons for calling him a Lightless bastard."

Roland swallowed, saying nothing.

Pierre's fist came down with a crash against the table. Roland flinched, not expecting his father's outburst. A few glasses shook, one falling over and spilling. Peter reached out to try cleaning it up, but his hand immediately retreated when Elizabeth shook her head.

Wetting his lips, Roland opened his mouth to answer. He couldn't think of anything to say.

"I didn't know he was dying," he finally admitted. He fought back a wince as his father laughed mockingly.

"I suppose that would make it all right then, not knowing that." He sniffed and rubbed his nose, then placed both hands out on the table. "But, since you seem unable to distinguish what is and is not proper, I'll provide you some counsel: You're to respect King Gerard's wishes, and you're never to dissuade the Lady Gwenivere again. Any and all communication with her must cease, or it is you who'll be deemed Lightless."

He turned back to his food, continuing to eat. Roland sat quietly, knowing he'd be further reprimanded if he got up and left the table. He stayed, then, accepting some bandages from the servants his mother called in. The rest of the table eventually started speaking again, but all joviality was gone. No one, not even the calloused Natalia, could come back from hearing the King of Peace was dying.

There are many differing beliefs on auroras. *Most agree that they are seen in what many refer to as "the mind's eye," and are what people pull from to draw elements and create* called *weapons. However, it is still undecided if these* auroras *are the same ones that appear roughly three days after someone has died.*

From the studies of Deladrine, the Lady Oracle

CHAPTER 3

DIETRICH

SADIE

Dietrich stood within the shadows, what little existed in the hospital room, and watched the *auroras* emerge from the corpse before him.

He'd waited some time for them to expose themselves, their colorful, haunting presence like a derisive dance. Most found the emergence of *auroras* calming, tranquil even, believing they were the pieces of a person's soul on their way to the afterlife.

Dietrich could never believe such tales. *Auroras* didn't just emerge from the righteous and kind folk of the world. They emerged from anyone and everyone: thieves, rapists, murderers. Even fiends. How could a man such as he, forced to face such evils, possibly condone such a belief? How could he live knowing the enemies he'd slain now watched him from a place of peace?

He never could. At least, he'd never wanted to before that moment.

I'm sorry, Dietrich thought, grimacing as he looked at the corpse's neck. A clean, dark line lay dried against it. *I'm sorry they came for you.*

He stepped out from the shadows and walked toward the body. The *auroras,* swirling upward in an array of color, sighed woefully as he neared.

You didn't deserve this. He swallowed and reached his hand out, hoping terribly he would feel something, anything, as he touched the lights. He wanted to know the woman before him, his beloved, raven-haired Daensla, would live on. He wanted to sense her presence, her goodness, wanted to believe it truly was her soul that existed in the ascending *auroras.* He held his breath and extended his palm to touch them. He waited.

Nothing. Not coldness. Not emptiness. Not even a shiver.

The lights were nothing more than a solidifying display of Daensla's death.

"Yeltaire Veen?" a hesitant voice called. "It's Sam. May I enter?"

Dietrich took several breaths, his eyes still stuck to the jagged gash along Daensla's throat. Perhaps such a thing wouldn't exist if Yeltaire Veen were the only name she'd ever known to be his.

"Forgive me," Sam said, shimmying into the hospital's drifting room. He hardly glanced at the body, enough time spent with the ill and dying to grant him comfort with corpses. "When Prince Abaddon heard of your presence, he immediately sent word for you."

Dietrich nodded at hearing his brother's name. The *auroras* continued to pass through his outstretched palm. He pried his eyes away from them, facing the babbling healer.

"I'd thought you would be elsewhere, sir, somewhere else within the hospital," Sam continued. "Thus my haste. Otherwise, I wouldn't ask of you to leave your . . . this woman."

Dietrich stood motionless. "I didn't know her."

Sam's brows furrowed over his spectacles. No one touched the ascending *auroras* of someone they didn't know. It was a horribly intimate intrusion on the deceased.

"Um, well, best to let her *auroras* drift in peace then." Sam clutched at the parchments in his hands and pressed them to his chest. "I suppose we should adhere to Prince Abaddon's callings. I'm sure this woman's family wishes to see her before she fades completely."

She had no family, Dietrich thought bitterly. *She had a grand-mother who survived the Prianthian enslavement, but that was all. No siblings, no parents. No one to remember her now that she's gone.*

"It was the Redeemers who killed her," Sam said. It seemed the longer Dietrich kept quiet, the more Sam spoke. "That's what her neighbor told us when he brought her body in. He never actually saw them, but he heard her speaking ill of them often. Sad, but I suppose that's why we have our Assassin Prince. Perhaps *he* can bring her vengeance now."

Dietrich's angered musings were stifled as he heard his title. No matter how many years he lived in disguise, no matter how long he walked and talked among the people of his kingdom, he never could grow used to hearing them speak of him as the Assassin Prince. They all knew he existed. They all knew he fought the insurgence that threatened their alliance with the West. They simply didn't know his face. They only knew Yeltaire Veen, or whatever given alias he chose to share.

At least I'm spoken of with hope, he thought. *Father would be so proud.*

He grunted in amusement at the thought. The healer's brows laced further, but he otherwise ignored the reaction.

"I pray peace be with her," Sam went on, dipping his head toward Daensla. The spectacles along his nose dipped too. "I pray she finds solace under the Creator's grace."

Dietrich continued to say nothing. He looked at the eerie remnants of Daensla one last time, looked through her now nearly translucent form, then turned away and nodded.

Sam stood still for a time, unsure it seemed whether he should lead or follow. Dietrich eyed him with an unenthused expectancy until the healer at last pressed onward.

A distance formed between them as they walked out of Daensla's drifting room and into the hospital's hallways. Though he was never accustomed to his uncloaked guise, Dietrich kept his chin up and his neck high. His confident strides revealed nothing but prestige. Sam's nervous steps were a perfect opposition, his head snapping back from time to time to ensure Dietrich still pursued. It was an odd pairing, but the prince gave it no mind, knowing it was better the healers throughout the hospital thought him wonderfully unaware than exceedingly perceptive.

They did whisper, though.

"Is that Master Veen? Is that the fiend hunter who aids Prince Abaddon? He killed a cyclo'ghul just a moon ago . . . "

That was how it usually went, followed by, "My, he's quite scary, isn't he?"

Blissful naivety. He wore it convincingly.

"How fares the queen?" he asked, at last breaking the silence with Sam. It was a dull question, he knew, but he grew bored of eavesdropping on the people they passed. He needed to distract himself, needed to forget about Daensla. He already knew how Queen Lenore fared, though, as he'd just seen her a short time ago, but probing Sam for insight might prove wise. Gossip spread among the living in places where they fended off death. If Dietrich was to gain an idea of how much the people knew about his sick mother, the hospital was a good place to start.

"Is she here?" he continued. "Does she accompany Prince Abaddon today?"

Sam fiddled with the parchments he clenched. He nearly stumbled as he began his climb up the hospital's stairs. "Uh, no sir, she does not."

"How strange," Dietrich said. "You speak as though mention of Queen Lenore is forbidden."

"I know little of the queen and her state," Sam answered. "Anything I would say would only be speculation, concerned musings, if you will, and I think it best not to share such things. Gossip, it is, and better not said, I was told."

Dietrich tensed. "Told? By whom?"

The healer looked down, waving his hand.

"Uh, no, sorry, not ordered silent, if that's the impression I gave. I merely meant, uh, broader. In general, my parents always said it's best not to share something if I didn't know it to be true."

"I see." Dietrich couldn't resist the smile that pulled at his lips. "At times, though, sharing concerns can help prevent misunderstandings from occurring. If you think something not right with the queen, you can certainly trust my judgment to differentiate your thoughts from truths. Wouldn't you agree?"

Sam turned his head slightly and bit his lip, then shrugged.

"I've just noticed her absence from aiding the weary here as of late. She hasn't joined Prince Abaddon in his work, and the prince has seemed . . . ill at ease. Some of his patients, they're very sick, and he can't seem to find an elixir to cure them. He has managed to keep them alive, his genius prevails, but none have been completely healed—"

"You believe the queen to share their illness?" Dietrich interrupted.

The healer nodded.

That was bad. If Sam had been able to figure out Lenore was sick, who was to say the Redeemers hadn't? Or the Prianthians? Their enemies were always looking for a chance to strike, and now, with Lenore weak, this might be the chance. The Light knew his father wouldn't be coping well with her illness.

"Sam," Dietrich said, quickening his pace. He caught up after a few strides, grabbing the young man's shoulder. Sam winced but halted.

"Thank you for sharing this with me," Dietrich said. "You're intuitive, clever; it's made you good at your work." He forced a smile, a pleasant, convincing one, then released the pressure of his grip. "I do, however, think you correct in your earlier statement: sharing such an idea is perhaps not wise for Sadie's well-being. The idea that our first queen since the Prianthian enslavement might be ill could give our enemies a newfound hope. And with Redeemers always amiss, heartfelt expression could be an invitation for their assassins.

"Know I say none of this as accusation. It was my fault to press for your confession. Retain your wisdom and remain silent." He patted Sam's arm and widened his grin. "Your parents were astute in such a command."

Sam hunched slightly and clenched his parchments tighter. His eyes were wide behind his spectacles. "Y-yes Master Veen." He swallowed, then attempted his own smile. It staggered as much as his speech. "I-I will say nothing of the sort again."

Dietrich nodded and pulled his hand from Sam's shoulder. Meagerly, the healer reached up and rubbed it.

"You may return to your work," Dietrich said. "The sick need you down below."

Sam finally propped his frames from the tip of his nose back to its bridge. "Yes, of course. Good day to you, Master Veen. My warmest regards to Prince Abaddon."

"I will relay them to him." Dietrich held his smile and watched as the healer walked away. He stood silent as he listened for the young man's retreat, shifting back and forth from his heels to his toes. When the clumsy patters ended, he lifted his hand and knocked on Abaddon's door.

"My Lord?" he sang cheerily. He tapped rhythmically and

randomly, knowing full well the incessant knocking would annoy his brother. "It's your good friend, Yeltaire Veen. I was informed by the healer Sam that you requested my presence."

He smirked as the door opened abruptly. Abbadon faced him, lips tight and eyes squinting.

"Well hello," Dietrich said. He peeked his head around his brother's shoulder, the study behind him filled with vials and vials of different colored liquids. Stacks of parchment lay strewn about, some in a straight line along shelves, others scattered in piles across the floor. Dietrich straightened and turned back to Abbadon, distressed suddenly as he looked at him again.

He wasn't just glaring from the annoying knocks. The dark skin around his lids was puffy, his jaw lined with black, unshaved stubble. His green eyes looked laden as they shone a bloodshot red.

"May I enter?" Dietrich asked. He tried to keep his jesting tone, tried to stay upbeat, but his voice had unintentionally softened.

Abbadon stepped aside and let him in.

"It's good to see you, Dietrich." He lifted his foot and kicked the door shut behind them, his dark robes nearly catching along the door's edge. Dietrich looked around and stood with unease, not favorable to sitting in any of the seats with backs facing the door.

"You should not refer to me as such with others so close." He grabbed a chair and turned its angle, fidgeting uncomfortably as he sat down. He hated chairs, hated all of them. They left him so terribly, terribly vulnerable. "Veen is the only name of which you should speak when I'm here."

Abbadon rubbed his face and plopped down in his own seat. He stared at Dietrich, more than likely waiting for him to stop shifting the chair's legs across the floor.

"Yes, well these walls are plenty thick."

The chair screeched.

"Especially in this room."

Another screech.

"It's not anything . . . for the Light's sake! Cease your worries, both in your mind and your chair. If sitting so ails you then stand!"

Dietrich cleared his throat, sniffed casually, then halted. "Forgive me. I'm not fond of chairs. "

Abaddon chuckled. "Caution is good, but in excess it's unbecoming. You can't maintain such a demeanor when you go to Xenith's masquerade."

The masquerade. Of all the things for Dietrich to go to.

"I still think this a mistake," he said. "*You've* actually crossed the expanse of the desert before and gone through the Dividing Wall's mountains. *You've* sold your elixirs to the nobles of the West. *You've* charmed their material minds into believing such items are more valuable than the metals in our caves." He poked at a vial of exceptionally red liquid, then smelled its rank contents and pushed it aside. "You are a name and a face they trust. I . . . " he leaned back and poked at his own chest. "They've never so much as met."

Abaddon slicked his fingers through his hair and rested his foot atop his knee.

"You heighten my abilities to persuade and diminish my intelligence by insisting goods for armor are more valuable than liquid life. If not for my elixirs, the West would be plagued with illness."

Words. Abbadon used a great many of them.

"Come now," Dietrich countered with a pointing finger. "You know that even the most practical of things requires one to believe them to be of such. Reduced famine would be more favorable for any kingdom, yet feasts for royal mouths still seem more desirable for the noble classes. The begging hungry are not enough to outweigh a clever chef."

"A clever chef has more senses on his side." Abaddon leaned forward and tapped his own finger to his nose. "The hungry merely appeal to our pitying sight. Food appeals to our sight as well as our nose."

Dietrich held up his hand to end their continuous cycle of besting. "We stray. My point is that you have a connection with westerners. They don't even know who I am."

"You insult your reputation!" Abaddon's lips pulled into a grin. "Surely you're aware of how intriguing your story is. Perhaps it's more a legend than a truth now, but still. The names the Shadow, the Cloaked Prince, the Assassin—they've all preceded you. People are curious of the Sadiyan peasant-prince whose face is unknown."

Dietrich scowled, at last denying the comforts of his chair. He rose and walked toward the window, looking out over the bright reflections of Sadie's capital. He knew it was odd, but he felt more at home within its streets than within the luxuries royalty might have otherwise bestowed. How intriguing he was indeed. What common royal preferred sleeping in the crevices of his city's roofs and the arms of a whore?

Dietrich blinked. The latter of such dwellings was gone.

Eager to cast his thoughts aside, Dietrich turned back to his younger brother. Quickly he noted the heaviness that resided below Abaddon's eyes, the difficulty with which they fought to stay open. He was weary. Fatigued.

The search to cure their mother's illness was consuming him.

"I must admit, I'm hesitant to take the Dagger," Dietrich confessed. "I know we wish to save Mother, but the Xens and the Mesidians believe their roles as Guardians have blessed their nations. Faith and perception may be falsely intermingled, but it nevertheless guides their actions." He waited for Abaddon to interrupt him, waited for him to try and dissuade his uncertainty. His brother just sat silent.

Doesn't even want to argue. Light, he really is tired.

Dietrich ran his hands through his black hair, the strands rough as he slicked them from his face. He thought back on his and Abaddon's last discussion, and the one before that, each visit since their mother had fallen ill having been filled with possible ploys.

It had been Abaddon's idea to draw on the Dagger of Eve's immortality. He wanted to try and convince its Guardian that Sadie's predicament was of merit.

Dietrich hadn't believed he could possibly be so persuasive, but Abaddon had been insistent he at least try. The younger prince knew as much about royals as he knew about remedies, and he was convinced that Roland Laighless might forfeit the Dagger if it meant he could marry Gwenivere Verigrad. Convince her to aid them, pull her to their side and have her promise herself to Roland, and the Dagger was as good as theirs.

To Dietrich, it was all just chatter.

"I understand Roland and Gwenivere may love each other," he said, "but I can't believe such an ordinary feeling would break the celestial force that qualifies their roles. The prosperity of their nations is instilled in them more than anything else. Temptations of the common man cannot so simply sway those beliefs."

Abaddon peered for a moment, his eyes turning away and looking at nothing and everything that lay atop his study.

Quick to persuade, but never quick to give a hasty reply. Not for the first time, Dietrich was glad their father wasn't opposed to Abaddon being the possible heir. Better the genius prince takes the throne someday than the peasant one.

"Do you remember the night the Redeemers first came?" Abaddon asked, tapping his fingers. "Do you remember how shocking it was, after our very father had freed Sadie from Prianthia, that some of our own men had been persuaded to risk their lives in an attempt at ours?"

Dietrich stood motionless. Only his eyes moved to face his brother's pressings.

"I would not forget that night, Abaddon," he answered grimly. "What game are you playing to ask such a thing?"

"Not a game." Abaddon stood from his chair and joined Dietrich by the window. "Just an effort for you to see the truth."

"I've lived that truth for the past fourteen years," Dietrich said. "I see it with every Redeemer who falls by my blade." Daensla flickered into his mind again, her slit throat weighing down on his conscience. He pushed the thought of her aside. Guilt was useless to the dead.

"And yet," Abaddon said calmly, "after killing so many people, have you managed to put an end to the Redeemers? If you have, why have you not returned to the palace? Why do you still walk among the shadows, nervous to sit with a door at your back?"

Dietrich ground his teeth, his shoulders heaving. He opened his mouth to respond but quickly stopped, reminding himself where he was. If any healer came to ask advice, came to inquire about some herbs or elixirs, they might find it odd to hear Abaddon being spoken to so forwardly. And about things vastly different from what the fiend hunter Yeltaire Veen would speak of.

Dietrich turned back toward his brother, his muscles tense.

"You know as well as I that Navar still lives," he said coldly. "You know the Redeemers still obey him. If you believe my efforts to kill them have failed, just say so. Don't dance about it."

Abbadon held up his hand and shook his head. "You misunderstand my meaning." He grabbed two glasses from the alcove below his window and filled each with a dark, golden liquid. Dietrich shook his head slightly in refusal. Abaddon shrugged and drank both himself.

"Is that bottle full because you drink from it so rarely?"

Dietrich asked. "Or because you have recently opened it after finishing another?"

His younger brother evaded the query with a guilty grin and wave of hand, then poured himself another drink. "We digress. I didn't mean to offend before, Dietrich. I'm sorry if you took it as such. I hold nothing but the highest respect for you.

"However, the inevitability of the Redeemers' growth has become more and more apparent to me as of late. They are formidable, both in number and in skill. They don't answer to their blood. Their eyes and tongues don't define them." He swirled the liquid in his cup before raising it up and swallowing.

"Their leader is the only man to have ever succeeded in unifying the eastern peoples," he continued. "While his cause is unjust, his ability to ally people from both Sadie *and* Prianthia is something that cannot be denied. Who else do you know who has accomplished such a thing?"

Dietrich didn't answer. He hardly wanted to reflect on all the Redeemers had done. They'd emerged during his youth, sent their men after him and his mother and Abaddon when his father had first left to pledge alliances to the West. The Redeemers believed the western kingdoms plagued the East with war and carnage. Worse yet, they believed the West was responsible for the East's turmoil, that any and all who associated with them were subject to death.

Their convictions were nothing if not committed. Their following had indeed grown, despite Dietrich's attempts to end it, the whole purpose of his cloaked guise continuing to lose merit the longer they lived. They'd not yet pieced together his alias to his face, not completely, the identity he portrayed in Yeltaire Veen still somewhat safe from their assassins. Dietrich had heard whispers, though, and tortured confessions, that the insurgence had their own assassin now, some Victor of the Black. The man's features were supposedly chosen for their resemblance to Dietrich's own. How the Redeemers had discovered his looks—or at least discovered what he ought to look like now—he didn't know. They clearly had though, to some extent. Daensla's slit throat was testimony to that.

"The majority of our people are loyal," Dietrich insisted. He shuddered as he forced his mind blank. "Navar is led by the Fallen One. He only succeeds in unifying cowards, traitors—"

"Warriors, academics!" Abaddon's voice practically echoed against the walls. "Navar himself was a scholar, a man who advocated for the freedom of our people from his own. Though it might've been our father who freed Sadie from Prianthia, it's not always the names of the righteous that are remembered in the present."

Dietrich opened his mouth to argue, then decided to remain silent. Abaddon had, after all, let him ramble on about his concerns to take the Dagger. He could do his brother the courtesy of staying quiet while he relayed his concerns about their kingdom.

"The Holy Book itself reveals of a time when the Creator gave man miracles," Abaddon said. "It speaks of the Creator appearing before our very eyes, and still, within a century, we returned to our false gods." Abaddon looked to his desk, a torn copy of the Holy Book sitting atop its surface. Its pages were yellowed, its spine bent. Dietrich wasn't sure if he believed in its teachings, wasn't sure if he believed in its Creator, but he could at least respect that his brother did.

"That's what Navar is," Abaddon went on. "He's the evil that intrigues the content when too many a blessing has befallen them. He's a voice that makes them question, makes them go down a path of good intentions but leads them to the Fallen One. He's our people's false god . . . and I'll be damned if he convinces our kingdom of his heresy."

Dietrich remained silent, not bothering to sway his brother's better judgment as, once again, Abaddon filled his glass.

The image of Daensla, of her emerging *auroras*, continued to flash across Dietrich's mind. Their colorful streaks painfully agreed with Abaddon's words.

If only the necessity of Dietrich's role had been triumphant, the endless chase for Navar's life and the Redeemers' insurgence ended, how peaceful his life could be again. He picked up the glass his brother had offered, not bothering to give an explanation as he too poured himself a drink.

"What do you propose then?" He barely winced as he took a swig, the liquid burning down his throat. "I came to express my concerns for our mother, perhaps reverse our decision of the Immortality Dagger. Instead, I'm being reminded of our enemies' success."

"A success that will only grow when the pillars of this nation fall." Abaddon's response came with a clinking of glass, his hand striking his full cup to Dietrich's own. "Your pillar is already being taken by the vines, barely visible as they consume your royal stature."

Dietrich took another drink and narrowed his eyes, but kept quiet.

"My pillar," Abbadon continued, "mine is strong, albeit not as much as yours." He gestured to Dietrich's taller, larger physique. "But it's free of . . . foliage.

"Then there's Harold and Lenore, our great parents, the foundation of their pillars joined only to be separated at the top. They provide twice the strength, yet if so much as a crack begins to climb through one, it will weaken the other. If that pillar begins to falter, if the foundation breaks apart, it will force them both to crumble. I know not what you think, Brother, nor shall I ever, but I'm afraid you and I may not be strong enough to hold what's left of Sadie without them."

Dietrich nodded along, though he wasn't quite sure he followed his brother's analogy. "So, draw on the Dagger's immortality to mend the 'crack' that is our mother's illness, and ensure Sadie remains strong. Is that what you mean?"

Abaddon shrugged.

"I can't seem to find an elixir to heal Mother," he said. "I have patients. I experiment. Nothing seems promising. I fear what will happen to this nation if we lose her—if Father loses her. And I worry about you. I often lie awake, wondering if I even have a brother left to pray for."

He paused, not meeting Dietrich's eyes. He licked his lips, staring down into the contents of his glass.

"So what say you, Brother? Will you try to bring the Dagger of Eve back for us?"

Dietrich let out a sigh, hardly able to look upon the defeated image of his brother. Once, before the Redeemers had come, the world had been theirs, the future a promising adventure the two would embark upon with sword and shield in hand. Wooden swords, and pillows for shields—those had been all they could wield as boys—but the vision they'd seen had been noble all the same.

He drank what remained of his cup, set it down, and faced his brother. He couldn't abandon that vision now.

"I will," he answered

Xenith is described as The Realm of Scholars. Gustav Halstentine is among the most famous of Xen's people, having written many—if not all—the common teachings on auroras. *His most popular work is known as* The Art of Calling.

From the curriculum of Garron Hillborne for the Princess
Gwenivere Verigrad

Chapter 4

GWENIVERE

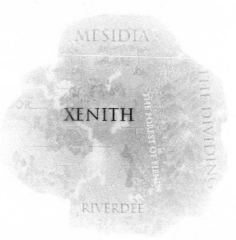

"We will be within the capital in about a day's time." Gerard's booming voice carried easily through the forest path. "I've sent word of our departure. I believe the people in Voradeen will be welcoming us when we arrive."

The king's knights grunted their approval, each beginning to talk to the men closest to them. Gwenivere didn't bother listening to their conversations, her mind occupied by nothing more than the royal garb she'd been forced to adorn.

"Curse my father, Garron, curse him his persistent ways!" She desperately tried to loosen her bodice. It was absurdly tight, especially given that the day was to be spent riding. "I hate these damned clothes. So bloody uncomfortable."

"Yes," her knight said dryly. "Your clothes must be very uncomfortable."

The princess looked up, catching the rare smile beaming across Garron's face. His face was the only thing she could see, his ceremonial armor covering the bulk of his body as his element-resistant chainmail covered what was left. A mighty sight it was, the Golden Knight almost glowing from atop his stallion's back. But he was, no doubt, enduring far more discomfort than she, a quick glance down reminding her how fortunate she was. Her tight bodice was really the only pestering article she wore besides perhaps her crown, which lay pinned in place against her red hair. Everything else she wore was made from nothing but the finest and softest materials.

"Albeit dreadfully heavy, I do admit your gallant attire quite fitting of you." Gwenivere grinned cheerfully, then cocked her head toward Garron's horse. "I pity Druke, though. I can't imagine he cares much for all that weight."

"He's a horse, and a fine one at that. I doubt he cares for much but a full belly and a caring rider." Garron's armored palm patted the horse's neck, clinking against the metal it too was forced to wear. "But to respond to your prior kindness, I would tell you that no number of jewels or lace would ever be fitting of your stature."

Gwenivere looked down and blushed, her smile replaced by sudden concern. *He is over twice my age, and my knight, but people are fools.* Garron's voice was deep, and had likely gone unheard, but the princess still looked around with unease. *If any of the men were listening . . .*

"I am grateful for your sentiment and your kind words, Sir Garron, but perhaps you've been too bold. I know where your heart lies, but other men do not. They will question our friendship if such words are exchanged often." Her statement was said under her breath, her eyes darting around the nearby band of knights. She hoped none of them had been in earshot.

Garron, as he always did, veiled whatever thoughts or emotions had surfaced.

"My apologies, milady, I only meant to return the compliment I'd received."

"I know," she said. "Forgive me. I just I don't ever feel like I know what is and isn't proper to say. And with this masquerade coming up . . ."

Garron met her eye sternly. "Complimenting you on your nobleness is very proper. It's a reflection on your abilities as our future queen. You haven't been around many men in your lifetime, but to remark on such things will occur often. You should learn to become accustomed to such flattery."

Gwenivere scoffed. Flirtatious banter with men was nothing she had ever mastered, the idea of it a useless and daunting chore only befitting of royal trends. She missed the days of her childhood when improper behavior was tossed off as youthful naivety. "I'm not sure I could ever become accustomed to that."

"Well you'd better start," Garron said simply. "Men will be complimenting more than just your stature at the masquerade, and you need to know which of those compliments are fitting."

"And what shall I do if their remarks aren't fitting?"

The knight glanced over at her, another rare smirk sneaking through his beard.

"Just call for me. I will do to them everything a lady of your dignity cannot."

Gwenivere laughed at the thought, a small part of her now hoping crass behavior would unfold in her direction. She recalled specific faces, specific noblemen, their less-than-courteous glances having made their way shamelessly across her figure. How she had wanted to rip their eyes out, burn them with a lick of fire or shock them with a bolt, but alas, it was not the way of a lady. Perhaps she could find one of those men at the masquerade, take her knight up on his word. What a pleasantry that would be.

"Let us have some fun, shall we?" Garron said. Gwenivere's vengeful thoughts were quickly forgotten as she glanced at her knight. She craned her neck and squinted incredulously.

"Your version of fun is never fun. When you say *us*, do

you really mean *you*?"

"Don't be selfish. No one cares for a prissy noble."

Gwenivere smiled and gaped, then released a quick bolt of lightning Garron's way. It would hardly do anything, she knew, his elemental armor merely absorbing it, but the tingle it gave him was well worth her efforts. She laughed as she saw him squirm in his saddle.

"That's perfect actually," he said, scratching at his beard. "Element practice was what I was going to suggest."

"Now?" she pressed. "In the middle of the forest?"

"Do you have a better way to pass the time?" His tone was as much a taunt as it was truth. "It's not a dreadfully long trek to Voradeen, but it's long enough. Besides, we haven't trained in a while. If a fiend attacks and you do nothing but cower behind your dress, I'll be the one to blame."

"This dress would be the last thing I'd cower behind," she countered. "There isn't a thread in it that could absorb an element. My crown on the other hand, I might cower behind that as it's made of element-resistant silver, but certainly not my dress—"

"Gwenivere—"

"All right, fine!" The princess held her amusement in, knowing very well she shouldn't mock her knight's good intentions. "What element, and where?"

The swift trots of horses behind them interrupted Garron's reply. They came from Aden and Maximus, who gained ground toward where they rode. Gwenivere waved at them and smiled as she noted her brother's armor. The little prince looked more like the toy soldiers he played with than a royal boy.

"May we join?" Maximus asked. Gwenivere didn't bother looking to Garron before nodding, too excited to share in her training to risk her knight dismissing it.

"I so rarely see my brother's abilities," she answered. "I welcome them."

"A challenge!" Aden raised his arm in excitement. In truth, it attempted to rise, but was cut short halfway up by the bulk of his armor. "I bet I'm as skilled as you now, Sister."

"My, my, must everything be a competition to you?" Her eyes rose from Aden to his knight. She squinted at him with feigned disgust. "Typical tykes, always turning tasks into trials. What've you been teaching him, Maximus?"

The young knight's cheeks reddened despite her tone, the color at odds with his broad face and square jaw. Gwenivere decided a man as big as he needed something to soften his build, something to keep people from thinking him a muscled brute. Even bears had their honey.

"Quite a lot, actually," the knight answered, giving Aden an approving nod. He chanced at a grin, matching Gwenivere's own as he pointed to a tree up ahead. "See that branch there, the one hanging over the road? Use your air to shake its leaves onto Sir Nicolas when he passes beneath it. Whoever succeeds in doing so first shall be the victor."

Garron grunted beside them, clearly entertained by Maximus's choice of victims. Nicolas was a pretty knight, so much so that he almost looked like a woman, the smooth skin on his face without hair and his lashes thick. Other knights matched close to his looks, but none his demeanor, the rest of the men too mindful of being proper to risk having pride. Gwenivere imagined Garron would love doing the deed himself if not for the lesson he was trying to teach.

"Deal," she said. Aden echoed his own agreement immediately after. She closed her eyes, took a deep breath, and attempted Maximus's request.

The *auroras* shone brightly in her mind, the colors swirling fancifully with one another. They danced, in a way, some twirling slowly, others swiftly, their auras an alluring ballroom of celestial lights. Garron had told her everyone's shone uniquely, that each individual saw their *auroras* in their own way, all dependent on how in tune they were with them and how much time they dedicated to seeking them out. Anyone could find them, he'd said, anyone could control and draw from them. How well they did so was mostly determined by the training they had.

Gwenivere, under his watchful wing, had gone through plenty.

Air, air, where are you? She rummaged through the *auroras*, searching through the maze of colors for the clearness of air's light. The colors matched each element, the red and oranges of fire and the crackling white-purple of lightning always overly prevalent in her mind. The hues of blue were second to the others, the snow and water that came with them always relatively easy for her to find. The greens and browns of earth were third after that. Air, drawn from the clear *auroras*, always gave her trouble. It tricked her as it hid behind and beside the other lights.

It usually did, at least. The memory of the window shutting in her father's chambers flashed through her thoughts. She quickly pushed it away. She was determined to beat her brother in this match.

With her eyes still closed, Gwenivere snatched the first few air *auroras* she could find, opening her lids when she had her grip. She was tempted to cast her hands toward the branch, but she refrained, fearful her young brother would hurry his attempt along if he saw her do so. For all she knew, clear *auroras* were the easiest for him to find. She inhaled deeply, tried to keep her gaze steady, and slowly released her element.

The sensation drained her, if only a bit, the effort not enough to cause her fatigue. She beamed when she sensed contact with the branch. Her mind forced her element to twitch beneath her hold.

Just as the first leaves began to fall, Aden's armored arm shot forward. The slight shaking in the branch was quickly dominated by the strength he released. His element was too strong, though, the thinness of the tree's limb not able to withstand his force. It broke with a loud snap, the might of the air's gust propelling the branch forward and atop Sir Charles's—*not* Sir Nicolas's—back.

"Dammit!" the old knight yelled, turning to find his assailants. The royal siblings froze. Maximus and Garron pointed at them from either side. Charles shook his head, furrowed his brow and frowned, but said nothing more as he grumpily snapped his stallion's reins and hurried away.

When he was out of earshot, Gwenivere, Aden, and Maximus all burst into laughter.

Garron's beard shifted slightly.

"I might cry I'm laughing so hard," Gwenivere said, dabbing at her eyes. "Though I would've enjoyed that falling on Sir Nicolas, I think Sir Charles was a good second. I suppose it serves him right for always correcting you for cursing, Maximus." She grabbed at her bodice, the muscles of her stomach tense, and cleared her throat.

"Aden might not have much control yet, but he certainly has strength." She turned her gaze to the prince's knight, nodding to him with a grin. "I have no doubts as to where he learned that from."

Maximus blushed again, his gaze cast down as his broad shoulders hunched. Garron leaned in toward Gwenivere, gently whispering, "Quite the little flatterer you are," before sitting back up in his saddle. The princess's cheeks took their turn to beam.

"Not bad, Aden," the Golden Knight said, returning their fun to learned boredom. "But has Maximus taught you your academics on *auroras* and elements? Have your tutors? Have you read *The Art of Calling* by Gustav Halstentine?"

Gwenivere groaned, and Aden shrugged with indifference, outing his knight as he answered, "A little."

"A little, eh?" Garron attempted to give Maximus a glare, but the young knight seemed to suddenly find interest in the trees. "Perhaps I shall quiz you then: What happens if too much of an element fills into elemental armor?"

The little prince smiled, clearly knowing the answer. "It explodes!"

Garron furrowed his brows but didn't correct him. His answer was close enough.

"Which nation is known for having the strongest elements?"

Gwenivere rolled her eyes. She thought she was five again as Garron questioned her brother.

"Um . . . " Aden looked at her for help, and she obliged by tapping the Amulet on her chest with a wink. He squinted, confused, before piecing her hint together and smiling triumphantly. "Eve!" he answered. "The Land Across the Sea!"

"Correct, though perhaps next time you shan't have assistance."

Gwenivere met the chastising look she knew was coming, smiling coolly as the Golden Knight shook his head.

Gwenivere opened her mouth to tease him but stopped when she noticed Sir Charles and Sir Nicolas urging their mounts hurriedly up ahead. The trio beside her joined in her worried glance, a heaving cough breaking through the cantering of their horses' trots. The princess panicked as she realized the sickly sounds were coming from her father. She didn't wait for the Golden Knight's approval as she hastily quickened her mare's pace.

The cough had become violent. Gwenivere tensed as her father's empty hacks morphed into harsh, forceful barks. His hand rushed from its civil place in front of his mouth to a clenched grip against his chest. With no command to steady his still trotting mount, he slowly began to lean to the side, his body bending more and more.

He's going to fall, Gwenivere realized. *He's going to—*

He collapsed from his saddle, landing with a heavy thud on the ground.

"Father!" Gwenivere's yell was accompanied by a quick dismount, and she hastily ran to the king's side. Aden leaped from his horse and ran forward as well, attempting to follow her, but Garron's swift hand was there to hold him back.

To fall off of one's horse was a great embarrassment, a dreadfully belittling act to occur in front of so many dutiful men. Gwenivere knew Gerard was loved by his knights, though, and none in that moment thought shame upon him. They only appeared to want insight on his wellbeing, each inching forward to help but halting as Gwenivere blocked their way.

"I'm fine, really," Gerard insisted, waving his hands as his cough ceased. "It seems I've forgotten how to breathe in my old age!" The men around him laughed hesitantly, uncertain relief washing over them as the king began to rise. He patted Gwenivere's shoulder and smiled, then headed back to his now still horse.

"Father, if you are not in good health, we should turn back around." Gwenivere followed behind him, careful to keep her words quiet and her voice low. The knights were already beginning to settle back into their places, likely too far to hear her words, but she heeded caution nonetheless. It would only do her father's image more harm to have her questioning overheard.

"Really darling, I'm fine." Gerard cupped her face in his hand and smiled at her again. Quickly he kissed her on the forehead, turning himself back to his horse and hoisting himself into the saddle. Gwenivere's breath caught as she noticed small specks of blood covering his sleeve.

"Your tunic, it has—"

"Enough Gwenivere," he interrupted firmly. "Go back to your mare and ride."

The princess stood still for a moment, her turquoise eyes glaring. Her father wasn't in good health; she knew he wasn't, his weariness evident in the way he held his shoulders with lingering fear. She readied herself, told herself to defy him in that moment would be to exert sensibility, but such an opportunity wouldn't come. The Golden Knight was already there, pulling her gently away.

Gwenivere looked down, her father already straying from their standstill. Cursing her weakness, she took the reins Garron held out to her, not bothering to look him in the eye as she returned to her saddle.

It's not at all strange for you to question the forbidding of marriage between Xenith and Mesidia. There is much behind the history of the decision, and there are many different aspects that come into play. Let us for now say the root of the decision lies in the power of the Artifacts.

From a letter between Dorian Cliffborne and Prince Abaddon Haroldson

CHAPTER 5

ROLAND

MESIDIA

"Where's that bloody wench?"

Roland chuckled as Peter glanced around, eyes darting about. The young noble sat atop his horse and scratched his head, shaking it in frustration before at last reaching for the wineskin in his satchel.

"Are you mad?" Elizabeth scolded, snatching the leather pouch. Peter scoffed, throwing his hands up in protest.

"What? It's just a bit of juice is all."

"I'll be damned if that's juice!" She unscrewed the top rapidly and brought her nose down to smell the contents. Based on the way her face scrunched, it would seem it wasn't juice.

"That's enough," William said. He took the wineskin from his sister and placed it in his own satchel. "And get off your horse, Peter, for the Light's sake. We haven't even said our goodbyes."

"Not true. I said all mine this morning."

"No you didn't."

"Yes I did."

Roland smiled as he approached his cousins, unable to hide his amusement at their constant bickering. He knew he should be more concerned about Peter's drinking, and William's for that matter, but for now he would just relish in the humor it produced. He turned toward the ambassador beside him.

"How long till they notice us?"

Dorian chuckled and shrugged. As if sensing they were being talked about, Elizabeth looked over and spotted them.

"Oh, hello!" She quickly lifted her hand and smacked her squabbling brothers. William stood tall, politely nodding to Roland and Dorian, while Peter continued to stay on his horse.

Dorian smiled, tapping Roland's shoulder as he whispered, "Wish me luck," and made his way to join the trio. The prince laughed and walked behind him, then curled his finger and beckoned Elizabeth over.

"Me?" she mouthed, pointing at her chest. Roland nodded, the parchment beneath his cloak held firmly in his grasp. He took in a heavy breath as his cousin approached, unsure still if he would go through with his plan.

Elizabeth was standing before him before he was truly certain.

"Hello, Roland." Her voice was sweet and pleasant. Roland reached one arm around her and hugged her tightly, pressing a kiss to her forehead.

"You know you've always been my favorite, yes?" He gestured to her brothers, and she giggled quietly.

"Of course I am. I'm the only one who's ever sober enough to remember the conversations we have."

Roland laughed, his breath clouding in front of him from the chill of the morning. He hardly felt it, hardly noticed the way it bit at his ears and nose or evoked shameless tears in his eyes. He felt the parchment under his cloak and nothing else, the smooth seal of the Mesidian leaf protruding from its even surface. Elizabeth continued to smile, too kind to question his silence. She stood shivering as the sun refused to warm her little bones.

"I have a favor to ask," he said finally. He revealed the parchment, his lungs filling with another deep breath before he placed the paper in her hand. She glanced down at it, biting her lip, but remained quiet.

"It's a letter, to the Lady Gwenivere. I know it's been ordered to keep such things from her, but I promise I only wrote to assure her of Mesidia's allegiance. When the day comes for such concerns."

It was treason, what he asked of her, his words to Gwenivere forbidden by both Pierre and Gerard. Elizabeth had every right to refuse, had every right to tell him she would not partake in such an act. Instead she just smiled and bobbed her head with reassurance.

"Of course, Roland." She took the envelope, then placed it in the satchel at her side. Grabbing the edges of her skirts, she gave him a jesting curtsy, then rose back up and kissed his cheek. He pulled her close and squeezed her tightly, noting how her small body shook. He hoped it was simply from the cold morning.

"My, my, Elizabeth, your own cousin?" a voice called.

Roland and Elizabeth pulled away from each another, both turning to find Natalia Barie approaching.

"I must say, I hadn't thought incest within your capabilities," she said. "I have to admit, though, it does explain a lot."

She smiled coyly and gestured toward Peter, who—still atop his stallion—struggled to keep it from turning in circles.

Elizabeth's cheeks colored. "I was just saying goodbye."

Natalia continued to smirk. With Peter cursing like a drunk at his horse, Elizabeth didn't have much to say. She gave Roland one last look, her round eyes conspiratorial, then made her way back to her own horse.

"You really can't be pleasant for even a moment, can you?" Roland asked.

Natalia shrugged irrationally bare shoulders, waving the query off.

"Did you know our fathers spoke recently?" she asked.

Roland frowned. Her question seemed genuine and amicable, and her questions were never genuine and amicable.

"It's true," she went on. "They were meeting with the leaders of your Elite. My father was discussing something with yours he thought important enough to cast aside our families' rivalries for. Don't bother asking what they discussed. I wasn't able to pry that out of him. Just know that, regardless of what impressions your family might have of my father, he is indeed a decent man. My mother, perhaps not, but my father cares a great deal for this kingdom. Somewhere my ancestors are cursing him, no doubt, but be careful, and don't waste his extended hand. Whatever he felt worth mentioning, it more than likely involves all of us."

Roland continued to stand silent. It was almost too difficult to believe the cold duchess-heir would show any form of camaraderie. Her loyalty was to her Victorian lineage, and she always pinned Pierre and Rosalie as the enemies.

If he knew something that endangered their people, though, wouldn't he share that with her? Mesidia would always come before petty attempts at the throne. He could certainly believe her capable of that mindset as well.

"Thank you, Natalia. I shall." He nodded his head respectfully. "And . . . the same to you."

She tilted her head. "Hard for you to say it, isn't it?" She breathed into her hands, brushing them together before sliding on a pair of riding gloves. "Don't think this makes us allies, Prince. If you will not have me for a wife, you should still consider me an enemy."

"I would think of you as such regardless."

Natalia laughed, genuinely, the sound a much more pleasant one than what usually came from her. Its showing nature was gone as quickly as it had come.

"Dravian Valcor, Rellor Bordinsua, Odin Iceborne, and Markeem the Mute," she said, listing off names of his father's Elite. "They're all accompanying the al'Murtaghs and Dorian and me until we part ways at the Forest of Fiends. Before that, I shan't need to be careful—your father's Elite will be careful enough for all of us."

She grinned again and blew him a kiss. Coming from her, the cloudy breath it spawned seemed fitting.

Roland stood motionless as Natalia grabbed her stallion's reins and gestured behind them. From the gates of Stonewall Castle came the troop of Elite, the finely trained men and women who wielded no *touched* swords and bore no *touched* shields. At their head rode a dark-haired man, the only one among them to adorn armor. The garb was not meant as a defense but merely a means to distinguish him from the rest. Roland knew him as Dravian Valcor, the Inquisitor and leader of the Elite. He nodded to Dravian as he approached, and Dravian nodded back, but gave no other respecting gestures. He met Roland with a cold stare, then led his soldiers toward Natalia, Dorian, and the al'Murtagh siblings.

Roland gave one last look to the duchess-heir, her eyes filled with knowing warning, and resigned himself to the castle. If Natalia had been telling the truth, he'd need to find out what her father had told his own, and why some of their best soldiers had just been sent away.

There are a great many kinds of serpent fiends throughout the deserts of the East.

An excerpt from *Fire and Fiends*

Chapter 6

DIETRICH

SADIE

Dietrich awoke in the same manner he had the days prior—overheated and covered in sweat. The desert sun came like a wave over the chill of night, the brightness blinding. He looked up to his horse, the stallion smug as it accepted the heat it'd been bred for, no sweat trickling from its brow as it did Dietrich's own. Envious, he wiped his forehead and ripped a piece of cloth from his threadbare blanket, wrapping it against his head in an effort to keep his eyes free of sweat. A few adjustments granted him comfort, but eventually he pulled the hood of his cloak up for more cover.

It hadn't even been that many moons since he'd left Sadie's capital, but he already hated this quest.

He looked out over the dunes, his eyes still at war with the light in their efforts to settle. When they did, his cracked lips

gave way to a smile, the pain of their splitting a small deterrence to the sight ahead of him.

"See there, Zar." He pointed toward the mountains ahead
of them. "A day's ride, two at most."

The horse continued to stand steady, indifferent to the
merriment that overcame his master. Dietrich patted him
roughly in triumph and cast his squinting eyes at the wondrous heights that towered beyond. Centuries had marked the
Dividing Wall's mountains, centuries still unseeingly altering
their paths, their immovable conviction distorted by the dancing of the heat's waves.

The prince packed his belongings quickly, a newfound energy pulsing through him. Just within the mountains' depths
the landscape would change. Rocky, jagged cliffs would be replaced by rolling hills and lush forests. Leaves would be turning colors and ice, cold and unbearably harsh, would be melting from peaks and plummeting into streams.

The prince hoisted himself onto his stallion and tried not
to create the vivid musings in the mirages of the sands. Excited, he rallied himself and the horse onwards. Zar, who usually
complied, stood locked in place.

"Zar, friend, come now, we must make haste. Go!"

He urged the stallion forward again, kicking his heels and
clicking his tongue. The mount didn't obey.

Sighing, Dietrich decided Zar must have grown fatigued
from carrying his weight after so many days. He patted him
on the neck and began to dismount.

Sensing his master's return to the ground, the stallion
turned toward familiar sands. Dietrich was barely still on as
Zar began running.

"Whoa whoa whoa, settle down!" Dietrich tried to turn
the horse back, but the stallion wouldn't listen.

Defiantly, he erupted into a frantic gallop.

"Zar, stop!" Dietrich yanked against the reins, desperately

attempting to get his mount under control. The horse fought against him, thrashing his head. Not knowing what else to do, Dietrich *called* a gust of wind, using it to force Zar back.

When they'd turned back around, Dietrich at last caught sight of what Zar had sensed.

A fiend.

Motionless, and praying his horse would keep still, Dietrich watched the massive serpent emerge from the sands. Its body was covered in golden scales, and seven long, sharp tails unwound from its back. Lowering himself against Zar, Dietrich tried to comfort him, the horse's hooves treading fearfully in place.

He'd seen three – and four-tailed serpents, even a five-tailed serpent once, but never a seven-tailed. Just his luck he'd find one during his venture to Xenith. The serpent, at least five times larger than Zar, didn't appear to have seen them yet, perhaps not even heard them. Slowly, carefully, Dietrich began guiding Zar onward, his eyes never leaving the fiend as they attempted to slip away.

Its tongue flickered. Its head twitched.

It knew they were there.

Dietrich waited. He'd fought his fair share of fiends before. The alias he portrayed in Yeltaire Veen had granted him more than enough encounters with the creatures outside the capital's walls. Anything from teradacts to cora'cahn had fallen victim to him, but an encounter with a seven-tailed serpent had not yet made his list. Accounts of the serpent family were all classified together in *Fire and Fiends*, the Holy Book for fiend hunters, but such a lumped categorizing was highly unhelpful. Even a four-tailed differed greatly in ability than a five, and which elements proved useful and which proved useless were not fleshed out.

Uncertain which tactic would be best to follow, Dietrich kept the expanse between him and the hissing seven-tailed serpent large, searching through the *auroras* in his mind.

Red, red, red, he thought, reaching out to the blazing flashes. They were there, crackling brightly within his mind. He rallied them together, his focus strong as he brought them to life in his hands. With a thrust he cast the flames forward, a whirlwind of fire burning against the fiend's scales.

His energy drained, but the serpent reeled its head at the attack. An ear-piercing shriek escaped its throat.

Dietrich smiled in triumph and gathered his *auroras* again. Before he released them, he caught sight of the first wave dimming. The flames were sinking and retreating into the serpent's body, making it glow red. Its scales absorbed the fire until nothing remained of Dietrich's attack. The menacing slits of the serpent's eyes now also burned a reddened hue, hungry, it seemed, for Dietrich's blood.

"Go!" he yelled, leaning low against Zar's back. The fiend was much faster than the mount, its body gaining ground at an alarming rate.

The prince pinned his legs down firmly. With one hand clutching tightly against the reins, he freed the other. He began *calling* his crossbow, trying to imagine the weapon as he and his stallion raced against the fiend. He could see it in his mind, feel the infinite bolts that took aim within its grips, the perfect weight forming itself into existence. When its structure was complete, the prince sent his and Zar's path at an angle, took aim, and fired.

The first bolt stuck into the fiend's neck. The tip pierced through the beaming scales as the creature neared them. It reeled back, another shrill call stabbing through the air as Dietrich steadied his grip and released again. The fiend slowed its retreat, bolt after bolt holding true.

As Dietrich readied another shot, a wall of fire formed in their path and forced Zar to halt.

The sudden stop sent the stallion on its back legs and

Dietrich to the sands. He grimaced and lost focus. His cross-bow faded as he clutched his now-aching stomach. Weapon-less and exposed, the serpent slithered toward him.

Dietrich dodged the first of the serpent's tails, but another struck where the first had failed. He rolled quickly to his side, one tail shredding through his cloak. He managed to get to his feet, then caught sight of Zar.

The horse was trapped in one of the serpent's tails. Faintly, through the cloud of dust and sand, Dietrich could make out the muscles of the tail tightening.

"No!" He snatched a blue-white *aurora* from his mind and cast out a sheet of ice. It'd been an instinctive *call*, but it proved resourceful as it cut through the serpent's tail. Writh-ing, the serpent retreated. Its wall of fire vanished.

Dietrich knew he could take it then, knew he could slay it if he advanced. Instead, his feet foolishly went to his steed.

He unwound the severed tail that lay wrapped around Zar's body. The horse whinnied and trotted helplessly, but Dietrich managed to get it freed. He summoned more *auroras*, creating a barricade of ice to protect them.

The defense wouldn't last long. Already Dietrich could feel it draining him. He released one side of it, the other still block-ing the fiend out, and smacked Zar harshly against the back.

"Flee!" he yelled, striking his horse again. It whinnied and kicked its legs in protest, refusing to leave his side. Dietrich panted as his elements continued to drain him.

"Zar, go!"

The horse snorted, but at last ran. When he was far enough away, Dietrich turned toward the serpent. He *called* a sword into his grasp and a sturdy, circular shield. He released his melting barricade and revealed himself exposed to the beast, weak and alone.

The serpent propped itself up, flicking its slit tongue. Di-etrich stood unfaltering, waiting for the creature to strike as each of its remaining tails encircled him.

Before he could blink, the bladed tails were upon him.

He rolled and pivoted, narrowly avoiding being slashed and stabbed. If his feet failed him, his shield was there. If his defense proved futile, he swung his sword. He would err eventually, he knew, the rapidity of his guard already waning. He searched again for his clear *auroras*. Summoning what small amount he could, he cast it out, a narrow whirlwind thrusting against the blade-like tails.

Seeing the fiend reel back from the element, Dietrich dashed toward it. He lifted his sword, fighting to preserve his blade, and plunged it toward the serpent's body. With a heavy strike, he severed its neck.

A single tail, errant and unyielding, pierced through his uncovered shoulder.

With thick adrenaline pulsing through him, Dietrich grabbed hold of the tail and ripped it out. The serpent's body, headless now, swayed slightly. After a moment it fell to the sand.

Dietrich tossed aside the tail he held, well aware that the pain of his wound had yet to reveal itself. There was too much energy in him still, too much thrill from the fight. He refused to look down at his injury, afraid it might worsen somehow if he did. Instead he stood back up, only then realizing he'd collapsed to his knees, and whistled between bloodied fingers for his stallion's return.

"Zar!" he yelled, trudging toward where he'd cast the horse away. As he lifted his feet, the sand seemed to grow deeper, each step sinking farther and farther than the steps before. He tried to keep his legs moving, tried to continue his triumphant trek, but his muscles would move no more. He once again fell to the ground, the pain in his shoulder at last beginning to surface.

"Zar," he muttered weakly. His vision began to blur, his eyes finally traveling down to inspect his wound. Small specks of black were all he could see. He closed his eyes then, grateful his tattered cloak kept the burning sands from searing his skin, and allowed himself to fall into the seductive call of slumber.

A mild nudging interrupted his attempt at rest. The darkness faded as the light of the day brightened once more. Dietrich inhaled deeply, his focus lost, something reflexive forcing his eyes to open. Through his dim sight he could see the black outline of his stallion, the wetness of its nose waking him from his feeble state. Energy sparked through him, his muscles strengthened as he rose back to his feet. He leaned against his devoted companion, his hands shaking as he hoisted himself onto its back.

"Ride," he whispered. Faithfully, the loyal horse obeyed.

Roland Laighless

At times Roland feels more like a brother to me than my own brothers. Perhaps it's just that I wish he were my brother, as I love him dearly. He's a good man, and an honest one. He's not boastful, despite being a Guardian, and he's the only man of noble birth I've met who has a way of being liked by anyone.

He is destined for great things. And I don't believe that solely because he's my cousin.

From the sketchbook of Elizabeth al'Murtagh

CHAPTER 7

ROLAND

"They say this tapestry belonged to Daniella Corrins, my ancestor, and hung in Castle Goddjvek before it was sacked." Roland examined the tapestry he stood before, his hands behind his back.

"My great grandmother said her great grandmother had found a servant who had stolen this when the castle was being destroyed, a man by the name of Redfroi, who was hoping he could sell it and make a fortune off of it. Instead, my great grandmother's great grandmother and Redfroi fell in love, and he gave her the tapestry as a wedding gift. It is said he's the part of my lineage where the Laighless name comes from. Apparently he was 'without law' because of his thieving ways."

Roland paused from his tale and glanced over at the quiet Elite beside him. He waited for the man to respond, give some kind of nod or noise of acknowledgement, but his expression continued to stay hard and squinting as he stared at the tapestry.

"What do you think, Merlin?" Roland asked. The man

always seemed to know something about everything, when he actually spoke, though such a thing was always a rare and interesting occurrence. The prince was genuinely curious what the soldier thought of his lineage's legend.

"I think this Redfroi fellow was a great liar," Merlin answered. Roland raised a brow, surprised the man didn't show more respect to his blood's past. It didn't make a difference if he did. Merlin was a good soldier; he followed orders, and he executed them well. That was all he really needed to do.

"Why's that?" he asked.

"When Castle Goddjvek was sacked, it was burned," Merlin answered. "The ruins are still black from the ashes, and the fields around where it once stood still don't grow trees, only thick blades of wheat-grass. Do you really mean to tell me that Redfroi managed to get this tapestry out of the burning castle without even a bit of soot marking its face?"

The Elite didn't laugh, not aloud, but the peculiar twinkle in his eyes meant he thought of something amusing. The look was practically a guffaw for the reserved man.

"What?" Roland pressed.

"Perhaps Laighless shouldn't have been his name," Merlin said. His mouth twitched at a grin. "Perhaps it should've been Honorless."

Roland cocked his head as the soldier stood expectant.

"Because he was without—"

"I understood, Merlin, thank you."

"You're most welcome."

Roland took a few more moments to admire and ponder the tapestry—and ignore his Elite's uninspiring brand of humor—before at last walking away. His father had said the night before that he wished to speak with him and Merlin when the sun rose. What he wished to speak of Roland didn't know, but he'd tossed and turned throughout the night pondering what Pierre wished to share.

The warning Natalia had given before her departure still rang clearly in Roland's mind. The idea that her father, Bernard, had cast aside their families' feuding bloodlines to share counsel with his own father was a strange and terrifying thought. What could be so awful that the duke would be willing to abandon his pride for? What could have happened for him to extend an aiding hand?

Roland and Merlin made their way to the center room of the castle. The War Room, as it was called, was a room with no windows or doors save the one they walked through. Pierre was there, his body looming over the room's large stone table. Torches along the walls flickered shadows along his weathered face.

He hardly glanced up as Merlin and Roland entered.

"I believe I asked you to be here when the sun rose." Pierre finally abandoned what he was examining on the table, his gaze now resting scornfully on Roland. "The sun has not yet risen."

Roland smiled, if only to keep from cursing.

"You're right, Father. I apologize." His voice held little sincerity, but the glare the king shot him was not expanded on further. Instead Pierre stepped away from the table and extended his arm out toward it, a set of maps revealing themselves from under his shadow. Merlin crossed his arms beneath his chest, resting his dark eyes where the king pointed. Roland looked too, but didn't take much interest in what he saw. Two of the maps were of Mesidia, and one of the entire continent, but besides a few markings that had been etched into each, none looked to be anything peculiar. Roland tried to remain patient, the drama of his father's actions making him anxious.

"I've sent Dravian Valcor and his soldiers to our sister nation in Riverdee," Pierre said, tracing his finger along the map of the continent. The nation he spoke of, Riverdee, rested on the coast, more a neighboring nation to Xenith than Mesidia. The easternmost point of the sea-trading kingdom did extend up to Mesidia's southern border, though, the chunk of land called the Forest of Fiends. It was dense with coastal trees and mighty mountains, and despite never having been there himself, Roland knew it was filled with fiends.

"Bernard spoke with me," Pierre continued, "two nights before the al'Murtaghs, Natalia, and Dorian left. He told me the reason the Duchess Yvaine hadn't accompanied him to Stonewall was because she'd fled to aid the rebels. According to him, the Victorians are planning to attack Riverdee soon."

Roland cursed. Natalia was certainly unpleasant, but her mother was far worse. He'd always suspected she was plotting more than just slanders.

"Why attack Riverdee?" Merlin asked. "Why would it matter to us? The nation is good for trade, but Mesidia has allies in other places. Riverdee as well. Even if the rebels are successful in an attack, there are a handful of nations that would come to her defense."

"Xenith certainly would," Roland added. He glanced at the map again. "Riverdee is the only nation on the entire continent that has no enemies. If someone attacks it, as Merlin said, surely other nations would intervene."

Pierre placed a firm finger against Riverdee's place on the map. "Yes, but not until *after* an attack has occurred. As her ally, Mesidia can't just sit back while innocent people die. Riverdee is good to the world, one of the few nations that is. Someone has to rise up to protect her."

Roland was about to protest again, insist that it was foolish to split their army over a rumor, but Merlin's voice chimed in first.

"It's a trap," he said. Pierre glared at the soldier, a glare fierce enough to turn a man to stone, and Merlin quietly added, "Milord."

"I agree," Pierre said, "but even if it is, half of our soldiers in Stonewall and half in Riverdee are still enough to defend us against a rallying of rebels. The Elite are the highest trained element wielders in Abra'am. The Victorians are uneducated farmers and stable hands who get worked up by rumors and lies. Besides, Stonewall has withstood countless attacks before. She never fell during the War of Fire, and she won't fall now. Those are chances I would bet on."

Merlin chewed on his lip and Roland sighed, neither man having much retaliation. It was true what Pierre said of the rebels. They were mostly ignorant and poor, a vast majority of them only having their qualms to unite them. No leader had ever emerged from their ranks. No one rose up to guide them with strategic tact. They really only held influence over a small plot of land to the south, and even that wasn't much to worry them.

Roland wondered how many of the rebels even knew how to *call* a weapon or draw from their *auroras* to cast elements. All he could imagine were straw-chomping men, pitchforks in hand, standing outside Stonewall's fortress as they pondered how to get in.

And all because they felt Natalia's ancestors should've been given the Dagger and the throne instead of Roland's.

"Why would they bother attacking Riverdee at all?" he asked. "If it would bring about the fury of the entire continent, shouldn't we be . . . glad, they are plotting this? After all, there are some nations who wish the Barie family were in power. Perhaps this would be the perfect opportunity to show them we deserve to rule."

Pierre's lips thinned. "So you propose we just let innocent people die? You propose we let the Victorians continue their ruse because it's convenient for the Laighless name?"

"No," Roland answered, forcing down frustration. "I'm trying to agree with you. Aiding Riverdee's people *would* be the right choice. I'm just pointing out that there has to be more to this, more than just the possibility of an attack on

Riverdee or a trap for us. The Duchess Yvaine is too smart a woman to plan something so foolish."

Merlin nodded his agreement.

"I believe that as well," Pierre said. He rested his weight against a chair beside him, his blue eyes narrowing as he slowly shook his head. "In all the years we've held the throne, there has never been anyone as deceitful and malicious as Yvaine. Know that I know this, Roland, for it's the very reason I gave you the Dagger of Eve instead of Dorian. Blood doesn't define my heirs. Dorian is my son, and he would've made a fine king. But Natalia is Yvaine's daughter, to her very core, and Dorian fell victim to her seduction when he named her his betrothed. Had I given him the Dagger, I would've been handing our kingdom over to her."

Roland shifted his weight. His father had never said those things to him before. It felt strange to finally hear it, especially with Merlin standing next to them.

"You did what was necessary," he said quietly. He watched as Pierre nodded, surprised at the regret in his gaze.

"So," Merlin said, rubbing his chin, "what do you think the duchess is plotting? What's her purpose in splitting our men if she can't take advantage of it?"

Pierre's jaw moved slightly as he ground his teeth. "That's what I want you to find out."

He reached down to the maps on the table, settling on one and pressing down its corners. The ends seemed eager to roll themselves back into a scroll.

"Bernard said Yvaine is hiding in the old castle ruins in the heart of the rebel lands. He said he's followed her before and believes she meets with some of her allies there. Who those allies are, he wasn't sure, but he said he didn't think they were Mesidian. He said they looked too pale and had too dark of hair."

"Didn't think anyone got paler than us," Roland said jestingly. Merlin and Pierre just stared at him, unamused.

"Yendorians have dark hair," Pierre continued. "And they've always seemed eager to be involved in our politics. I don't think it could be them, though. Their skin is too olive to be considered pale."

"Agreed," Merlin said. He stared at the maps, noting the different countries that pressed against Mesidia's borders.

"It certainly couldn't be the Arctic tribes," Pierre continued. "Their hair is white and their skin is black. Exactly the opposite of what Bernard described."

"Theatia's people aren't all that pale either," Roland added. His own hand now settled against his chin, his face scrunching as he tried to think who the mysterious allies of their enemy could be.

"Regardless," Pierre said, lifting his hand, "exactly who they are is not our most pressing concern. What we need to know is if Yvaine is indeed plotting something against us, and, if so, what that might be. Bernard said he believes Yvaine is staying in the castle ruins now, and that, if haste can be made, perhaps we can catch her in her deceit. I would trust this task to our soldiers, but now that they're split, I can't risk dividing them any further. Two men, though, two men I trust—perhaps they could get through the rebel land unnoticed."

Roland's head rose and his eyes widened. He looked to his father, then to Merlin, then back to his father again.

"You mean to send us? Just us?"

The words came out excitedly. He hadn't meant for them to; he knew what Pierre was asking was dangerous, and he knew it was serious. Still, the idea of sneaking through Mesidia's ruins and capturing the duchess in her deceit seemed quite enticing.

"Aye, Roland," Pierre said. He looked at him, the corners of his mouth turning, and clasped him on the shoulder. "Aye."

Smiling, Roland glanced down. He'd have to start paying attention to the maps his father had set out.

A few hours later, Roland and Merlin collected the notes they'd taken from Pierre and made to leave. It'd been a productive conversation, and a telling one of what Pierre must have been like back during the War of Fire. Roland had only ever known his father in times of peace, but he'd heard stories. Pierre Laighless, according to most older nobles, was not a man to make enemies with.

"Roland," Pierre called. "Stay back a moment. I wish to speak with you alone."

The prince sighed, nearly to the door. He was eager to be on his way, but beyond that, he was tired of being in the War Room. It made his eyes weary from the dark, and his skin slick with sweat.

He didn't admit any of that aloud, though. He merely nodded and waited for Merlin to leave.

"I want you to know that I'll send another if you wish it," Pierre said. "Say the word and you'll stay."

Roland stood silent, his mouth agape for a moment before the taste of soot rested on his tongue. *Merlin was right,* he decided, sealing his lips. *There's no way the tapestry could have come out of the burning castle unscathed.*

"I wish no such thing, Father. I'm honored to be assigned this task."

Pierre's shoulders sank. He looked down and pinched the bridge of his nose before rubbing his temple.

"All right. I think that's a fine choice." He brought his gaze back up, the piercing blue of his eyes almost orange as the flames glowed against them. "It's a dangerous mission, what I ask of you, and one that could risk you being captured by the very people who wish us dethroned. These are people without honor, without merit, and they will kill you if they have the chance."

"I know, I—"

"Hush Roland, listen." The king raised his hand for silence, then slowly brought it back down. "We can't allow the Dagger to be in the rebels' hands. I need you to leave it here, in case you're caught. Don't take this as an assumption that you'll fail, I just . . . "

Roland stepped forward, swiftly reaching down as his father's voice trailed off. He removed the Dagger from its sheath against his thigh, his leg instantly feeling lighter.

"Don't fret, Father," he said, trying to sound reassuring. "The rebels won't capture us."

Pierre nodded, reaching out and taking the Dagger. Roland tried to meet his father's eyes, hoping to see confidence in them, but Pierre just stared absently.

He didn't seem convinced.

There is much debate on when the Elite were first established. Some believe they date back to the breaking of Mesidia, when the son of Daniella Corrins needed protection against the Victorians. Others believe they should be credited to King Pierre and the War of Fire, as Mesidian soldiers were incompetent with calling *when compared to the soldiers of Concord and Tiador. Thus they had to master the art in order to turn the tides of war. As King Pierre himself was not an expert in* calling, *he captured those who were best with the skill among his enemies' ranks and forced them to teach his soldiers.*

Mesidian Historian

CHAPTER 8

ᴇLIZABETH

Riding through the rainy hills of Mesidia had proven dreadfully dull. The land was beautiful in the fall cycle, the skies a constant shade of grey against the falling leaves and darkening grasses, but it was a sight Elizabeth saw far too often. Sharing the blood of a king made her and her brothers constantly called upon for local endeavors, each season often frequented by saddle-sore bums and achy backs.

Continental affairs, however, were few and far between.

The titles she and her brothers held—or, rather, the title their *uncle* held—did little to grant them worth in the eyes of most nobles. It didn't help that Elizabeth's mother was her relation to Pierre, and thus her surname was that of her father's. Al'Murtagh was a poor man's name, and common, images of fiddle playing, pale-skinned halfwits coming to most people's minds when they heard it. Elizabeth wanted to bring it honor, prove the worth of her beloved mother Catherine and her witty father Joel, but her brothers Peter and William always seemed to diminish any good deeds she managed to accomplish. She glanced up from her sketchpad and watched them, both singing loudly as they drank with her uncle's Elite soldiers around the campfire. Peter's tunic was already stained red from all the wine he'd spilled.

Elizabeth might have been more bothered by the act if she wasn't so distracted by Natalia's dancing. The duchess-heir swayed her hips and flung her hair to the song the soldiers were singing, her clothes far too revealing for the cold of the coming night. She had taken off her shoes, her bare feet covered with dark soil, and when the song ended she fell into one of the men's laps. She laughed and stroked his chin, her slender fingers pointing and beckoning for him to wash the dirt away from her skin.

Peter and William banged their mugs together and began their pitchy singing again, neither of them seeming to notice how terribly Natalia acted. Elizabeth suppressed her annoyance, insisting to herself that it was only her brothers' nature to be so oblivious.

I'm just holding a grudge. She turned her attention to Ambassador Dorian, who sat quietly by the campfire. He was sitting near the finest of the Elite's men, Rellor Bordinsua to his left and Odin Iceborne to his right, but he still appeared lonely as his lips remained sealed. She looked to Natalia again, watching as the beautiful woman leaned in and whispered in the soldier's ear whose lap she sat on.

I cannot blame Dorian for being reserved, she thought. *I would be quiet too if my former betrothed whored about like a bar wench . . . That was cruel of me. Forgive me, Light. I don't mean such things.*

Elizabeth was startled suddenly as a thud of footsteps sounded beside her. She clutched her drawings to her chest and looked up, surprised when the dark eyes of a man met her own. She recognized him as Dravian Valcor, the Inquisitor and leader of the Elite, the soldier supposedly known for his ability to glean truth from any captive. The heaviness in his stance, and the hard way his jaw was set, did little to dispute the reputation.

Peter and William had told her stories of the man, recalled gruesome tales that were too bloody for her to bear. She tried not to shudder as he sat down a few feet to her side, his scarred hands opening up the binding of a large book. When his fingers flipped the pages, Elizabeth could hear his calluses scrape against them.

"I can move if you'd like," he said, eyeing his story. "I don't have to sit here."

Elizabeth knew Dravian was speaking to her, but still she asked, "Away from me?"

She felt dull as soon as the words escaped her lips. The soldier glanced up from his book with a nod and what she assumed was a smile. She was not entirely sure, though. His mouth only curled up a little, and only on the left side. For all she could tell, the right side—unseen from the position he sat in—still looked hard and foreboding.

"You can sit wherever you please." She tried to sound sincere as she gave her statement, but she couldn't help feeling she'd belittled his stature. *Light, what a snob I must seem. But goodness, he is frightening.*

"I know I frighten you," he said, as if knowing her thoughts. "Rest assured, my book will read the same here as it would over there, or there, or there." He lifted his dark-haired head toward different directions around them. "Not over there, though. The story would be utter nonsense over there."

Elizabeth furrowed her brow until that half smile grew larger, the soldier's grey-blue eyes looking to her. His head moved too, revealing the other side of his face. It seemed to be grinning as well.

He's jesting, she realized, forcing a smile to her lips. *Perhaps I was wrong to judge him. What do my brothers know, anyway?*

"So," she started, pointing a finger to where he'd gestured, "what would be wrong with your book over there? That is the eastern part of the camp. Perhaps the book would suddenly be in Prianthian?"

The Elite raised his hand and waved it dismissively.

"No, no, it has nothing to do with direction, and it's far more difficult a language than that."

"Ah, Concordian? Alivadian?" She felt herself relaxing as she played along with his jest. "I've heard Alivadian is very hard to learn. The same word can mean five different things depending on how high or low your voice is when you say it."

He pursed his lips in thought. She realized then it wasn't his smile that was crooked, but his nose, likely broken from his years as an Elite.

"Well," he started, "I suppose I don't know those languages, but I'd reckon the Old Evean tongue would be the most difficult to translate. And that's what my book would be if I sat over there. Old Evean." He paused, his head shaking with feigned dismay. "I'm afraid I don't read a lick of it."

Elizabeth laughed and nodded, responding with, "I suppose you can sit here then," as she eased her sketchpad back against her knees. She looked up at the campfire, the loud, jolly singing of her brothers having faded as Peter began to vomit. William patted him on the back and guided him away from flames, but his lips held a mischievous grin. The rest of the soldiers guffawed hysterically at her younger brother's expense.

I will never understand men, Elizabeth decided. She blushed as Dravian turned toward her, the stifled smile on his face and a raised brow revealing she'd spoken the words aloud.

"I can fill you in a little," he said. "I know what motivates a great deal of those men."

"All right," she said, anxious to be rid of her embarrassment. She gestured toward the men near the campfire. "That one, with the reddish-blond hair sitting beside the ambassador. His name is Rellor, yes?"

Dravian's jaw twitched slightly. "Indeed. Rellor is the second youngest of the Elites' leaders. He's my second when we take prisoners captive, and he . . . delights, in what he does."

Elizabeth felt a chill run down her spine as she looked at the wiry man again, his gaze almost aglow from the blaze of the fire. The ghastly thinness of his cheeks made his face appear sunken in, his mannerisms sharp and manic as he looked between the other men. Elizabeth almost wished she hadn't asked of him.

"He is better than I at what he does," Dravian continued, "when the victims are to his liking. Most men fear hurting someone if they're unsure of their faults, or if they don't know the entirety of their crimes. At times it even alters our interrogations, these fears, because the shame of harming someone who should never have been harmed is a guilt unlike most others. Young people barely older than children, a woman with child; those are all people who are difficult to bring justice upon. Rellor loves those kinds of prisoners, the ones most of us are too afraid to touch. He has never failed in avenging the people who died from the blades of those who look innocent. He is crazed—cruel, most would say—but many more would be dead if his sanity were clearer."

Elizabeth swallowed, her fingers trembling. She'd not thought her uncle would allow such a man in his Elite, let alone be the second in command. "Someone else then," she said hurriedly. She was eager to stray from the disturbing images she envisioned. "Odin Iceborne, the older man on Ambassador Dorian's other side. He is a leader too, yes?"

"The lowest ranking of the four, after Markeem and Rellor, yes," Dravian said. "He fought alongside King Pierre and King

Gerard in the War of Fire and is said to be the only man the Golden Knight of Xenith could not defeat in a duel."

Elizabeth relaxed slightly at the mention of the Golden Knight. Sir Garron had always ruined her and the Xen princess's fun when they were girls, his constant insistencies of Gwenivere's training still a vivid remembrance in Elizabeth's mind.

Dolls are fine, dear, but if Xenith is ever attacked, the dolls will not be able to save anyone. Painting is pretty, yes, but Gwenivere really must read The Art of Calling *by Gustav Halstentine.* It was not often that Elizabeth got to see Gwenivere growing up, especially not after Queen Rose passed, but when she had, Garron had rarely allowed his charge's time to be rededicated to her guests. Swinging swords and casting elements were far more important to him.

"So, Sir Garron cannot defeat him," Elizabeth said. "But has anyone actually seen Odin defeat Garron? Or has it just been determined they would finish at a draw?"

Dravian's forehead wrinkled. "Well, the rumors are they finished at a draw after Odin made an insult to Sir Garron. But while he might be an Elite and one of my men, I would not put Odin against the Golden Knight now. Garron trains with the princess of Xenith almost every day, hones both her skills and his own in *touched* and *called* weapons and shields. Odin's gut grows wider from his drinking and his coin purse lighter from the brothels. He would tip over before Garron even nudged him."

Dravian turned to Elizabeth and motioned toward her drawing, his half smile returning as she realized her now crossed legs revealed its image. She yanked the sketchpad up frantically, embarrassed that it had almost been seen, and hoped the soldier had not been able to decipher any of it in his quick glance.

"Perhaps I shall speak of you now," he suggested. "Women are hard for many people to understand too, you know."

Elizabeth swallowed roughly as her hands shook.

"All right, go ahead," she said defensively. She had ridden with Dravian and his soldiers for some time, their shared paths having yet to part, but not once had she engaged in conversation with any of them. Certainly Dravian could say nothing of her that was above whispered assumptions and queries among the men. Certainly not . . .

"You are kindhearted," he started, "but you seek to find strength for your family's name." He held out his hand and lifted a finger, as if she could be summed up in a handful of qualities. "You chastise your brothers because they bring you dishonor, but if anyone were to speak ill of them, you would be fiercer than they in their defense. You mentioned the men you asked me of in relation to where Ambassador Dorian is sitting, which means you either hate him or fancy him."

Elizabeth's cheeks flushed as she opened her mouth to protest.

"Fancy him," Dravian gathered. "And you despise the duchess-heir Natalia because . . . because you know in your heart the ambassador still loves her. But if not for that, you would pity her for being the daughter of the Duchess Yvaine and would try to befriend her."

Dravian stopped, his amusement seeming to soften as he took in Elizabeth's saddened appearance. She had not wanted to ruin what was only meant as a jest, knowing the man only meant to be cheery, but the truth of what he'd said made her happy spirits falter. She hadn't thought her feelings for Dorian were so obvious.

"There is a reason the title *Inquisitor* goes along with my name," Dravian said, his hand reaching out and nudging at the drawings she clung to. "Rest assured, girl; the ambassador doesn't know."

Elizabeth nodded as she at last let him see her sketch, the scene she'd depicted hardly different from that of the men just beyond them. The flames of the campfire rose into charcoal smoke, soldiers laughing jovially as Peter and William sang in the background. In the forefront was the skinny outline of Natalia, her breasts purposefully uneven and her back arched awkwardly in her dance. Her face held a laugh, her eyes squinting with seduction, but the tail of her dress and the ends of her hair were caught afire as she danced too close to the blaze.

Dravian burst into a booming chuckle, his hand releasing his book as he clutched to his chest. After a moment, Elizabeth eased her stiffened shoulders, her hesitant giggle abandoned for a fullhearted laugh.

The two quickly stifled their amusement as the camp took its turn to stare.

As someone who is praised for creating healing elixirs, you would think I'd have discovered more in regards to regenerative healing. Alas, I seem to be behind in the advancements of our enemies, as reports have indicated some among their ranks have succeeded in making such concoctions.

From the journal of Abaddon Haroldson

CHAPTER 9

DIETRICH

The weavings of darkness interlaced with the piercing splendor of light. It came with agony, pressing Dietrich back into the calm of black. He saw his beloved Daensla there, her raven hair falling like waves along her back, her golden skin gleaming in the candlelight. And then she turned, eyes cold, lips pale, the jagged scar along her neck open as blood poured out of it.

"You knew I would die," she whispered. "You knew they would come for me." She rose, her nightgown stained in crimson, and stabbed a blade at his shoulder.

"Why would you not leave me?"

Dietrich yelled, screamed in guilt and pain, the light returning as he reached up to hold his beloved Daensla.

"Rest," a voice soothed, pressing him back down to his bed. "Rest."

The prince obeyed the voice, its tone unfamiliar but kind, and slowly let it guide him back down to the softness of his pillow. He tried to open his eyes, eager to know who it was who spoke, but only a blurred outline would reveal itself.

The darkness beckoned with every blink.

"Do you remember your name?" the voice asked. It was fading now, his mind returning to the haunting of his dreams, but still he tried to answer the query with his alias. Whomever he spoke to could not know he was the prince.

"Vvv . . . vvvv . . ."

Veen.

"Shhhh," the woman commanded, something cool dabbing at his chest. "It's as I thought."

Dietrich nodded, continuing to hear the woman speak. He thought she said something about Prianthia, about his triumph, but his mind was foggy and his thoughts likely misconstrued. He kept motioning his neck in agreement as the pain subsided, heavy lids once again casting out the light.

Dietrich awoke quietly, his eyes skimming the room as he tried sleepily to decipher its contents. It was morning, the dawn sneaking its way through the clamped windows, the shielding drapes assisting in keeping the light of sunrise at bay. He wished terribly one window would open, the rank smells of blood and sweat trapped within the still air. He glanced down, the warmth of his blanket covering the dampness of his bed, the former white of its sheets now a faded scarlet and copper. If the colors were any indication, it would appear the smell was coming from where he lay.

"Ah, you're up," a voice said cheerfully. Dietrich leaped from his sheets and *called* instinctively for a blade as the air chilled his skin. Enough nights seeking out the traitors who led the insurgence in his lands made him accustomed to sudden bouts of wakefulness.

The woman before him smiled, her round, green eyes looking away courteously as she pointed to a wardrobe beside him.

"I fetched you some new attire." She sounded as though she were holding back a laugh, dimples forming against her cheeks. "I couldn't wash the blood from the things you adorned before."

Dietrich looked down, at last realizing the absence of his clothes. He *vanished* his weapon hastily and reached for the things she pointed at.

"Wait!" she said, shaking her head in scorn. "You will dirty them if you don't bathe first. Come, I have prepared a bath."

The prince didn't reply, still unsure of where he stood. He looked around the room, his eyes and mind now less under sleep's grasp. He ignored the woman's insisting hand as she urged him to follow.

"Why are my things covered in sand?" he asked, recognizing his satchels on the floor, "Where am I?"

The woman laughed, walking over to him and nudging him along.

"It will come to you soon, I promise." She was careful to only touch the skin along his back. "But first, the bath."

Dietrich at last obeyed, allowing the woman's hands to guide him forward. He rattled his brain, tried desperately to remember what had occurred, but the sweet smells of soap and the steaming warmth of water were all he could think of. He slipped into the bath's hold, muscles he hadn't known were sore gratefully unwinding. He heard the woman mutter something about the water being too hot as she put a hand in it, then saw a bead of sweat form along her forehead as she *called* the smallest bit of ice.

She wasn't good with elements; the visible effort she put into getting the water the right temperature proved that. That was helpful to know. While she might appear to be helping him, it might be a ruse. Maybe she wanted something from him, or maybe she was just keeping him alive until someone she worked for came to question him. Well, he'd just have to accept that. Being naked and disoriented, he doubted he could do much to defend himself. Best to regain his strength.

Gradually he allowed himself to close his eyes, his lungs taking in the steam as his head rested against the bath's edge. Perhaps he would heed the woman's words, let the memories come to him. No need to rush them while such perfection tempted.

"Better, is it not?" she asked. Dietrich glanced up. The woman's dress now rested at her feet, her smooth figure joining his scarred one as she lowered herself into the lavish, perfumed waters. He watched without a word, only admiring the stranger as she sat across from him. She smiled, catching his silent gaze, and unfastened the tie that held her hair.

"Truly," Dietrich said, grinning, "where am I?"

The woman laughed again and closed the distance between them. She took a cloth from beside the water's edge, filling it with the soap before wiping it across his chest. Gently she brought it up to his shoulder, a slight pain resonating through him as she cleaned off the blood.

"It still hurts, I see," she said, noting his grimace. She removed the cloth and set it aside, fingering the spot with careful examination.

Healers never did this *in the capital,* Dietrich thought, glancing down at where her hand rested. The dull remnant of a quarrel revealed itself from beneath her fingers.

The image of the desert fiend, of the serpent, flashed back to him. He saw it then, the blade-like tail puncturing through him, his sword severing through its scaled neck. How long ago had that been? The wound was already a scar.

The woman's hand was suddenly against his jaw, bringing his gaze up to meet her own.

"My cure healed you," she said. With a comforting smile she gestured over to a tray of elixirs at the room's edge.

"You haven't been here all that long," she added, reaching once more for the cloth. "The Dividing Wall, that is. I know you asked earlier." She glanced up at him and grinned again, holding his gaze for a moment before continuing on.

"I found you and your stallion on the outskirts of the city. You were near death, and I was not sure if you would make it, but here you are."

She ended her words with a chuckle and added some kind of small, dried petal to the bath before continuing with her self-appointed care.

Dietrich tensed. Why was this woman doing this, taking him in when he had given her no payment? What incentive did she have to help him, a man she knew nothing of and had nothing to give?

Dietrich's initial intrigue faded as rightful caution took its place. He quickly grabbed the woman's wrist, peering up at her searchingly as her smile vanished.

"Who are you?" he demanded, rising above her. "Why are you aiding me?"

The woman winced, her hand unwillingly releasing the cloth from the pressure of his grasp. It sunk in the bath's warm waters.

"Brelain Sandborne," she stuttered. She fought to free herself as his other hand grabbed her. "I know who you are. I know to keep your name and your purpose hidden. Thus I have aided you, as is my calling, hoping to assist you where others might intervene."

Dietrich watched her as she spoke, her words spilling out with a tempo that begged for release. He felt her pounding pulse in his hands, but it was not from deceit that it carried so quickly. She feared him, feared the ferocity with which his dominance held. He eased his grasp and released her, knowing her words weren't a lie.

He hardly understood, though, hardly comprehended how she knew his true self or his cause. He must have revealed it when she had first found him, ramblings often evoked when one was near death.

He had no memory of it, though.

Just be thankful she's not a member of the Redeemers, he thought, noting her quivering lips. *You wouldn't be alive, or sharing her bath, if she were.*

"Forgive me," he whispered. He swallowed and lowered himself back into the steaming waters. "I know not whom to trust."

The woman—Brelain—remained silent, her body still as she looked over him with mercy. Her hand cautiously rose, her green gaze watching him as she returned her fingers to his skin. Slowly, gently, she traced the scars scattered across his chest.

It was not the first time a woman had discovered him Sadie's eldest prince, and it was certainly not the first time a woman presented her loyalty through such intimate means. He felt guilt at such offerings, yet a life of solitude often pressed him to oblige. How else could he, the Cloaked Prince and peasant nobility of Sadie, ever think to find companionship? It wasn't as though he could pursue women as his fiend-hunting alias. Any courtship then would simply be a façade, and one that, as Daensla's death had shown, could ultimately prove fatal.

Casual acceptance of an offered bed, implied as it may be, was best. Dietrich rested his fingers against Brelain's side, grabbed her waist, and pulled her with eager agreement toward him.

Hours later, after having parted with Brelain and walked about the streets, Dietrich decided night came too quickly in the Dividing Wall. The town rested at the base of the monstrous mountains, and they seemed to devour the sun just as men began to withdraw from the mines. Soot and grime lined their faces, their pickaxes thrown carelessly over their shoulders as they made their way to the brothels. Eager was each for the warmth of a drink and the skin of a woman, all taking pleasure in the flattery and lies their rich voices spoke. Few of the men could afford to hear more than words, their coin purses dry as their glasses filled, yet words were all they needed, a pleasant compliment more payment than a bed shared. They sauntered home, drunk and happy, none paying any mind to Dietrich as he quietly strode past them.

Brelain had been helpful in providing him guidance for the Dividing Wall's towns. She gave him back his coin purse—still full save for the expense of the new clothes she'd bought him—along with a few vials of elixirs and a somewhat detailed map that she'd marked up with where she recommended he get supplies. She claimed she knew of his mission to Xenith's masquerade, which must've been another apparent, barely conscious slip of tongue, and suggested he try finding Zar at one of the stables along the outskirts of town. She apologized profusely for not having remembered where Zar was taken, but Dietrich insisted it was fine. Her almost religious means of aid had far exceeded what he expected, and he made certain she understood her preparations in assisting him were worthy of nothing but gratitude.

Her preparations for him had been so well organized that

he might have thought her expecting them to meet, if not for the chance happenstance that it clearly was. Still, despite her hospitality and his genuine appreciation for her efforts, he could not bring himself to share any more time with her than was necessary. As soon as their passion had ended and his items and memories had returned, he'd promptly departed.

Even then, rude as it was, she seemed to expect it.

"My, my, well what can I do for you?" a woman asked Dietrich as he walked into a building with a sign naming it THE MERRY LADY. It was the barkeep who had spoken, a stalky woman with pinned up hair, and Dietrich noted with a sense of swollen pride that she looked him up and down appreciatively. No one ever looked at him like that, even the women whose beds he shared. They examined his scars and admired his build, and occasionally commented on the tiny flecks of blue in his green eyes, but few ever seemed pleased by his appearance. He was frightening, like his father, and attractiveness was rarely a trait he thought of for himself. Feigned as it may be, Dietrich appreciated the barkeep's attempts to make him feel wanted. He reached into his vest's pocket and placed a generous amount of coins on the counter.

"Food," he said with a grin. "And a drink, if you've got it."

"Well of course we do, handsome." The coins were gone before the words were spoken. "And handsome you are. You want someone to keep you company while you dine tonight?"

Handsome? Dietrich smiled again at the lie, wonderfully entertained by the lack of formality. He shook his head politely, glancing at the scantily clad women throughout the room. They were pretty, all with good figures and varying appearances, their voices like songs and their laughter like instruments. They evoked a permanent grin, an unfaltering sense of happiness, but the temptations of their merriment would only be temptations at most. His morning with Brelain had left him plenty satisfied.

It took him a second glance to see that—despite *lady* being in the brothel's name—some of the workers were men. That was common enough in Sadie. Their nation had endured so much, and had so little, that no one was going to condemn what little joy each person found. Not during enslavement, and not now.

"Hey, I know you!" someone called. Dietrich glanced over, more curious than concerned, the voice having clearly been that of a young boy. He thanked the barkeep as she returned with his food, grinning at the wink she gave him before turning to face the small finger pointing at his side.

"How's that?" Dietrich asked, taking a drink from his glass. He looked around the room and searched for the boy's parents, hoping to find a concerned mother rushing through the door or a scolding father scurrying in. No one did. He looked back to the blue-eyed boy, clearly western, and lifted his glass to his swollen face. "And where'd you get those bruises? You try to fight me or something?"

The boy waved his hands and shook his head. "Nah, them is from my master."

Dietrich stopped chewing for a moment, enraged at the thought. After years of hearing his father speak of the beatings he'd endured as a slave, of the lashings and the abuse, Dietrich's blood boiled knowing it still happened. Especially to a child.

He forced himself to calm and gestured for the boy to continue.

"Yeah, you's was that man who rode in all bloody. The healer lady said she'd take care a' you, and that I should take care a' your horse. And I did, sir. He's been rowdy for my master, but he's been good to me."

Dietrich nodded and patted the chair beside him. He thought about sitting himself, but the simple fact that the chair's back would be facing such a crowded room of people sent a shiver down his spine. Awkward as it may be, he'd continue to eat standing. "That's what you do?" he asked, watching as the boy hopped to reach the stool. "You're a stable hand?"

His query was met with a bobbing head, the boy's small hand reaching out and taking a swig from Dietrich's glass. Dietrich knew he was faster than the boy, and he knew he should likely stop him from consuming so strong a drink, but for curiosity and amusement alone he let it happen. The squinting eyes and squished features, and the *bleh* sound that escaped the boy's chapped lips, were almost enough to offer him more. He motioned to the barkeep and smiled at her kindly, pointing to his plate before nodding at the boy.

"So if you work in the stables," Dietrich continued, watching the barkeep scurry back to the kitchen, "what are you doing in a place like this?"

The boy shrugged and swiveled in his chair as he glanced around. "My ma works here. She's usually done by now, but I guess she's busy."

Dietrich thanked the barkeep again as she brought out another plate and placed it on the counter. The boy already had half his bread consumed before Dietrich could give the woman his payment.

"So, young man," he said, leaning over, "riddle me this: If your mother works here, then why did I just buy you that food? Couldn't you have gotten it for free?"

The boy stopped his persistent stuffing and paused for a moment as he met Dietrich's questioning stare. He looked back toward his plate and finished the bite in his mouth before smiling again.

"I like Josie," he said, lifting his scabbed chin toward the barkeep. "She's nice, she gives my ma money and a place for us to sleep. If you's willin' to pay her, I's willin' to let ya."

"Ah, well, clever enough," Dietrich answered. He hoped the bed the boy and his mother shared was not the one she lay in now. "How about this then: If you're the one who's good with my stallion, and you're here, then does that mean you left my Zar alone with that master of yours? The same one you said is no good with him? The one you said hits you?"

At this, the boy hurriedly looked back down and shoved bite after bite into his mouth. Dietrich nodded, patting his hand on the boy's shoulder as he placed another coin on the counter for Josie.

"That's what I thought. Eat with haste, my friend; we're going to the stables."

The boy—Zain, as Josie eventually called him—did as he was told, inhaling his food as though it were the only food he had. Josie reached down and grabbed his freckled face in her hands, whispering to him quietly as she glanced back up at Dietrich. Her flirtatious grins were now abandoned, her eyes only conveying warning as she kissed the boy goodbye.

"Be safe, and swift," she told him, nudging him onward. "Your ma should be back soon." Zain nodded, holding his face where her hands had clenched, and looked back up to Dietrich with obvious embarrassment. The prince kept his grin withheld, at least on one side, his amusement emerging with a single curl of lip.

"How far are the stables you tend to?" Dietrich asked, saving the boy's pride. Zain pushed the door of The Merry Lady ajar, holding it for a few soot-covered men before allowing himself to exit.

"Well I tends to a lot of 'em," he said, sure-footedly walking into the torchlit streets. "The Dividing Wall's a bad name for this area, 'cause it's a name for everything. Them mountains is the Dividing Wall, this town is the Dividing Wall, all the towns north 'a here's the Dividing Wall. *Everything's* the Dividing Wall. So I goes between all the stables in a lot 'a the towns, mostly the southern ones, and help whoever has the most work. Used to be that I helped the north ones—they's have more Mesidian's up there like my ma and me, but they's also got more Prianthians. Some of 'em was pretty nice, but some of 'em were them Redeemers, and they started killing all the western folk." Zain pointed to himself, his finger circling his blue eyes.

"My ma moved us down here, said the farther south we went, the less of 'em there'd be. More Sadiyans down here, like you, and she said Sadiyans ain't about killing their own. She was wrong about that, though; the Redeemers started persuading some of you green eyes, and now, blue eyes, green eyes, brown eyes—it don't matter. We don't know who to trust.

"But still, Ma says it's safer down here, less chance of them killin' us. So some 'a the stables is far, but most 'a the ones I tends to are pretty close."

Dietrich sighed and took in the boy's ramblings. He knew much of his capital's tendencies, knew which parts of the city to bear caution and which parts to bear pride, but he had little knowledge of the towns to the west. It would seem his killing Redeemers in Sovereignty, Sadie, were pushing them to new places.

"And which towns' stable has my stallion?" he asked, clarifying his prior query. "Is that stable far?"

"Nuh-uh, that one's here." Zain looked up for a minute, glancing between the signs above the shops. His eyes squinted, his sight obviously bad as he tried to decipher the words on each hanging slat. He pointed to one and turned back to Dietrich questioningly.

"Do you think that shop there sells nice fabrics? My ma, she don't have much nice things, and I's been savin' to buy her somethin' nice, somethin' she can make a nice dress outta. All her dresses are torn and dirty."

Dietrich read the sign FINEST FABRICS and saddened as he realized the boy's illiteracy. He smiled kindly, nodding his head as he glanced inside.

"I believe they do," he said, "but it doesn't appear they're open. Perhaps you can go tomorrow?"

Zain shrugged, then looked back to the ground and continued on.

"So how'd you get all bloodied up anyway? And how'd you heal so fast? The pretty healer lady do that with her cures?"

"She did," Dietrich said, taking in all their steps. *First a left, then a right by the currency station, then another left by the plaza with the shops.* "She's quite good with elixirs. Prince Abaddon himself would be impressed by her work."

"You know him?" the boy asked. The torch lights flickered in his gaze.

"I work for him," Dietrich answered. "I fight fiends, fetch him their blood, their fangs, their poisons, and he makes elixirs from them. That's how I was injured, by a fiend, outside the . . . Dividing Wall."

"Sounds pretty hard," Zain said, his voice filled with wonderment. "I hears lots of people been attacked recently. Like the fiends are preparing for something. Was the one that attacked you like a panther, a big cat with bluish whiskers? I hears a lot about a big cat recently."

"No, a serpent." *Slight left at the baker, right at the seamstress.* "Interesting beast you describe, though. I have a book, a categorization of sorts, that helps healers and fiend hunters know what fiends will give them what they need. It's called *Fire and Fiends*, and it's quite an interesting read. There are a great deal of paintings in the book, and descriptions, but unless I'm mistaken, I don't recall ever coming across a fiend of that sort before."

"You's lucky then," Zain said. "You probably wouldn't 'a lived if you had, and if you did, you'd have had some strange black marks on ya."

Zain stopped suddenly and lifted his hand toward the battered building in front of them. The whinny of horses sounded from inside. "This is it though," he said, "the stable with your horse."

The prince glanced up, a sign reading STABLES and the smell of hay confirming the boy's words. He could hear a commotion stemming from within its slatted walls, vile shouts and curses directed at the rowdy steeds inside. It was Zain's master, more than likely, the one who had delivered the bruises on his face.

Dietrich leaned low to the ground, anxious to free Zar, and grabbed the boy gently by the arm.

"I am greatly indebted to you," he said. "First you helped care for my horse, then you went out of your way to bring me here. Many grown men wouldn't be so courteous."

He opened the boy's dirtied palm, reached into his vest, and transferred a small fortune into his hand. Zain stared at it in shock, his blue eyes wide beneath his swollen skin.

"Listen to me very carefully," Dietrich instructed. "There's enough there to get you by until the next half moon, and enough for you to buy your mother something from that shop. But"—he stopped, raising one finger and pointing it sternly— "you have to promise me, *promise me*, that you will not return to this stable. Not ever. Do you understand?"

Zain said nothing, only standing silent for a moment before nodding profusely. Dietrich smiled, returning to his full height and patting the boy kindly.

"Go on now, you've done your share. I'm sure your mother is back by now, and probably very worried."

Zain nodded and shoved the coin into his trouser pocket before hurrying back to The Merry Lady.

Dietrich stood still and watched protectively over the boy, waiting patiently until his footsteps were lost somewhere between the baker's and the seamstress's shops. When he could hear them no more, he headed for the entrance to the stables, cast out what little light the torches around him held, and *called* a black blade to his grasp.

The stable master would not beat another child after he was through.

"You're back?"

Brelain's voice was high, surprised it seemed to find Dietrich standing at her door. Her heavy lids lifted as she saw the bundle of hay he held and the black stallion a few yards behind him, which was tethered loosely to a post outside her home.

"Forgive me for disrupting you on this late hour," Dietrich said. "I . . . "

"'Know not whom to trust?'" She stood to the side and smiled, beckoning him indoors with a wave of hand. "Come. I don't wish to let the night air in."

The prince set the hay down and removed his cloak's hood, then quickly followed Brelain inside. The smell from his wounds still clung faintly to the walls of her home. He wondered how long it would be before the remnants of his injuries completely departed.

"Your elixir, the one you healed me with," he unfastened the clasp of his cloak and rested it against a nearby chair. "Does it only work on flesh wounds? Or does it also aid the sick?"

If it heals the sick, I won't have to continue with this foolhardy quest. I can just take this back for Mother—

"Only wounds," she answered, snatching his cloak and draping it over her shoulders. She grinned as she caught his glance, then sat beside a modest table in her study. "It regenerates flesh, quickly, as you discovered, but it does little else I'm afraid. And speaking of such things, have you gone killing tonight? The tunic I gave you has blood."

Dietrich started at her forwardness, never once having had

a woman so casually speak of his deeds. She was not a typical woman, though, he supposed, the very brilliance of her work distinguishing her so. Nonetheless, he leaned against a wall, choosing a spot where he could see every entrance to her home, and shook his head.

"What I do in the night should not concern you." He wished then that he still had his cloak to shield his tunic. Evidently, he was incapable of keeping his clothes without blood.

Brelain said nothing, only abandoning her chair and walking toward a few glasses beside her window. Dietrich watched her, intrigued by how little she seemed to ponder his words. She looked through a cabinet of liquids, hand on hip as she studied each bottle, then reached for a red one and filled two glasses. Cheerfully she returned to where he stood, handing him a cup as she began drinking from her own.

"Answer or don't. It makes no difference to me." She wiped her mouth and gave him a grin. "The masquerade is not for some time, and I know that's where your travels take you. If your feet bring you here each night until its arrival, I find no inconvenience in that."

The prince didn't answer, only drinking from the glass she'd given him. He swallowed the liquid with surprise, not having expected its tart flavor.

"I am a creator at heart, I suppose," she said, noting his interest in the drink. "I seek to make all things better. Would you like another glass?"

"I have had my fair share of drinks already this evening." Dietrich placed the empty cup on the table and cleared his throat. "Thank you, though." He glanced back over at her, realizing for the first time how little she wore under his cloak. He quickly turned away, too late it seemed, her proposition to house him more tempting as his mind conjured less noble thoughts.

"More reason to stay," she said. She finished what was left of her glass, then took their cups and placed them within a small basin. She washed them quickly, drying them with a thick cloth before placing them back perfectly where she'd found them.

"My injuries have set me back," Dietrich said, trying to ignore the healer's implications. "My time with you has as well."

"Are you blaming me?" Brelain asked teasingly. She leaned against the wall beside her, the edges of his black cloak opening slightly. The sight did little to cast away his thoughts.

"No," he said, smiling. His neck strained to stay up. "Though you don't seem eager to dissuade."

Brelain shrugged, dimples forming in her cheeks.

"My calling is to aid you, and aid you I have done. Forgive me for taking pleasure in my task."

Dietrich looked away and laughed. He'd not shared with Brelain his mother's illness, nor had he been foolish enough to share his and Abaddon's ploy for the Dagger, but somehow the healer seemed to understand the weight of his venture. He was going to the masquerade, she knew that much and he hadn't denied it, but that seemed the extent of her knowledge. He supposed asking her for a bit more guidance would do little to harm his cause.

"I don't believe I'll make it to Xenith in time for the masquerade," he admitted, still averting his gaze.

Brelain pulled the fabrics of his cloak back over her shoulders, seeming serious now as he relayed his concerns.

"You say the masquerade is not for some time, but it's coming sooner than I think possible for me to attend. And I don't know how to quicken my trek's pace."

Brelain lifted her hand up to her chin.

"You could befriend the Dragon Keeper," she said. "I've heard of some people riding his dragons before. Though I suppose I've never heard any firsthand accounts."

Dietrich stared at Brelain for a moment, surprised when what he assumed was a jest was not expanded on.

"Dragons?" he asked incredulously. "Fiends?"

"Well supposedly Zoran's are tamed," she countered. "Zoran is the Dragon Keeper."

"Fiends?" he asked again, tapping his shoulder. Despite the elixir's healing, the wound still ached when he touched it. "I should befriend fiends, after one just nearly killed me?"

"Or you can stay here with me," she said with a grin. "It's not as if you have an obligation to our people or anything."

Dietrich glowered at her, the healer seeming more entertained than fearful. He tossed her dismissal off.

"So how do I find this Zoran?" he asked, humoring her suggestion. "Does he have stables?"

Brelain shot him her own glare, clearly noting the mockery in his tone.

"The Path of Dragons is somewhere in the mountains. Zoran is thought by many to have sold his soul to the Fallen One for the power to command his dragons. Speak of him to the wrong people, and they will have you bound with element shackles."

Dietrich shuddered. Element shackles were what the Prianthians had used to keep his people in slavery, what they'd used to suppress his father's and his ancestor's elements.

Brelain, seeing his dismay, held up a finger.

"Speak of him to the right people, though, and perhaps you'll find some aid."

Dietrich closed his eyes and shook his head. "So you can't just walk me up to his dragons' lair and convince him of my merit? You can't solve *all* my problems? My, my, aren't you proving useless."

"Useless, eh?" Her fingers undid the ties of his cloak and revealed her thin garb beneath. "I suppose you're right. I've only saved your life, let you stay in my home, gifted you with elixirs and poisons, and let you taste the wonderful drinks I've created." Her dimples formed again as she smirked. "I thought, when you brought your horse and hay, that perhaps you were going to dismiss me of my uselessness and keep me company. But if you feel so compelled to leave, I suppose my heart will bear it."

She tossed him his cloak before walking into her sleeping room. Amused and convinced, Dietrich rose from where he leaned, set his cloak aside, and followed.

I'm not a Redeemer sympathizer—I think what they preach is detestable. However, I would be a liar if I didn't admit that wealthy Western women are the absolute worst when it comes to providing decent payments for working girls like myself.

Dividing Wall serving girl

Chapter 10

DIETRICH

After a lingering farewell with Brelain, Dietrich led Zar from the southernmost end of the Dividing Wall and headed to the northern towns. Traveling by horse was a much more preferable means of transport through the old mining towns than walking. Beggars were less likely to ambush riders than simple men afoot. Thieves also grew wary of robbing men on horseback, most knowing it was far more difficult to escape the canter of a mount than the sprints of a man.

A few *touched* daggers, each strapped in plain sight along Dietrich's thighs, were certainly a deterrent as well. No one was foolish enough to disrupt his leisurely ride about the towns. Leisurely it was, albeit only in appearance, the careless stroll meant to detract any attention a more purposeful one would bring. With purpose it was, the Assassin Prince intent on the destination he sought.

Intent, and penitently nervous.

The north of the Dividing Wall's towns had much reason for Sadiyan men to be afraid. Solitude was enough to mark them outside the Redeemers ranks. More parties of brown and green eyes appeared the farther Dietrich's travels took him, the strange alliance of Prianthian and Sadiyan men a result of the insurgence's hold. Zain's words had proven true, it seemed, the constant hunt for the radicals in the capital indeed having led the hateful group into the Dividing Wall's borders. With confidence they spoke, no apprehension in their words, former Sadiyan slaves speaking in the tongues of their previous Prianthian captors as openly as men bargained for goods. Dietrich kept his cloaked green eyes cast to the ground, grateful Brelain had gifted him with more poisons and elixirs.

Nightfall came dreadfully early, Dietrich cursing the wondrous mountains for stealing the sun so swiftly. Without the burning heat of day, more people withdrew their hoods, at last allowing their features to feel the crispness of dusk before the bitter cold of darkness came. Suspicious he would seem, then, to keep his cloak up, but he had little choice, his wiser thoughts telling him it was better than risking recognition among such crowds. To the inns he retired, his belly full from their food and his muscles eager to continue moving. He read, he drew details on his map and documented the seven-tailed serpent and the panther-fiend Zain had described, then attempted to greet slumber. It was always elusive and infrequent as his *touched* blades rested within his grasp.

Few miles remained after moons of travel, the character of the northernmost town different from those he had visited before. Hardly a Sadiyan strode through the streets, blue eyes of westerners taking the place of green, golden skin replaced by white. More blond and red hair rested atop heads and through brows than any Dietrich had seen before, a colorful contrast to the black he was accustomed to. He drew back his hood, comforted to see the Redeemers' victims outweighing their men, and tethered up his horse.

"Pardon me for such a bold request," he said, spotting a solitary blonde as he walked into the inn. "But may I join you?"

The woman looked up with bright blue eyes, her face pale and mature despite the deceptive youthfulness of her face's powders. It almost made him nervous just to see her, so obviously western, in an area where Redeemers dwelled so near. They hated westerners, believed them responsible for pitting the eastern nations against one another. He rarely witnessed western women in the East who didn't have to hide who they were.

"I am a traveler from Sovereignty, Sadie," he continued, "Yeltaire Veen is my name. I plan to travel to the West, but I'm afraid I know little of their customs. I shall pay for your meal in exchange for your knowledge of such things, if you would be so kind as to share them."

The woman stared for a moment, then placed down her book, *From the Victor's Victims*, and pushed out the seat beside her.

"It would be a delight," she answered. Her voice was somewhat deep, but held an enchanting lilt. She leaned back and caught the eye of a server, waving her over to her table. "No need to buy, though," she said, looking back to Dietrich, "I am a wealthy woman who enjoys the company of interesting men. I shall pay."

"Is that custom in the West?" Dietrich teased, quickly ordering a grand meal from the young girl who approached. He eyed the seat the woman had offered, hating the idea of sitting in the middle of a tavern, but he supposed a fine meal might be enough to distract him as he sat. *If you's willing to pay her, I's willing to let ya.* Zain had been wiser than he had seemed.

"For our women to be wealthy, or for us to pay?" the woman replied with equal jest. Dietrich grinned, already amused by the company he'd chosen.

"Either. Both."

The woman took a sip from her glass, handing the empty one back for the server to fill before waving her off.

Not the politest woman, it appeared, but the server would be paid handsomely.

"To answer the first query," she started, "no, it is not custom for all women to be as wealthy as I. Though many in Mesidia do not struggle and earn what they deserve. On the contrary, Xenith has many women of my stature, and many more above mine. Most, if not all, are highly educated."

"What of you?" Dietrich asked, finally removing the cloak from his shoulders. "You speak with formality, you read historical books, you drink wine when most drink mead. Are you well educated?"

"Indeed," she answered, not bothering to thank the serving girl as she brought back another glass.

The prince made sure to whisper, "My gratitude, dear," as the server handed him his drink, her eyes twinkling at his notice. She shot a glare at the woman, unbeknownst to her, before scampering off dutifully.

"I grew up in Mesidia," the woman continued. "I excelled in my academics despite having farmers for parents. A wealthy patron took interest in me when I was fifteen, said he would pay for me to attend his school in Voradeen, Xenith. I accepted and went on to be educated there. I told myself I never wanted to be poor again, so I married the patron's brother, a wealthy man good with coin."

"How did you end up here then?" Dietrich asked. "Seems a rather unlikely place for such an intelligent western woman."

"Yes, well," she shrugged the compliment off. "My husband is good with coin, but not in the most traditional ways. He finds opportunity where others don't. The mines here, for instance. No one's to properly manage them now that the Prianthians don't use your people for slaves. Barbaric it was, certainly, but you cannot denounce their effectiveness to loot anything of value from here."

Dietrich nodded, if only to keep from standing up and walking away. He had nothing against the westerners, but comments like those were why the Redeemers felt the West's people were so callous and evil. It was how they were convincing others to forsake alliances with westerners and keep loyalty to the East.

After all, how could a decent person speak so casually of slavery?

Her parents were farmers, not slaves, he told himself. *She doesn't know what it's like to hear the stories of her ancestors in chains.*

"My husband, Gregory, came," she continued, not noticing his internal rigidity, "seeing it was only adventurers, treasure hunters, people of that sort, that came to the caves here. He figured they needed someone to manage their plunders. He deals with traders in the West, helps the miners sell their profit, and in return gets a heavy portion of their coin. Smart, really, seeing as most of the miners are dimwitted and don't realize how much he cheats them. But it pays for me to live in luxury, and no one is really harmed in the process. So, to answer your former query, no, most women do not pay for men's meals. But my husband is older, and a cowardly bastard, so I snatch the company of any fascinating guest I can."

Dietrich grinned. He was simultaneously annoyed and entertained by the woman's selfish confidence.

"So I'm fascinating to you?" he asked. He dug his knife into the meal the server brought and took a purposefully large bite. He was almost tempted to eat the meal with his hands, see the look of disgust the woman would give him, but he decided against it. She possessed knowledge he wished to gain. It was best not to dampen her ready tongue.

The large bite, though, forcing him to chomp loudly, did earn him a haughty glare.

"I have heard the name Yeltaire Veen, read it rather," she answered, cutting her meal with delicacy. "Gregory doesn't just trade in elemental metals, or jewels or rocks, but in anything my people are willing to pay for. Your Prince Abaddon, many of his remedies travel here, travel through my husband's hands, and I often see the name *Yeltaire Veen* listed as one of the chief aiders. You fight fiends for a living, but you are intelligent enough to know what parts of them to keep before they drift. So yes, Veen, I find you very fascinating."

Dietrich used his meal as a reason to swallow. He cursed his younger brother in his head.

"I had not realized my name had gained so much recognition. Prince Abaddon should not humble himself to such lengths and give others so much credit. He is the true genius behind the elixirs." *But not a genius when it comes to discretion.*

"Humility is a fine quality for a noble to have, although I agree that one in your country's predicament should not be so keen to make it known."

Dietrich paused. "Our predicament?"

The woman took another tiny bite before sipping her wine. Her painted lips stained the chalice. "Well yes. It was not so long ago that the Prianthians held your people in chains, and even a shorter time ago that they sent their troops to your borders. King Harold was smart to slaughter them in the streets, torture them for all to see. It scared the Prianthians away. The true Prianthians, that is. Now you have the Redeemers, bloodthirsty Crossbreeds eager to unify the East by shutting it off from the West. They blame the West for the brokenness of the eastern peoples, claim that the West's wars have turned Prianthia and Sadie against each other. They hate your King Harold because he has allied himself to the western peoples, and they hate the Prianthian royal family for the same reason. They want to overthrow the current nobility and try to unify the East as one nation, and though their tactics may be brutal, the idea of unity is one that appeals to a great many people."

I know my country's history, Dietrich thought irritably.

He kept eating his meal.

"With such strong opposition from this cult," the woman continued, "Prince Abaddon should not be so eager to hide his intelligence, as you've stated. I mean, for the Light's sake, your eldest prince, Dietrich Haroldson, is now reduced to a glorified vigilante. Effective in the capital, certainly, but the Redeemers seem to have plenty of men at the ready in most of the Dividing Wall's towns."

Dietrich wiped his mouth with a napkin and took a swig from his glass. Was this the kind of conversation he had to look forward to when he reached Xenith? Would all the wealthy westerners be like this woman? He wasn't sure he could continuously feign tranquility while he, his family, and his people were spoken of so absently.

"Do you fear them?" he finally asked, trying to steer them to a slightly different topic. "The Redeemers, I mean. Are you afraid of them?"

"I would be foolish not to be," she muttered, her confident aura slipping as she looked at the reflection in her cup. "But to live in fear is foolish, especially when I live such a grand life. If they kill me, at least I can say I enjoyed my time alive."

Dietrich drained the remains of his own drink. "Interesting perspective."

The server was there in an instant, filling his glass promptly before hurrying off and escaping any requests the woman might have.

"I don't believe refills are free," she noted, her eyes falling to Dietrich's second glass. "You are a man of opportunity, I see, snatching up the chance to gain what you can from my generosity."

"It's your husband's money, is it not?" he pressed. He held

the glass up to her, tapped it to hers in cheer, then took a sip and exhaled contentedly. "And if you take him to be a cowardly bastard, then I believe you. So yes, I will seize the chance to take from a man that you take from daily."

The woman's brow arched, her red lips pulling into a smile as her forehead lines deepened.

"Cheers to that," she stated, taking a drink of her own. "Now what things do you wish to know? I'm afraid I've spent a dreadfully long time speaking of myself and my own thoughts."

"None of which I haven't enjoyed." Dietrich forced the words with a feigned grin. He finished what was left of his meal, wiping his mouth again with his cloth before setting it atop his plate. The server was there before suddenly whisking away, she and the dirty dish gone before he had time to thank her.

"You seem to know much of politics," he started. "I'm interested in such affairs. Rumors, facts, gossip—all of it. I assume you have gained a great deal of this in the trading industry, yes?"

The woman nodded and shrugged modestly as she called for more wine. "One might say that, I suppose." When the server returned, she ordered two delicacies, despite still having her plate half full. The server nodded and rushed off.

"I shall start with Mesidia, as I know much of its history.

"Currently Pierre and Rosalie Laighless rule, and their son Roland is the heir to the throne and Guardian to the Dagger of Eve. Duke Bernard the VII and his wife Yvaine are thought to be the true royal bloodline by many, though not enough to evoke civil war. Yet."

"Why the discrepancy?" Dietrich asked. "And which do you believe?"

"Oh, I care little for one side or the other. Mesidia is relatively well off, not as much as it once was, but enough that I think it proper to keep the Laighless—Pierre's bloodline—ruling. But if it switched, and the Barie family did just as well, it would make no difference to me.

"The feuding bloodline started before my lifetime. I have read many texts on the matter, though many have a different bias depending on the author. Bias aside, the story is that, years ago, King Veldigar and Queen Victoria could not conceive a child. Veldigar took a second wife, Daniella Corrins, and had a son with her. Five months later, Victoria, his first wife, gave birth to her own child, a boy as well, and insisted Veldigar divorce Daniella and denounce the second wife's child from their bloodline. Veldigar refused, keeping both women for his wives, and both children as his son's. Fourteen years later, Victoria died, and Daniella was now the sole queen of Mesidia—"

"How did Victoria die?" Dietrich interrupted. "Sounds as if Veldigar wished to be rid of her. Picked a convenient time too. Both sons would have been old enough to inherit the Dagger."

"Precisely! And many historians would agree with you. Some say it was the plague of that time that took her, others say Veldigar poisoned her. Nonetheless, it was she who was the former Guardian of the Dagger, and therefore it should've been her son to take the title. But Veldigar did not heed the counsel of his advisors, or his late wife's will, and gave the Dagger to Daniella's son. He made a lot of enemies when he did that, made a lot of enemies for his remaining wife and her child as well. Attempts at the throne have been made by Victoria's descendants, the *Victorians*, as they're called, ever since."

"Hard to blame them," Dietrich said. "If I was one to care about bloodlines and political honor, I'd have to agree that Victoria's ancestors should have the throne."

"I too, though Pierre is more kingly than the duke. Although recently, if such gossip intrigues you, the throne was almost returned to the Barie family."

"Oh?" Dietrich bit into the dessert as the server set it down. It was cold and sweet, different from anything he consumed in the capital. Nothing stayed cold there for long. "How's that?"

The woman sat up, almost giddy, like a youth sharing secrets with a friend. "For some time, Pierre and Rosalie could not conceive, and they took in a Yendorian orphan by the name of Dorian and raised him as their own. Though he was a peasant, he was charming and witty enough to pass as otherwise, and many were not in opposition to name him the next king, even when Rosalie did finally give birth to Prince Roland. However, after years of holding back, Pierre decided to give the Dagger to his son, much to Duchess Yvaine's contempt. Natalia, Bernard's daughter, was betrothed to Dorian. When Pierre named Roland heir, Natalia and Dorian's engagement was broken."

"Seems Pierre didn't want to hand back the Dagger to the Victorian bloodline."

"It would appear so, yes," the woman agreed. "Though Mesidia is the closest it has ever been now to erupting into civil war. Yvaine has started a campaign of ill-thought on King Pierre, spread rumors and gossip of his 'betrayal.' I pity her daughter Natalia, always being thrown back and forth between whomever her mother needs her to bed. Some said she truly loved Dorian."

"Prince Abaddon has shared accounts of their meeting with me," Dietrich recalled, remembering the unnecessarily detailed descriptions his brother gave of the duchess-heir. Most were about her looks, and most were inappropriate, but laced between Abaddon's fondness of her appearance was a dislike for her tongue. "He said Natalia was cunning. And cruel."

"I would be too, in her position." The woman shrugged, seeming to contemplate what it would be like to fill the duchess-heir's shoes. "Perhaps not."

You would have more coin and your beauty would be greater, Dietrich thought, smiling at the server from across the room. She blushed, but not before smiling back. *Those seem to be the only things you delight in.*

"What of Roland?" he asked. "I've heard he pines for the heir to Xenith."

"All men pine for the heir to Xenith," the woman said bluntly. An odd annoyance sounded in her tone. "She could be hideous—or a man for that matter—and every nobleman would still desire her. She is attractive enough, from what I have heard, and bold, a characteristic I admire in other women, but she is to inherit the wealthiest and most powerful nation from the King of Peace. Wealth and power are enough to sway men's hearts as it is. Add a decent-looking girl in, and the chance to father the next Guardian of Eve? As I said, all men pine for that."

Dietrich's jaw tightened, his nerves unsettled. "You believe Roland's romance for the girl stems purely from political greed? You don't believe he truly loves her?"

"I know naught," she answered, finally finishing her first plate. She pushed it aside and placed her knife neatly at its edge before taking a sip of wine, dabbing her lips, and breaking into her dessert. "Love for nobles is not the same for common folk. It has to be practical, it has to uphold expectations. Rarely are such things fulfilled for those outside the royal sphere."

"I see," Dietrich said, trying to hold back his frustration. Their conversation had been informative, despite the woman's slights, but nothing up to that point had been anything he could take advantage of. Delicately, he tried to probe for more.

"Do you believe Gwenivere loves him?" he asked. "I've heard Roland is quite the dashing young lad."

She shrugged. "I met him once; he is quite fetching. Tall, rugged but beautifully handsome. For such a guarded, protected girl like Gwenivere, I could say it's possible she believes she loves him."

"Why do you say she's guarded?" he asked. "Is she guarded any more than the past heirs of Xenith?"

"Goodness, yes, far more! King Gerard's wife, Queen Rose,

passed giving birth to their son Aden five or so years ago. After that, the king moved his family from the palace in Voradeen to their castle fortress in the forest. He became very protective of his daughter, overly so one might say. On a side note, if you are to venture to the capital, you should tour the palace. It's the grandest thing I've ever laid eyes upon. It overlooks a lake, waterfalls are visible from all its balconies, the finest paintings adorn its walls. And the gardens—I've never seen so much color in one place. Really, it's a marvel. Breathtaking."

Dietrich sneezed, twice, grateful for the abrupt disruption to the woman's elegant and useless musings.

"Pardon me, where were we? Ah, yes, Princess Gwenivere. Tell me, um . . . "

"Fiona Collinson," the woman said, answering his nameless beckon.

"Yes, tell me, Fiona, do you think Gwenivere and Roland will try to marry? I know it's forbidden, they both being Guardians, but I am curious about all the speculation and gossip around such a thought."

"They would be foolish to try," Fiona said, "though nobles have done things more foolish in the past. Their families would never allow it, and I believe both to be too wise to pass their Artifacts on to someone so they could wed. They would lose too much power, too much prestige. Most nobility are smart enough to know no human is worth that. Not to mention it's treason. There are treaties that forbid Xenith and Mesidia from unifying. They were one nation in the past, before the marriage of Guardians was forbidden, and the amount of strength their unity possessed sent the rest of Abra'am into peril. Greedy hearts always brought war to their borders, and even if they were nearly indestructible, their people were not. It was better to be allies, in castles and palaces of their own, than to share in the title of king and queen for such a large landmass. Not only that, but the Dagger of Eve grants immortality, and

Gwenivere's Amulet is the only thing that could reverse it. If they were conquered, and someone drew on the Dagger's powers, the conquerors would then possess the one item that could nullify it. No one would ever be able to end their reign."

Dietrich said nothing, his full stomach suddenly queasy. Fiona carried on, still too infatuated in her telling to notice his sudden shift. The red of her lips faded with every bite and drink she took.

Curse you, Abaddon, to convince me of this ploy. Dietrich shifted uneasily in his chair. *Use the Dagger to heal our mother? I'll have your head for sending me on this implausible quest.*

"Do you think the Dagger only grants immortality?" he asked, cutting off whatever useless thing Fiona rambled on about. "Or do you believe it makes one invincible as well?"

She stopped eating for a moment and looked up in thought. "Why, that is a peculiar thought, isn't it? It's never been used, not to my knowledge, so I'm afraid I don't know for certain. I'd imagine it grants some sort of invincibility, though. The two go hand in hand, do they not?"

"I don't know," Dietrich said, forcing a smile. "You're the educated one."

"Well," she said, smoothing out her skirts. "To be immortal means never to die. One's body must always be healing itself, cleansing itself of wounds that might cause infection or viruses that might make them ill. Now, if the wielder were beheaded, or his or her heart ripped out, I'm not so sure."

"Those are quite gruesome depictions you paint."

"I've read worse."

Dietrich noted as Fiona's eyes looked down at the book she'd been reading when he'd first approached. She seemed suddenly lost in it, likely thinking through some morbid, fascinating tale from it she would impress someone with later.

He took a deep breath, trying to take in everything she'd told him. Was this quest Abaddon had convinced him of even possible? Would Princess Gwenivere ever help them persuade Roland to give up the Dagger?

Likely not, he thought, fighting off disheartenment. His doubt was confronted with the way his mother had looked when he'd last seen her, the way her bones had so prominently stuck out from beneath her clothes and the way her eyes had looked on with such fatigue. How much longer did she have? How much longer until their enemies knew she was ill?

This plan isn't going to work, he told himself, taking another breath. *It isn't going to work . . . but I still have to try.*

"To change the subject," he started, stealing back Fiona's attention. "I have a query of a more local sort."

"I've learned a great deal of that as well," she said smugly. "What is it you wish to know?"

Dietrich looked around the room and leaned in close to Fiona, curling his finger toward himself. She glanced around the room herself, her expression a mixture of annoyance and curiosity, then slowly leaned in too.

"The man they call Zoran," Dietrich whispered. "The Dragon Keeper."

"Ah." Fiona grinned as she declined the server's attempt to fill her glass. Dietrich cursed under his breath, assuming the refusal of drink meant their meal ended. *Speak of him to the wrong people, and they will have you shackled,* he heard Brelain say. He was nervous now that Fiona was one of those people.

"I no longer wish to be here," she said, gathering her things. "Though I do wish to spend more time with you. I shall tell you all you wish to know, but perhaps as pillow talk, rather than table talk."

Dietrich stood up as Fiona did and noted how little she left on the table for the server. He glanced at the band along her finger, a sizeable elemental diamond atop it as she clenched her book. He forced a smile, neither agreeing nor dismissing her request.

"You are married, to a wealthy man who takes good care of you."

"I'm married to an old man," she countered. "One who only takes care of my financial needs. He hardly satisfies me any other way."

She grinned, then turned her back and headed confidently toward the exit. Dietrich pulled some coin from his pocket and left it atop her pay, winking at the server as he followed behind. Truthfully, she was more a temptation than Fiona.

"I shall accompany you home," he said, holding the door open for her as she walked. "But I'm afraid that's all I can do."

"A shame," Fiona said, though the seductive lilt in her voice still held. She smiled and laced her hand through his. "Perhaps another day then. Now go on, ask away about the Dragon Keeper."

Dragons are amongst the rarest of known fiends. From all accounts of them, they are intelligent, dangerous, and able to absorb any elements forced upon them.

An excerpt from *Fire and Fiends*

CHAPTER 11

DIETRICH

Many a road connected the East and the West, some mighty as they swiftly rose to great heights, others moderate as they slowly wound and twisted about. To the north led voyagers to Yendor and the Arctic, snow always present as an endless winter grasped their lands. Few took the paths that led there, even fewer willingly, most footsteps marking the chained feet of prisoners sentenced to bitter deaths.

The southern roads led to cheerier lands, well-crafted signs indicating the pleasantries that awaited varying trekkers. Adventurers, eager to find purpose throughout the world's corners, would pass through to see the wonders, checking off their maps hastily as they searched for the next marker to set. Others, more inclined to complete their faith's callings, journeyed to the temples of Alivad and Stormhold, giving their bequests to the priests and priestesses before slowly venturing to the next points of their pilgrimages.

It was neither for pleasure nor for religious fulfillment that Dietrich traveled along the mountains. His was a journey still set in obligation, forcing him to imagine the lands beyond each path he passed. A rose with no thorns, the image of Xenith, nearly bloomed before his eyes, the vivid reds and dark shadows along the sign's slats almost enough to sway him to lean in and smell its budding petals. He sat atop Zar for a time, bringing the horse to a standstill as he gazed at the rocky road beyond and tried to convince himself he and his steed could hasten through its terrain.

Had time permitted it, he would have gladly accepted the coolness of the cliffs over the heat of the desert, but time itself discouraged his hopeful thoughts. His injury had set him back, too many days gone by and too many nights wasted in the comforts of taverns' beds. Afoot, or along Zar's back, it didn't matter. A different creature would have to bring him across the borders.

"Damn Abaddon and his mad plotting," Dietrich muttered, kicking Zar along. It wasn't really his brother's fault, he knew, as his own dabbling in local matters had been the true source of his altered travels, but he was too fatigued to blame himself.

Grey hair, grey beard, even grey eyes, he heard Fiona say. *Grey eyes. Rare, wouldn't you say? I myself have never been so close to see them, but I've seen the man from afar. And when the mountain man is among us, his dragons linger in the sky.*

Dragons. Fiends. Ancient beings from the Age of Old, susceptible to no element, in control of all. Highly intelligent, many said, or more accurately many read, few having actually laid eyes upon them.

"Ah, my dear brother, if only you knew what you asked of me," Dietrich said, his eyes lost in the words before him. Another sign, a good distance from any of notable passage, stood erect, strokes of blood conveying the words PATH OF DRAGONS

in several tongues. With warranted caution, Dietrich dismounted from his wary horse, gently tugged on the reins, and sang
nervously as he led them down the narrow path:

> First there were many, ladies aplenty,
> Come, they came, each to my door.
> Prudes there were few, my experience new,
> Come morn, come morn, they left a bit sore.

Dietrich grinned, the words to the old song slowly coming
back to him. His and Abaddon's watchman Culter had sung it
to them as boys, the meaning of the lyrics lost on the younger
prince. Dietrich had been of age, though, laughing as much
at Culter's crudeness as he did his brother's humored but confused expressions. He paused his singing for a moment, realizing Zar had calmed at his voice, and continued.

> Then there was Lassie, a lady so classy,
> Come, she came, in the cover of night.
> But she fell from such squander, over cliff down yonder,
> Come morn, come morn, her head wasn't right.

> Then there was Crole, a beautiful soul
> Come, she came, a book in her hand.
> 'Twas poems she talked, then the bed she rocked.
> Come morn, come morn, she could hardly stand.

Zar gave an approving snort. Dietrich laughed, singing
louder as the tenseness in his muscles loosened.

Haggard or dumb, more still seemed to come,
Over and over, to the neighbors' dismay.
We tried to be quiet, but still caused a riot,
Come morn, come morn, no more words they could say.

Then there was Klister, this one a mister,
Come, he came, for the sleep he had lost.
With a yell and a roar, I was knocked to the floor,
Come morn, come morn, my manhood the cost.

In the end there was none, the ladies all done,
Come, they came, to Klister's dwelling.
Now *I* had to listen, to all the fun *I* was missin',
Though come morn, come morn . . . he'd be itchy
and smelling.

As the song ended, a loud call took its place. Instinctively Dietrich ducked and pulled the bucking steed over to the mountain walls, *calling* a crossbow and scanning the sky. He lifted his weapon to take aim, but the Path of Dragons had plunged them deeper and deeper into a narrow canyon.

His view was obstructed by the rocks surrounding him.

Quickly Dietrich cast up a thin wall of ice, tall enough to ensure Zar couldn't flee. The stallion whinnied, begged for them to be free, but Dietrich kept his element steady. He stood still, made sure the balance on the ice and his weapon were set, and slowly tiptoed forward.

Silence, aside from Zar, was all he heard. The air was painfully still. Each tiny step he took thudded like stomps, the thin gravel sliding beneath his feet. He held his breath. The canyon was winding farther down as it curled, his view of what lay ahead narrowed even further. He crouched down, sweat beating down his brow, and lunged around the corner.

Nothing.

He held his weapon up, adrenaline forcing his heart to pound violently. He kept his stance, his feet sturdy beneath him. His eyes darted across the new clearing. With a hesitant grimace, he lowered his arms and *vanished* his weapon.

The call returned, louder now, fire suddenly plunging toward where he stood. Dietrich ran, barely able to outrun the swooshing of wings. The shadow of them closed in on him as he tried to return to his stallion. He stumbled on the jagged path, scarcely managing to keep his balance, but the ice element he held dissipated as his grasp on it faltered. Zar was nowhere in sight. Dietrich was left with the feebleness of his own feet to escape.

He could feel the heat of the flames behind him. The fiend barely missed him as its breaths of fire cascaded down. He *called* back his crossbow, slowly but steadily, cursing each dreadfully long second that passed. Knowing he couldn't outrun the winged beast, he took aim and released. Bolt after bolt fired with frantic precision. The flames ceased, replaced by a wounded bellow. The dragon above him crashed into the canyon's depths.

Dietrich watched, his chest burning as he took the moment to refill his lungs. The scaled creature cried out in pain, dust and dirt swirling around it.

Guardedly, the prince stepped forward, one foot cautiously following the next as he held up his weapon. The dirt and sand floated into nothingness, the sight of the injured dragon now laid out before him.

It looked at him with slit eyes, almost humanlike, surveying him as he neared. Mesmerized, Dietrich released his crossbow and took in the mystic creature, its watchful gaze an icy blue against the charcoal of its scales. He sensed its suffering, felt compelled to ease its pain, somehow as much a part of him in that moment as it was a part of the dragon itself. He stepped closer still, warily, his own eyes watching the fiend's as they followed his every step.

Its wings. That's where the bolts had struck. There was no evidence of the now-faded bolts, but dark blood spilled from where they'd pierced. Anywhere else and the bolts would've likely been deflected, the thick scales like a suit of armor around the dragon's body. The wings were thin, though, a skin-like substance no different perhaps than a bird without its feathers. Dietrich thought of Brelain's elixir, tucked somewhere in his satchel along Zar's back. Perhaps if he found the stallion and retrieved the elixir, he might be able to use it.

Not likely it would work, he thought, oddly tortured as the beast lay wounded before him. *It's not meant for fiends.*

The dragon was large, bigger than Zar even in its curled position, but not as large as he'd expected.

A swift death would be the more compassionate choice.

He exhaled in lament and leaned down beside the beautiful creature. He extended his hand out toward where it lay. It didn't move, though he knew its legs and body could, instead lying still as his hand met its neck. The scales were cool, despite a sense of warmth beneath them, likely remnants of the fire it had cast. He stroked its side, comforted it, wishing terribly its slit eyes would look away as he reached for one of his *touched* daggers.

I am not your enemy, a voice said. Dietrich froze, instantly releasing the hilt of his blade. The dragon continued to stare, knowing he had heard, yet Dietrich couldn't find it in himself to believe it as truth. It was a trick; dragons were known to deceive men, trap them within their lairs with elemental metal and fortune only to devour them. That was what this was, a mind game, some form of element from the Age of Old. Fearful, Dietrich again reached for his dagger, this time with no hesitation as he released it from his sheath.

As he raised his arm to deliver the fatal strike, a heavy blow fell against his head. Blackness, and the knowing eyes of the dragon, were the last thing he saw before he collapsed to the ground.

Drummers, from the desert tribes, pounded on their drums, their garb laden with colorful layers of pinks and greens and blues as their jewels sparkled from the sun. The women danced and spun, sheer cloths shielding their faces and stomachs as their feet jingled with repetition. The constant pounding, never ceasing, never ending, the twirling and jumping never stopping . . .

Dietrich at last opened his eyes from his dreaming, vertigo bringing about what little rested in his stomach. When he'd finished, the smell of his breath nearly made him hurl again.

"You're dehydrated," a man said. "You'll feel better soon."

Dietrich hardly heard, the pounding still continuing to pulse against his head.

"I hadn't thought you'd be out for so long," the man continued, "but it seems I struck you harder than intended. You must forgive me of that. You would've done the same if a blade was about to be cast on your loved one."

Dietrich sat back and wiped his mouth with his sleeve until the sensation of vomiting subsided. He opened his eyes again and squinted as he tried to keep the light from beaming against him. Slowly he brought his gaze to where the man stood, the body of a dragon lying calmly beside him. It hardly moved aside from the steady rise and fall from its breath, its reptilian lids keeping its eyes hooded.

"You're Zoran," Dietrich muttered, noting the man's grey

beard and hair. The man said nothing, only continued to mend the wounds to the dragon's wings. He didn't face him, more concerned with his strange pet, but Dietrich was certain grey eyes would peer at him if he turned.

Curious, he glanced around, not looking for but a moment before the glare of another dragon faced him. It was larger than the other, and darker, not a blink or a twitch to distract it from its guarded watch. Dietrich sat motionless, knowing the creature despised him, something startlingly human emitting from its stance.

"It attacked me," he said, as much to the man as to the new dragon. "I had no choice."

Zoran remained silent. He looked down at the dragon he tended, met its stare, then spoke again.

"Savine thought you were another," he said simply. He walked away from the wounded dragon, draping a blanket over its back before wiping his hands clean in a washbasin. He grabbed a towel and padded his hands dry before tossing it to Dietrich.

"Clean it," he demanded, cocking his head toward the floor. "I've had my share of tending to the mess you've made."

The man walked to a chair in the corner of the shed and fell into its embrace. The prince did as he commanded, careful not to lean forward too quickly as he wiped his vomit up. When he completed his task, he looked back over to the man, wordlessly asking what to do next.

"There is a waste bucket over there," he said, pointing.

Dietrich stood carefully, trying not to get any closer to the glaring dragon than needed. As he walked across the room, he knew the eyes of the beast followed.

"Who are you?" Zoran asked, leaning back in his chair. Dietrich thought on the question, never fond of revealing his stature, but one quick glance at the fiend beside him and he knew which name to give.

"Dietrich, son of Harold, son of Rorik, prince of Sadie."
He grimaced slightly, the titles sounding overly pompous to
him. With as many times as he had heard Abaddon introduce
himself in such a way, he hadn't thought he would hate it so
much when he spoke it of himself. The Dragon Keeper seemed
to care little of the formalities, though, his grey eyes glancing
over at the larger dragon briefly before turning back to him.

"I believe you, Dietrich, son of Harold, son of Rorik."
There was a hint of mockery in his tone. "I am Zoran, son
of Eva'uhl and Vorin. I have no ancestors beyond them." He
grinned slightly. "Why have you come here, Prince? What
purpose do you have with me?"

Dietrich looked regretfully at the wounded dragon—Savine, as Zoran had called her—before responding.

"I wish to make it to Xenith, by way of your . . . dragons." It sounded foolish, now that he said it aloud, but he
kept going. "I have pressing matters that involve the royalty of
the western peoples, matters that concern the continuation of
Sadie's prosperity and freedom. I would take the footpaths to
Xenith, but a fiend attacked me early in my crossing and made
travel by horseback . . . " he paused, nervous suddenly as he
thought of Zar. Where had the stallion gone? Had he made it
out of the canyon, or had the other, larger dragon . . .

He didn't want to think about it.

"Making travel by horseback too slow."

Zoran again turned to look at the other dragon. They
stared silently for a time.

"Your stallion is safe. He's residing in my stables."

Dietrich furrowed his brows, daunted by how strangely
perceptive the Keeper seemed to be. As if to mock him, the
larger dragon showed him her fangs.

"As for whether you can make passage by way of dragon,"
Zoran continued, "that depends on whether Seera can forgive
you for what you've done to our beloved Savine."

The prince met Seera's icy glare, somewhat defensive as she glowered with unwarranted hatred. After a moment he traded her vengeful eyes for those of the resting Savine's, remorseful as he took in the sight of her tattered wings.

"Will she fly again?" he asked quietly. Oddly, despite it having been her who had attacked him, it was she of the two dragons he felt drawn to. *The other can rot in darkness.*

Zoran exhaled loudly. "Dragons heal, but slowly. There are few flesh wounds that can truly harm them though. She'll be fine."

Dietrich nodded in relief, grateful his defense had not been fatal. He wanted to reach out to Savine, feel her tranquil spirit again as he did in the canyon, but he refrained. He didn't need to do anything impulsive after the damage he'd caused.

"You said she thought I was someone else," he started. "Who comes against you? Perhaps I can aid you in exchange for your—for Seera's help."

Zoran grinned, as if Dietrich's very offer amused him. He shook his head, his chair rocking as he rested his hands in his lap.

"The people I fear are not insurgence members who meet in the alleys of Sovereignty, Sadie. Your enemies are dangerous in their own ways, I do not contest that, but they aren't as powerful as the beings I seek solace from. Your offer is appreciated, but useless. Seera will decide your worth on other terms."

Dietrich nodded in acceptance, surprised by how much the elderly man knew of Sadie. He supposed Fiona and Brelain had both mentioned his passing through the towns, the man likely gathering what little he needed from the shops and the markets. News of the continent was likely something he overheard from conversations of passerby.

"I am tired," Zoran announced suddenly, rising from his chair. "I, unlike you, haven't been asleep the past few hours. Drink some water and drink some tea with my herbs if your head bothers you. I'm going to rest."

The Dragon Keeper brushed past the prince, not bothering to say any more as he walked away. Dietrich grinned uncomfortably at Seera, his hands clenching tightly as he remained alone with her and Savine. He headed toward the cabinet Zoran had pointed to, curious of the different herbs the mountain man possessed. With nowhere to go and nothing to do, the prince grabbed an herb, smelled it, and decided to indulge.

I am writing to you from the halls of Voradeen's palace. It is the most remarkable of things, though I write that with the limited experiences of a former slave. I'm sure to you, my beautiful queen, this place would pale in comparison to your sky city. That still doesn't make it any less wondrous to me.

Queen Rose is an avid supporter of the arts and has told me she will commission a painting of the palace so that I may show it to you. Hopefully it will not be damaged when I make my return to Sadie.

I gave your gift to the princess. She seemed quite fond of it.
All my best to our sons. Kiss them each for me and tell them I love them.
I pray safety for all of you.

A letter between Harold and Lenore of Sadie

CHAPTER 12

ᖲWENIVERE

XENITH

Gwenivere lay in her bed, birds singing their songs as the sun peeked through her window. She stretched with invigoration, every morning waking in Voradeen's palace like waking up to a dream. It was such a contrast to the castle fortress, which had prisonlike walls that seemed to keep the very thought of the outside world at bay. Her mother had hated it too. She'd insisted, over and over and over again, that unseen mold made her lungs ache. Coughs would follow her complaints, and a convincing hand would press at her chest, but as soon as Gerard's gaze drifted away, she'd give Gwenivere a wink.

They'd both preferred living in Voradeen's palace.

Gwenivere lazily rolled from her bed, the carpet at her feet sneaking through her toes. She scrunched them tightly, pulling the soft fabric tight against her skin, then strolled to her window and pulled the drapes open to her balcony. With a firm press to the glass, the window creaked slightly, the cool breeze of morning slipping through. She took a deep breath, listening to the sounds of her capital, and watched as it slowly began to wake.

This was what she loved. This was what she cherished.

She wondered how often she'd have moments like these when she held the throne.

And then it hit her, the memory she'd tried so hard to forget. The specks of red, the terrifying bark of her father's cough. The horse he'd fallen from as he'd clung to his chest . . .

I need a distraction. Gwenivere shut the window harshly, blocking out the pretty song a bird was about to sing. She headed toward her library, the crammed shelves running from floor to ceiling, and searched for something to read.

A vast array of history texts and religious teachings lay unevenly scattered, fantastical stories mixed in throughout. A ladder was needed to reach the highest of them, though what lay on the top shelves and what lay on the bottom was in no particular order. As a girl, Gwenivere had insisted her mother hide the most boring texts where she couldn't reach. The queen had happily obliged, even going so far as to tell Garron the ladder was a fearsome and unsafe mechanism to be used by a small girl. It was a constant battle then, Rose against the Golden Knight, both moving the books they thought worth reading to the most accessible places. Meanwhile, Gwenivere would steal away to the balcony, blissful in her moments away from tutors and training as she stared at the pictures of her favorite books.

Without thinking, she reached out and grabbed the first binding she saw. She brushed off the dust and read the title, *The Breaking of Mesidia*, holding her breath to keep from sneezing. When she was sure the dust had settled, she opened the cover and stared at the first page. Squinting, she read through a handwritten note that had been placed inside the text.

Your tutor has an ass for a chin. I feel like a scoundrel just looking at him.

It was jest, from Roland. She laughed at the writing, the elegant penmanship so opposing to its words. She'd tried so hard to shut out memories of Mesidia's prince and fellow Guardian that she'd nearly forgotten the spring he'd spent studying alongside her. Her father had thought it wise, and Roland's too, to have her best friend around in the months after her mother had died. It had felt perfect at the time, as if her broken heart had found its mending, but now . . .

She forced the book shut and shoved it back where she'd found it. She'd find a different book.

After a quick scan of everything eye level, Gwenivere decided to search on the ground. The shelves up high were filled with more books from her studies, more boring texts like the ones Garron insisted she read. She was certain more jests and flirtations from Roland lay within their covers, so she opted for the texts she'd read as a girl. Surely something for a child couldn't harbor solemnity.

The Tales of Eve, she read, kinking her neck to see the tiny spine. The book stuck to those surrounding it as she pulled it out, too many seasons having gone by with it lying untouched by human hands. This would be good then, for her and the book, as she needed her thoughts occupied and it needed reading. Stories weren't meant to go untold.

Quickly, though, Gwenivere realized she couldn't read the text. Many of the pages were in another language—an ancient one, if the different letters were any indication—and the ones that were readable had been too damaged to make out. The paintings themselves were stunning, though, vibrant and vivid, and she remembered cold winters by the fire, curled up beside her mother, guessing at what was happening in each scene. She could practically smell her then, the scent of wildflowers on her hair and vanilla on her skin. It was a fond memory, and one, unlike those that recently plagued her, that she allowed herself to see.

What do you think this is here, Gwenivere? What do you think is happening on this page?

Turquoise water, gently crashing against the white sand of a beach. And at its edge, just out of its reach, stood a man and a woman with grey eyes, both looking back at a forest of long-leafed trees with tears along their cheeks.

I think they're leaving Eve for Abra'am. And I think they're sad.

Gwenivere stared at the page, pushing it down to marvel at its beauty. *Light, I was a dreary child,* she decided, remembering her reply. She flipped to the next painting to see what came next, to hear her mother's velvety voice in her head as she took her turn to decide when a knock at her door interrupted her musings.

"Milady, it's Becca!" a voice called. "May I enter?"

Sighing, Gwenivere shut the *Tales of Eve*. She adored Becca, loved her as closely as an heir could love a servant, but the girl's incessant chatter was enough to make her ears bleed. She'd want to discuss all the royals, all the handsome men who had come to negotiate at the Peace Gathering and dance at the masquerade. And Gwenivere would want to bury herself in the ground, hoping there was enough soil between her and Becca to keep her endless ranting unheard.

"A moment," she answered. She trotted across the room and swung open the door, her chambermaid waiting with hands twirling between her hair.

"You're . . . blond?" Gwenivere said. Becca, once having hair a red shade similar to her own, giggled and flipped her head.

"I used pepper tree leaves," she whispered, leaning close as if it were a secret. She pulled a small bag out from her waist pouch and lifted it up, her blue eyes wild with excitement as she opened it for Gwenivere to see.

"I brought some for you!" she exclaimed, answering Gwenivere's raised brow. "I remember how you used to tell me you didn't think anyone in all of Abra'am would know who you were if it weren't for your hair. So, I thought, hmm, perhaps we should test that theory before you're married and chasing after tykes!"

Gwenivere shuddered at the thought. She smiled at her servant, though, deciding the offer was kind enough, and hoped the girl didn't see the dread the image had evoked.

"Thank you, Becca. You're very considerate."

The servant beamed, only hearing the words and not the tone.

"What's that?" she asked, pointing as Gwenivere accepted the bag of leaves.

The princess looked down, confused, before realizing she still held the *Tales of Eve* in her hand. "A book I used to look through as a child."

Becca gaped, staring at the story eagerly. Gwenivere handed it over, watching her servant's mouth hang open as she flipped through its pages.

"It's stunning!" she said. "Where did you get it?"

Where had she gotten it? She stood silent for a moment, raking through the hundreds of people who had bestowed her gifts on their ventures through Xenith. Most often the gifts had been portraits of boys her age, sons or nephews foreign kings thought would make good husbands for her when the day came. Few royals had brought her gifts she enjoyed. There had been one, though, a bear of a man, the memory of him slowly sinking back into place. She remembered her mother's hands rigid against her shoulders at their meeting, the man's golden skin stretched from muscle and lined with scars. He'd had a beard, a bird's nest compared to her fathers trimmed one, and his face looked spotted from years in the sun. But his eyes, dark green beneath hooded lids, had held an air of kindness and hope.

"King Harold," she answered, "from Sadie."

Becca looked up in shock. "Sadie? I wouldn't think the desert slaves had anything this nice."

Gwenivere snatched the book back. She wanted to chastise Becca, tell her off for being so poorly informed, but instead she chose to hold her tongue. The girl was hardly past her sixteenth spring, and with three sisters and a mother to look after, she hardly had time for an education. Besides, Garron had scolded Gwenivere herself enough times for saying something she shouldn't, and she'd always felt the fool for it. She softened her voice as she answered, "Harold was nice, and so was his gift."

Becca's head bobbed. Her now-blond curls bobbed too.

Behind her, casually striding down the palace's halls, a foreign diplomat approached. There had been a handful of them since Gwenivere had come to the capital, many having arrived early in hopes they might speak with her father privately. The Peace Gathering would be a public affair, a jumbled mess of ambassadors and monarchs arguing on behalf of their nations, and the masquerade would simply be to celebrate the fact that no one had killed one another negotiating. It was already plenty for the King of Peace to offer, but greedy nobles were still eager to snatch him aside for themselves in hopes of secret arrangements. Xenith was powerful, and wealthy, a nation of scholars amid ruffians and thieves. No other nation was regarded so highly or sought after so fervently for political pull.

The man's pace quickened down the hall, and Gwenivere hurriedly tried to usher her servant inside her chambers. She'd been told not to engage with other royals if it could be avoided, not without Garron or her father himself around, but before she could get the door shut—

"Lady Gwenivere!" the man called. He waved jovially and trotted over, his long legs placing him feet away. Gwenivere held in her sigh, placing her best smile on her face before turning back around and facing him.

"Edifor," she said, dipping her head. With all the nobles about, she was sure she'd forget at least one person's name, or mispronounce them. There were already hundreds of foreigners residing within the palace, and most weren't even people of significance compared to who would attend the actual events. But Gerard had been insistent she learn to place each name with each face, and Garron had been adamant in following the king's orders. She'd flipped through page after page of portraits, running over again and again who each person was, what nation they resided from, and what they likely wanted to gain from the Peace Gathering. Edifor of Yendor, a lean, sharp-eyed man with round spectacles and snug clothes, was one of the few whose interests her father had decided she shouldn't know.

It made him all the more intriguing.

"You're up and about early, milady," he said, gesturing toward the sun through the hallway's windows. It was far from early, and her sleepwear certainly confirmed she wasn't "about," but Gwenivere supposed he couldn't say she was lazy and should be dressed. Especially when she had a reputation for being temperamental.

"I enjoy the palace," she answered, "my chambers most of all."

She hoped he would get the hint, intriguing as he may be, and leave her and Becca alone. The chambermaid, however, looked as if she were starving for him to say more. She'd likely never heard a Yendorian accent.

"As do I, of my own chambers," he said. "Your father is most hospitable to allow us to stay."

Gwenivere smiled weakly. She stood silently for a moment, hoping the awkwardness of it would make him scamper away, but again he stayed put. His eyes, gold beneath his spectacles, looked down at her chest, resting there far too long. She felt her cheeks flush, her throat bobbing as she remembered her knight's words on their woodland trek: *Just call for me, and I will do to them everything a lady of your dignity cannot.*

She opened her mouth to scold him, to rehash a foul jest she'd heard of Yendorian men, when she realized what he was staring at.

Her Amulet.

"I may be bold to say this," he started, "but I've been told you would have married Prince Roland of Mesidia if not for both of your Artifacts." He raised his eyes, his expression inquisitive as he awaited her answer. Beside her, Becca tried to hold back a gasp. Unsuccessfully.

It was bold, and rude, the red *auroras* in Gwenivere's mind brightening. *Let us burn him,* they seemed to say, *let us sear his flesh! How dare he speak to you of such intimate affairs!*

She pushed the *auroras* down, however tempting they might be to *call,* and gave him a warning grin.

"He's a dear friend," she said. "But I suppose Mesidia wasn't ready to place a Yendorian on its throne."

The reference to Dorian Cliffborne was low, she knew, but she hardly cared. The ambassador was her friend, a brother figure to Roland and a likeable man, but Edifor shouldn't have asked of her marital prospects. Drawing on Dorian's Yendorian roots, implying it was his blood that kept him from being fit to rule, was an insult to Edifor and his people. She stood steadfast, hopeful his pride was damaged enough to bid her farewell.

Instead, he met her false grin with one of his own. His gold eyes practically glowed.

"Perhaps you're right, milady," he said. "Although, the way I saw it, King Pierre's decision to bestow Roland the Dagger and the throne was more to keep Natalia Barie from being Mesidia's next queen. It's certainly no secret she and Dorian were once betrothed." Edifor pulled a hand from behind his back, glancing at his nails before giving her a bored glance.

"Perhaps the conclusion then is not that Mesidia needn't have a Yendorian on the throne, but that it needn't have a Victorian. But I suppose we shall see about that soon enough."

He nodded to her, then to Becca, his spectacles dipping down his nose as he wished them a good day. Gwenivere leaned against her door, her chest rising and falling with angered breaths. What reason was there to bring up Mesidia's civil disputes and her romance with Roland? She looked to Becca, hoping she might voice her concerns, but the girl's gaze was following the Yendorian until he was out of sight.

"What was *that* about?" she purred. She seemed more fascinated at the implying comments then worried. "Interesting, wouldn't you say?"

Gwenivere pulled at her lace robe, folding the fabric over her Amulet. She wished the fabric was thicker, if only to shield the incessant, shifting glow.

"Yes," she replied, staring down the massive hall. "Very interesting indeed."

Though her mind had been consumed with the morning's encounter, Becca's restless chatter eventually pulled Gwenivere out of it. The chambermaid spoke more about her new blond hair, the blond men she'd seen and thought handsome, and then of any men she'd found handsome. Gwenivere knew her servant wasn't simpleminded; the girl's conversations were often petty and shallow for Gwenivere's own benefit. Most of her days were filled with sparring Garron, honing in her skills with *touched* weapons and shields, *called* weapons and shields, and elements. If she wasn't doing that, then she was reading about all those things, and usually from that Light-forsaken book Garron loved so dearly, *The Art of Calling*. From there it was more reading, researching fiends and languages and histories, then it was dancing and etiquette, then harp lessons, then whatever other thing her father could fit in her days. He wasn't around often, the calls of war so tempting for other nations that they needed his wisdom to help ease their quarrels. Philanthropic ventures consumed most of his time, and thus, knowing she had no one but her younger brother Aden to speak to, he used her academics to pass the time. She was lonely without her mother, and she was burdened without Roland to write to, so an unending, tireless routine was his solution to make her forget.

She didn't forget, though. Not with the Amulet hanging around her neck to remind her.

Becca may like to chat, but she does it to help me. She glanced at her servant through her vanity's mirror, waiting patiently for the girl to catch her gaze through her intricate braiding. Anytime one of Gwenivere's hairs didn't quite stay put, Becca would—with great effort—*call* a bit of heat to smooth it down. Given how inept she was with elements, Gwenivere used to think Becca would burn her hair off, but the servant seemed to have mastered *calling* just enough to control it for varying hairstyles. She did love hair so very, very much, and thus, it took her a great deal of time to pull her attention away from it long enough to notice Gwenivere's stare. She beamed at the smile that accompanied it, then carried on.

"I forgot to say so earlier, but I believe the al'Murtaghs have arrived. Isn't that grand? They're very kind, and amusing, especially Peter."

Gwenivere had spent her fair share of time with Roland's cousins, and she loved them each as her own family. Peter, she decided, *was* especially amusing.

"I'll have to seek them out later."

"Yes indeed. Natalia is with them, though, but so is Dorian.

He makes up for her awfulness, wouldn't you agree?"

Gwenivere looked at Becca through her mirror again. She knew that tone, knew the implication of it. She wasn't in the mood to speak of marriage, though, or the fact that her father expected it of her so soon. Circumvention, unfortunately, had never been easy with Becca.

"I agree that Natalia is awful, yes," she said. She winced as Becca tugged at her hair.

"And Dorian? What do you think of him?"

Gwenivere sighed, confined to her chair and trapped into speaking. She gave the query time, thinking through how best to answer her servant. She wanted to make it very clear that she had no intention of marrying Dorian. Not when Roland thought him a brother.

"I have no sisters," she started, "not like you. I only have Aden, and he's fifteen springs my younger. For many years, when the al'Murtaghs and the Laighlesses and I would get together as children, I only had Elizabeth, and she only had me. We're both twenty springs, and we're both girls, and I hold her very dear to my heart.

"It's a secret to most, but Elizabeth is very fond of Dorian. She may even love him, though I doubt she'd ever admit that. So, to answer your query, I think he is a fine man, and I hope someday he and Elizabeth find happiness with each other."

Becca grunted, chewing on her lip as she stared at her own reflection. She pondered the hair atop Gwenivere's head, looking at it from multiple angles, then nodded. Whether to the braiding, or the answer to her question, Gwenivere wasn't sure.

Gratefully, before Becca could toss in more implicative questions, a knock sounded at the door. Gwenivere shrugged at the expectant look Becca gave, uncertain who else might have come to visit. Garron had been given the day off—or she had, depending on how she looked at it—and Aden had insisted Maximus teach him more about elements after their challenge in the forest.

To Gwenivere's delight, when Becca opened the door, a fresh-faced Elizabeth stood waiting.

"May I enter?" she asked.

Gwenivere laughed, hurrying from her chair to greet her friend. The two embraced tightly, the smell of a bath still clinging to Elizabeth's skin and her satin gown. The fabric was likely impossible to wear in Mesidia's colder climates. It was flattering, though, the soft curves of Elizabeth's body outlined nicely where thick wool and fur normally lay.

"Well I have to be going now," Becca said, cutting in. She gave Elizabeth and Gwenivere a warm farewell, then left the room.

"She seems very kind," Elizabeth said. "I remember her from when we were children, when I'd visit you here in the palace. She's the one with all the sisters, and the father who left her mother?"

Gwenivere stared at her friend, perplexed at how casually she referenced a memory she had no need to store. Becca had, after all, only interacted with Elizabeth a few times over the years, and always very briefly. The serving girl had waited on her once or twice and had been around Gwenivere often enough that Elizabeth was bound to see her, but the intimate details of her life were nothing most nobles would bother remembering. Gwenivere admired Elizabeth, for her kindness and her retention. Few others possessed such traits.

"Yes, unfortunately, and I've often tried to give her extra coin beyond her wages, but she always refuses. She says she's only worth the work she does, and she won't accept any more than that. Respectable, certainly, but she's very stubborn— and chatty."

Elizabeth gave a sheepish smile. "Stubborn, hmm? Sounds like someone I know." Her smile broadened to show teeth, her cheeks rounding. "Chatty, though; that's less like the person I know. Does she speak of anything interesting?"

Gwenivere blew air from her cheeks and shook her head. "Marriage proposals," she answered. "Not my favorite topic as of late, but it's the only one anyone seems interested in." She headed toward a set of chairs and ushered Elizabeth to follow.

The pleasant smile Elizabeth wore slipped, her fingers fidgeting as she folded them neatly in her lap. "Whom did Becca suggest? Sometimes those servant girls have better insight than we do."

Gwenivere wished she had a glass of wine, if only to have something occupy her. Before she had wished to brush off Becca's attempts to find her a suitor, but her admittance of Elizabeth's feelings had not been a convenient deterrent. Elizabeth did indeed fancy the ambassador, and while Dorian hadn't the slightest insight, her fancying continued nonetheless. Catherine al'Murtagh, Elizabeth's mother, would never approve. Not with the way Pierre's reputation had been put in question when he'd accepted Dorian into his home, and certainly not after Dorian had courted Natalia Barie. Those years had been difficult for Elizabeth, and Gwenivere was the only one she'd been able to confide in. Peter and William wouldn't understand. If they were sober enough to listen, they would simply tease her, or call her incestual, despite there being no true blood between Dorian and them. And if they weren't sober, they would likely let the secret slip. Someone as sweet as Elizabeth couldn't face the protective wrath Natalia would put on her. The duchess-heir might have broken off her and Dorian's betrothal, but she still preyed on those who stole Dorian's glances.

"No one worth mentioning," Gwenivere said. She gave Elizabeth's hand a reassuring squeeze, then leaned back in her seat. "Though I always enjoy your visits, I'm a bit surprised to find you here so soon after you've arrived. What bit of gossip are you so eager to share? Or is it that you've at last abandoned your pining of men and decided, 'to the darkness with them all, let us see how ladies differ?'"

Elizabeth's cheeks flushed as she shook her head profusely. Gwenivere grinned, amused at her friend's sensibility, and tried with little success to shun her jest's delight.

"I-I have a letter," Elizabeth stuttered. She reached into a pocket in her dress and pulled out a parchment. Along it's top, elegant and sapphire blue, lay a four-cleft leaf. "From Roland."

Gwenivere stared at the letter, blinking at it silently. After a moment, she frowned, and glared viciously at her friend. "Why would you bring this? You know my father has forbidden this, do you not?"

Elizabeth winced, her throat bobbing. "Aye, I do. But please, Gwen, I come with good reason. Roland only wanted to convince you that you still have Mesidia as your ally, regardless of whom you marry." She stared at the letter, ran her fingers over the wax of the leaf, and extended it out for Gwenivere to take.

I can't, she thought, peering at the beautiful leaf she'd wanted so badly to see again. *I can't. Father forbade it, Pierre forbade it . . .*

But there it lay, perched so tightly in her friend's grasp. Gwenivere knew she should leave it unopened, leave its words unread and its seal undone, yet the pain of such a thought was almost more than she could bear. She had longed for this, ached for it even, and though she refused to admit it, she had prayed that the Light might grant her one last word with her beloved. They had practically been betrothed for so long. How did he fair now after so many moons? Would he hate the man she married? Would he respect him?

She looked back to Elizabeth, the girl's eyes wide as she shifted her weight in her chair. Her lips tightened, beads of sweat trickling down her cheeks.

If she says it's only to assure alliances, surely there can't be any harm.

She took the letter and tore its seal.

To my Dearest Gwenivere,

Forgive me my unable hand and persistent ways. Shame resides in a man who disobeys the will of his king, and certainly more so the will of his father. Yet I could not sit without action, allowing you to believe I had accepted this fate without protest. Albeit difficult, I have come to accept the words of Gerard as truth, the marrying of our great nations too dangerous so long as we both hold the title of Guardian.

Know that it is with sincerity I admit my disdain for such an outcome. Though it makes no difference to state, none of this would have come to pass had my father given Dorian the Dagger of Eve. He is deserving, noble and strong, yet the woman he had chosen to take as his queen would have ensured my bloodline no longer hold the Mesidian throne. My father made his choice, and though its outcome has negatively altered our fates, he did, as any king should, what he felt was best for his nation. I know Gerard has done the same.

My intention for such statements is to assure you I hold no ill-regard toward your father. The King of Peace is a leader beyond many, his heart mighty and his sword merciful. Yet he commands with the power and respect deserving of his name. I hold no contempt for him, and I hold no contempt for you as you search to find another.

Know that, though it's no longer proper to say, I love you very dearly Gwenivere. I will forever hold you with the highest reverence. Your name will always hold nothing but admiration in my mind.

If ever another were to come along whom I could trust to take my place, so it would be, our hands no longer forbidden from one another. Though, be it that we both still hold our titles, I am afraid such a longing will likely never come.

Trust in faith and reign with justice.
Your ally and friend,
Roland Laighless

Gwenivere read the last paragraph over and over, hardly able to withhold her tears at the possible proposition it presented. She folded the letter back up in defiance, refusing to humor the thought of another taking Roland's name as Guardian. The suggestion alone could be seen as treason, especially under the circumstances it had been delivered. She looked back over at Elizabeth, shoving the parchment in its envelope and slamming it in a drawer.

"Have you mentioned this letter to anyone? Does anyone else know it exists?"

Elizabeth shook her head.

"Good." Gwenivere rose from her chair and pointed toward the door. "Speak of this to no one and be gone from my chambers. Best we not give the servants any more to talk about."

So shall be the beginning of destruction, when the city of the sky will fall, and all the world will know evil.

From an Evean Prophecy

Chapter 13

X'ODIA

X'odia sat in the alcove beside her window, the glass propped open to let the ocean breeze come into the room. She lay with her back against the wall, her feet out in front of her and a large book in her hands.

She'd been staring at it for a time before finally realizing that she'd not registered any of the words. Closing it shut, she gazed out over the expansive mass of blue beyond her window.

From where she sat, X'odia could hear the gentle crashing of the water against the sands. The occasional call of a bird, lost from its flock, was the only disruption to the repetitive calm. As the wind brought the taste of salt to her tongue and the Day Star gazed down at its distorted reflection, she wondered if someone else on the other side of the world shared the sight.

She longed to see Abra'am, the dark shores across the sea. How marvelous it would be to feel the snow that fell there, to see the blinding brilliance atop the dark mountains. The trees too would be a wonder, foreigners telling tales of building homes within the trunks and decks across the branches. Even the deserts, filled with grains of gold, stretched as far as the eye could see, an ocean of sand where water dared not saunter.

How different everything would be, so much grander, so much harsher. Continuous contradictions, nothing in harmony. Even the people were provoked by the constant conflict of their kingdoms.

X'odia thought of her father, wishing then that she could speak with him of those troubled peoples who had once brought war on their lands. Alkane of Old, the Savior, Protector, and Guardian of Eve, had lived for centuries, his heart and body made to beat ever-strong by the jewel within his Shield. The darkened barbarians of his time were brought down by his strength, the restoration of a tattered nation preserved.

He was a myth to most, a hero told of in Evean books such as the one she held. X'odia was among the few who knew her father's existence to be truth. It was a hidden truth, the innocence of her people not permitted to know a man of such Knowledge still reigned supreme in the High Council. Her life was one of seclusion, then, as was his, the swirling of her gaze and the nearly ageless body she inhabited proof of the Shield's powers in her veins. She glanced over at her mirror, its likeness the only companion she had, and watched as the colors of her eyes shifted like those in the Shield's jewel.

She cast her ponderings aside and looked back out her window, at last setting her book down and walking outside her cottage. She gently kicked off her sandals and sunk her feet into the warm sand, the tiny white grains falling smoothly between her toes. The ocean crawled to where she walked, extended out to her dark skin, her path hardened as the sand beneath her turned to mud. She smiled and swiftly slipped off her outer garments. Her slim legs carried her from the sun's warmth to the ocean's cover. With a paranoid glance, she crouched down, hid her exposed body under the waves, and submerged herself fully into the clear waters.

As she brought herself back up to the surface, everything around her began to spin. Her swirling eyes glowed brightly, their shifting colors reflecting with a blinding radiance off the surface of the sea. She tried to bring her hand to her head, tried to make the sudden spinning stop, but every muscle in her body now refused to move.

No, please, no, she begged, *I don't want to See anymore!*

She tried desperately to cast away the painful vision she knew was coming. Struggle as she might, she couldn't keep it away.

The Sighting was excruciating. It sucked on every ounce of energy, every bit of strength and endurance she had. When it was over, she came to with a convulsion of coughs. She gasped for air, trying to remove the water that'd crept into her lungs. Hurrying out of the sea, she collapsed onto the shore, her eyes burning and her muscles aching. Her bed called to her, the comforts of its soft sheets begging her to rest, but she couldn't keep what she'd Seen from the council of her people.

When she could control her legs again, she rushed over to her clothing, hastily snatched a few of her belongings from her cottage, and began her trek to the High Temple.

"X'odia Daer'dee, Born of Nevaeh, Sky City of Eve . . . "

X'odia listened to the formalities of her presence, silently praying the old councilman announcing her would hasten his speech. Her thighs and calves burned and her feet ached.

Her priestess's gown was what she'd chosen to adorn, the veils easily suppressing her swirling eyes. Unfortunately, the thinness of her garb did little to hide the impatience her shifting weight conveyed. She clenched tightly to her soft skirts and hoped the dampness of her palms wouldn't transfer to the elegant threads.

"Watcher of the Guardians," the councilman concluded. He looked up, the wrinkles in his forehead deepening, and turned his gaze to her. "What reason do you have to come before us today?"

X'odia nodded her gratitude. "Father Cid Orloff, I thank thee for the moment to speak." She slowly raised her arms up, lowering the veil she wore from her head. The High Council gasped, at last revealed to her dimly glowing eyes. They were among the few who knew of her existence and the Sight that plagued her, the illumination of her gaze signifying the short time since her vision's occurrence. "As you can see, I've been gifted this day."

Cid Orloff nodded. The other twelve members whispered their concerned murmurs. Some of the elders' whispers were not whispers at all, merely muted words spoken in the direction of their neighbors. The sounds echoed against the smooth marble and glass along the floor.

X'odia inhaled deeply, released her breath, and tried to press on through their oblivion.

"Lenore Daer'dee," she said, "former High Councilwoman and Daughter of Eve, now wife of Harold Rorikson and Queen of Sadie, will pass with the Changing Star." More gasps followed her announcement, but X'odia continued on. "I saw King Harold of Sadie with Lenore as her *auroras* began to surface. He sat still beside her bath while the remnants of her body drifted to the Land of Light. He shared in word with his youngest son, Prince Abaddon of Sadie, and . . . and was seen falling by his son's blade."

X'odia paused and allowed the startling statement to have the moment it deserved. She looked down, the vision of the weeping prince piercing his sword into the belly of the king overwhelming her mind again. The image was not as clear then, more like a blurred moment from a dream or a forgotten memory, but it was vivid enough. She held her stomach, her exhaustion doing little to combat the disturbing scenes.

"I saw the Cloaked Prince, Prince Dietrich of Sadie," she went on. "In a second vision, a ripple to the first. He too was killed by Prince Abaddon, somewhere in the deserts of his land, but it was not by the same blade."

The room fell silent, each in their youths and their years fearing what words the Watcher would speak next. She held that moment, a chill overwhelming her as all breaths remained still in the High Council's chests. She looked back, noticing for the first time as her father Alkane stood silently in the shadows. He was always nearby the Council, always watching, his dark skin nearly hidden in the shadows as he bore witness to the fate of his people. X'odia wished she could reach out to him, ask him for strength and guidance as she faced the Council's pressing stares, but his cold eyes gave her no reassurance. His shoulders just heaved, up and down and up again, the Shield of Eve heaving with them as it rested against his back.

"The prophecy of our demise will begin," X'odia started again. She swallowed, saliva feeling like a boulder as it slid heavily down her throat. She pulled her gaze away from her father's and met the fearful ones of her leaders.

"Prince Abaddon will slay Prince Dietrich with the Dagger of Eve."

Hush and keep your tears
Keep your tears from falling
Look upon the dawn, see the sun
See the sun
Rise and break your chains
You are free my daughter
Rise and break your chains
You are free my son

Sadiyan slave song

CHAPTER 14

DIETRICH

*F*oolish boy. *That's all you are. A pity you can hear me.*
Dietrich grabbed at his head, his legs curling as his mind
spun. He opened his eyes for a second, the darkness of the
night making it difficult for him to make anything out, but
he thought he could see a set of icy eyes looking back at him.
Quickly he tried to clear his hazy sight, identify the body
holding the slit gaze, but the sudden twist of hunger in his
belly began to consume his thoughts. He sat up, his hopeful
stomach instantly forgotten as a sharp pain in the back of his
skull forced him to vomit.

The icy eyes were there again, mocking in their watch as
Dietrich wiped his mouth. For a moment he remembered his
trek, remembered the mountain man and his dragons and his
herbs, yet his mind only seemed to remember for a few seconds. He forgot an instant later, the icy eyes terrifying him as

he lay back down to rest. He wrapped his arms around himself and told himself he saw nothing, shutting his lids in a panic as his weary body forced more attempts at sleep.

Nothing but a fool...

"Again with this?"

The prince blinked a few times as he fought against the brightness of morning. Zoran stood above him, his head shaking with disapproval as he said something to his dragons. Dietrich nearly *called* a weapon as he saw them through his grogginess, then remembered the events that had recently transpired. He sat up slowly, a foul taste in his mouth and an ache in his head.

"You're a prince, are you not?"

Dietrich turned to look at Zoran. His hand was stretched out before him, his fingers gesturing toward the smelling pile of vomit laden with flies.

"Is this any way for a prince to behave?"

Dietrich slowly rose from where he'd slept. "No." He didn't need to be told to clean up his mess more than once. He reached for the rag he'd used to gather his vomit from the day before and began wiping. "Though it wouldn't be the first time."

He attempted a grin at the old man, but his attempt was only met with a scowl. That, and the cold gaze of the dragons further back.

With those looks one might think I'd shat all over his things. Dietrich bent down, his nose wrinkling as he wiped up his mess. He peaked back over at the trio, their expressions riddled with contempt at the smell they had likely endured all night. *I suppose it certainly doesn't smell much better than if I had.*

No, it does not.

Dietrich's neck shot up as he heard the woman's voice, but the Keeper was already making his way off, the two dragons following behind him. Had it not been for the grueling headache he felt or the herbs still lingering in him, he might have been more concerned with the voice. In that moment, though, Dietrich decided maddening thoughts were likely side effects of the herbs. All that really mattered then was that he scrub up his mess and gain Seera's approval.

If he could get that, he could get to the masquerade in Xenith.

The next few days proved better than the first. Dietrich did what he could to help Zoran aid in the recovery of Savine's wounded wings. The Keeper would make him hunt, make him spend the day bringing back as much game as he could, only to then feed it to his dragons and send Dietrich back for more.

It was tiresome, the mountainous terrain straining on his lungs, but Dietrich enjoyed the opportunities to explore the cliffs and the canyons. Streams of water trickled through, some small, some flowing, all of them a contrast to the expanse of sand that existed only a few lengths beyond. The birds were different too, their bodies rich with colorful feathers, their songs melodic rather than ugly and cackling. His horse Zar seemed to enjoy the environment too, his trots lighter as they strode through the trees. The soil beneath his hooves was no doubt more pleasant than the hot sand within the desert.

Most of Dietrich's ventures weren't carried out alone. The steady swoosh of Seera's wings were never far from wherever he sauntered. She was always there, her presence somehow known even when he couldn't see her. There was something about her and Savine, something the Sadiyan prince felt drawn too, yet he couldn't explain what the feeling was. He had always been good with animals, good with the horses he rode and the strays he fed. This was different though. He wondered if it was just the mountain air playing tricks on his mind, or lingering effects of the herbs he'd consumed that first night.

Not tricks, Dietrich heard a voice say. It was not so much a voice but an impulse, his own mind convincing him to accept the insanity. He looked up to the sky to see Seera, her wings gliding effortless overhead. Zar hardly cantered any differently, apparently having already grown accustomed to the scaly fiend's presence. Dietrich shook his head and guided them along, trying to convince himself his sanity was still in check.

Maybe it was that damned elixir Brelain gave me, he thought, fingering where the seven-tailed serpent had left his newest scar. *Maybe it's made me crazy.* He smiled as he thought of the woman, his mood instantly lighter as he allowed himself to reminisce. He all but forgot the strange feelings in his head as his thoughts drifted to simple musings.

"Have you ever had deer?" Zoran asked one evening. Dietrich politely put down the map he'd been drawing, shaking his head as he folded the unfinished parchment.

"No," he answered. He had only caught small game like rabbits, or the occasional fish from the stream. He wasn't sure what had evoked Zoran's query until Seera landed beside them, a deer in her jaws. Her icy eyes looked almost playful as she trekked over to Savine.

"We shall skin it soon," Zoran said, beckoning Dietrich over. "First, help me with Savine's wings."

The prince hurriedly did as he was told, making his way over to where Zoran and the two dragons sat. The Keeper pulled off the blanket wrapped over his dragon and dabbed ointment onto her wounds. He placed the jar between where he and Dietrich sat, his grey gaze gesturing toward Savine, then to it, then back to her.

"You hit her a few times," he said. "There's more wounds than just the one I'm mending."

Dietrich nodded and reached into the jar, surprised by the pleasantness of the ointment's scent. He had thought everything that helped healing smelled bad, though he supposed all he'd ever smelled were the elixirs Abaddon made. Perhaps the things toward the western parts of the world simply smelled better.

Savine opened her eyes for a moment when Dietrich patted on the ointment, her throat releasing a deep, purr-like bellow. He wondered if it stung, if it was painful in any way, his approach taking after the mountain man's as he rather forcefully rubbed the ointment in. Dietrich gave Savine a sympathetic smile, regretful as his calloused palms ran over where his bolts had struck. Her lids closed shut again, her purrs ceasing, but something in her scales seemed to convey a semblance of forgiveness. Dietrich could feel it, could sense the odd connection he'd felt before, heightened now as his fingers rested against her. He inhaled deeply. The strange sensation of Savine's voice was somewhere in his mind before the sound of Zoran's own snapped him back to focus.

"Tell us of yourself," he insisted.

Dietrich's brows rose at the man's use of *us*. He chuckled and gave him a grin before stumbling to find an answer.

"I don't speak much of myself to people," he admitted, glancing over at Seera. The larger of the two dragons stared at him coldly, the lightness of her eyes seeming brighter against the darkness of her charcoal scales. The iciness in her gaze lost some of its sting as the blaze of a fire burned beside them. "I suppose I don't know what to say."

"How did you become the Shadow?" Zoran waved his hand Dietrich's way. "How did you become the Cloaked Prince—the Assassin Prince?"

Dietrich followed the wordless command to release Savine as Zoran placed the blanket back over her.

He felt oddly empty after his hand pulled away from her scales.

"Well," he said, unsure how to start. Zoran hardly seemed to be listening, occupied instead by the carving knife he pulled from his ankle sheath and the body of the deer he now walked toward. Dietrich would have remained silent if not for the expectant grey gaze that pressed him to follow.

"My father, Harold Rorikson," he started, "led a slave revolt nearly thirty years ago and freed Sadie from Prianthia's enslavement. When I was a boy, nearly fifteen years of age, my father took his first trek to the West, said he wanted to learn from the diplomats and the scholars of such righteous and enlightened people. He desired to make Sadie strong, keep the minds of its people sharp and the blades of our swords sharper. He believed the people of the West might help him do that.

"Many of my father's advisors told him not to go, insisting the western peoples are a troublesome lot, and the East would be better off without them. Though nations like Xenith helped us gain our freedom, many stated they had also turned a blind eye to us when they reaped the profits of our shackled feet and beaten backs. The War of Fire tore the West apart, and they tore Prianthia and Sadie to pieces with them. Such a thing might've been true, though perhaps it might not have. Either way, my father was set on seeking more aid and allegiance from the West. He disregarded the warnings.

"Nights after his first departure, the Redeemers' assassins

came. We didn't know such an insurgence existed at the time, and we didn't know the advisors' warnings had been sentences for my family's deaths. Culter, my father's closest watchman, managed to keep the assassins from killing my mother, and I kept the assassins from killing me and my brother, Abaddon. I ordered the assassin Culter had captured to be left alive and . . . I tortured him, until he confessed to us everything about the Redeemers and their cause.

"He said they wanted a purified East—a unified Prianthia and Sadie—without the influence of the West to tear us apart. They had hoped they could persuade my father not to taint a new Sadie with the West's ways, but when my father had refused to listen, they had decided to try taking the throne.

"Many of the Redeemers were our own people, and the threat of them existed in every corner of every street. Our enemy was no longer made clear by the darkness of their eyes or the harshness of their tongues. We had no way of knowing who among us were loyal, and who among us were traitors.

"When my father returned from his venture and discovered what had happened, he asked me to start wearing this." Dietrich gestured at his cloak and the cover he normally wore over his face, surprised by how easily he had forgotten to dawn its cover. "Nearly everyone in Sadie wears these, uses them to shield themselves from the desert's sun. As I was only fourteen, my father decided that if I began to wear one, perhaps the world would forget my face, and I could blend with the people as the people, and aid him in killing our new enemies.

"It wasn't long before the streets themselves became my new home. But the insurgence only began to grow. For every life I ended, two more followers seemed to arise, the message their leader Navar spoke seeming to resonate with those who'd forgotten what my father had done. They didn't care that they only lived freely because of his hand, that their lives were good because of him. All they heard was the ramblings of a madman, and the Fallen One took over their minds and cast my father as the enemy."

Dietrich stopped suddenly, not sure how else to go on. He supposed that was all there was to his tale, to his dark beginnings, the rest a shadowed dream of deaths and tortures. He thought of Daensla then, thought of her raven hair and soft touch. He wished he'd been strong enough to leave her before she'd discovered who he was.

Perhaps the Redeemers would never have found her if he'd let his love for her fade.

"You have lost much in this life."

The prince looked up at Zoran, surprised by the knowing tone in the Keeper's voice. He didn't bother looking at Dietrich, still too occupied with his task, but the eyes of his dragon Seera looked to him in his stead. Dietrich pondered the odd way the man seemed to always have glimpses of what he was thinking, reminded then of how strange his first day was when the Keeper had questioned him. Dietrich swallowed, turning his eyes away from the dragon's watch.

"Yes," he said quietly, still thinking of Daensla. The view of her *auroras* drifting, of the dried line of blood streaked across her neck, still frequented his mind. "I have."

Days passed. Morning after morning continued as each morning had before. The air was noticeably colder than it had been when Dietrich had first arrived in the mountains. Itching to move, to do something other than the monotonous actions he'd begun performing each day, he grabbed the axe he'd watched Zoran use to cut wood and began chopping up the pile of logs beside a tree stump.

Axe up, eyes down, cut. Toss the pieces into the pile, grab another, repeat. Axe up, eyes down, cut. Toss the pieces into the pile, grab another, repeat . . .

Dietrich kept his focus steady and tried to ignore the sweat that dripped into his eyes. He could've sworn he'd only been doing the act for a few minutes, twenty or thirty at most, but the sun was higher in the sky when he glanced up. He took a few deep breaths and returned to his chore.

The nights had been cold, the elevation holding the crisp air into the day, and the Dragon Keeper seemed to need this kindling at the start of each new morning. When the Day Star faded away, he would use the wood to warm Savine. The injured dragon had hardly moved since Dietrich and Zoran had rubbed the ointment into her wings.

With few words exchanged between the two men since then, Dietrich's patience was finally beginning to waver. His short timeline was growing shorter still, and he had yet to gain the elder dragon's judgment.

Axe up, eyes down, cut. Toss the pieces into the pile, grab another, repeat. Axe up, eyes down, cut. Toss the pieces into the pile, grab another, repeat . . .

"You needn't bother yourself with that," Zoran said, walking out from his home. Dietrich had yet to see what the inside of the house looked like, still secluded to the shack under Seera's watchful gaze. The smell of his vomit had finally faded, but he still found himself longing for something better than the glorified shed. Though with half his life secluded to the rooftops of Sovereignty's homes, he supposed a covered room wasn't half bad.

"I insist, really," Dietrich said, cutting another log. "You've been kind enough to take me in after what I did to Savine. It's the least I can offer in return."

Zoran stood steady and sipped his tea. "Tell me, boy, have

you ever heard anything from the fiends you've killed?"

Dietrich narrowed his eyes.

"Your alias, Yeltaire Veen," Zoran continued, "you're supposed to hunt fiends, yes? You use their poisons and such to aid your brother in creating his elixirs. Have you ever heard the fiends, spoken with them, as you have with Seera and Savine?"

The prince pounded another log in half, cursing at the unevenness of his cut. He rubbed more beads of sweat away and shook his head.

"No," he panted. "I usually kill the fiends I hunt quickly, give them peaceful deaths. I don't enjoy watching creatures suffer."

"I see," Zoran said, looking over at Seera. "Dragons are from the Age of Old. They are smarter than most beasts. I suppose it would be easier to hear them over most fiends."

Dietrich nodded, though only out of courtesy. He'd decided rather quickly that Zoran's words were nothing more than odd ramblings. He had no doubt there was some strange connection between the mountain man and his dragons, the constant way they seemed to share in unspoken exchanges proving that. But the prince took such occurrences as nothing more than instinctive tendencies. Even Zar had come back for him when the serpent had attacked. Surely some relationship was there between Zoran and Seera and Savine, but nothing too far beyond what the prince and his horse shared.

"You have a great many scars," the Dragon Keeper noted, Dietrich's back exposed as his shirt lay off to the side. He shrugged in response and grabbed another log from the pile.

"I'm careless a great lot." He smiled in jest as he cast the axe down. He tossed the broken halves aside, at last pausing from his task as he wiped the sweat from his brow. "Will this be enough? Or shall I cut more?"

Zoran glanced where he pointed, took a sip of his steamy drink, and shrugged.

"Tis enough for now."

Dietrich nodded, resting the heavy tool down as he grabbed his shirt and placed it above his head. From across the way, he could see Seera glaring.

"Doesn't seem I've gotten on her good side yet." Dietrich lifted his chin toward the dragon and glanced at Zoran, hoping his statement would elicit some response.

The man simply blew at his cup, attempted to take another sip, then blew on it again.

"Does the fire help Savine heal?" Dietrich asked, trying his luck with a direct query. Zoran peered up from his mug and shook his head.

"Not all dragons are the same. Seera and Savine, they are very susceptible to the cold. It makes them weak. Even these mountain climates are a bit tough for them in the winter, but they make do. It's the only place I feel I can dwell in safety, in peace, so they choose to reside with me. Savine only needs the extra warmth because she's frail. Her scales need the heat more now because her body fights so much to heal her." Zoran stopped and looked over at Seera for a moment before glancing back at Dietrich. "She doesn't hate you, not like she did at first. It's more that she mistrusts any that share our abilities."

Dietrich rested his arms against his sides as he attempted to regain his breath. The mountain air still didn't seem to agree with his straining lungs.

"Our abilities?" he asked.

Zoran turned back toward his tea, blowing at it again and nodding.

What abilities? Dietrich thought angrily, looking back at Seera. The dragon hadn't moved from her post beside the canyon wall.

Still you don't know? a woman asked. Dietrich's breath caught, his eyes darting back toward the Dragon Keeper to see if he'd heard too. The man said not a word, only continuing to look at nothing and everything as he stood content within the crisp morning air. Dietrich returned his gaze to Seera, the cold expression of her charcoal-scaled face seeming to have softened.

"She knows you hear her," Zoran said, admiring the changing colors of the sunrise. "She senses the Elder Blood in you."

Dietrich's blood boiled. "I know nothing of what you speak. I don't understand why I supposedly hear their voices in my head—how *you* know I hear their voices. I don't understand why fiends would protect a man, or why a man would protect fiends, and I don't know what the *Elder Blood* is." He sighed, exhaling heavily as he licked his dry lips. "I mean no disrespect to you, or to your dragons, but I need some answers, and I need them soon."

The mountain man took a heavy breath, holding it high in his chest before slowly releasing it.

"All right Dietrich, let us speak of such things.

"You are, as am I, a descendent of the Ageless. They were and are the original High Council of Eve, all but forgotten by the people of today. They possessed the ability to control fiends, summon beasts from the Age of Old, live for eternity without illness or disease. As a son of the Ageless, I have inherited such abilities, or a variance of them I should say. I can speak to fiends, understand them, feel what they feel and see as they see, but I cannot force my will upon them. Seera and Savine, they are enhanced, intelligent, and they have forbidden themselves from eating the flesh of men, instead feasting as any other animal might. They are disciplined, in control, and human in a way, and they seek our companionship. *Our* companionship, mind you, not just mine, as you too share this gift."

The prince stood silent, his body unmoving as he took in the old man's words. A far-off tale, a fantastical legend—that was all Dietrich was capable of interpreting. Everything Zoran had said sounded like the stories in the Holy Book, stories of Ageless beings and strange magics.

Dietrich did his best to hide his reservations.

"I am the son of one of these people?" he asked incredulously. "These Ageless?"

"It would seem so," Zoran said. "Your mother is from Eve, not Sadie. I hadn't thought the queen would be one of them, but I suppose it makes more sense than Harold."

"My mother does age," Dietrich argued, patience straining. "And she grows sicker as each day passes. Forgive me my misgivings, Keeper, but I hardly believe she could be one of the people you describe."

"The Ageless lose their immortality when they bear children," Zoran defended calmly. "And they pass on fewer of their abilities when they bear the child of a mortal. Or so it would seem. Both my parents were part of the original High Council, thus the many years I've lived upon this land. You seem not to have inherited such defiance to time, though. You look every year your age."

The prince laughed hopelessly, believing less and less of what the man spoke the more he said. How had he let himself be convinced this was the better route? His stallion's pace would have been too slow, his hooves far less capable than the wings of the dragons, but at least Dietrich would have been progressing forward. At least he would have had a chance of reaching the masquerade in time. Now all he had was the ramblings of an old man, crazed by his solitude and driven insane by the silence of his chosen companions.

"My mother would have told me," he insisted, as much to himself as to the Keeper. He caught the gaze of Seera then, her eyes somewhat sympathetic, but he ignored them. "Are you saying that my mother can talk to fiends?"

Zoran, infuriatingly, just nodded.

"And you can too," Dietrich continued, "to some degree, because you're a son of these Ageless? These Elder Bloods?"

"Yes." Zoran looked down at his cup, saddened it seemed that it was now empty, and he added, "As are you."

Dietrich sat down atop the stump he'd labored on, burying his face in his hands with defeat. Flashes of his family flickered in his mind, his mother weak and feeble as she lay dying helplessly in her bed. He thought of Abaddon's fears: his father driven mad with despair, the Prianthians declaring war against Sadie, the Redeemers striking at them in their sleep. If those things happened, the people of his kingdom would beg for a leader, beg for someone to save them, succumbed once more to the hands that enslaved them or the assassins that fought to overthrow their reign. And there Dietrich would cower, alone among the shadows, so fearful of being the king who lost his nation that he would rather watch it fall from his throne of darkness.

Cold scales, from one of the dragons, suddenly stroked against his booted foot. Dietrich pulled his hands from his face and glanced down, realizing it was Seera.

Stand tall, Prince, the woman's voice he'd heard before whispered. Dietrich looked up, Seera's slit eyes gazing at him with what seemed like empathy. She nudged her head against his belly, her body cool through his shirt as she began propping him up. His hands clung to her neck as she aided him to rise. Silently she pulled back, looking at him and through him, knowing everything he thought and everything he felt.

Dietrich sensed it then, the calm, slow beat of her heart and the steady pulse of her blood. He felt the way her scales took in the sun, felt the cadence of her breath and the depth of her thoughts. Entranced, he stretched his arm out to her again, desperate to clench the feeling of her very being in his hand. As much as logic combated what he'd been told, his instincts could no longer deny the serenity he felt. Reason and sense were abandoned as the knowing of what he and the dragon were resonated within him.

You need not be atoned for my companionship, Seera assured. *You are worthy.*

I found some interesting books today. They washed up on shore near my home. I expected them to be ruined on account of them being wet and all, but they'd been carefully bound.

From the journal of a Riverdian townsman

Chapter 15

X'ODIA

The ocean seemed different. The waves pressed against the sand, their never-ending tides pleading onlookers to stay back. They had not always been that way. The waters had once beckoned curious feet out toward the warmth of their shores. They did nothing of the sort now. The salt in the air stung X'odia's eyes, and the wind howled past with aggression. Even the birds' calls, once so peaceful and serene, sounded like nothing but grotesque warnings.

Perhaps her quest to Abra'am was not meant to be.

You're simply nervous, X'odia told herself, clutching the books she held to her chest. *It has always been your wish to see the Dark Shores. Have you not dreamed of it since you were a girl? Do not be such a coward; consider it a blessing the High Council has ordered you there.*

Despite her self-assurance, X'odia's skin tingled.

Up ahead, the crewmen of the *Seagull* were preparing her sails. A delicate name for a ship, certainly, but Eveans were known as docile people, and the name seemed fitting. The sailors themselves, dark in skin and cut with muscle, seemed nothing of the sort, but the smiles they wore and the banter they spoke revealed them soft. X'odia took a sharp breath as one approached, hesitant to speak with someone outside the High Council. She knew it was a foolish fear, the men having all been selected for their relations to the High Council, but knowing that did little to combat her fear. She bit her lip and hugged the books in her arms tighter, wondering what the approaching man would think when he saw her swirling gaze.

"Lady X'odia," he said, bowing his head. He gave her a smile that consumed his entire face and placed his hand on his chest. "My name is Ravel Orloff. Allow me to welcome you on behalf of the Seagull's crew."

X'odia released the forceful bite on her lip and returned the smile. "Orloff, you say? As in Cid Orloff?"

She hardly needed the answer; the young man shared the same dark skin and braided hair as the councilman.

"Yes, my lady," he answered. "I am the High Councilman's grandson."

You certainly don't assign an unnecessary amount of titles, though, she thought, remembering how long she had stood weak-kneed during Cid's greeting. The old man had never seemed to take notice of her annoyance when she stood before the Council.

Aloud, X'odia simply answered, "I see."

Ravel gave her another grin, even fuller than the one before, and extended his hand toward the *Seagull*. If he was transfixed at all by seeing her swirling eyes, he did nothing to show it.

"Shall I accompany you to the ship?"

X'odia opened her mouth to say yes, eager to be on her way, but the gentle swaying of the ship ahead forced her silent. The last time she went in the water . . .

"In-in a moment," she stuttered. She smiled, more to shield her nerves than to show kindness, then tried to find the words to explain her Sighting.

"If I could, I would like to speak to the captain before

boarding. My most recent venture near the sea made me a bit—"

"Sick?"

X'odia stared for a moment, wondering if he had somehow known of her vision's occurrence, then realized the mistake.

"Seasick!" Her cheeks flushed with embarrassment for what must have seemed so obvious to the sailor. "Um, yes, I grew seasick."

Ravel laughed and patted her gently on the shoulder.

"Do not fret, Lady X'odia. They say once the sea has gripped you, you are no longer plagued by its sways." He turned and pointed toward the *Seagull*. "I shall go fetch Captain Bronal."

X'odia thanked him and let out a breath. Her mane of curls clung to the sweat along her neck. She wanted to curse the cloak strapped across her shoulders, blame it for its immense heat, but one of the councilwomen had insisted she take it to Abra'am. *The north of the world is a dark place,* she had said, *and a cold one at that. Why else are the people there so bitter and misguided?*

Certainly not solely from the cold, X'odia thought, lowering her cloak's hood. She felt immediate relief as the wind caught her skin, the sweat dripping down her neck now a lovely chill.

As she waited, X'odia looked over the books in her hands. The High Council had forced her to take the first, *The Prophecies*, explaining she might need it as a reference if more visions plagued her. She hadn't been able to argue. Her mind might have easily held the images of all the Guardians she had seen, but new visions would relay people and events she knew little about. That, or they would reveal visions she knew a great deal about, like the one that had her standing there now. It would do her good to have *The Prophecies* handy.

The *History of Eve* lay beneath *The Prophecies*, its cover faded and its spine creased from years of wear. It was a children's book, a foolish thing for someone grown to cherish, but X'odia clung to it with more fondness than *The Prophecies* above it. Her mother had read her a similar book as a child, before she had left her and her father for Abra'am. When X'odia flipped through its pages, she could practically hear her mother's voice. The original book only had the one copy, and *The History of Eve* was the closest thing X'odia had to it. Childish or not, she wanted to have the book in her hands when she landed on Abra'am's shores.

A small binding of *The Holy Words* was at the bottom of her stack, the wisdom of the Light written across its humble pages. Solitude had pressed her to read it again and again, the book more disheveled than *The History of Eve*. Though she knew the Creator would accompany her to the darker side of the world, it still comforted her to hold the text. Surely her painful visions had been granted so that she might someday aid the people of Abra'am, keep the violent prophecies from coming true. She was the Watcher. She was the daughter of Alkane Daer, Keeper of the Shield. In her blood ran the power of the Shield's stone. The day to ease the world's pain, to begin her journey, started now.

I have spent too many nights reading, X'odia thought, scoffing at the grandeur of her musings. *What grown woman thinks herself the hero of tales?*

A lonely one, she decided mockingly. She clutched her things tighter and wished she hadn't lowered her hood.

"Lady X'odia," Ravel said, returning with a man behind him, "this is Captain Bronal."

The captain, broad shouldered and stout with muscle, simply nodded. He had no hair on his head, just a simple, glistening dome, and what he lacked in attractiveness he made up for with an air of command. X'odia, though comforted by Ravel's kindness, was relieved a harsher looking man was guiding her to Abra'am.

"Greetings, Captain," she said. "I thank you for accepting

this quest. I'm eternally grateful."

The captain nodded again, though his neck was so short it was hard to see. "Eve is grateful," he said tersely. The gruff strain of his voice hardly matched his formality.

After he didn't say more, X'odia pulled a map from one of her books.

"I have a map," she stated dully. She held back annoyance at herself as Ravel reached out to take her other things. Thanking him, she opened up the folded parchment and tapped her finger on it.

"Here," she said, "Riverdee. It's known in Abra'am for being a nation of peace, and I'm told it welcomes the sails of any kingdom to its docks. Though it's Sadie I seek, they don't embrace such foreign spontaneity."

She stopped suddenly, uncertain how much the captain knew of her quest. The High Council had told Bronal and his crew who she was, the necessity of such a thing made obvious by the unusualness of her gaze. What other information they had bestowed, though, of her mission and her destination, she knew naught.

"Riverdee does, however, share a border with the Dividing Wall," she continued. "Getting into Sadie's capital, Sovereignty, from there, without being seen as a threat, should be easy."

"As you command is as we've been told," Bronal replied. "Our sails are set for Riverdee. We will not dock with you, though, as the High Council has ordered we return to Eve without stepping foot on Abra'am's shores."

X'odia nodded.

"We shall be ready to depart shortly," Bronal continued. "You may rest below deck in the cabin if you so please. The men have made the space tidy for you."

"Thank you; your men are too kind." She looked down as Ravel held out his hand and motioned to the map. X'odia folded it and passed it along. She was unaccustomed to being pampered, especially after practically raising herself when her mother had left. The Light knew her father could only spare her so much time.

"You say the sails will be set for Riverdee soon, yes?" she asked.

"Yes."

"Good. Once they're ready, your men may rest below deck if they please. The waves will abide by me."

She walked past both men and took a deep breath, the last full breath she would get of Eve, and headed toward the *Seagull*. Terrified, and excited, she pushed her shoulders back and stood a little taller.

You can do this, she told herself, now ignoring the men beside her.

You will *do this.*

The blue *auroras* in her mind raged as they begged her to pull at the sea. She obliged, reaching out with her mind, and readied herself for her voyage to Abra'am.

When people speak of calling weapons and shields, they often say that one must be a master of said weapons and shields in order to call them. It is like muscle memory, they say, which is true, but one does not need to be a virtuoso performer to claim they know how to play an instrument.

Do not lose courage then. Mastery will make calling easier, but it is possible even with only some experience.

Excerpt from *The Art of Calling* by Gustav Halstentine

CHAPTER 16

DIETRICH

If you call yourself a fiend hunter, how were you so easily defeated by the serpent?

Dietrich opened his eyes at the voice, his hand lifting at the sunlight. The air was crisp from morning, more than he was accustomed to in the desert, and he felt the sudden urge to pull his blanket over his head. It was rough and still held the scent of vomit, despite never being the thing he'd vomited on, but the smell was bearable and the thick weavings of its thread helped block out the cold. After years waking up on the flat clay roofs of Sadie's capital, it was easy to forget he now dwelled in the Dividing Wall's mountains.

He swallowed and grabbed for the pitcher of water next to his makeshift bed. Zoran must have left it for him before continuing his daily ritual of tending to Savine. Wiping the grogginess from his eyes, Dietrich took a sip of the water, yawned, then grabbed his shoes and the freshly washed shirt he'd left out for himself the night before.

"Forgive me, dragon," he said, pulling the shirt over the element resistant vest he'd slept in. He could sense Seera beside him, somewhere, but she wasn't anywhere he could see. He figured if he'd been able to hear her projected voice, though, then she'd be able to hear his spoken one.

I have a name, halfwit, she answered. *Have you forgotten it already?*

Dietrich chuckled and readjusted the buckles of his *touched* knives' sheaths along his calves and thighs. He wasn't used to having Seera's voice in his head, not in the slightest, but years of having Abaddon as his brother at least made him accustomed to banter.

"Yes, I'm afraid I have forgotten your name. You see I was born with this affliction, a terrible thing really, where once I bond with a fiend, I completely forget its name. Please, mighty beast, enlighten me as to whom I speak."

He waited for the snide response. Seera said nothing.

"Ah, have I finally silenced you? I didn't think such a thing was possible."

Is your brother such an ass too, or is it just you?

Laughing, Dietrich grabbed his cloak and fastened it around his shoulders. He'd not needed it when he'd first arrived, but the days were growing colder, and he'd found it best he continue the habit of wearing it to prepare for the West's colder temperatures.

"Abaddon is a far bigger ass, I assure you."

He walked out of the shed that'd become his home the last few weeks and looked around, expecting to find Seera perched on top of the shed's roof. She wasn't there. He held his hand to his face and looked to the skies, shielding his eyes from the sun and looking for her scaled figure in flight, but he didn't see her there either. Perplexed, and not wanting to ask her of her whereabouts, he made to find Zoran.

No, prince, she chided, *you can sense me. Find me that way.*

He grunted, annoyed at the inability to keep her from his thoughts. He did as she instructed, though, closing his eyes and searching for the invisible tether that connected them to each other. It was much like searching for the *auroras*, for trying to find the various colored lights for the desired element. Only this time, instead of grasping at an internal light, he was grasping at a feeling.

After several seconds of concentration, he found it.

That's Savine, Seera said. Dietrich opened his eyes and puffed air out his cheeks, his foot having lifted to take a confident step forward before settling back. He couldn't tell for certain, but Seera sounded somewhat amused.

"Alright. How do I tell—"

Stop speaking aloud. You'll look like a fool if people see you constantly talking to yourself. I'll rephrase: You already look like a fool and in front of me, a mighty beast from the Age of Old. That's far more embarrassing a thing than looking foolish to some human.

Dietrich opened his mouth to retort, then quickly shut it. Grumbling, he scratched at the stubble on his face from a shave-less morning and took a breath.

All right, he thought slowly. *Am I . . . am I doing this right?*

Thinking? Yes, although if you don't know how to do that after twenty-eight years of existence then there are far more things I'll have to teach you than I realized.

"Light above," Dietrich cursed. He heard—or felt, rather—a sort of laugh coming from Seera. He latched onto that, hurriedly making his way in its direction. The feeling shifted to something else a moment later, something more along the lines of annoyance, then shifted again to what he thought might be pleased.

Very good, she said.

His pride swelled at the compliment, much the same way it

had the few times his father had given him praise. It'd happened rarely, but when it had, Harold's approval had made him practically giddy.

I'm not your father, boy. For starters, I'm a female.

How in the Light's name do I keep you from doing that? From hearing everything I think?

Seera once again did what he decided was indeed laughing, then made a clucking sound.

There is of course a way to keep me from your thoughts. But for now we are working to solidify the feeling of each other. I won't teach you to block me out when you only just started letting me in.

Dietrich nodded, realized Seera likely couldn't see him, then ducked beneath a few low-hanging branches. He'd been so set on following her presence that he'd not initially taken in where he was going with his usual attentiveness. Straightening from his ducked position, he stopped and looked around for a moment, analyzing the sway of the trees surrounding him. He'd hunted a number of times in the forests surrounding Zoran's home, often being tasked with getting them their daily meals, but he didn't remember ever having gone this way. The trees were closer together here, and with dark, thick trunks, the texture of which was oddly soft to the touch. It was from dew, he realized, something he never really experienced in Sovereignty, Sadie, save perhaps the coldest times of the year, and only if he ventured to the coast. That was rare, though, as the cliffs near the ocean were known to harbor fiends that hid in the crevices and caves along the shoreline. Since Abaddon had rarely required anything from the fiends that dwelled there for his elixirs, Dietrich had rarely gone.

It's beautiful here, he thought, more to himself than Seera. She still responded with a low, agreeing purr.

Wait, that wasn't a feeling, he realized, noting as the sound immediately ceased. He smiled to himself, turning in the direction he now knew Seera had made real sound from. Or an out loud sound . . . a sound outside his mind? He still didn't know how to wrap his head around hearing things internally from another being.

It's confusing, I know, Seera comforted, landing in a meadow nearby. Her wings were nearly silent as she descended to the ground, the charcoal depth to her scales oddly blending with the shadows the forest cast. Dietrich smiled triumphantly as he approached her.

What was it you asked me earlier? he asked, reaching out a hand to her. She lowered her quilled neck and leaned into it, a sort of greeting he'd often had with Zar.

I'm not your horse, she snorted, snapping her head back. *And I'm assuming you're referring to the query I presented that awoke you.*

Dietrich pulled his hand back to his side and rested it against the hilt of a *touched* blade.

That's the one.

Her ice-colored eyes took him in for a time, the intensity of her slit pupils almost making him back away. There was no longer the fear in him, though, not in the way there'd been when he'd first seen her. She was fearsome, no doubt, her sheer grace of movement and intelligence not fitting of something so powerful. Yet there was something that went beyond that, something strange and ethereal that connected him to her. He'd pushed it away before, had balked at its outlandishness, but now that he had it he didn't want to let it go.

Seera lowered her head back down and nudged him—rather forcefully—in the stomach. He stumbled back, barely catching his balance before instinctively gripping his knife's hilt tighter.

I asked you how you could call yourself a fiend hunter if you were so easily defeated by a serpent.

She lunged at him, jaws snapping. He had to throw his full weight to the ground and roll to get away.

What? he asked, surprised when he heard his mind's voice

projecting the same panting in his body. *How do you know about that?*

He tensed as Seera feigned another lunge. She slowed then, circling him, and he tentatively pulled the *touched* knife from its sheath. He'd be more afraid, more confused, if he didn't feel the parental spirit behind her movements.

You're very dense, she said, showing her claws in response to his knife. They were nearly as long, and likely sharper, the color almost glistening. *I can see inside your mind whether you will me to or not. And at the end of your slumber you were having a nightmare about the serpent you fought. The one that pierced a tail into your shoulder.*

Dietrich leaped as Seera lashed her own tail at him, then fell roughly to the ground as she brought it back and smacked it against his side. The air knocked out of him and his knife nearly fell, his fingers only knowing to keep hold from years of training.

I'd never fought a seven-tailed serpent before, he managed, quickly trying to get back to his feet before she struck again. He wasn't fast enough. She pounced on top of him and roared, her face inches from his.

But you've fought, yes? she mocked. *You trained for years alongside your father, a man who survived enslavement? A man who led his people through a rebellion?*

"Yes."

And you learned from tutors as a boy? Learned the ways in which to fight fiends—to defend yourself against them?

"Yes!"

Then fight back! Use your knowledge. Use what—

Dietrich didn't hear what came next. He fought against the weight of her on top of him and forced his knife up toward her eye.

She immediately reeled.

And don't forget to speak through your mind, she said, a

smile sounding through her reproach. *Our bond is stronger than your voice.*

He was on his feet now, still holding his knife, but nodded at the command.

Do you mind me asking what this is? Why you're suddenly attacking me in the middle of a meadow?

You heard what Zoran told you, she said, her stance suddenly easing. He didn't trust it at first, thinking it some kind of trap, but the tether between them told him it wasn't. He lowered his blade slowly, then slid it back in its sheath.

Zoran told me many things, he said, careful to keep his words respectful. *Which thing is it you reference?*

She pulled her legs in and laid against the grass, her posture suddenly like that of a cat. Dietrich took her relaxed position as an invitation. He lowered himself to the ground, already aching from their abrupt training, and crossed his legs beneath him.

There are those out there who can possess us, she said. *Other fiends like myself, I mean. I have gained a better amount of what you call sentience through my tie with Zoran, and that makes it more difficult for me to be possessed, but it can still happen. If at some point my mind is not my own, you need to be ready to defend yourself.*

Dietrich began to nod, then quickly stopped. He supposed that—if she really could sense his every thought—nodding would be like saying the same thing twice.

Yes, it certainly would be, she said. *And I'd ask that you stop comparing me to animals. Just because you have a limited mind doesn't mean you should try to force limits on me. I'm a dragon. Dra-gon. Not horse. Not cat. A dragon.*

Dietrich bit his lip. Then tried his best not to think of anything at all.

Ah, you're gaining manners. Good. I hadn't thought with all that whoring around you do that you had much of those.

You've seen that too, have you? he asked. He felt a bit of heat flood his cheeks. Although his mind had occasionally wandered back to his time with Brelain, he hadn't thought he'd been so explicit in his thoughts around the dragon. Had he remembered things in his sleep? Had he dreamed of the healer—

Her and your former lover Daensla, yes, Seera cut in. *And might I add that you aren't very bright for someone who's been hunted most of your life? Why didn't you question the healer more? Why didn't you ask her how she knew so much about you? I know there are holes in your memory from having been wounded—foolishly, I might add, as you're supposed to be some master fiend hunter—but you shouldn't just ignore rightful suspicion the moment a bed-hungry girl crosses your path.*

Dietrich stared directly at Seera, trying with as much strength as he could to think of absolutely nothing. That was difficult. In raiding through his thoughts, Seera had begun seeing the images of him with Brelain, of him indeed casting aside his uncertainty of the girl for her smile and tempting beckons. The heat he felt in his cheeks deepened. It was like having his mother walk in on him in the middle of—

While mother is closer than father, that's not what I am to you, Seera said. *What I think you mean is it's like having a dragon point out both your stupidity and your inability to keep physical urges suppressed.*

I didn't sleep with Fiona, he offered jestingly.

She stared at him. He stared back. If she had eyebrows, he imagined at least one of them would be arched.

Let's return to the conversation about the serpent, shall we? she asked.

Eager to be rid of the most discomfort he'd faced in years, he projected his agreement.

All right. What should I learn?

You should know the basics of your elements, she said. *You should know when* calling *a weapon is better than using one a blacksmith has made.*

I know that, he said. *I learned it when I was—*

Why did you strike at me with your blacksmith knife? she interrupted. *Why did you choose to use that against me instead of a* called *one?*

Blacksmith knife? He suppressed a grin. *You mean a* touched *knife?*

She let out a throaty sound. And, if dragons could roll their eyes, he supposed that was what she did. It was reminiscent of a slit casing a reptile's eye as they went beneath the water; not a complete closing of her lid, but a protective cover over it. It made him almost laugh to see it.

I don't know what you humans call them these days, but whatever a manmade weapon is referred to as.

We refer to them as touched *weapons,* he said teasingly, no longer holding in his grin. *I believe I just said that.*

She must have sensed the way he noticed her reaction before, because this time she made neither noise nor movement.

The point of the question still remains: Why did you use your touched *knife against me rather than a* called *one?*

Dietrich didn't answer right away. It was a serious tone with which she asked the question, and he wanted to show her he took her words to heart. Well, that he took some of her words to heart. Mainly the ones that weren't jest or jab.

I panicked, he admitted. *If you'd tilted your head slightly, I wouldn't have hit your eye, and my* touched *knife likely wouldn't have even pierced your scales. Had I* called *a knife, though, that would've actually harmed you. That's the whole reason the black auroras* were given to us—to use them to create weapons and shields in our defense.

You're lack of knowledge is astounding, Seera answered. *But . . . that is not your fault. And in truth, it is best you believe such fanciful tales.*

Dietrich couldn't help himself; he held his hands up in question.

You're eluding to having truths behind called *weapons and shields, and you aren't going to tell me? My, my, you are quite teasing. Can you at least tell me why I can* call *a weapon into existence—a sword, a crossbow, a dagger—but I can't call, say, a fork?*

Seera gave him a flat stare.

A fork?

Yes. The utensil humans use to eat.

I know what a fork is.

Then why ask?

Because I was giving you a chance to retract that question rather than commit to how ludicrous it is. But again, I suppose the root of why you're asking is not so absurd. Mastering a blacksmith—a touched *weapon—allows you to then gain the muscles memory to form a* called *one with the black* auroras. *So in your mind, you're wondering how something you've gained muscle memory with from everyday use cannot also be called into existence.*

Yes, exactly.

I wasn't asking. Nonetheless, that logic would imply that you could call *any possible object into existence if you have enough training with it. Which you can't. And the reason has to do with the limitations of the black* auroras *and the intent. You may have the intent to use a fork as a weapon, but the limitation does not allow you to create such a thing. Weapons are things that have existed long before your time, and only a select few were given the ability to be* called.

I see, he answered. He placed his chin in his hand, thinking through her explanation. It made good enough sense, he supposed, or at least it aligned well enough with what he already assumed was true. The Holy Book Abaddon was always reading from mentioned the very same kinds of weapons mankind still used now. It made a strange sort of sense then that if those weapons had been vaulted, in a manner of speaking, then it would be from that same vault humans could draw from now.

A question came to him then, but before he could ask it, Seera was already answering.

I will not tell you if there are other objects that can be summoned besides the typical weapons you call now.

In a way you are answering, he said, pointing his finger. *If the answer was no, then why not just say no?*

Perhaps I want you to think a little for yourself. Perhaps I want to give you the gift of imagination.

How honorable.

Seera stood then, and Dietrich immediately stood with her. He half-expected her to lunge at him again, his mind racing for the black *auroras* this time rather than his *touched* knife, but Seera merely stretched out her wings. He kept his stance up, though. Just in case.

There are many more things I wish to teach you, she said. Dietrich had the immediate thought that she hadn't actually taught him anything, only chastised him and talked circles around his mortal knowledge, but he quickly halted it. She eyed him, noting the beginning of what he'd been thinking, but when he successfully kept his mind on whatever she wished to say next, she began speaking.

I understand that your current predicament requires a hasty departure? she asked.

Dietrich kept his mind clear.

That was an actual question, Prince.

Oh. Yes, I do require haste.

She opened her wings again, the glossy charcoal color practically absorbing the sunlight that snuck through the trees around them, then lowered her neck to the ground.

I suppose you ought to learn how to ride, then.

I saw sweeping darkness
I saw pillars black
Then I saw the soldiers
Whack, whack, whack

I saw auroras drifting
I saw buildings fall
Then I saw the widows
Bawl, bawl, bawl

A poem from *The Breaking of Mesidia*

CHAPTER 17

ROLAND

MESIDIA

"For someone who so despises the Dagger, you sure reach for it a great deal."

Roland grimaced, retracting his hand from the empty hilt at his side and returning it to his lap. It'd been moons since he'd left Stonewall, Mesidia, but still he found himself reaching for the Dagger of Eve. He hated the thing, and he'd been relieved to temporarily give it back to his father and fulfill this quest he and his Elite had been assigned. Despite that hatred, it was still the Dagger his hand itched to hold.

"Habit," he admitted quietly. He looked out the window of his and Merlin's hideout and noted the dark skies thickening with clouds. For days they'd waited for such weather, both men knowing the small drizzle and light greys that frequented Mesidia's southern reaches wouldn't be enough for their task. They needed a storm, murky and unrelenting, not so unlike the one he examined now. Albeit a burden to his desires, reaching for the Dagger had become a comforting tendency in times of such turmoil. It made him uneasy not to feel it there.

His Elite hacked and spit to his side. "You needn't worry. The Dagger is safe. If tradition didn't require him to bestow Guardianship while he still lived, your father would be guarding it now anyway."

Roland pulled the edges of his cloak further over his shoulders. The creaking wood of the shack did little to shield the cold from his bones.

"My father was a finer Guardian than I shall ever be. It's not the Dagger's safety I fear."

Merlin harrumphed mockingly. "What then?" He twirled his blade. It was *called*, as was every weapon the Elite used, the soldiers never weighing themselves down with the heavy metal of *touched* swords. So engrained was his blade, though, present in his grasp since their venture had begun, that it was difficult to believe he could release its existence with the swiftest of thoughts. Roland had learned to brush off the feelings of deprecation he felt in Merlin's presence.

"I fear our task," he confessed. "I fear being caught."

"You fear the duchess? Skinny wench is hardly more than a stern tongue."

Roland tapped his fingers, annoyed. "You misinterpret my admittance." He tore his gaze from the window, royal eyes meeting those he commanded, and wished just once the Elite would speak to him with the respect he deserved.

"Yvaine has brought many under her beliefs," he clarified. "No matter how many hungry mouths my father feeds, no matter how many people he protects or wars he ceases, the people cannot stand united under him. They hear her words, her slanders and maligns, and they believe them. All because her husband is of the Victorian bloodline." Roland stopped, a flicker of lightning flashing through the cracks of their shelter. Thunder would follow soon.

"If she catches us," he continued, "if she discovers our

ploy, there will be little we can say in our defense. Many will be eager to swing their swords and end my father's name."

Merlin listened, likely as much to Roland's words as the thunder's echo.

"Better to risk that than allow Yvaine to kill," he answered simply. "If the duke were telling the truth, we need to know. If it was deceit he aimed for, we should know that as well." He grabbed a water skin from his satchel and took a swig before tossing it to the prince. "Drink. The storm will be upon us soon. We must ride when the hooves of our mares cannot be heard."

Roland nodded and swallowed what was left of the cold liquid reluctantly. He knew his body would thank him later, the ride to the old ruins a quick but tiresome one, yet all he wanted was something to warm his bones.

Mead, ale, wine. Light, anything but this. He grinned, memories of when he'd snuck Gwenivere her first drink flickering through his mind. *She practically spat it out she hated it so much.* He hurriedly pulled up his hood to shadow his amusement.

"Are you a man who believes in prayer?" he asked, tightening the straps of his *touched* blades. Merlin stared at him with cold eyes before finally stilling his sword.

Another web of lightning flashed around them.

"I believe the Creator sends me where prayers go unanswered," he said. "Not a beam of light ever seems to shine where I amble."

The thunder erupted.

"We must go," Roland said, not waiting for the Elite to say the words for him. He gathered what little they had brought into the shelter. His hands were numb, forcing him to put his gloves back on. With a howl the wind burst the door open, the storm itself seeming to insist they begin their trialing gallop. Quickly Roland pulled his cloak tighter around his face, the piercing cold forcing tears from his eyes. The mares, tied up nearby, thrashed their heads and whinnied as the storm raged.

Roland patted his girl reassuringly as he took to the saddle, not bothering to hear Merlin's order before wrapping unfeeling hands around the reins and kicking her onwards.

The ruins lay within sight, though Roland could see little as the malevolent rains pounded against him. Flashes of lightning were all he had to determine his reins still guided with precision, blurs of the stones growing larger as he and the Elite grew nearer.

Few and sparse, the ruins were remnants of a castle shared before the feuding bloodlines began. As the two approached, Merlin waved Roland down, gesturing for them to halt. He did so gratefully, his muscles aching and his chest burning as he peeled his rigid grip from the reins.

He wondered if Yvaine and her mysterious dark-haired companions, the ones Pierre had been told of by Duke Bernard, would be inside.

Without a word, Merlin motioned for Roland to follow him to the outskirts of the fortress. An old tunnel was there, a means of escape in the event of an attack. Vines and leaves nearly covered its entrance. Merlin tore open its latch, surveyed it, then tied his mare to some stone columns nearby. Roland did the same, the brief calm allowing him a chance to wipe his eyes and stretch. When he was ready, he nodded to his Elite and followed his descent down the tunnel's steps.

The temptation to *call* on his fire was almost irresistible as the path fell into complete blackness. It smelled of mold, the stones along the walls slimy as they brushed against them, but the cold air was a pleasant replacement to the raging winds outside. Their footsteps grew louder the further they went, the sound echoing dully as the storm's cries faded above ground.

"Halt!" Merlin whispered. Roland did as commanded. The small glow of an element emerged in Merlin's hand. Roland squinted at the light, adjusting his eyes to the bright flame as it crackled lightly. Merlin's other hand, visible now with the blaze, held firmly to his sword.

"This leads to a wardrobe within the royal quarters," he said, slowly meandering forward. "What's left of them at least."

Roland nodded, though for little point. The Elite was already a few paces ahead.

The tunnel eventually evened its descent, the stones along the floor traded for soil and the small scurries of rats. Most avoided Roland's strides, few more than little scampers, but the occasional one would attempt to crawl up his legs. He shook them off with annoyance, already missing the whirling air outside.

"How do you know all of this?" he asked Merlin, kicking a rat away. The smell of their droppings quickly replaced the smell of mold. "You always seem to know a great lot about Mesidia's history."

The Elite shrugged. "My father was a historian. He wrote books about the breaking of Mesidia's royalty. He journeyed to ruins like these often, he and his team of scholars, and he brought me along with him when I was a boy." He paused suddenly, turning around with reddened eyes. Roland immediately brought down the hand he held to his nose, embarrassed as the rugged Elite stood steadfast before him.

The Light burn him, I know he smells the droppings too, he thought, quickly trying to seclude his breaths to his mouth. As soon as Merlin turned his back, the prince once again succumbed to the relief of his plugged nose.

"Unsheathe your blade, Prince, and hold steady to my cloak. I must relinquish this flame. There are voices above us."

Roland obeyed and cast aside all pride as he dutifully clasped Merlin's cloak. As silently as he could, he stripped his sword from its place along his hip, grateful he didn't need to *call* one of his own. It would've weighed less, certainly, the imaginary always perfectly balanced as it breathed life within its maker's hand, but his mind was in no state to maintain such creations. His other senses were already too drained from their quest.

With little patience, the Elite silently stepped forward. Roland went forth with each small tug. The voices Merlin mentioned grew louder the closer they stepped, their ascent through a new staircase now seeming dreadfully exposed. Roland was sure the people who spoke would hear their boots as they made their way up. His boots, in truth, as the Elite's steps were nearly nonexistent.

"Yes," someone said. The prince froze, as did Merlin, both men hearing the voice above them now with perfect clarity. They stood still, neither moving an inch as the person continued.

"Natalia is traveling with them."

Roland's heart pounded, his breath held high in his chest as he at last recognized the voice.

It was the duke's.

They were supposed to catch Yvaine in her treachery, not him. Why would he lead them to his own deceit?

"Fool," a woman answered. Merlin grabbed Roland's arm firmly, the duo cautiously climbing the last few steps of the stairs. A small light peeked through what appeared to be the wardrobe Merlin had mentioned, the slim line of its doors only wide enough for one man to look through at a time. Merlin pointed to him, then back at the light, nodding with reassurance and nudging Roland toward it.

"You understand why we wanted her here with us?" the woman asked. Roland scanned the room quickly, the keenness of his ears reaffirmed as he indeed saw the stoutly duke. The man sat on his knees, bloody and beaten, his hands bound together by shackles. Glowing, elemental shackles.

The metal that trapped and withheld elements.

Roland felt a shiver run down his spine. Never in his life had he seen the strong man brought to such disgrace. He all but forgot the woman beside the duke until she spoke again.

"She may not know it yet, but she's strong. She'll aid the Xens when we attack."

Roland examined the woman closely, trying to etch her appearance into his mind. The sudden movement of someone behind her, a tall, bulky man, stole his attention. The newcomer's features were nearly identical to the woman's own.

Pale skin, Roland noted. *And dark hair.*

The duchess Yvaine's allies.

"What-what do you mean?" Bernard stuttered. His bloodied face was plagued with horror, his eyes wide and his lips quivering. "What're you to do there? They possess the Amulet, nothing more. The Amulet can only reverse the effects of the other Artifacts. It's useless!"

"To your wife perhaps," the woman answered, running her fingers contemptuously through his hair. "But bearing your child has stripped Yvaine of her immortality." She glanced back gleefully to the other man—her twin, more than likely—a twisted smile emerging on her face.

"I did as you asked," Bernard said, his voice rising. "Pierre has sent troops to Riverdee—his best men! Stonewall is weak without them!"

No, Roland thought, fighting to stay calm. *No, no, no, it was a trap. The men sent to Riverdee, the threat of an attack—it was all to weaken our defenses.*

His pulse pounded wildly against his skull.

"You shouldn't have sent your daughter away," the woman scorned. Her amusement vanished as she lifted a hand to Bernard's cheek. He cried out in pain, flames emerging where the woman touched. Roland's muscles twitched as he made to stand, desperate to act, but Merlin's hand was there to pull him back. The prince looked to him insistently, grimacing at Bernard's screams. The Elite just shook his head.

It was an agonized eternity before the shouts ceased.

We have to help him, Roland thought. *We can't let him die.*

If there's a threat heading toward Stonewall, he's the only one who can tell us what's going on.

He turned for a brief second to Merlin, wishing there was some way to convey his thoughts. The woman's voice returned before he could.

"You shouldn't have sent your daughter away," she repeated. She pulled out a blade from her side, the metal singing as it cut through the air. "We have no need for you now. You'll serve us better in death."

With swift impulse, Roland burst through the wardrobe and lunged to save the duke. It was foolhardy, rash and reckless and dangerous, but it didn't matter. Stonewall was going to be attacked—his *home* was going to be attacked—and he knew next to nothing of who or when or why. Only Bernard could provide them insight.

As he tightened his grip on his sword, the tall brute standing beside the woman lifted his arm and released a gust of air. The element struck Roland, his body unable to move as he crashed against the wall. His shoulder slipped out of place as he hit the stones. Merlin was beside him in an instant, casting up a fortress of lightning as he helped the prince to his feet.

"Run!" he ordered, pushing Roland back toward the wardrobe. The large, dark-haired man walked through the crackling wall of lightning. His air element overpowered Merlin's own as he made his way forward. The two dueled, swords ringing loudly together, both men lunging and dodging the other's attempts. Roland barely looked up in time to see the woman standing above Bernard's body, his head rolling across the floor.

"No!" Roland shouted. He ignored the pain in his shoulder and reached for his red *auroras*, casting out a blaze of fire. The woman hardly moved from his element, the air she *called* gathering into a whirlwind before sending the fire back toward him. Roland ducked. The heat burned through parts of his clothes, the scent of scorched fabric strong. The element resistant armor beneath his cloak absorbed most of the flames.

He instantly released his fire. It still came toward him, the woman seemingly adding her own. Frantic, Roland pulled at air. He could feel his body draining as he forced up a small shield to deter the flames, but he didn't have any other choice. If he let the flames keep soaking into his armor, eventually the metal would be overwhelmed. If that happened, most of the fire would be released anyway.

Miraculously, the woman stopped, Merlin having stolen her attention away. Roland blinked away his dizziness, trying to regain his bearings. When his vision began to refocus, the woman was there.

Bernard's blood was streaked across her face.

Instinctively Roland lifted his sword to strike. He wouldn't win in a fight with elements, his first attempt confirming that. He leaned in, putting as much weight behind his thrust as he could manage, but something held his feet in place. Barely able to keep himself steady, he looked down, cursing.

Ice. The woman had cast ice around his feet and ankles.

Panicked, he *called* his fire back. The ice held steady, as if his element was a mere candle flame trying to melt a glacier. The woman smiled, her expression crazed as he struggled to break free.

Then her amusement vanished. Her eyes, wide and manic, began to glow.

The ice at Roland's feet melted.

He wasted no time escaping the trap. His legs and feet were numb from the frost, but they worked enough to get him free. He made to take the woman in her weakened stake, take advantage of whatever had consumed her, but a sudden glimpse of his Elite behind her stole his glance.

Merlin was kneeling in front of the giant man, blood spilling from his stomach.

The dark-haired man lifted his blade and struck.

"Merlin!"

Enraged, Roland thrust his sword at the woman. His blow was again deflected by the woman's elements. It was air this time, not ice, but it was weaker. It didn't knock the sword from his grasp.

She was still stronger than him, though, despite whatever was plaguing her. Defeated, Roland did what Merlin had commanded.

He ran.

Guilt tore at him. He didn't want to flee, didn't want to abandon the duke's headless body or Merlin's cut open one, but he knew he would do their deaths little justice if he wound up dead too. Weak, and fighting not to stumble, he *called* his fire and sprinted down the darkened stairs behind the wardrobe.

He twisted around corners he hardly remembered, running back to the tunnel's exit. Moldy, wet steps reappeared beneath the raging storm. The mares were still there, their snorts and whinnies growing louder as Roland rushed to their sides. He unsheathed a knife at his hip and cut their ties, careful to hold tightly to the reins as he hoisted himself into the saddle. He shouted through clenched teeth at the pain of his wounded shoulder. Grimacing, he straightened himself and kicked his mount onward.

He took a remorseful look back. He hoped he'd see Merlin behind him. He hoped the man would come running, telling him he'd defeated the two Lightless beings. Instead, he saw the dark tunnel, rain, and webs of lightning.

Merlin wasn't coming back. Duke Bernard was dead.

And his father's soldiers had been sent away as a trap.

Part Two

An Image of Peace and Turmoil

I succeeded in my mission. I wish I hadn't.

Gwenivere Verigrad
My closest friend. We don't have a lot in common, but she is like a sister to me, and I love her dearly. I was saddened when Roland was given the Dagger, as I know he loves her, and I'd always fancied the idea of she and I being related.

From the sketchbook of Elizabeth al'Murtagh

Chapter 18

GWENIVERE

Gwenivere knew she was sheltered. Her father rarely allowed her outdoors unless it was to learn survival practices or hunting tactics, and even those were heavily monitored by his knights.

Today she was rebuking that.

She was in her capital, and she had every intention of seeing it. Garron didn't enjoy the idea of her traipsing about the city, but he was her knight, not her father's. If she ordered him to do something, and Gerard hadn't outright refused it, then he wasn't in a position to disobey.

"Don't fret so much," she'd told him. "I promise Father will be so consumed with the guests he won't even notice I'm gone. And if he does, I left a note with Sir Charles. Runners will come fetch us if I'm needed."

He hadn't seemed convinced.

She'd been determined, though, and prepared, proudly proving it to him by displaying her *touched* blades, element-resistant bodice, and hooded cloak, all of which were adorned over commoner's clothes she'd borrowed from Becca. Her boots, stiff and dirty, had switches in them to produce blades in the soles if she needed to kick someone.

Garron hadn't been pleased, but he had been impressed with her preparation. He'd gone and changed into his own rugged clothing and let down his hair to look less polished, then begrudgingly agreed.

"Look at all those knives," Gwenivere said, pointing at a nearby juggler. He stood on a platform in the middle of a plaza, his face painted with an artificial smile. "Light, it's a wonder he never lost a finger learning such a trick, wouldn't you say? Oh, is that another knife?"

The man did indeed pull out another knife, adding it confidently to his current set. The crowd gasped and clapped, a few onlookers tossing him coins and cheering. Gwenivere stood on her tiptoes to get a better look.

"Do you find him entertaining?" Garron asked.

"I do. His talent is both impressive and unusual."

"I'll teach you then."

Gwenivere furrowed her brow, amused as she surveyed her knight's rigid physique.

"You? Forgive me my disbelief, but I hardly take you to be a juggler." She glanced at the flamboyant performer one last time and tried to picture her knight clad in his colorful tunic and pants. She smiled at the thought and turned away.

The next area greeted her with a sign labeled VENDOR'S AL-LEY. Despite its name, it was more a street than an alley, and hardly an inch of it lay bare as dealers and buyers lined up along booths and tables. The cold of the day didn't seem to bother anyone, bustling bodies creating warmth as blacksmiths' forges burned. The hammers of armorers and the banter of bargaining merchants competed noisily, and fiddlers, with cases set out, played cheerful tunes. It was madness but it was beautifully clad, flowers and art coloring what bits of the street weren't filled with metal and wood and people.

Gwenivere gaped at it all like a child. She noted people buying and adorning masks and turned to Garron, saying, "Perhaps I'll find a mask here for the masquerade." She looked back to see if he'd heard but found his forehead wrinkled and his lips scrunched.

"I don't care for these crowds; they're dangerous."

Gwenivere scoffed, leaning in close. "The Amulet is hiding well beneath my dress, and few can distinguish me without seeing my hair." She tugged at her cloak's hood for emphasis. "Besides, none of these people could match you in skill or in valor, or myself for that matter. You needn't fret so."

He opened his mouth to protest, but Gwenivere ignored the ominous possibilities he began listing off. She caught bits and pieces of them—poisoned knives, poisoned darts, poisoned something or other—and found his discomfort escalated the further into the street she walked.

Blocking him out, she approached a table of glasswork and fingered at the various shapes on it. Fiends and animals were laid out on one end, each bright and exquisitely detailed, while simpler things, like feathers and leaves and prayer symbols, were laid out further along.

"These are beautiful," she said. She looked up to find the seller, a small, elderly woman, who beamed at her with bag-ridden eyes.

Wanting to keep the woman's spirits high, Gwenivere turned to point the glasswork out to Garron. He was now looking away, though, admiring the work of a sword crafter.

Bloody traitor, she thought with a smirk. She looked back to the glass and let her fingers wander. The fiend ones would likely impress Aden, but they were so delicate she decided to leave them be. Her father might fancy the regal ones, like the lions or the birds, but buying him something would reveal she'd left the palace. She'd not been lying to Garron about the note she'd left with Charles, but she'd rather not have the topic arise at all if she could avoid it.

About to walk on to the mask maker's stand, Gwenivere stopped, swallowing and lifting the piece her fingers had drifted toward.

A rose, she realized, admiring its petals. *Like my mother.*

She forced away the thought. Setting the piece down, she thanked the elderly woman, crossed her arms beneath her chest, and made her way to Garron.

"What happened to all that talk of being murdered?" she asked. "Not so concerned an arrow will poison my heart when a fine *touched* sword is in your view?"

He looked at her for a moment before placing the blade he'd been admiring back on its stand.

"They were not that fine," he replied. His beard shifted with a grin, though only slightly.

"So you really used to juggle?" Gwenivere asked, pulling him onward. "I don't believe it."

He said nothing. When they neared a food vendor, he unlaced Gwenivere's hand, bought an armful of random fruits, and handed over the allotted coins. He shifted the fruit from one arm to the next, rolling up his sleeves, then stood shoulder-width apart, tossing the fruit in the air.

Gwenivere stood wide-eyed. Passersby poked their heads in their direction, seemingly intrigued, before shrugging indifferently and walking away.

"My, my, what other things do I not know about you?" She snatched three of the fruits from him and attempted the pattern she'd seen him do.

All three pieces ended up on the ground.

"I sing," he answered, picking the fruit up and handing

it back to her. He grunted as she dropped them again, her second try worse than her first. "Or at least I think so. There you go, there you go. Here, now try with a fourth." He threw another piece at her, hitting her in the stomach.

"Curse your burly arms!" She plucked the fruit from the street and tried again. "You say you sing, though?"

"I do. Though my wife always said I croaked like a crow."

Gwenivere started. "You were married?"

Garron opened his mouth, as if to say something, but the vendor behind them cut him off.

"Could you move? You're blocking the way!" The man's voice was laced with annoyance, and he pointed at them aggressively. Gwenivere stepped forward, about to curse him, but Garron's arm was dragging her away before she could.

"A meal," he said, gesturing toward a tavern. "It's been a long day, with a great deal of walking. My feet could use the rest, and my stomach the food. I'm sure yours could use the same."

Gwenivere fumed but agreed, following him out of Vendor's Alley. She tossed the fruit in a wastebasket and wiped her now-sticky hands on the kerchief he handed her. He took it back after she'd rid herself of the fluids, using it to wipe his own hands. When they reached the tavern he'd suggested, he opened the door for her and followed her to a table.

"So you were married?" she asked, sitting down. "I never knew."

He nodded and gave the approaching server their order, already knowing Gwenivere wanted elk. When the man hurried off, Gwenivere relaxed into her seat and made to remove her cloak, but realized she'd need to keep it on if she wanted to continue hiding her hair. She glanced around at the tavern's other patrons and hoped the raised hood wasn't reason to grant unwanted stares.

He still has his up, she thought, noting a hooded man

across from them, *and he adorns a mask as the others did in the street. Ah, and now he's caught me staring.* She tilted her head in greeting, then smiled slightly as the man grinned courteously in return.

After a while of silence, the server returned with their food. Garron thanked him and reached for Gwenivere's plate and drink, grabbing a fork and smelling the meat before placing it in his mouth. He didn't chew at first, only tasted, then sipped her water. When he deemed each was safe, he scooted them back and gave her a nod.

"Thank you," she muttered, watching as he washed it all down with his own drink. "And I'm sorry for prying. I was just taken aback. We don't have to talk about—"

"She died," Garron interrupted. He took a bite from his plate, his eyes lazily looking about the room. "She was killed, during the War of Fire. I enlisted in your father's ranks shortly after."

Gwenivere bit into her food, tasting nothing. "I'm sorry. You must've been quite young when it happened. Only . . . sixteen or seventeen springs?"

He nodded but kept quiet. She looked at him, waiting for him to say more, but his thoughts were visibly elsewhere.

"What was her name? If you don't mind my asking."

Garron sighed, swallowed the contents of his cup, and motioned to the server for more. It took a moment for Gwenivere to realize he wasn't drinking water.

"Her name was Marie," he answered. "It was a simple name, nothing grand. My name was Luthier Hill."

Gwenivere gaped, then quickly covered her mouth with her napkin. "Luthier you say? I rather like it. I never knew Garron wasn't your birth name." She grabbed his hand and patted it gently. "Marie and Luthier—a very lovely sound. I'm sure she was perfection."

Garron took another drink. "She was."

He didn't say anything more. Gwenivere took her hand

back and gave him his silence, only exchanging polite pleasantries with the server as he occasionally checked in. She kept
track of the tankards Garron cleared, grateful when, after four,
he refused another.

He always just seemed my honorable knight, she thought,
eyeing his ever-stern expression. *How terrible of me, never considering the man before the armor.*

When they'd finished their meal, he set coins on the table
and rose. Gwenivere followed, attempting an encouraging
smile as he opened the tavern's door for her.

"Miss?" someone called. Gwenivere turned, the cloaked
man she'd noticed before holding out a small pouch to her.

"You dropped this," he said, his voice thickly accented.
Gwenivere eyed the pouch distrustfully, deciding it best to slip
on her gloves before accepting it.

"Thank you," she said. She narrowed her eyes at the man
as she took the pouch, hoping to remember his face, but it was
hard to see it through his cloak and mask. All she could make
out were green eyes and dark, golden skin.

"It was my pleasure, milady," he answered. "Good day."

He was out the door Garron held open before Gwenivere
could say anything more. The knight immediately slipped inside
when he realized it wasn't Gwenivere who'd walked through,
the encounter happening so fast he'd barely had a chance to
witness it. His movements turned frantic when he saw Gwenivere holding the pouch, but she smiled at him and held up her
now-gloved hands, assuring him she'd taken precautions.

"What did he give you?" he asked, hovering protectively.
"Give it here, I'll examine it for you."

"Light, you're so paranoid! You're as bad as my father." She
undid the pouch's tie and peeked inside, careful to keep it
out of his sight. When she realized what it was, she hurriedly
cinched it back shut, feigned a calm grin, and insisted they go
back out.

"It's just some coins," she said, tying the pouch to her side. "I must've dropped them earlier."

Garron narrowed his eyes but didn't press her. She was grateful. She was rather certain that, if he'd asked her anything more, she'd have broken down and admitted her lie.

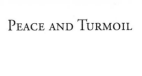

There's nothing the paintings don't see, Gerard. While we gaze upon one moment of their existence, they gaze upon thousands of ours. What an interesting irony, don't you think?

From a letter between Rose and Gerard Verigrad

CHAPTER 19

GWENIVERE

Profligacy at its finest and multitudes of wasted coin—that was how Gwenivere viewed her palace quarters, the *Queen's Quarters*, they were called, which had lavish decorations lining everything from the ceilings to the floors. The room was large, absurdly so for just one person, and she often argued that it should be divided up and used to house poorer staff members. Her father thought it a generous proposition but insisted the palace's splendor was a tiresome but indispensable act to show the height and achievement of their nation.

Gwenivere wished terribly that her father would've succumbed to her persistent tongue. She knew that somewhere, within the room's vast darkness, the green-eyed man was waiting.

As the sun had given way to darker skies, she'd expected to see him again, every step through her city a step gone by without his appearance. Further and further her feet had carried her, back down the crowded plazas and swarming squares, across the bridge to the palace and up the stairs of its floors until finally, with shoulders to her door, she stood unmoving.

She'd taken her gloves off, feeling inside the pouch he'd given her. The object inside was the glass rose, the one she'd admired from Vendor's Alley, along with a note reading *Do not fear me, I await when the night comes.*

Silencing her nervous breath, she reminded herself of Garron's presence just opposite her wall. If she thought this something too dangerous to consider alone, she could warn him. He was only inches away on the other side of her door.

She stood motionless, running over again and again what to do. The rose proved the stranger had been watching her for some time, yet he hadn't harmed her, and he hadn't tried getting her attention as she'd ambled through Voradeen's streets. It wasn't until she'd stood aback from Garron that he'd made his presence known, and even then he'd only attempted to subdue any panic his intended meeting might bring.

None of that mattered, though. He'd followed her, and he needed to suffer the consequences of his actions.

But if she told Garron, and her father found out . . .

She took a deep breath, exhaled, and opened her door.

"Garron, I must confess something to you."

The knight turned to face her, brows furrowed at her abrupt return.

"In the plaza, in Vendor's Alley, I was looking at a glassmaker's stand while you looked at swords. I found a rose," she held up the glass, "and bought it, because it reminded me of my mother. Being here, back in the palace, is bringing back all these memories of her, and I'm finding I miss her a great deal more than I have for some time."

She looked up to see if Garron believed her, surprised when his hand lifted and patted her heavily on the shoulder.

"Rose was a fine queen," he said, returning his hand to his

side. "And a loving mother. It is understandable to reflect on her absence. Would you like me to call one of your servants to your room? Becca perhaps? Or maybe Lady Elizabeth? I'm certain they would be happy to accompany you."

Gwenivere felt a wave of guilt. She forced a smile to cover it, wiping at the false tears threatening to fall.

"No, thank you, but I do have another request."

He stood tall, nodding dutifully.

"There's a blanket," she started. "A thick, red one my mother and I used to curl up in when I was a girl. It's in Aden's room now, but he hardly fancies the thing. Could you perhaps get it for me? It would only take a moment."

She bit her lip, watching her knight's expression shift as he contemplated the task. Time fulfilling her request meant time away from his post, any and all terrible dangers possibly befalling her in that time. He scrunched his nose, clearly displeased at the thought, but eventually nodded.

"I'll return with it in a moment. I'll have knights standing guard at either end of the hall while I'm gone."

"Thank you, Garron. I appreciate it."

He gave a parting nod before heading off.

Gwenivere wiped her eyes again, inhaling deeply as she caught sight of the new painting along the hallway's wall behind where Garron had stood. It depicted a naked woman in a garden, alone and unclothed with nothing but leaves and flowers to cover her. She looked as if she knew Gwenivere's deceit, her painted eyes chastising.

Even in her nudity she has less to hide than I, Gwenivere thought. She groaned quietly as she turned away, walking back into her chambers and shutting the door.

Knowing Garron would be back soon, she *called* fire and lit the sconces on her walls. Beside one of her windows, with mask and cloak still adorned, the green-eyed stranger stood.

"You have but a small time to reveal your intentions,"

Gwenivere told him, hoping her voice sounded more steadfast than she felt. The man closed the window he stood by, holding his hand out and gesturing toward the room's door.

"You mean until your knight returns?" His speech was clear, though obviously foreign, the unusual lilt almost musical. Its charm hardly fit the circumstance of their encounter.

"That man could slice you in half with a broken blade," Gwenivere said. "As could I. Speak ill of either of us and I shall see to it you find out."

The stranger grinned, much to her annoyance. He withdrew from his place beside the window and slowly walked across the room, his steps silent.

"You seem rather eager to inflict pain on me," he said, picking up the *Tales of Eve* from atop her study. "Do you always make threats so hastily?"

"I am a person of civility. If I seem eager, it's only because I wish to do what is just."

The man glanced up from the book, cocking his head toward her hands. Gwenivere followed where he looked, her body tingling with embarrassment when she realized she'd started *calling* fire again. She scowled and forced the element away.

"Did my father give you this book?" he asked, holding up the *Tales of Eve*. "He must have; my mother said this was the only copy."

Gwenivere squinted, staggered by the simplicity of his query. She examined him again, what little she could see beneath his hood and mask, and realized who he was.

"Dietrich," she said slowly. "Dietrich Haroldson."

The man nodded, grinning as his father had in her memories.

"I see. And what exactly do you want from me, Dietrich Haroldson? Are you here to assassinate me? I've been told that's what you do."

The prince looked up from the book again, at last seeming to note the insistence in her tone. He closed the book and gently placed it atop her study, facing her but saying nothing.

"Why are you here?" she pressed. She winced as she realized the words came out with audible weakness. She fought the urge to lick her lips and made to speak again, but stopped when she saw Dietrich's head tilt. He was no longer looking at her, but to the ground, listening.

"Your item, milady."

Gwenivere jumped, spinning around to face Garron as he pressed open her door. It creaked loudly and she rushed toward it, seeing Garron's eyes widen as he took in the lightened sconces throughout the room.

She looked from him back to Dietrich.

He was gone.

"Gwenivere?"

With a heavy breath, the princess took the blanket from her knight. She didn't notice until then that she still held the rose, its stem now disfigured from the fire she'd unintentionally *called*.

The Xen palace is by far the most magnificent structure I've seen. The architecture is exquisite, the artwork is stunning, and the backdrop of the lakes, waterfalls, and forests is breathtaking.

Fiona Collinson

Chapter 20

DIETRICH

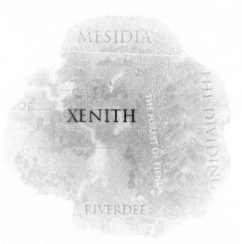

*Y*ou, *Prince, are a ball-less bastard.*

Dietrich pounded his fist against a tree and released a small grunt of frustration.

Thank you, Seera.

He still hadn't grown accustomed to her constant searching in his head, but he tried his best to ignore it now. He ran over the meeting with the princess again and again, trying to understand how he could've possibly revealed none of his intentions to her. He cursed the moment he'd wasted, shaking out his hand.

You said your name at least, Seera offered. She curled up closer to their campfire, more concerned with warming her scales than discouraging his blame. *Actually, you didn't. You got her to say it. Very useful indeed.*

Dietrich shot her a glare, though for little purpose. She

already seemed disinterested in his failure.

He blew air from his cheeks and sat down beside her, pulling the hood of his cloak up in an attempt to cast away the night's chill.

It's freezing here, he thought, inching closer to the flames. He'd only been in Xenith a short time, the flight atop Seera's wings having left him plenty of time before the masquerade, yet he'd still not grown accustomed to the cooler climate. He repositioned some of the logs, hoping to expand the blaze, but his efforts yielded little results. He gave up after a few tries, sighing in defeat and tossing in several more branches.

Our king is patient
Our king is kind
Our king is witty
And very sound of mind
His guests are spoiled
His guests are crass
His guests are violent
With sticks up their ass

Xen tavern song

CHAPTER 21

GERARD

The halls of the Xen palace bustled with noise. Maidservants frantically ran errands for their noblewomen, diplomats argued over historical controversies, and ambassadors discussed ways to ease tensions. Anyone who was someone had finally arrived, and it would seem by the booming echoes throughout the main chamber that they were all gathered outside the Assembly Hall.

Many a treaty had been signed in that room, and many a man and woman had argued from dusk till dawn, hair proper and done upon arrival, and unkempt and untidy upon dismissal. Gerard remembered the story of one gathering lasting so long that the late King Carlisle of Xenith had left with bruises on his hands, not from fighting the men he shared the chamber with, but from pounding his fists in outrage against the table. A painting of the scene was displayed on the wall inside the room, with Carlisle sitting silently while the nobles around him bickered and argued.

Gerard loved the story. He felt it exemplified the very spirit of Xenith's people.

"My lord?" a voice called. "Would you like me to report?"

Gerard turned away from the painting, giving Sir Nicolas a nod of acknowledgment. "Yes. How are things?"

The knight glanced at the king with a smirk, almost too pretty a smirk to belong to a man, and laughed. "With myself? Or with our guests?"

Gerard bit his tongue, knowing such retorts were simply in the young knight's nature. He was a fine guardsman, and when Gerard had fallen from his stallion during their trek from the castle, Nicolas had been the only man who'd come to him after and demanded he be told the truth. He was bold, with enough forwardness for ten men, yet his insistencies were only out of devotion.

"With the guests," Gerard answered.

Nicolas laced his hands behind his back, standing straighter. "Most are fine, milord. They discuss, they laugh, they . . . examine, but there are of course a few who seem far from calm. There are feuding rivals among one another out there. I imagine they can only wait so long before elements begin to illuminate the halls."

Gerard nodded and took a deep breath in, knowing full well the amount of fury he'd have to ease. He glanced back up at the painting, Carlisle the only person in it whose knuckles were white, with everyone else's red from throwing strikes.

"Send them in," he said, walking to his throne. It was an imposing and salient seat, bigger and mightier than any of the rest throughout the semicircular chamber. He loathed the seat in part because it was so pretentious, but also because Gwenivere often stuck her nose up at it. She despised anything that displayed obvious wealth, and when she despised something, it was infectious.

He leaned against the throne's back, hating how cushioned its seat was, and took a tense breath. His chest burned. His breathing was noticeably loud in the empty chamber, despite his efforts to keep it quiet. It felt shallow, too, like his lungs were constricting and limiting his air. He swallowed and told himself to relax, realizing suddenly that Sir Nicolas was still standing before him.

"Why do you not obey me, boy?" Gerard asked. "Were my orders unclear?"

"No, milord," Nicolas started, looking to the floor. "It's just—you aren't in good health. Are you certain this is wise?"

Gerard rested his arms against his throne, the tension of his breaths agreeing with the knight's qualm.

It wasn't wise, but what choice did he have? He was the King of Peace. He couldn't allow the leaders of other nations to intervene on his behalf. How would it look, insisting he was impartial, to then allow someone else's king or queen to take his place? What message would that send?

Perhaps he could ask Gwenivere to lead the event. She was certainly intelligent and capable. The Light knew she'd studied each kingdom and its quarrels as much as any of his scholars.

But no. She wasn't ready yet. She couldn't do it.

It had to be him.

"Send them in," he ordered, pointing toward the doors. The knight nodded, not doing a good job of hiding his grimace. When his back was turned, Gerard held his chest with one hand, let out a strained breath, and clutched the arm of his throne with the other.

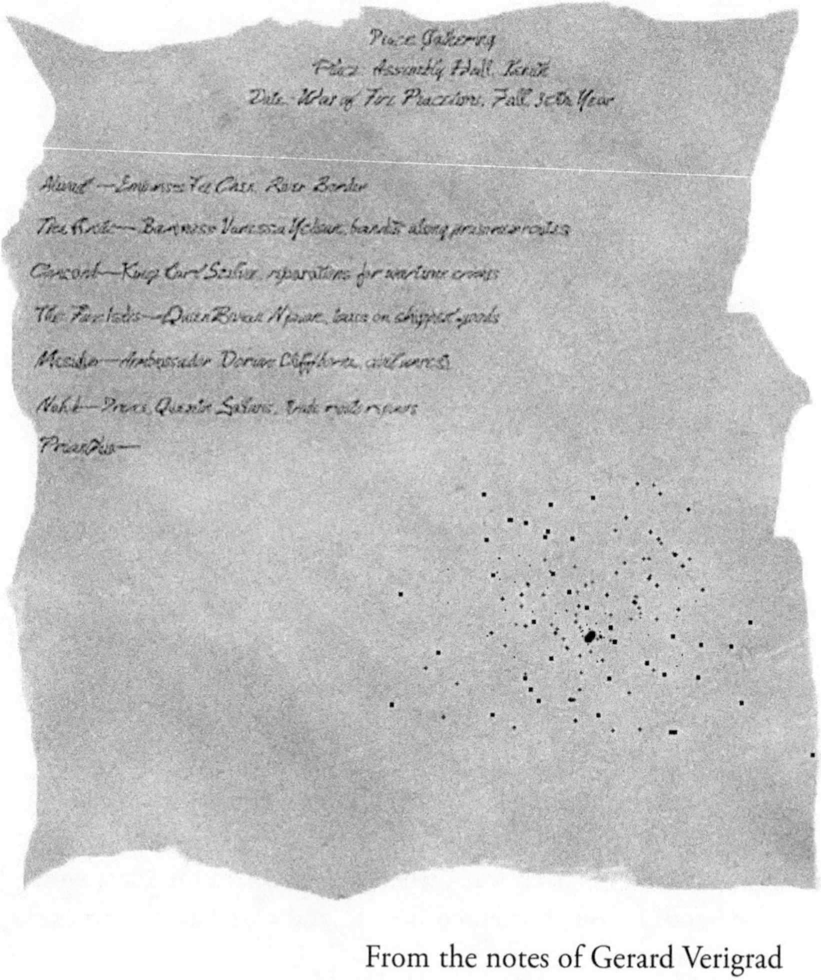
Peace Gathering
Place: Assembly Hall, Kenth
Date: War of Fire Placations, Fall 30th Year

Alurat—Empress Fei Chen, River Border
The Krule—Baroness Vanessa Ycleave, bandits along prisoner routes
Concord—King Carl Scalus, reparations for wartime crimes
The Fire Isles—Queen Bivana Nguae, taxes on shipped goods
Mosiko—Ambassador Dorian Cliffhorne, civil unrest
Nakk—Prince Quentin Saliers, trade route repairs
Pranthia—

From the notes of Gerard Verigrad

CHAPTER 22

GWENIVERE

Not a moment of sleep had graced Gwenivere through the night. She'd wrapped herself in the warmth of the blanket she'd asked Garron to bring her, then cracked her door ajar and sat in a chair at its side, fearful of Dietrich Haroldson's return. The Golden Knight never retired to his chambers, politely dismissing the other men who came to take his place. Not a word had been spoken between them, not a glance shared or a gesture exchanged, but there'd been a silent understanding that he was needed nearby.

"Your scrolls, milord."

It was Sir Charles who spoke. Gwenivere started, half-asleep, and remembered it was the day of the Peace Gathering. She wasn't in her bedchamber any longer—she was in the Assembly Hall, beside her father, who was sitting in his obnoxiously large throne. Her own wasn't much better, though at least it had fewer unnecessary intricacies in its frame. It was considerably smaller than her father's, which she was grateful for, as she hated the idea of people thinking she thought herself better than them.

There was one additional throne, an empty one, where Aden would have sat. Her brother wasn't present though, as Gerard had deemed him too young for the political event. Gwenivere wished he hadn't. It would've been nice if her brother and his knight Maximus were there since she was often surrounded by older men. She longed to have more young people nearby—young people who weren't Sir Nicolas, who currently stood near her father's throne. She didn't care for him, finding him far too arrogant for her liking. If she weren't so tired, she might cast him a glare.

Maybe Garron can glare at him for me, she thought, sneaking a look at her knight. She was surprised to see he was already looking at her, eyes narrowed. He was either dreadfully tired himself, or he was worried about her lack of sleep.

Not liking his scrutiny, she turned from him and glanced over her father's arm, trying to see the scrolls Sir Charles had brought. Gerard caught her stare, setting the feathered pen in his hand down and smiling.

"I can see you're overwhelmed, dear, but don't be afraid. I never read through all of them. That's what Sir Charles is for."

Gwenivere sat still for a moment, confused. She furrowed her brow, about to shake her head, then realized her father's jest.

The scrolls. That's what he thought her daunted by.

She returned his smile, saying nothing. It was best her father thought what he did rather than knowing she'd disguised herself as a commoner, trekked about the capital, and let a stranger into her bedchamber. *Willingly* let a stranger into her bedchamber. Like those fool girls she hated in stories.

I wonder if Dietrich's here, she thought, tensing as she looked around the Assembly Hall. Any fatigue she'd felt before was gone now, replaced by prickling fear. She took in a breath, trying to steady the trembles in her hands, and sat back in her throne.

When all the incoming nobles had settled, Gerard stood up. He nodded to them all in greeting, politely waving down any who were about to stand with him. Once everyone had quieted, he sat back down and spoke. "Thank you all for being here today. Welcome to Voradeen, Xenith."

Translations for foreign tongues followed.

"For those whom I have never met, I am filled with gratitude that you've graced my home with your presence. Although this particular gathering is one of politics, I look forward to speaking with each and every one of you in a much more . . . endearing fashion, at the masquerade."

His speech was laced with a hidden humor, and many nobles snickered. Even those of different languages chuckled, delayed by their translators' words. Gwenivere smiled as well, supposing that was the right thing to do, before Garron leaned down and whispered in her ear.

"Peace Gatherings are often filled with tension," he explained. "On the contrary, masquerades are filled with wine. Your father is implying that everyone will be much more at ease when they have a glass in their hand."

Gwenivere nodded, then flushed with embarrassment that she had. She shrugged and waved her hand at him, pretending she'd already known.

Garron either grunted or laughed—it was too short a noise to determine which. He returned to his upright position beside her, hands behind his back.

"To those whom I have met before," Gerard continued, "it is an honor to have you here again. As each of your invitations indicated, this is a time to honor and celebrate Abra'am's thirty years of peace. It's also a time for us to come together to ensure our wonderful calm continues." He paused, allowing his words to settle. Scribes and translators hurriedly whispered to catch his place.

"We shall begin our commencement with introduction. As a nation is called, the representative shall state their names and titles, as well as the topic they or their leaders wish to discuss. Each nation shall be called in order by the letters of Common tongue. This classification is in no way an insinuation of my feelings toward any one region or peoples."

Gerard accepted a full container of ink from Sir Charles and unfolded a map of Abra'am's nations. Dipping his quill in the liquid, he skimmed the map and lifted his head to the hall.

"Who represents the nation of Alivad?"

Near the back of the hall, hardly seen, a small woman rose.

"I, Empress Fei," the woman answered gallantly. Gwenivere perked up, intrigued by the tiny noble with the powerful voice. She grinned, wondering if the blade-like sticks in the empress's hair were for decoration alone.

"Thank you, Empress," Gerard stated. "What matters do you wish to discuss today?"

"The River Border," Fei replied. She sat back down, not waiting for the Xen king to grant her permission. Then, with snarled lips, she glared toward a few men below her. From the bitter expressions on their faces it would seem they were from the nation she shared the River Border with.

Rude and improper. Gwenivere rather liked her.

As the king ran through the list of names, each went along in a similar fashion: he'd ask who was representing where, a representative, his or her translator, or a combination of both would rise, and boiling feuds or economic crises would follow.

Gwenivere recalled meeting many of the guests throughout the halls of the palace in the time since they'd arrived. Names had been exchanged in those encounters, all of which she'd carefully stored in the back of her mind. Every person she'd met had been attached some small characteristic, a great deal of them coming back to her as they were called.

Vanessa of the Arctic is a head taller than most women. And men.
Carl of Concord is old with an alarmingly young wife. And
was Xenith's main enemy during the War of Fire.
Bevani of the Five Isles has intricate braids.
Dorian of Mesidia is, well, Dorian of Mesidia.
Quentin of Nahl. Ah yes, Quentin of Nahl . . .

Gwenivere scowled as the impish man stood. He was exactly as she'd remembered him: pale, confident without reason, and sneaky-eyed. He glanced down at the bosoms of women below him, inhaling with satisfaction before looking to Gerard. Gwenivere snuck a glance at her father, her grimace replaced with a grin as she saw him mouth something behind his scroll. She didn't catch the words but she knew by his twitching jaw they were nothing of praise.

"Who represents the nation of Prianthia?" he called, his shoulders relaxing when Quentin at last sat. Across the hall, in the very utmost corner, a group of people stood. There were five in total, three women and two men, each sharing the same black hair and harsh, demanding stares. They were almost Sadiyan in appearance, with the exception of their eyes, which even from a distance Gwenivere could see weren't green. The women were tall, slender yet curved, and the men beside them were hardly men at all, both like bears in their heights.

"My name is Alanna," one of the women said. "I am the daughter-heir of Prianthia." She looked over at her companions, pointing to each as she said their names. "My sisters: Anastasia and Alexandria. My brothers: Nicolai and Rokinoff. Rokinoff is the leader of our armies." She paused, lacing her hands in front of her. "We are here on behalf of our parents, Rimsky and Anya, leaders of the East."

Gwenivere scoffed. Leaders of the East? Thirty years of freedom for Sadie evidently meant nothing to them.

"Thank you for being here today," Gerard answered. "I must admit, I expected your parents, but nonetheless, it is an honor you have endured such a tough passage to be here."

"Yes, they wish they could attend. However, as we speak, they mourn the death of our brother Pasha."

Gerard nodded, genuine grievance crossing his face. Many in the room had similar expressions, sighing in sympathy or whispering commiserations. Few did nothing at all.

"My condolences to all of you," Gerard said endearingly. "And to your parents. May your brother rest peacefully in the after—"

"No!"

It was the smaller of the two brothers. Gwenivere shot him a glare—Nicolai, she recalled—and felt Garron's hand pushing down on her shoulder as she unwillingly began to rise.

"His killer is still loose," Nicolai continued. He looked around, meeting the eyes of those around him. "And Prianthians do not rest until justice has been brought."

The hall stirred. Gerard said nothing at first, his expression still but his gaze strong. Gwenivere looked between him and the Prianthians, five against one, and swallowed. The chamber slowly fell back to rest.

"We will do our best," Gerard said, "to assist you in finding your brother's killer. This I assure you. Now, if there's nothing else you wish to discuss, you may return to your seats."

Nicolai slammed the table in front of him. Those around him gasped, inching their chairs away.

Garron's grip on Gwenivere tightened.

"No more waiting to hear the pointless problems of the West. 'Silk is hard to come by,' 'Our libraries, our books, are too old.' Curse you westerners and your soft hands. My brother is dead! We will discuss this now."

The Prianthian ended his outburst with a glower. Leaders and nobles sat anxiously, each staring with wide or narrowed eyes to Gerard. Gwenivere burned to shield him, knuckles whitening with clenched fists, but she knew shame would be the only thing to come if she defended him.

"As I've stated," Gerard began, voice steady, "I mourn for your family. I can only imagine how unbearable the pain must be for all of you, but even more so for your parents. To lose a brother is difficult. To lose a child is unfathomable.

"I know how much you wish to capture the one who has caused you this heartache, but understand that discussing a solution now versus only a little while later will not change the plan of action in the end. A few more minutes will come soon enough."

Gwenivere stared at Nicolai. The young man's shoulders still heaved, his breaths heavy.

Be calm, Gwenivere thought. *Be—*

"You misunderstand my brother's eagerness."

The words came from Alanna, the one who'd introduced them. Her voice was velvety but firm, and she glanced at the king with pressing reserve. Gwenivere cursed under her breath, watching Nicolai's chest and shoulders return upright.

"You must understand," Alanna continued, "it is difficult to remain quiet, listening to all of your guests' problems, when the man who slit our brother's throat may be here in this very room."

Disarray followed her statement. Men dabbed at the sweat trickling down their heads while women, opening fans, frantically cooled themselves from the heat of the words.

Then weapons began to form. Gwenivere leaned forward, ready to unsheathe the hidden *touched* dagger beneath her skirts while the knights around the room quickly reached for their swords. Everyone stood on guard. Garron's hand no longer rested against her shoulder, cast instead to the hilt of his blade.

"This is madness!" a man shouted, pointing a finger at the Prianthians. "If you know who this assassin is, call him out. Zren is not one to let killers sit among kings."

"Hear, hear!" another voice called. Alanna lifted her hands

in defense, lips parting to speak, but her words were interrupted.

"Rest assured!" Carl of Concord shouted, clutching to his young wife. "You all saw how well this room was guarded. King Gerard would never let a traitor through those doors."

"I suppose Concord would know about traitors, wouldn't it?"

Carl rose to his feet, squinting and pointing at the insulter. "You Tiadorians wouldn't know a thing about grace if the Creator were sitting at your dinner table."

"Do not bring the Divine One into your quarrels!" a priestlike diplomat yelled. He shook his head vigorously, the dark garments around his face swooshing into a blur. "Such statements are blasphemy. Blasphemy! The people of Concord never respected the Church of the Divine. It is high time you learn to repent for your sinful ways!"

"None of you seemed to have minded our swords, or our 'blasphemous' ways, when we protected you from being taken by the Theatians!"

Gwenivere's focus shifted from one infuriated royal to the next. She looked over at her father, waiting to see what ingenious actions he would take or soothing words he would speak. His stature was no longer tall, though, but slumped, his shoulders and back lifting sporadically as he coughed into his sleeve. The embroidered tunic he wore began to dampen, blood turning the elegant cloth redder and redder with every heave of his chest.

Gwenivere thought she heard a woman scream, and a punch thrown, but all she could see was her father as he collapsed from his throne.

She ran to aid him. Garron and Nicolas reached him first. Both men grabbed him and lifted him from the ground, pulling him upright. Charles opened the door to another chamber and led them away. Before Gwenivere had a chance to follow, a man grabbed her roughly by the arm and spun her around. She instinctively raised her fist to strike, stopping when she realized it was her brother's knight Maximus.

"What?" she yelled, yanking her arm free and making for the door her father had been taken through. "Maximus, I don't have time for this, I—"

The knight fell to the ground, clutching her leg. "Milady!"

The word was practically buried beneath the noise and violence around them. Gwenivere turned back to face him, gasping as she took him in.

There was blood pooling from gashes in his stomach. He held a hand to them, the other still holding limply to her leg. She knelt beside him, examining his wounds. They were deep, and uneven and jagged. They ran across his entire torso, stretching from his ribs to his hips. She pulled out the *touched* knife strapped to her leg and ripped strips of cloth from her skirts, trying to work around his bulky frame to seal the wounds.

Her efforts were useless. The pieces of cloth were barely big enough to cover a single slash. The fabric was soaked through instantly, and any bit she moved Maximus only seemed to make his blood spill out faster.

She kept trying anyway.

"Hold on, all right?" she said firmly. She lifted her hands for a moment, trying to wipe away the tears blurring her sight, but only succeeded in streaking blood across her face.

If everyone would just be quiet, she thought angrily. *If everyone would just stop fighting!*

"How did this happen?" she asked, watching as Maximus began to spasm. "Who did this to you?"

The knight shook his head. His chest heaved and blood spurted from his lips.

"Fiends," he spat, grabbing her wrist. Gwenivere swallowed, looking behind her at the squabbling knights and nobles. No fiends resided in the hall. The only things around them were rivaling men and women.

"Fiends?" she asked, turning back to Maximus. She could see the life fading from his eyes, his muscles growing limp.

She pulled him against her. If she held him long enough, someone would come. Garron maybe, or a medic. Or Light, even Charles. Someone. Anyone.

Maximus can't die, she thought, shushing him as he coughed up more blood. *Maximus can't die. He's Maximus. He's Aden's knight. He's Aden's best friend. He's . . .*

"Aden," she whispered.

Maximus hadn't been stationed in the Assembly Hall. He'd been assigned guard over Aden, told to walk him through the palace gardens. And if this was the state Maximus was in now, and he was here, then where was her brother?

Where was Aden?

Opening eyes she hadn't realized she'd closed, Gwenivere grabbed Maximus's face and forced it toward her.

"Where is he?" she asked. "Maximus, where's Aden?"

A hand clenched at her shoulder, but Gwenivere ignored it. Maximus was paling, and she needed to know where her brother was. Remorseful, she lifted her hand to the side, prayed for forgiveness, and lightly slapped him.

"Where is he, Maximus? Where is he?"

"Safe," he managed. "He's in your father's quarters. But the city . . . "

He spasmed again. It was more violent this time, more jolting. Gwenivere held back a sob and leaned in, whispering consolations. She didn't know what else to do.

"Rest, my friend," she whispered, kissing his temple. "Rest."

If something was attacking her city, she couldn't stay here with him. She turned to the frenzy of nobles throughout the hall, half of them racing to escape the gathering, the other half swinging swords and casting elements.

Ignoring them, Gwenivere looked up to the ceiling. The domed roof of the Assembly Hall was lined with glass, but the light of the sun that normally shone through was smothered by the wings of fiends.

How did no one notice?

Gwenivere looked back to the people around her, searching for someone to guide her. There was no one. The Golden Knight's sword wasn't there to strike for her, and the King of Peace had no words of aid. It was only she, surrounded by unknowing fools, to lead them against the sudden attack.

"Silence!" she yelled, rising from Maximus's side.

The nobles didn't respond

"Silence!"

When they again didn't acknowledge her, she shut her eyes. In her mind, the bright lights of *auroras* flashed. She latched onto the first ones she saw—cackling specks of lightning—and held on, forcing her eyes back open. Taking a deep breath, she held her hand up in front of her, steadied herself, and released.

Lightning struck. The blades nobles and knights lifted toward one another halted.

"Save your swords," Gwenivere demanded, pointing toward the ceiling. "We're under attack."

The element was beginning to drain her, so she *vanished* it. In its place she *called* her sword, feeling the perfect balance of it coming to life.

I'll avenge Maximus, she thought. *I'll protect my city.*

When her sword was fully formed, she adjusted her grip, rolled her shoulders, and strode purposefully forward.

She didn't bother looking to see if anyone followed.

My grandson, be kind to the Watcher. She's lived much of her life in solitude.

From a letter between Cid and Ravel Orloff

CHAPTER 23
X'ODIA

Dark eyes rested coldly in heavy lids. The hairs on X'odia's neck stood as the eyes, aglow from the torches nearby, made their way to her.

She knew what to anticipate, could feel an understanding of her predicament without knowing how or when she'd gotten there. But she knew, knew that what she anxiously awaited, what she dreaded, would occur soon. The man just needed to give his command and it would happen.

The pain she felt inside, the overwhelming sense of betrayal, was quickly brought to life as a fist rose to strike her.

"X'odia!" Ravel shouted. "X'odia!"

The Watcher put her hand to her cheek, sure she'd find

swelling where the blow had landed. She scanned the area around her, noting damp objects and the smell of salt. In a mirror across from her, her eyes were glowing.

"You've had a vision," Ravel whispered. X'odia nodded, the motion making her sick. She rested herself back on her pillow, annoyed to find it damp with sweat and ocean dew.

Abra'am, she thought, rubbing her eyes. *I'm on a voyage to Abra'am.*

"I-I would let you rest, but," Ravel paused, his voice frantic. "X'odia, something is not right in Riverdee."

She sat up slowly, looking to the sailor. "What's happened?"

"I'm not sure." He hesitated, biting his fingernails. "The people of Riverdee—it seems they're being attacked."

"What?" She made to stand, but her weakened muscles forced her back. Ravel reached out to help her, guiding her to a beam for support.

"We have to help them," she insisted. She waited for her strength to return, then grabbed her cloak and fastened it over her shoulders.

Ravel stood wincing, fumbling with his hands. "I'm sorry, but you don't understand. Captain Bronal is going to turn us around."

X'odia stared, then hurriedly brushed past him. He protested as she went, shouting for her to stop, but she didn't listen. They couldn't turn around—couldn't. It was imperative she reach Abra'am keep the Dagger of Eve from being *called* on.

The sunlight blinded her as she cleared the stairs and reached the deck. She squinted, allowing her eyes a moment to adjust. She staggered when they did.

Riverdee wasn't under attack. It was being slaughtered, and by an army of fiends.

The sensation of vomiting came, but X'odia clung to the *Seagull's* railings and pressed it down. She forced herself to look out again, noting the blood that turned the shoreline red. Tentacles pulled at people near the sea, and winged fiends flew overhead as land-faring beasts charged. Corpses lined the coast, ragged and torn apart.

"X'odia." It was Captain Bronal who spoke, his hardened eyes lost as beads of sweat trickled down his neck. "I'm sorry, but we can't risk docking. We have to turn back."

"We can't turn back," she said helplessly. She released the railing and shook her head, her hand lifting to her chest.

Any sympathy in Bronal's face vanished. He stepped forward, lips curling, and pointed to her forcefully. "If you want to fight, then fight, but my men are fathers and husbands. Their lives need not end today."

X'odia grimaced. She glanced back at the crewmen, each looking to her and the captain for orders. Those within earshot held expressions of reservation.

I have to do this, she told herself, willing herself a little straighter. *I have to help the people of Abra'am.*

"I have one command, and one command only," she yelled, facing the sailors. "Take me ashore. From there, you may do as you wish. If you choose to fight, know the Creator will not punish you for your valor. And if you choose to stay behind, know Eve is grateful for your efforts, and that you are loved just the same."

Bronal put his hand roughly against her shoulder, but she ignored it. The men nodded, some looking ashamed at their fright, others stern, but all obediently returned to their stations to prepare the ship. X'odia shook off Bronal's hand and walked to the edge of the deck, waving away Ravel when he came toward her. When she was sure he was gone and none of the men were looking, she grabbed hold of the railing and steadied herself.

Creator, give me strength, she prayed, making herself look again to Riverdee's coast. She could hear the screams now, and the sounds of people dying. Her legs trembled beneath her.

I need every bit I can get.

Stonewall, Mesidia has been deemed impenetrable. Someday we'll prove that wrong.

Victorian rebel

CHAPTER 24

ROLAND

Roland forced his mare onwards. The pain in his shoulder throbbed, continuing to swell as he barely kept hold of his reins. But he had to keep going, had to warn his father of what he'd discovered from Merlin's and Bernard's killers. He couldn't let his parents share their fate.

As he cleared the top of a hill overlooking Stonewall, body sore and muscles weary, he felt his heart twist. Columns of smoke and mocking black clouds rose from within the city's walls. The air was so filled with ash he could taste it.

"Oh no . . ."

He remembered the duke's head rolling on the floor, and Merlin's slashed stomach, and he threw up over the side of his mare. He couldn't let his parents die like they had. They had to be alive, fighting somewhere on the outskirts of the city.

When he finished emptying his stomach, he wiped his mouth and sat up. Groaning at the pain in his shoulder, he wrapped the reins around his hands, took a deep breath, and yelled at his mare to keep running.

Teradacts are one of the most well-known species of fiends, but they're generally reclusive. If encountered, do not use elements on them, as it will only make them stronger. Instead, use touched *or* called *weapons, and aim for their wings.*

An excerpt from *Fire and Fiends*

CHAPTER 25

GWENIVERE

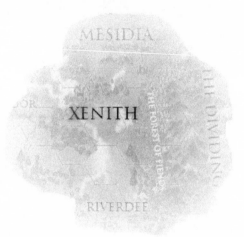

Gwenivere's *called* sword rested perfectly in her hand. There was no fear in her heart, no hesitation in her stride. There was no room for it. Garron had told her that battle either created rage in someone, or terror, but the latter could never be an option for her. She was an heir to Xenith. She was a Guardian of Eve. Holding her head high, she made her way out of the Assembly Hall with relentless, unyielding fury, ready to fight the fiends that'd killed her brother's knight.

"Gwenivere!"

The shout came from Elizabeth al'Murtagh. Gwenivere didn't hear her friend's voice, didn't realize there was someone calling out to her until the girl was there beside her. She froze at Gwenivere's side, mouth hanging open as she took in the view of the city from the palace windows.

"Light protect us," she whispered.

There were hundreds of fiends, thousands, all attacking the people of Voradeen. They lined every street and swarmed every building, pinning down anyone crossing their paths. Just beneath where Elizabeth and Gwenivere stood were bands of knights, fighting through the chaos in an effort to push their way into the city. They were confined to the palace grounds, though, unable to help those further out.

Gwenivere turned to her friend, noting the hopelessness that resided in her gaze. Over her shoulder, Elizabeth's pallor was reflected in those that'd followed them out of the Assembly Hall, each petrified and distressed as they took in the sight outside the windows.

I have to do something, Gwenivere realized. There might be the occasional citizen who was skilled with weapons and elements, but few could do more than the most basic of tasks. They certainly couldn't do enough to defend themselves against this onslaught. And this was her kingdom—her city. No one was going to rise up and defend it for her. Not while her best knights were with her father.

"You three," she said, pointing to the trio of Prianthian sisters, "and you, Dorian; I need someone to protect Aden. He's in my father's quarters on the other side of the palace. Elizabeth." Gwenivere turned, taking her friend's arm and squeezing it tightly. The Mesidian girl looked at her with wide eyes, her throat bobbing. "Elizabeth, I need you to lead them there. You know this palace better than anyone else here. Will you do this for me?"

Elizabeth looked back at the massacre.

She hurriedly looked away and nodded.

"Good." Gwenivere turned back to the other nobles, trying to decide how best to group them for battle. So many of them had just been throwing punches at one another. Would they even listen if she ordered them to fight?

You know them, she told herself. *You read about them. You studied their faces over and over and over. Hedford is the commandant of Theatia. Vanessa is the baroness of the Arctic. Peter and William—*

The glass behind her shattered.

Shouts erupted. People ran. Gwenivere collapsed to the ground and threw her hands over her head, small shards of glass cutting through her clothes. The grip on her *called* sword faltered.

Hastily she looked back toward the window. Recovering from their dive, opening flesh-like wings and scanning the room, four teradacts stood.

Their skulls peeked out beneath stone-like flesh, every twist of their necks grinding like metaled armor. Only their wings resembled skin, black pulsing veins weaving from their bases into dark, feathered tips. They weren't susceptible to elements; casting them would only grant them strength.

That left blades, *called* and *touched* alike. As they turned toward Gwenivere, yellow eyes ravenous beneath shadowed sockets, she tried to reinforce the grip on her sword.

Elizabeth was still there beside her, tripping over her dress in an effort to get away. Gwenivere set her jaw, pressing through the painful pieces of glass in her skin as she pulled Elizabeth to her feet. Knowing her friend was there, that she was in danger and that somewhere in the palace her brother was in danger, made the rage inside her stir.

"Go." She shoved Elizabeth away, *calling* again on the black *auroras* to steady her sword. The dark lights held and reformed the pieces that flickered out. The fiends headed toward her, talons scraping the floor.

A second passed before they were there. Gwenivere hardly had time to lift her sword as wings folded around her, her blade slicing through flesh. Blood dripped onto her from their wounds, mixing with her own. One beast let out an ear-piercing shriek, then another, more blood spilling as she slashed and dodged.

Parry, she thought, evading their claws. *Parry!*

Another shriek.

Roll. Roll! Duck. Swing.

A feral yell.

Without losing her footing, she wove out from under their shadows. Two of the teradacts collided together, one ripping open the other's throat.

That leaves three, she thought. With a vicious growl, she *called* another blade, readied her stance, and waited for the next attack.

Species of Wyvern are among the easiest to distinguish. Much like auroras, *the color of their scales coordinates with elements they can* call.

An excerpt from *Fire and Fiends*

Chapter 26

DIETRICH

To seek one's prey in the still of night, to hunt among the shadows as the victim sauntered about, blissfully unaware of the blade that would soon end its life. That was the killing Dietrich understood, the steps that'd become so common he could retrace them without effort. It was as though he'd made footprints along the shore, so easy to take, so easy to follow, and even when the tide washed them away, his feet would again sink into the soft moldings. It was gentle, malleable, and there seemed to be an elegant dance to it, a morbid waltz only he knew the count to.

This, however, this scene of chaos and disorder, this frenzied party of allies and enemies, was not in tune with the steps he knew. His feet felt clumsy beneath him as he walked into the disarray.

Seera! he called, reaching out to the dragon. He doubted

she could feel his thoughts from such a distance, yet within this bubble of bustling bodies, it was she he wished to ally himself with. *Seera!*

He stood still for a moment, trying to feel her presence. He couldn't. A wall in his mind seemed to block his voice from hers. Cursing, he glanced at his surroundings.

He was accustomed to finding crevices to press into, railings to climb and awnings to cushion his falls, but this was so different. So frantic. How did one even survey a setting of this sort?

Look around, he scolded, taking in the fearful trembles of those beside him. *None of these people know.*

"Help!" someone screamed. Dietrich spun toward the voice and caught sight of a group of servant girls, each huddled together helplessly before a red-scaled wyvern. Muscles flexing, the creature pounced, forcing the servants to pull away from one another in an effort to flee. Four managed to escape, but one fell, body pinned to the ground by the wyvern's weight. She kicked and cried out, trying to shield herself, but her thrashing ceased when the wyvern's teeth found her neck.

Dietrich's stomach knotted. The attack had happened so fast, so suddenly, it was hard to believe the girl's life was really gone.

Enraged, he *called* his crossbow, bolts of metal firing into the wyvern's back. The creature writhed in pain and released its talons from the girl's chest, opening its wings to fly. Dietrich kept his aim strong. He felt himself in each bolt, felt the moment each point sunk through the wyvern's scales. It attempted to *call* fire to shield itself, but the flames were wild and frantic, and only managed to set ablaze the ground it stood on.

With one bolt after the next, Dietrich pinned the wyvern's wings to the hallway's wall. The blaze it *called* turned to smoke, clouding the air, and Dietrich stepped forward, lifted his crossbow again, and fired.

He felt the *called* bolt sink into the wyvern's heart. Then he felt its heart stop beating altogether.

Joy to me
For the currents of the sea
Joy to me
For the waves

Woe to me
For the serpents of the sea
Woe to me
For our graves

Riverdian sea chanty

CHAPTER 27

X'ODIA

"Why've we stopped?" X'odia shouted. The waves had grown heavier the closer they'd gotten to the coast of Riverdee, the *Seagull's* crew now soaked through.

"It's not us!" Bronal called, bracing himself for another rush of water. When the wave passed, he shook his face, wiping the droplets from his eyes. "Something has the ship caught!"

X'odia fought to hear his voice over the ocean's roar. She turned back around, squinting to see out over the deck. There was nothing to explain their unwarranted standstill.

"Watch out!" Ravel yelled. He grabbed Bronal, shoving him to the ground. Inches from where the captain had stood, a red tentacle crashed, crewmen nearly plummeting overboard from its impact. X'odia clenched tightly to the railing by her side, two more tentacles slithering onto the deck and suctioning to the *Seagull's* wood.

She screamed, thrusting a gust of air under the creature's

limbs. She expected the force to unleash its grip, but the suckers along the tentacles held firm. Grimacing, she refocused her strength. She *called* her element again and sent it against the creature's limbs, feeling its resistance, but, little by little, she could see one of the tentacles start to rise.

With one hand held tightly against the deck's edge, she shot her other hand forward, *called* a third rush of air, and cast it out.

The limb unlatched from its place.

The force of the release knocked the *Seagull* back to its side. When X'odia's balance was steady, she let go and extended both hands forward. She shot a sharp blade of ice toward the writhing tentacle, slicing it apart and sending it back into the sea. She let out a triumphant laugh, beaming proudly as she caught an approving cheer from Ravel.

"One down, two to go!" Bronal called, ordering a few men toward the remaining limbs. X'odia raced to join them, stopping suddenly as her foot slipped through a hole. She lifted herself free, grimacing at the pain in her leg. A series of holes trekked out from where she knelt, remnants of where the fiend's tentacle had clung. She met Bronal's eyes, waving him down and pointing.

"These go all the way down the ship. We'll sink!"

His mouth fell open, but he acted swiftly. "You, and you!" he yelled, grabbing a few crewmen. "Get below deck. We need to drain the floodwater. The fiend—"

Another wave crashed against them. X'odia no longer had anything to brace herself with. The water launched her helplessly against the ship's beams, crushing her back. She fought for breath until the water receded, her body collapsing against the deck's floor. Hastily she glanced up, the salt and the sun stinging her eyes. She let out a small cry before prying them open again and catching sight of another wave about to make its fall.

With a shout, she pulled at every clear *aurora* she could find. A current of air escaped from her, battling back against the oncoming water and pushing it back to the sea.

Pausing to regain her strength, she glanced around and took in the status of the crew. Most had taken heed of her mistake and fought to slice apart the remaining tentacles with *touched* knives rather than air.

One more strike and they'll plummet overboard, she thought, running to aid them. *I have to kill it.*

The ship, though—the ship came first. The longer the creature held them, the faster the water would flood through the punctures.

X'odia planted herself as sternly as she could against the slippery planks, blocking out the chaos surrounding her. She closed her eyes, searching again for the clear *auroras*. The sensation of holding them, embracing them, filled her every muscle, and she worked them until they held the shape of a sphere. Opening her eyes, she extended them out, forcing them around the edges of the ship. When she was certain they'd hold steady, she wiped her brow and stood a little taller.

They wouldn't sink now. Nothing beyond her barricade would touch them.

Nothing but the still clinging serpent.

"Move!" she yelled, praying the sailors could hear her. The curtain of air she'd formed was already draining her. "Move!"

Any crewman left fighting ended his efforts. Those who caught her pleas backed away, and those who didn't were pulled to safety. X'odia waited until they were out of her path, then stepped forward, facing the fiend.

Still holding air, she gathered sparks of lightning. They erupted from her like a blade, piercing into the fiend and jolting through its body. The sensation was unbearable, insufferable, as much a pain to it as it was to X'odia. She held it, though, waiting.

It only took a few seconds for the fiend to die. Letting go of her lightning, she fell to her knees and made an opening in her barricade of air. The fiend fell through it, limbs limply falling back to the sea. When it was gone, X'odia let out a laden breath, coughed up the seawater in her lungs, and closed the barricade back shut.

The sailors around her cheered. They patted one another triumphantly and embraced, ecstatic in their victory. X'odia ignored them. She clung to her chest, the sorrow of killing enveloping her. One of the men sat down beside her, resting his arm comfortingly against her own, but pulled it away and rose when she didn't acknowledge him.

"Don't celebrate just yet," Bronal called, returning from below deck. "The ship won't make it back to Eve. We'll have to join the fight ashore."

X'odia, from her collapsed position, held back tears. With her eyes locked on the red-stained coast and her body weakening from her elements, she reached out for blue auroras, calmed the sea around them, and pressed their ship toward the battered coast.

The shore was worse up close.

From a distance, the water had looked an even, crimson red. Now, close enough for the crew of the *Seagull* to disembark, the color wasn't as spread out. It lingered in ominous pools, indicating where people had been dragged into the ocean by fiends. X'odia fought the urge to vomit, keeping her gaze up.

"I need everyone off," she choked. She cleared her throat,

her voice weak. "Everyone!"

The protective shield of air she'd cast had been sustained for too long. Her body was beginning to shake, her knees wobbling. The grip she had on her elements wasn't going to hold much longer.

"X'odia," Bronal said, leaning toward her. His men stared back at him, some openmouthed, others hurling over the Seagull's edges. None had the determined look of men ready to fight.

"My crewmen weren't intended to dock with you," Bronal said. "If they disembark and join this battle, they'll likely die."

X'odia grimaced, squeezing her hands to her head.

"If they stay on this ship, then death is certain. At least out there they have a chance."

As her words ended, the ship swayed. The captain quickly turned to his crew, ignoring the horror written on their faces as he pointed to the docks.

"Off—now!" he ordered. From the midst of crewman, Ravel came forward, nodding to his captain and walking to where the docks met the *Seagull*. Others followed, though none looked purposeful.

X'odia groaned. She couldn't release her elements until every last man was off the ship. If she stopped now, the currents she'd been fighting might crash their ship into the rocks further down the shore. They'd have no chance of survival then. But it was so tiring, so draining, to hold so many breaking pieces. Her barricade was decaying into an airy mist. The opening she'd made for the sailors to disembark was turning into a gaping hole. Her gut, tight and twisting, turned over beneath her chest.

"Captain—hurry!" Ravel called. "Everyone's off!"

X'odia opened her eyes, forcing down the rising bile. Instantly her body started to recover, her blood pumping with newfound strength. Bronal was there, helping her forward.

Without her elements to steady the ship, the waves took control and struck against the *Seagull*. Both she and the captain struggled to stay afoot.

Just a little more, she told herself. *Just a little more!*

Bronal reached the edge of the ship, one hand stretching out to his crew, the other to her. With a heaving pull, they both collapsed onto the docks.

Before X'odia had a chance to react, Ravel was there, pulling her back up.

"We have to move inland." he said. "There are fiends beneath these docks."

X'odia's legs were barely recovered enough to run again, but she nodded. Ravel was right; they had to move inland, and quickly. There'd be more fiends inland, but they wouldn't be able to hide beneath the sea. It was far better than awaiting an ambush.

"All right," she said. "Let's go."

The waves and calls of the sea faded as they ran. They were replaced by the sounds of battle, of swords clashing against fiends and arrows piercing into flesh. Once X'odia had breached Riverdee's city, she took cover from the chaos, finding refuge against the scattered remains of a fiend. Its fur was coarse, and its body still warm. She shuddered as its blood seeped through her clothes, but she swallowed and took a staggered breath, reaching for her *auroras*.

There was a slight stab of fear when she realized none of the other crewmen had taken cover near her. She wanted to seek them out, to hide and stay huddled beside them until the battle faded, but there was too much smoke from fire and lightning to see out clearly beyond a few paces.

I'm the one who insisted we help, she told herself. *I can't let that choice be for nothing.*

Determined, she glanced over the back of the corpse she hid behind. Through the smoke she caught sight of an armored man, a dark-blue cloak fluttering from his back. Behind him, with predatory grace, a fiend stalked.

X'odia grabbed the white-blue *auroras* in her mind and shaped them into sharp shards of ice. With a deep breath she stood, focused her aim, and launched the shards at the fiend.

They pierced into its stomach, sending it howling. The blue-cloaked soldier spun around, alarm evident in his stance. He growled, lunging forward, and finished the fiend off with an elegant swipe of his sword.

X'odia remained where she was. She wasn't eager to move out into the open, despite the horrid smell of the dead beast she nestled against. The decision to move was forced on her, though, a fiend overhead flying toward her.

As she made to evade it, she met the eyes of the blue-cloaked soldier. A brief flash of recognition flickered in her mind, but she didn't know from where, or how, and she didn't have time to dwell. She sprinted for a nearby stairwell and hurried up its steps, ascending to a balcony. She looked around for a moment before collapsing behind a series of barrels, a plum liquid leaking out of them. It was wine, she realized, a drink she'd read of in her stories of Abra'am. She'd have to take caution with any fire elements, lest she cast herself ablaze.

"Help!" someone yelled. "Help!"

Across from where X'odia hid, clustered together atop another balcony, a trio of women crouched. Two winged fiends had perched themselves at their sides, a burly man walking between them. X'odia halted the instinctive element she'd begun readying, holding it steady as she watched the scene unfold.

The man stroked the beasts' wings. When he was through, he pulled his hand back to his side and approached the huddled women. They trembled and cried as he walked toward them, the eldest of the three pulling a blade out from a sheath at her calf. The man lifted his hand slightly, the dagger flying from her grasp.

X'odia strengthened the *call* on her elements, waiting with fury as the man grabbed the woman closest to him.

He didn't harm her, he didn't pull her away from her family or force himself against her. She struggled under his touch; that was the most he had to settle, lifting up her chin as he examined her. When he'd finished looking her over, he tossed her aside and did the same to the other two women. Unimpressed, he walked away, nodding to the fiends.

They leaped forward hungrily.

"No!" X'odia shouted. She at last released her element, the man's eyes finding it and tracing it back to her.

Then he smiled.

The women took their chance to get away. X'odia stood frozen, petrified as the man lifted his hands and beckoned something forward.

From the roof of another balcony, several more fiends emerged.

X'odia willed her legs to move. They did, just as the fiends began to make their way toward her. She sprinted back down the stairwell, hurrying to escape.

When she was safely off the steps, she *called* her orange-red *auroras* and cast out a blaze of fire. The wine barrels she'd kneeled against burst into flames, several of the fiends burning with them.

Before X'odia could take another step, the blue-cloaked soldier she'd helped before barred her path. She breathed a sigh of relief, grateful for an ally, but the feeling faded as she took in his face.

I do recognize him, she realized. His eyes, a dark shade of grey-blue, had met hers in her vision, just before he'd ordered her beaten.

Lungs restricting, she took a step back.

The soldier reached out, trying to grab her arm as one of the remaining fiends dived toward them. Thrusting his sword, he lunged toward the beast, striking it in the chest. He pushed his blade in further before quickly pulling it back out, pivoting gracefully and slicing his sword through the neck of another approaching fiend. Its severed head fell to the ground.

Two more fiends came. The soldier lifted his sword and shield, ready.

X'odia wanted to do something in his defense, despite what the Sight had shown her. Not every scene it depicted proved true, and there was a chance that future awaited her down a different path.

He's too entangled with the beasts for me to help him, she thought, watching as his body circled around the fiends. It was like a dance, his feet elegantly gliding across the stones beneath him as the fiends' thumped and stumbled. His blade plunged into one's chest, his shield lifting and falling as it sliced the head off another.

Panting, with the beasts dead at his feet, the soldier stood tall. In his armor was the reflection of something glowing. X'odia staggered as she saw it, legs suddenly weak. The man stared at her with furrowed brows, his exhausted breaths audible as he made his way toward her.

X'odia tried to rise, tried to will herself back up, but she couldn't move. It was another vision, she realized, like the ones she'd had in Eve and on the *Seagull.* The reflection in the armor was of her eyes, which glowed now as the Sight began to take her.

She made to explain herself, to tell the soldier of what was happening, but when she looked up, her voice died in her throat.

The man from the balcony was there.

No! she thought, pleading to the Light to cease her vision. *Please, I have to warn him!*

There was nothing she could do. The man opened his palm, and the blue-cloaked soldier flew back. He hit the wall of a building nearby, falling to the ground.

Unable to move, X'odia did nothing. The man from the balcony knelt down, smiling and leaning in toward her.

"Daughter of Alkane," he said, running his fingers across her cheek, "I have waited a long time to find you."

His hand was snatched away by another soldier, the Sight at last taking its hold on X'odia as she fell unconscious.

When using the horn, be sure to purse your lips together to create a buzz. Empty out the spit too, or the tone won't be clear.

Instructions for Elite horn players

Chapter 28

ROLAND

MESIDIA

The sounds of screams and the smell of smoke rushed to Roland. His legs and back ached, and his voice was hoarse from yelling his mare onward. It was cruel, the way he forced her, the animal likely close to death, but her state didn't matter. He had to reach his parents, and he had to reach them with haste. He cursed the Dagger's sheath that lay empty at his side.

I should never have left, he thought, grimacing as he felt the air above the Dagger's straps. His mind raced to the twins, to the evil woman, her glowing eyes and ominous voice still burning in his thoughts. Yvaine wanted the Dagger—that was what they'd said. Roland hated Yvaine, hated how she maliciously maligned his family and their claim, but he'd never thought her capable of such a morbid alliance. He shuddered, remembering Bernard's head as it had rolled on the ground.

He prayed his parents' fates wouldn't be the same.

"Faster!" he shouted, kicking at his mare's side. She whinnied, thrashing her head in protest, but still her hooves carried on. Roland's grip was numbing on her reins, his gloves rubbed through to expose raw, bleeding palms. He had to keep going, though. He couldn't stop to rest, couldn't stop to ease his aching shoulder. Stonewall was in his sight, just through the surrounding forest, and if he could just make it there—

The aching in his shoulder morphed into blinding pain. He hardly had time to react before the talons of a beast, sharp and unrelenting, thrust him from his mare.

As he crashed to the soil, massive jaws snapped at his flesh. He barely got his arms up in time as teeth punctured through his gauntlets. He tried to *call* his fire, his wind, his water, his anything, but the fatigue of his ride and the saliva dripping on his face kept his focus deterred. Hurriedly he pulled out one of the small *touched* daggers hidden beneath his gauntlets, stabbing it aimlessly up at the beast. He knew the moment he hit bone, the beast howling viciously as its jaws slackened. He pulled the blade out and stabbed again.

This time, the creature was silent.

Roland panted heavily, examining the creature as it lay lifeless before him. It was a fiend, its strange features marking it as such, no animal existent with such morphed parts. He winced as he felt the impact of its attack, the muscles beneath his shoulder aching. His torn flesh stung.

He looked around hastily for his mare, hoping the horse hadn't fled, but his eyes only caught the strange movements of more fiends coming. He took cover behind a tree, glancing around its trunk and watching their approaching trek.

There were scores of them, hundreds, each and every one trudging forward with hungry intent. It was rare for so many to hunt together, rarer still with different species. Roland ran from his tree's cover to another, anxious and fearful as he stalked the beasts' march.

Something was controlling them, he realized, something beyond the outskirts of Stonewall's borders. There was no other explanation, no reason for so many elusive creatures to seek out the city. He didn't want to admit it, didn't want to believe such a thing could be true, but in the pit of his stomach, he knew.

He pulled his cloak up and followed.

The creatures sensed him—he could see it in their twitching fur and slithering scales. He clenched his sword's hilt, fearful at any moment they would stray, but the pull of their hidden master never surrendered. Holding his breath, Roland peered over his spot of hiding, attempting to track whatever it was that moved them. He reeled back instantly, sweat dampening his back as a fiend sniffed near his side.

He could smell the blood on its fur and hear its intake of breath. He kept perfectly still, praying silently for his *auroras* to aid him. He found them—weak and flickering—then pulled at what little of them he could see. Slowly, cautiously, he began to *call* them to life. He watched as the green and brown lights in his mind twitched the roots at his feet.

He'd have to time his attack perfectly, lest he attract the attention of more fiends.

He held his breath. Steadied his element. Waited.

The beast's head rounded the corner.

A note, blasted from a horn's bell, cut through the wind. The rumbling of hooves followed, shaking the ground. Roland exhaled, knowing the blaring tone and heavy steps to be the call of the Elite. The roots beneath him settled as he released his element. The fiend beside him fled from its hunt. Elite, lethal and stoic atop their mounts, emerged gallantly into the infested forest.

The soldiers who bore no shields and wore no armor cast elements into the air, flashes of lightning and towers of flames searing through the fiends. Knives and arrows, *called* from the dark, murky lights of their minds, flew gracefully, ripping through flesh with perfect precision. Beast after beast fell, shrieks and howls announcing their pain, even more falling silently as death greeted them. Roland, from his place of hiding, rose to his feet, unsheathing his sword and joining their attacks.

Liquid dripped, blood and sweat alike. Scales and hides burned in the air, the wind consumed with the smell of scorching flesh. The forest floor opened and closed to swallow prey whole, crushing their bodies as the soil retained its place. Amid it all, Roland fought, the blue of Elite cloaks blurring around him as they danced their dance. Death befell wherever they went, piles of bodies left in their wake.

Seconds passed, eternity passed, more fiends continuing to come. Roland stepped away from the battle to catch his breath, leaning his wearied body against the bark of a tree. He was too weak now to use any elements, too weak to conjure any weapons, the sword in his hand growing heavier and heavier each time he swung. He should continue fighting, he knew, continue fending off the fiends' attacks, but the support of the tree's limbs behind him felt so comforting. He slid down its trunk, his sight blackening.

With strained breaths, Roland fought to stay present. He could see swords clashing, but he couldn't hear them; he could see the Elite call for reinforcements, but no noise escaped their horns. Something in the first fiend he'd fought—something in its bite—was rendering his senses slackened, even his fingers forgetting the feel of his sword's hilt. He tried to stand and join his men again in battle, but the numbness in his bones pinned him to the ground.

Stand up, he told himself, willing his muscles to move. Even his thoughts felt weary. *Stand up, dammit; stand up!*

His body refused.

Confined, Roland glanced around, the Elite's cloaks a fluttering haze. Their deep blue blended with the browns and greens of the woods, every color rimmed with the black of his gaze. Soon it was all one colorless shade.

But then a different color, a different shade: gold. Roland furrowed his brow, battling to see. He weakly placed his sword in the ground and fought again to stand. This time his body listened, hoisting him upright with wobbling knees. He panted, too tired to wipe the sweat that dripped into his mouth, and looked again for that shade of silky, glimmering gold.

It was hair, he realized—exposed and flowing from a woman's head. Roland stumbled forward, rushing closer, cursing his weakened legs as he fell against another tree.

Natalia? he thought. He turned again, struggling, and squinted.

Not Natalia. Not the duchess-heir. It was Yvaine Barie, the duchess herself, standing steadfast with a wicked grin.

Wherever her eyes looked, the fiends followed.

"*Yvaine,*" Roland snarled, fighting through the venom in his blood. The duchess hadn't seen him—not yet, at least—and the sliver he had of his senses might not remain for long. He didn't know how she was doing this, how it was even possible for her to manipulate the beasts, but if he struck her, if he killed her, maybe they'd have a chance.

A bow, Roland decided, closing his eyes. *I need my bow . . .*

He'd *called* it before, time and time again, the feeling of it almost innate. Swords, spears, daggers—no other weapon had ever felt as natural to him as his bow. He was just so weak, so tired. Every one of his *auroras* hid behind his feeble state.

I have to do this, he told himself, conjuring every black *aurora* in his mind. *I have to do this!*

The black *auroras* slowly, tortuously, began to pulse. He pulled at them in desperation, willed them into being. Adrenaline rushed through him as the wood began to form in his hand. He dropped his sword, not caring to sheath it properly, and gripped the draining weapon, holding it steady until the thread of black lights finished their creation. He swayed then, dizzy from the feat, but kept his weight low and his stance steady. With only seconds before the bow would fade, he turned from his place of rest, took aim at the duchess, and released.

The arrow's point struck. Roland collapsed instantly after its impact, his bow disappearing as his knees hit the ground.

Every fiend reeled in disarray. Roland seized his chance in the frenzy and made his way toward Yvaine, the effects of the fiend's poison slowly starting to fade.

I'll kill her, he thought, vividly remembering Merlin's slashed stomach. *Light above, I'll kill her for what she's done!*

The duchess still stood, her hand rising to her shoulder where his *vanished* arrow had struck. She saw him them, saw him rushing toward her. She rose to her feet and lifted her arms. The roots beneath Roland bent to her will. Their limbs wrapped around his legs and ankles. He fell to the ground, thrashing violently against their hold, but his body was still weak and the roots pinned him easily to the ground. Yvaine grinned, suddenly there before him, and rested bloody fingers against his jaw.

"Tis a shame such a thing had to be," she sang, scratching his cheek. Roland reeled under her touch, grimacing as he continued to attempt his retreat. The roots wouldn't budge.

"If only Pierre had allowed my daughter to be queen," she continued, slipping her hand from his face, "this would finally be mine."

She reached for the sheath of the Dagger, her smile vanishing as she met nothing but air. She rose back to her feet, her face twisting into a scowl. Roland laughed, hopeless and beaten, pleased even in his certain death that the duchess hadn't gained what she'd wanted.

"Where is it?" she yelled, reaching to her wound. Blood spurted from it, drenching her pale skin as it seeped down her sleeve. "Where is it?"

The roots around Roland tightened. He hardly realized he

was screaming as the horns of the Elite blew again. Yvaine's head snapped back, the conquering call echoing through the forest. Roland smiled between shouts, knowing the sound signaled their victory.

The duchess *called* a knife and held it to his throat.

"Where is it?" she demanded, pressing the cold metal against his skin. "Where's the Dagger?"

A swift arrow pierced into her back. Her blade sliced Roland's jaw. The roots let go of their hold, setting him free.

The heavy trots of horses surrounded them and another arrow fell where Yvaine was about to step. Roland barely breathed as he saw his father, unharmed and unscathed, chasing his mare after where Yvaine ran. The king caught up to her in seconds, his reins pulled taught as he leaped from the saddle. She fell to the ground with a whimper.

"For the attempts on Stonewall," Pierre said, grabbing her golden hair and yanking her head back, "and for the attempts on my throne." He extended his hand out toward one of his Elite, the soldier quickly handing him the slim cuffs of element shackles. Yvaine screamed, cried out in anguish, begging and pleading Pierre to spare her from the chains. His expression never changed, though, his resolution merciless. The shackles buckled shut in triumph around her wrists.

"No!" Yvaine shouted, thrashing in Pierre's hold. Blood poured from her wounds as the bindings began to glow.

Roland remembered the duke, bound in similar chains before he'd died. His had glowed too, a sign he'd attempted to *call* his *auroras*, but the elements had lain trapped within the shackles' metal.

A fitting thing then, for the duchess to suffer as her husband had.

Pierre left her screaming for a moment, staring at her with hatred before finally striking her across the temple. Her protests ceased, her crazed, wild eyes shutting as she slipped from consciousness. Elite came forward as Pierre wordlessly beckoned. They lifted her limp body, the glow of her shackles fading.

"Tend to her wounds and lock her in the dungeons," Pierre ordered, his voice deep. "I'll meet you in Stonewall's castle." His men obeyed, taking the bleeding woman and tying her to a mare. The king looked down at where Roland knelt, waiting until the Elite had retreated before at last walking toward him.

Roland ground his teeth and tried to sit taller. He'd been bested by the duchess, unable to come home in time to warn his father of her attack. All the Elite had borne witness to his failure. What son was he of the Laighless name, falling to that of the Barie? What good had he done in keeping the people of his capital safe?

He breathed heavily. Everything hurt. He wanted to stand, to face his father on his feet rather than his knees, but his muscles were too weak. He waited then, covered in sweat and blood and dirt, no better than the fiends that lay dead around him. He held his chin high, the only respectable thing he could do, and met his father's gaze. The slash from Yvaine's knife dripped with mockery.

"Duke Bernard is dead," he said grimly. "And Merlin as well." He paused, his heart heavy as he recalled the dark-haired man's blade, wet and red with Merlin's blood. "I'm sorry, Father. I failed us."

Pierre curled his lips and swallowed, walking closer to Roland and kneeling beside him.

"My son," he whispered, voice choking. "You have failed no one."

He brought his hands to Roland's cheeks, holding them tightly, then forced him into an embrace.

This new knight you've assigned me refuses to tell me his name. I've decided to call him the Golden Knight, as he rides into battle without his helm, and his blond hair stands out. I think he hates the grandeur of it.

From a letter between Rose and Gerard Verigrad

Chapter 29

GARRON

"The plaza is safe, milord," Nicolas said, kneeling to his king. The Golden Knight knelt beside him, noting how the young man grimaced as he placed his palm to the ground. It was his first battle; his knightly duties thus far had been nothing more than training and guarding. His armor had likely never felt so heavy.

King Gerard nodded his response, though it seemed Nicolas's words had been for naught. The king took in the scene around them, the muscles in his neck tensing as his men carried away the bodies of the fallen.

Garron knew peacetime had softened Gerard's gaze. Years had passed since they'd had to survey such a sight. The bodies during the War of Fire were rarely anything but foot soldiers and banner men. The corpses before them now, ripped apart by fiends, were merely common city folk.

"And what of my daughter?" the king asked quietly, beckoning them to rise. Garron sensed Nicolas's gaze, the young knight likely wondering if it was he who should give the answer. Garron stepped forward in his stead.

"She's not here, milord," he said grimly. He swallowed, nostril's flaring, and cast his eyes to the ground. Everything during the Peace Gathering had happened so quickly; the princess had only been a few feet from him as he'd led Gerard away from the chamber. It had seemed only seconds had passed when Maximus had run to him covered in what had to be someone else's blood, and told him that Voradeen was under attack and Gwenivere was missing. Garron had been desperate to go after her, find her amid the chaos and bring her to safety, but he'd been needed in his king's ranks. Men like Nicolas were too young to know the ways of battle, too spoiled by a lifetime of peace to know what war was like. This was not a war the Golden Knight was accustomed to, but it was a war all the same, and he knew how to rally men's blades into the bellies of their enemies.

He glanced at the square, trying not to imagine Gwenivere's face in the bodies being carried away.

"We must find her," the king said, his voice hushed. He lowered his hand from his chest, dark-blue eyes cold as the sun hid behind the clouds. Garron glanced up, the hairs on his neck standing as he realized how far the Day Star had traveled.

Dusk was already upon them.

"Milord," Garron said. "We've detained a great deal of the city. Sir Charles can lead the rest of the men in my place; he knows the capital better than I. Release me of my services here. I will find her."

The King of Peace said nothing.

"I shall go too, milord," Nicolas added hurriedly. Gerard raised his brow as he glanced back, the young knight's fatigue hardly hidden as heavy breaths escaped him. He looked back toward Garron, awaiting his judgment.

"It's a battle of fiends, milord," Garron said. "No place is safe."

The king nodded, patting Garron's shoulder.

"Keep him alive, and bring Gwenivere back. I will not mourn my daughter."

The Golden Knight bowed, then turned to Nicolas beside him. He cared little for the young knight, cared little for the perfect way his teeth were settled or how flawlessly his lips pulled around them. His smug grin was almost always present, more it seemed when it need not be. He was loyal though, and filled with valor, foolish enough to be brave when he ought to be afraid.

And he's not smiling now, he thought, noting the way Nicolas stood tall. Garron pressed past him and unsheathed his sword, knowing the young man would trek wherever he told him to follow.

I remember fighting a dragon on one of the palace's balconies, then being woken up by my squire. I didn't have any serious injuries, nor any lasting headaches. I don't know how I could've fallen unconscious, but the knights I fought beside on the balcony reported the same thing happening to them.

Account from a Xen knight

CHAPTER 30

DIETRICH

The balcony! You must reach the balcony!

Dietrich started as Seera's voice at last came to life. The fiends around him were endless, one onslaught after another. With every wave a new pile of bodies formed.

I'm coming! he thought, pulling his sword from a were'ghul's stomach. The beast was a mix of wolf and corpse, and it let out a too-human howl before collapsing to the floor. Dietrich knew he shouldn't care about its death after all the people it'd come after, but with it and every beast he took, a sense of guilt overwhelmed him. They didn't seem much different than Seera and Savine, perhaps only more wild, like children not yet raised. What thoughts would he find in them if he reached out and grazed their minds?

You would find them lost, Prince, Seera soothed. *Now hurry to the balcony. The archers are readying their arrows at me.*

Dietrich didn't bother asking which balcony; their bond

answered for him. His feet carried him through the palace's massive halls, blood and bodies littering the ground. Some still breathed as he passed them, but he couldn't stop, couldn't stall to give them Brelain's elixirs. Flashes from Seera's vision kept playing through his mind as arrows flew toward her wings.

The glass leading to the balcony was shattered, four tera-dact bodies lying shredded among the shards. Dietrich started at the sight, impressed by whoever had taken the beasts down. The fabric of a woman's skirts caught to his heels, but he pulled it off, annoyed, and made his way to the balcony.

Seera circled above. Knights nocked their arrows. She deflected them with a simple *call* of air, then opened her jaws to release a warning roar. Some of the knights stilled, and others quivered, but again they began readying their shots.

Don't kill them, but take them out, Seera ordered, flying closer to the balcony's edge. *I can distract them for you, but I can't land until you take care of them.*

Dietrich smiled, ready. This battle, a battle against unsuspecting humans, was more to his strengths. Darkness would be better than the current pinks of dusk, but the light and open expanse would give him a challenge. He pulled a pin from his belt, the tip lined with sleeping poison, and stuck it in the first knight's neck.

No one saw him as he did the same to another.

The men didn't fall at first; the poison needed at least a minute before it would take effect. Dietrich had a short window to stick the rest of the men, lest the first two knights slip from consciousness and alert the others. He was careful to grab the pins from the correct side, never letting them prick his own fingers. He wouldn't feel it—none of them would—the points too small for them to detect. In a relaxed state, with nothing overt distracting them, they might feel them, but with a dragon circling above, absorbing all their elements and deflecting all their arrows . . .

Dietrich stood, waiting, and watched them all slink to the ground.

Seera paid him no thanks other than a landing and a closing of her wings. He quickly ran toward her, hoisting himself onto her back and grabbing hold of the quill-like spikes along her neck. The charcoal color of her scales had shifted slightly, a reddish hue pulsing beneath them. It was fire, likely, from the elements she'd absorbed. He could feel the warmth of it in her bones.

They're after the Amulet, she said, launching them toward the city. Other fiends flew through the sky, more teradacts like the ones that lay dead in the palace, but all were too occupied fighting humans to pay them mind.

Why? he asked. *Why the Amulet?*

Seera dodged a wave of arrows that came toward her, Dietrich nearly vomiting as she spiraled and dropped.

I don't know, but they are. I felt the pull of it before. Someone's controlling them.

There was something else there, something left unspoken, but Dietrich didn't press her. He could feel the clouding commands that tried to consume her.

We have to warn the princess, then, he said, releasing the breath he held as Seera headed toward the descending sun. At least now if any knights below tried to aim at her, they'd be blinded by the light.

I can still sense the pull of the Amulet, she said. *I can use that to find her. If you think you can actually manage to speak this time, I can get us to her.*

Dietrich scoffed, as much at the surprising jab as at the continued spray of arrows.

Speaking won't be the problem, he said, pulling up the cover of his cloak. The air tore at his skin and face, more than he could stand to bear. His eyes burned with withheld tears. *She's already wary of me, after how I made my introduction.*

Another wave of arrows came at them. Dietrich clutched Seera tightly as she wove between their paths.

Yes, such an introduction was likely inappropriate. You couldn't have simply pretended to be her suitor?

Dietrich said nothing for a moment, only hoping Seera's spiraling flight would cease. When it did, he still stayed silent, the only thought in his mind that of withholding the contents in his stomach.

No, he finally managed. *She's notorious for hating suitors. At least, according to my brother's sources.*

Perhaps your brother should be here. He sounds more informed.

Dietrich grunted, imagining his younger brother in his place. *The little bastard should be,* he agreed.

A smile seemed to play in Seera's thoughts, at least the semblance of one, but she kept quiet. The wind sang with the sounds of battle, and their words ceased, the pull of Gwenivere's Amulet forcing them onward.

Tortavel often live in lakes, and don't surface for years. If encountering one, be mindful of its backside. It tends to use its tail for defense.

An excerpt from *Fire and Fiends*

CHAPTER 31

GWENIVERE

*B*reathe *through your nose. You look weak to your enemies when they can see you panting like a dog.*

Memories of Garron's voice echoed in Gwenivere's head. The strong, *called* metal of her sword clashed against the armored shell of a tortavel. The reptilian fiend spun around, its spiked tail lashing out toward her. Gwenivere ducked and planted her feet. She held her ground as the heavy tail crashed against her shield. Her defense withstood the blow, just barely, the impact shooting pain through her arm. She stood up and backed away. Her eyes narrowed as she regained her strength.

You never hack with your sword, she heard Garron scold. *You never use it as a shield, or try to penetrate something that's too strong. The sword is graceful; the sword is elegant, refined. It should enter the flesh of the enemy with ease.*

The princess listened to the memories of her knight's commands. The tortavel's body she faced was covered with a hard shell, spikes protruding from nearly every inch of it. She'd circled it time and time again, advancing toward it when she found an opening between its attacks, but she always came away with a battered shield and a throbbing arm.

Roaring, the beast thrashed its tail toward her again. The boulder-like tip clipped the top of her shield, forcing her legs to buckle. She fell, her shoulder banging roughly into the street as her head barely missed the ground. She winced at the pain, then scrambled to stand before the tail returned.

When she peeled her lids open, the spiked creature was charging toward her.

Its stomach, she realized, at last noticing the small patch of skin under its shell. She grinned, *vanishing* her shield and *calling* a crossbow in its place. She took in a deep breath, keeping her hands steady as she fired toward the fiend's eyes. Her aim held true, the tortavel's head thrashing as a bolt made its find.

Calling her elements, she cast out a sheet of ice in a slim, straight path between the fiend's legs. She *vanished* her crossbow and unsheathed the dagger at her side, waiting until she and the tortavel nearly met before falling to her back and onto the slick ice. The speed of her impact propelled her down the slippery path, her body only feet from being smashed under the fiend's weight. She lifted her dagger and pierced it into the tortavel's exposed skin. She sliced through the soft flesh and cut down the length of its stomach, shutting her eyes as blood spilled onto her. When her path of ice faded into rough stones, she pulled out her weapon, scrambling to get up and flee.

Frantically she wiped away the warm blood that now coated her body. She sheathed her dagger and *called* back her sword, lifting it with weak arms.

The fiend stood motionless.

Gwenivere waited, sword raised, watching as the beast's

insides spilled onto the plaza street. After several agonizing seconds, it fell loudly to the ground.

Uncertain if it was truly dead, Gwenivere licked her lips and slowly inched closer. Breaths still rose and fell from the tortavel's chest, labored and heavy, but its remaining eye was slowly closing. With no other beasts in sight, Gwenivere stood, triumphant and bloody, and watched the tortavel die.

It wasn't as satisfying as she'd thought it'd be.

The plaza is clear, she thought, trying to cast away her guilt. She shouldn't feel anything for the fiend, especially not when it had caused so much destruction, but the nagging guilt was there. She snarled and spit on its corpse, *vanishing* her blade.

How many fiends had that been then since she'd first made her way from the Peace Gathering? How many monsters had she defeated since the teradacts had burst through the palace windows? There'd been four of them, then waves of beasts along the way, then the tortavel she stood over now. What were they all doing, swarming her capital with such fervor? Why would such elusive beasts attack her city?

She wanted to know, but the idea of resting, of kneeling down on the cobbled streets, was growing more enticing with each second that passed.

Cover, she decided, walking toward a building. The beams of it had cracks from missed attempts of the tortavel's tail, but it looked sturdy enough. She walked toward it, limping in what remained of her tattered dress, and shut her eyes. She didn't need to see to step forward.

Screams sounded from a few streets away, the ground beneath her suddenly shaking. Her lids burst open as she held her arms out, fighting to stay standing through the abrupt trembles. The building she'd been walking toward released a threatening groan, and the cracks along its beams spread. She stumbled back, tripping over nothing as she tried to escape the now-crumbling plaza. All around her, shops and homes and schools quivered from the earth's might.

With nowhere to go, Gwenivere stopped, realizing she was trapped within the damaged plaza.

Air, air, air! She reached for the element, begged for it, but her body was too weak and the lights too hidden. She lifted her hands above her head, just as Aden had during their challenge in the forest, and prayed a gust of wind would burst from her fingertips.

Nothing came.

She tried again.

Nothing.

The shadows of the falling buildings began to envelop her.

She is incredibly skilled at calling, *with the exception of* calling *air, which takes her a great deal of concentration and effort. She passed out today when I asked her to levitate a chair for ten minutes.*

A report of Gwenivere Verigrad's training from Garron Hillborne

Chapter 32

GARRON

"Gwenivere!"

Garron sprinted for the plaza. He'd just spotted Gwenivere's slender frame, surrounded by collapsing buildings, and made to reach her. Nicolas's hand pulled him back.

"We won't make it in time!"

Garron watched, hopeless, helpless, pleading that the Light would put him in Gwenivere's place. She couldn't die, not when she was so close to where he stood. Not while he still lived.

Despondent, Garron reached within his mind, forcing out every clear *aurora* he could muster. The ground shook too much for him to reach her before the buildings fell, and the expanse between them was too great. He could do this for her, though— he could try to let her escape. The buildings just needed to stay standing, to stay upright long enough for her to flee.

I have to save her, he thought. *I have to save her!*

The buildings my great grandmother designed are now destroyed.

Voradeen townsmen

CHAPTER 33

DIETRICH

We won't make it Dietrich! There isn't time!
We'll make it, we'll make it—
We won't!

Dietrich leaned forward on Seera's back, pressing her toward the princess. They'd barely caught a glimpse of her before everyone on the ground had begun to scream and fall.

Dietrich hadn't realized the severity of it from the air until it'd been too late. The buildings around Gwenivere were crumbling.

Even without trying to read her, Dietrich could hear the thoughts that pressed at Seera's mind. What good would it do them, do the rest of the city, if they died trying to save Gwenivere? It was her Amulet the strange pull was after. It wouldn't stop just because the Guardian was buried. If the two of them were buried alongside her, there'd be no one who could lead the threats from the rest of the city.

Dietrich knew it was true. But he refused to accept it.

Seera—now!

The dragon obeyed, closing her wings and diving between the buildings. It was too late. Dietrich knew it was too late, could feel it. They were shrouded by the caving stones, the buildings falling upon them as they made their way toward the princess.

Dietrich reached out. He grabbed at Gwenivere's waist, clinging to her. She gasped from the impact, the breath knocked out of her, but she didn't scream.

They weren't going to make it.

Seera *called* her air and Dietrich *called* his, pressing it against the buildings around them.

It shouldn't have been enough, but somehow, miraculously, they made it through.

Behemoths are creatures from the Age of Old. Tales of them are likely exaggerated.

An excerpt from *Fire and Fiends*

CHAPTER 34

DIETRICH

"Hold on!" Dietrich yelled, pulling Gwenivere's body up to his own. She didn't need telling more than once. Her arms wrapped around his waist as Seera narrowly avoided the collapsing buildings. The wind howled, tears streaming down Dietrich's cheeks. Behind them, without his and Seera's air, the plaza's buildings crashed to the ground.

Gwenivere, within his arms, stifled a sob.

Thank you, Seera, Dietrich thought, squeezing tightly to where he held. *You didn't have to save her.*

As if knowing his thoughts, Gwenivere's grip around his neck tightened. Her tears dampened his shirt.

Don't thank me yet, Prince, Seera said, landing atop a roof. The earth's shaking had ceased, the steadiness of the rooftop they landed on strange after their time in flight. Carefully Dietrich peeled away Gwenivere's hands, clutching to her wrists and meeting her gaze.

He hadn't had a chance to really look at her before, but he could see her blood-ridden face now. Everything about her looked of death, crimson smears streaked across her skin and down her clothes. Even her head was caked with it, the color so present it was difficult to know what was blood and what was hair. He wondered then, trying to convey comfort in his touch, if any of the blood belonged to her.

"Are you all right?" he asked. He likely looked menacing himself, his face half covered and his body garbed in black, but Gwenivere simply nodded.

Prince, Seera said, cocking her head toward the sky. Dietrich ignored her, pulling a dagger from his side and tearing off a piece of his cloak. He handed it to Gwenivere, giving her a moment to herself as she wiped her face clean.

Prince!

Dietrich looked up, his blood running cold as he followed Seera's gaze. Near the palace, gleaming against the coming of night, a colossal fiend hovered.

What is it? he asked. The beast was black, it's body snake-like as it flew without wings. Air, manipulated by its mind, kept it in the sky, the sheer force of it causing the lake beneath it to ripple with waves.

A Behemoth, from the Age of Old, Seera answered. *It was asleep in the lake beside the palace, but whoever wants the Amulet must have called upon it. The quakes likely started when it awoke.*

Dietrich stared, as much consumed by fear as he was by awe. He'd studied fiends most of his life, had seen and slain more beasts than most men had heard of, but he'd never seen anything like this.

Beside him, Gwenivere began to thank him, her face wiped clean of the blood, but she quieted when she followed his eyes. The hovering creature let out a deafening roar, the sound echoing through the battered city.

It's blind, Seera mused, studying its cry. She turned her

head, remorseful, the colors of her scales easing back to charcoal. *After years of slumber, it's lost its sight.*

"I have to get people to safety," Gwenivere said, hoisting her leg over Seera's side. Realizing she was about to slide off, Dietrich put out his arm, barring her from leaving his side.

"It's after you," he said, pointing toward her Amulet. "After that."

And currently it's trying to sense where she is, Seera said. *The longer we stay here, the faster it will find—*

"It's after my Amulet?" Gwenivere peered at him incredulously. Her demeanor had shifted, angry now, her gratitude lapsed. She went to move Dietrich's arm, but a warning growl from Seera kept her still. Her throat bobbed as she glared at the dragon, her hand lowering to the knife at her side.

"Listen," Dietrich said, reaching for her knife. Gwenivere gave him vicious scowl, lips snarling, and tightened her grip.

"I know it doesn't make any sense, but Seera"—he cocked his head to the dragon—"she can sense the pull on the fiends, the thing that's driving them all here. And that Behemoth, it's after your Amulet too." He let out a breath, cautiously pulling his hand back. "She thinks if we take you from the city, it'll follow."

Dietrich knew as soon as the words left his lips how absurd they sounded. If he were in Gwenivere's position, he wouldn't believe any of it. It'd only been a short time ago that he'd been in denial about his ability to speak with Seera.

"I know it sounds absurd," he said, sensing her distrust. "But that pull is how Seera and I were able to find you. We didn't just stumble across you by pure happenstance."

He stared at Gwenivere, awaiting her response. She stared back, lips pursed.

What would they do if she refused? Take her by force? Light, they would have to. Their only chance at saving Voradeen was getting her as far away from it as they could. He could see the contemplation written across her face, the suspicion, but he could see that paired with logic. Even if she didn't believe them, would she have believed an organized attack by fiends was possible if he'd told her just last night? Would she have believed a man could be allied with a dragon? Likely not, but there they were, victims of some ancient elemental forces. She had to see that. She had to.

Seera's muscles were tensing. His muscles were tensing. But Gwenivere's expression, twisted in hopelessness and confusion, finally eased.

"All right," she said, swinging her leg back over Seera's back. Dietrich breathed a sigh of relief. Then the reality of it all sunk in.

I'm going to have to fight that Behemoth, he thought, feeling feint. *Me, a dragon, and a tiny, blood-coated princess.*

Why had he ever agreed to this venture?

"Well?" Gwenivere pressed. Seera gave an amused grumble as Dietrich irritably guided the princess's hands to where she could hold on. In his head, not caring if Seera heard, he let out a stream of curses.

Any irritation he felt vanished as the dragon launched them back into the sky. The streets had mostly settled from the fiends' attacks, the grounds below quiet while people wept. Knights no longer nocked arrows toward Seera, instead guiding people to places of safety.

Dietrich kept his focus on the Behemoth, the wind pressing sharply against his eyes. The creature turned slightly, tilting its head to listen. There was a brief, tense moment as it blindly hovered in the air, motionless and silent. Then it ceased its hovering, angled itself toward Voradeen, and glided forward.

Seera responded immediately. She thrust her wings with vigor, racing to reach the ends of Voradeen's borders and lead the Behemoth away.

It was too late. The Behemoth opened its mouth, exposing long, slender fangs, and roared. Flames burst from its throat.

Within his chest, Dietrich's heart beat violently. Gwenivere said nothing, her knuckles white where she clutched Seera's spikes.

The fire from the Behemoth's breaths caught quickly to the rubble of the streets. The piles of fallen buildings were quick to burn as people sprinted away, screaming. Knights did what they could to douse the fire, but they were tired and weak. They'd been fighting all day, protecting innocent city folk from fiends. They couldn't possibly manage to fend off the beast before them now.

Dietrich held back a cough as the smell of smoke and ash filled the air. He clung to Seera, praying strength for Gwenivere and her burning city.

Who would want for something like this? Who would place the Amulet's worth over all these people's lives?

Mournful, Dietrich shifted his grip to Gwenivere's hand and squeezed. The princess did nothing in return, the speed of their flight too quick to warrant a returning gesture.

Behind them, the heat of the Behemoth's flames increased.

Whatever is controlling this thing—Dietrich thought to Seera, moving his hand back to her spikes—*keep fighting it. I can feel its pull for Gwenivere's Amulet now. Don't let it take you.*

A rumble sounded from Seera's throat. Beneath them, the outskirts of the city finally faded, the trees of the surrounding forest thickening. Hills and cliffs closed together, a river rustling gently in contrast to the roaring Behemoth. It stopped casting its fire, instead shifting its attention to them.

"We got it out of Voradeen," Dietrich said, as much to comfort Gwenivere as it was to comfort himself. Surprisingly, the princess released a hand from Seera, the beginnings of a weapon forming around her arm.

"How do we kill it?" she asked. There was a hunger in her voice that nearly made Dietrich lean away.

Well? he thought to Seera. She was still fighting, blocking out the pull on her mind, but she was present. *How* do *we kill it?*

Silence. The beating of her wings was frantic as another breath of fire escaped from the Behemoth's throat.

Seera?

I heard you!

She bolted toward the treetops, the thick reds and yellows of leaves enveloping them. Despite being blind, the abrupt change in flight seemed to alter the Behemoth's senses. The pull on the Amulet flickered.

Its mind only knows the commands it's being given, Seera said. She wove through thick trunks of trees, quick and agile. *If we can get it to attack itself—to cast its flames on itself—maybe we can kill it.*

All right, Dietrich thought. In front of him, the weapon Gwenivere *called,* a crossbow, solidified.

So what do you propose? he asked, examining the weapon. It wasn't quite as bulky as the ones he usually *called,* or as black, but it latched to her arm, just above her wrist, so she could still hold on to Seera.

Clever.

Perhaps we could just drop her off on top of it? Dietrich thought. *She seems rather . . . feisty.*

Seera kept quiet for a moment, her wings closing shut as she barely avoided the limbs of surrounding trees. Dietrich's heart fell to his stomach as she quickly opened her wings back out, barely keeping them off the ground.

Behind them, the Behemoth had caught their scent. The sound of breaking branches flew along the wind.

Seera? Dietrich asked. *What are your thoughts? Should we throw the Amulet at it and hope it burns through itself?*

"It's gaining on us," Gwenivere said. Her neck craned to see behind them, her cheek nearly pressing against Dietrich's own.

A bolt formed inside her crossbow.

Seera burst through the forest, a waterfall cascading down

into the depths of a canyon. Dietrich and Gwenivere both released a scream as the dragon descended headfirst down the mist of the falls. The river forming the falls ran at the canyon bottom, the rapids white and roaring against the rocks. It grew closer, closer, closer, until Dietrich swore Seera was headed straight for its depths.

Gwenivere screamed again. Dietrich pinned his elbows against her torso, his legs squeezing at Seera's side.

Then, just as quickly as their plummet started, it was over. The canyon echoed with the Behemoth's roar.

"It's fallen!" Gwenivere yelled. She and Dietrich both looked back at where the beast had crashed, blood darkening the river's waters. The princess's laugh filled his ears, her hand chancing a grip against his own as Seera circled around.

Is it dead? Dietrich asked. It was useless to ask; he could sense in Seera's mind that it wasn't. He was disappointed but unsurprised when she answered no.

As their flight turned back toward the Behemoth, Dietrich could finally see it's features clearly. The scales he'd mistaken for black were actually a flurry of colors, different, darkened *auroras* pulsating through them. Its head looked similar to Seera's: dragon-like, with horns extending back and sharp, menacing eyes. Not eyes, exactly, but sockets, where eyes used to be.

Your idea might actually work, Seera said. The Behemoth, grumbling now from its fall, summoned the air back around it. The mist of the falls and the bloodied waters of the river flew as its body slowly began to rise.

Gwenivere lifted her crossbow arm, readying her aim.

Which idea? he asked, watching Gwenivere's *called* bolts fly through the air and pierce into the Behemoth's scales. They were close to it now, close enough that Dietrich could see the tiny punctures the bolts made before they faded and were replaced by more. Dietrich *called* a dagger and thrust it at the beast, deciding he should do something to aid the princess.

It was like throwing darts at a mountain.

The one about the Amulet, Seera finally answered. *I think the Behemoth will burn through itself if we get the Amulet near enough to it, or even on it.*

So what, we dangle Gwenivere over it? He *called* another dagger, this one bigger than the first, and threw it down.

The Behemoth's air blew it back. And then it was after them again.

The steady pace Seera had set grew rapid again. Gwenivere's crossbow faded as she lunged back toward the dragon's body, Dietrich's own body pressed down against her. He wished now, as the Behemoth bellowed so closely behind them, that they were going down again instead of up.

No, Seera said, even her thoughts sounding breathless. *You're going to take the Amulet from Gwenivere—and then you're going to jump onto the Behemoth's back.*

Dietrich practically choked.

What?

Seera managed to break the line of forest she'd only come from minutes before, continuing upward over the height of its trees. *We can't make the girl do it; she and I can't communicate. It has to be you.*

Dietrich cursed aloud. The princess likely mistook it for fear of their continual climb, letting out fouler words than his.

I'm going to stop soon, Seera continued, *and then you're going to let go. The air the Behemoth is calling is what keeps it in flight. You shouldn't fall if you can get level with it.*

Shouldn't?

Correct. Seera halted her ascent, her wings opening to their full length.

Now!

Groaning, Dietrich let go with one hand, grabbed at Gwenivere's Amulet, and yanked it over her head. Before she could do anything to stop him, he looked down, cursed again, and let go.

This was his death. This was how the Assassin Prince was going to die. Not from the poisons of his enemies, not from a blade or an arrow. He would die splattered in a river, narrowly missing the pocket of air surrounding the Behemoth he dropped toward.

That, or he'd be swallowed alive by its massive, opened jaws.

Let that blasted princess at least tell them I died valiantly, he thought, letting out a yell. Through the curses and fearful doom in his mind, he managed to pull at his black *auroras, calling* them with panic. They fluttered like a dying flame, barely sparking to life before flowing into a rigid, slender blade. Dietrich clung to them, allowed them to fill his entire mind, his lungs, his stomach, until the black swarm of the Behemoth's body flew feet away, inches, seconds.

Dietrich shut his eyes, damning his brother and Seera and the Xen princess, and let out one last yell. Then he slammed into something hard.

My heart broke when I heard what'd happened in Voradeen, but I didn't realize the scope of it until I started seeing blood in the river near where I live.

Xen countryman

CHAPTER 35

DIETRICH

Dietrich opened his eyes, expecting to see whatever realm existed between the day of death and the day the *auroras* drifted from one's body. He'd died, after all, crashed into the body of some monstrous, ancient being. He'd listened to the dragon—the damned, bloody dragon—who'd told him to leap onto the back of a Behemoth.

A Behemoth.

His sight began to focus. Fluttering, shifting darkness moved in front of him. He ground his teeth, his shoulder throbbing.

Stupid fool, came Seera's voice. It was distant, like it had been when he'd first heard her outside the palace balconies. Could she speak to him even in death?

Are you always so theatrical?

Dietrich looked past the darkness in front of him and up toward his arm, one hand clinging tightly to his *called* blade. Its point stuck into the darkness. Thick, crimson blood dripped from where it was lodged.

In his other hand, metal imprinting itself into his skin, rested the Amulet of Eve.

It was the air you felt, Seera explained. *It felt like a wall when you hit it, but you're fine. You're* alive. *Now stop thinking curses at me and get a better grip. The Behemoth is going to strike.*

Dietrich hastily put the chain of the Amulet around his neck and did as he was told. There was another knife, a *touched* one, strapped to his thigh. His thoughts were too jumbled for him to balance *calling* two knives, so he pulled the *touched* one from its place and stabbed it through the Behemoth's scales.

They were surprisingly smooth, and thin, the knife puncturing through cleanly. More blood spilled down onto his face, but he ignored it, not wanting to risk letting go of his makeshift grips to risk wiping it away. He looked around, hoping to find Seera, but the view of the Behemoth's mouth was all he could see.

Dietrich yelled, brazen and unashamed, as billowing flames came toward him.

The heat from the flames was almost enough to make him let go. They didn't land directly on him though, so he held steady. He wondered if the princess, safe now atop Seera's back, mourned him or cursed him. How foolish he must have seemed, jumping off the back of his dragon and onto the Behemoth.

It's not foolish, Seera said, *it's working!*

Dietrich wanted to look up, but the elemental fabrics of his gloves and cloak were barely managing to absorb the might of the Behemoth's flames. If he risked looking, the skin on his face wouldn't be able to do the same.

He'd take the dragon's word for it.

It's torso, it's almost burned completely through! Dietrich, can you feel its air faltering?

He couldn't feel anything but the blaze above him and the

throbbing of his shoulder. He tried, though, tried to see if he could still sense that protective wall of air that propelled him and the Behemoth upward. He *vanished* the *called* blade and extended his hand out, trying to gain a sense of the beast's element.

It was still there. But it was fading.

Hold on, Prince, hold on!

He listened without protest, quickly returning his injured arm back to where the other still held his *touched* knife. The Behemoth breathed its fire, the flames growing hotter and hotter above and around him. The air began to disappear. Dietrich couldn't see what was happening, even if he tried.

Seera could, though. He reached his thoughts out to her and glimpsed flashes of what she saw.

The mighty Behemoth, the ancient beast from the Age of Old, was burning its own body in half.

You are, as am I, a descendent of the Ageless, he heard Zoran say. *They were and are the original High Council of Eve, all but forgotten by the people of today. They possessed the ability to control fiends, summon beasts from the Age of Old . . .*

The ability to control fiends. That's who was doing this then, one of the Ageless. And they'd done it all for Gwenivere's Amulet.

Dietrich, it's done, Seera said. He knew what she meant before she said it. The Behemoth's air had faded to nothingness. Dietrich was back to free falling, the sensation equally terrifying and petrifying as the Behemoth's body made its way toward the ground.

I'm coming, she said. Dietrich kept still, his fingers rigid as they hung from his knife's hilt.

And then his dragon was there, aiding him once more onto her back. The ancient Behemoth, split in two, fell back into the canyon below. This time when it crashed to the ground, there was no sense of gleeful triumph. There was only hatred, both in Dietrich's heart and in Seera's, for whoever had forced the slumbering creature to burn itself to death.

While good quality elemental fabrics and metals can absorb a great deal of elements, it is still important to switch them out. Otherwise they can overfill and become dangerous for the wearer.

Warning note on elemental armor

Chapter 36

GWENIVERE

As soon as the prince was safely back onto his dragon, Gwenivere grabbed her Amulet and yanked it from his chest. He didn't protest, instead looking down at the remains of the Behemoth below. Sadness seemed to cross his eyes, and his dragon's, both man and fiend looking downtrodden at the fate of the beast. Gwenivere had understood that feeling when she'd stood above the tortavel corpse, her stance of conquest but her heart sorrowed. It'd made her angry that she'd felt anything but hatred for something that had brought havoc to her city, but she had.

She didn't now.

Behind her, Dietrich suddenly began to fall back. The dragon leveled its flight as Gwenivere spun around and caught him, cursing when she saw how much of his clothing had been burned through. He was injured, somewhere, but she couldn't tell where. His black clothes were no doubt made of elemental fabric, but . . .

What happens if too much of an element fills into elemental armor? she heard Garron ask. And then she heard her brother's elated reply:

It explodes!

Garron had told her stories of threads and metals becoming so filled that they eventually burst. Perhaps that's what had happened to Dietrich. She grabbed his hood and pulled it down, only to find he wore another layer of elemental fabric underneath. She grunted and instead pulled at his shirt, the dark skin beneath bubbling from burns. The smell of charred flesh hit her as the breeze flew passed.

"He's hurt," she said. She spun back toward the dragon, uncertain how the prince managed to talk to her, and shouted, "Please—he's hurt!"

The dragon seemed to understand, or somehow already knew, her flight lowering to a stream within the forest. She landed gently, her claws slipping into the soft soil as her wings folded. Gwenivere jumped off and quickly grabbed onto Dietrich's shoulders, carefully pulling him off his dragon's back.

"I-I'm going to try and help him," she said. The dragon stared at her, its eyes a cool, white blue. Gwenivere looked to Dietrich, then back at the beast, unsettled at how saddened the beast seemed. It was a fiend; it shouldn't feel anything but hunger and fear for humans. Why did it look at them, then, as if they mattered?

Gwenivere put her fingers to Dietrich neck, praying for a pulse. It was there, a slow *pum, pum-pum, pum-pum*. She laughed, grateful and surprised, and breathed a heavy sigh of relief.

He was alive.

All right, now what? she wondered, peeling off the layer beneath his hood. She realized then that she'd never seen his entire face.

He was younger than she expected, likely not even in his thirtieth year. She supposed if she thought about the profile of him that she'd read in preparation for the masquerade, she'd know that, but the portrait of him then had just been from his boyhood. After everything he'd just done, after having saved her and her city, her people, she'd have thought he'd be older. More at peace with the idea of dying.

Why would someone she didn't know, who had no love for or affiliation with her home, risk his life for it?

"Don't die, all right?" she whispered. Her voice came out more choked than she expected, so she cleared her throat and began peeling back the layers of his clothes.

The extra tie around his head had saved his black hair from burning, but the edges of his face had lines of damaged flesh where the tie hadn't covered. He'd not been a beautiful man as it was, his features harshly masculine, but the scarring would make him especially fearsome. She pitied him, knowing it was shallow, but it didn't seem fair that he'd saved so many and lost the youthfulness of his golden skin. Some women fancied men like that, she supposed, men who simply looked rugged and dangerous. She would tell him so, if he awoke from this.

When he awoke from this.

It got worse the more clothing she peeled off. She was careful to keep his skin from peeling off with it, though she knew there were times the fabric was too meshed to prevent it completely. She let out a wince on his behalf as she carefully removed his clothes, the dragon making a similar noise behind her.

If the fiend was wincing, it had to be bad.

"You're going to make it," she said, as much to herself as to Dietrich. She looked back at the dragon—Seera, he'd called her—and gave her a reassuring nod. "He'll make it."

Fortunately, after she finally removed all of his shirt, she found a vest underneath. It'd been damaged too, though, so she began pulling it off, marveling at all the old scars already on his stomach and chest.

What've you been through, to have a marred body like this?
She ran her fingers over the scars. She pulled back quickly
with flushed cheeks, realizing she'd been caressing the bare,
muscular torso of a shirtless man. She swallowed and checked
the skin just below his belt, grateful when she saw he hadn't
been injured there. She wasn't sure she was ready to see that
part of him.

All right, I have to get him awake, she thought, trying to
keep focused. She couldn't imagine how she'd react if the roles
had been reversed, if he'd not only stripped her of her clothes,
but touched and examined her naked skin.

I'd be furious, she thought, dragging him over toward
the nearby stream. Winter would come soon, and the waters
would likely be a bitter cold from the cooling days. Perhaps
the feel of it would wake him, soothe the pain of the burns
that had most likely caused him to lose consciousness.

Yes, I wouldn't like that, she decided, trying to distract herself from the damage of his wounds. If they were as bad as they
looked, he might not wake up at all.

She panted and glanced back at his dragon, hoping the
beast couldn't read her thoughts. Then she felt the water
against her ankles and winced at its cold.

"Please wake up," she whispered, splashing Dietrich with
water. "Please . . ."

If all three layers of skin have been damaged, I recommend using the Blue Wyvern Elixir. It's expensive, but it will heal the wound quickly and prevent infection and scarring.

From Abaddon Haroldson's burn pamphlets

CHAPTER 37

DIETRICH

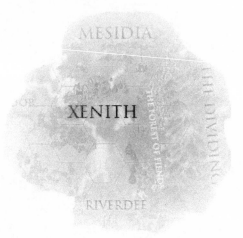

The prince awoke with a gasp. He instantly pushed Gweni-vere away and lifted a dagger to her throat. She held her hands up, watching him as his weapon fell from his hand and his body dropped back to the stream.

"Whoa, whoa, whoa," she said, catching him before he could fall. Pain dripped from his wounds, red seeping through his clothes and trickling into the water. Gwenivere helped lower him down and crouched beside him, urgently looking back to his dragon for help. Seera stood still, her nostrils flaring as she watched with icy sadness.

"Dietrich," Gwenivere whispered. She reached her hand out to his burned skin, her turquoise eyes filling with tears. He breathed heavily, pain pulsing through him, and fought to stay awake.

He would die soon; he could feel it. He would die a hero,

he supposed, having battled to save the grandest city from a Behemoth. People would tell stories of him, of his legacy, the titles that had haunted him abandoned for ones of heroism. He took a breath and looked back at Gwenivere, who wore a forced, hopeful smile as she held him.

Yes, I could die like this, he thought, noting her matted hair and tattered clothes. He lifted his hand and brushed her cheek, wiping the tear that fell from her face.

Your elixir, you fool! Seera yelled, ending his musings. Dietrich reached for his pouch and found a bottle of Brelain's cure still intact. He sat up and cast Gwenivere's hand aside, deciding he wanted to live more than he wanted to imagine a gloried death.

He poured every last drop of the liquid over his hands and body and face, reeling as an overwhelming pain took him. The princess attempted to ease his thrashing as she grasped his arms, holding him down. She observed him, brows furrowed.

Then her expression shifted. Amazement and wonder flashed across her face as the flesh of his burns began to heal.

"What in the Light is that?"

Her tone was hushed but firm. He relaxed his grip, not realizing he'd been holding his hands in fists.

"An elixir," he managed. He carefully propped himself up, inhaling deeply as the currents flowed over his mended skin. Realizing Gwenivere was still awaiting a more thorough explanation, he said, "It's not been tested on enough people to sell to the West yet."

That was the easiest answer he could give. Telling her of Brelain and the desert serpent would take too long, and claiming it was his brother's creation would be an outright lie. Not to mention a political mistake. Regardless of how good the terms were between Xenith and Sadie, he didn't think the heir to the throne would appreciate knowing the country they paid a great deal to for elixirs was keeping such a miracle cure to themselves.

This response was simplest. And for all he knew, it might be true. All that really mattered was that, after chewing on her lip for a moment, Gwenivere nodded.

"Well I don't know if they have knights in the East," she said, pulling her arms back to her lap. "But you're a proper knight, I'd say." She smiled and stood, extending a hand down toward him. He looked up, obliging her offer.

"We have watchmen," he said. He thought of his and Abaddon's watchman Culter, the man who'd taught him so many filthy and wicked tunes, and decided he was, indeed, a proper watchman.

Something's wrong, Seera cut in.

Dietrich froze, feeling what she felt.

It was the pull from before, the longing for the Amulet on Gwenivere's chest. He turned from her and unsheathed another blade, the muscles in his shoulder aching. He rubbed at them with his free hand, noticing for the first time he was no longer wearing his shirt or vest.

He gave Gwenivere an amused, inquisitive glance.

She suddenly found interest in Seera.

What's going on? he asked, noting as the pull to the Amulet grew. Gwenivere stood beside him, reaching for her own dagger.

The Elder Bloods, Seera sneered. Dietrich looked back at her, his blood boiling as hers did. A wave of hatred enveloped him.

The people who summoned the Behemoth? And the fiends?

Seera didn't answer. She didn't need to. He already knew what the answer was.

Yes.

"Seera is going to get you out of here," he said to Gwenivere. "It's not safe."

"Me? Why not us?"

The demand in her tone was back, so soon after he'd barely survived the battle.

"It's too dangerous," he said. Seera was there before he

asked, already prepping to take Gwenivere away.

"Come with me," she said, grabbing his arm. Dietrich was torn by the concern in her voice, desperately wanting to accompany her back to her palace and rest.

I still need the Dagger, he reminded himself. *And Gwenivere is the key to persuading Roland to give it to me.*

He looked back up, careful to keep his gaze on Gwenivere's face. Even that seemed to sway his thoughts.

The pull toward the Amulet grew stronger.

Seera? he asked. *These Elder Bloods—these are the same people who led all the fiends against Voradeen? Who called on the Behemoth?*

Seera bellowed a deep, low grumble. *Yes.*

So my chances of dying here quite high, correct?

Silence.

"Dietrich, come with me," Gwenivere insisted, tapping her Amulet. "I can feel it too now, whatever is out here. I can help you—"

She didn't finish her statement. Couldn't. Dietrich had closed the distance between them and pulled her close to him, swooping her up into his arms.

Before she could curse him or hit him—or stab him, by the look on her face—he carried her a couple feet, stuck one of his needles in her neck, and tossed her onto Seera's back.

Gwenivere Verigrad was seen with the desert scum's dragon. I can try to twist this in our favor.

A letter between Anastasia Verkev and an unknown party

CHAPTER 38

GWENIVERE

Gwenivere cursed as Seera lifted off the ground. The Sadi-yan prince still stood alone in the creek below.

Quickly Gwenivere thrust the dagger she held back in its sheath, clutching tightly to the dragon. The air was cold. It was made worse by the coming night and the water that still clung to her from the stream. She leaned against Seera's dark scales, tired and fatigued, and wished terribly Dietrich had come with her.

She grabbed tightly to the chain of her Amulet, the strange pull for it waning as the dragon carried her home.

She was so tired. When was the last time she'd slept? Had it really only been last night that Dietrich had met her in her chambers?

So much had happened. So many terrible things had happened. And she was so tired, and her body ached, and her mind was so weary from *calling* . . .

She closed her eyes, just for a moment.

And opened them again when Seera nudged her. On a palace balcony.

She'd fallen asleep? After all that had happened, she hadn't thought herself capable of that. She rubbed at her neck where she felt a numb, dull pinch, noticing a small needle sticking from her skin. Grimacing, she pulled it out and slid from the dragon's back. The needle must have come from Dietrich.

The dragon nestled her head against Gwenivere's stomach, seeming to know the distress that filled her. Gwenivere tensed at first, unsure as the beast pushed gently against her, then obliged when she realized its intent.

"Thank you," she whispered. She backed away, looking into her crystal-colored eyes, and nodded as she saw the pleading worry within them.

"Go save him," she said. The dragon turned away, dark wings opening. When she leaped from the balcony, it was silent and graceful.

"Gwen?"

The princess spun around, the scared, dirty face of her small brother staring up at her. She gasped gratefully and fell to the ground, embracing the young boy as he ran into her outstretched arms.

"Aden," she whispered. Her heart lifted as he draped his tiny hands around her. She hugged him, pressing his face against her chest and away from the scene of their burning city. He sobbed, his eyes red and his shoulders shaking. Someone's blood stained his clothes.

Maximus's blood.

Gwenivere shushed him and rocked him gently. She kissed his head, thanking the Creator he was alive and unharmed.

Just past them stood his protectors: Dorian and Elizabeth, the three Prianthian sisters, and further back, nearly a foot above them all, a bloodied knight, wiping tears from his eyes.

Was that . . . Maximus?

Gwenivere nodded to them all, knowing they had questions. And she had questions for them too, especially Maximus, who indeed stood seemingly unscathed behind the others.

That elixir Dietrich used—could that have been what had saved Maximus? Gwenivere remembered someone had put an arm on her shoulder when she'd been questioning Maximus during the Peace Gathering. Had it been Dietrich trying to get her attention, come to help her save her brother's knight?

It doesn't matter, Gwenivere decided, kissing Aden again. In that moment, all that mattered was that her brother was safely in her arms.

The pebble and petal will melt the ice, but break and wither with the winter. All because the Shadow will save the mortal heaven, only to be the name that tears it apart.

Evean prophecy

CHAPTER 39

DIETRICH

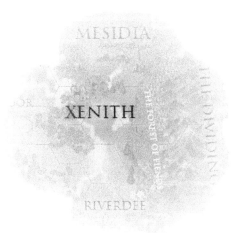

Dietrich stood tall, blind without the Amulet to give way to the Elder Bloods' presence. He knew they were out there, though, rapidly approaching. They were likely eager to confront the man who had defeated their Behemoth.

Perhaps I'll die after all, he mused, trying not to startle at the sounds of the forest.

"Dietrich Haroldson," a voice said. The prince looked toward where the voice had come from, chills running down his spine. There were only two, a man and a woman, both with pale skin and long, dark hair. They were siblings—twins more than likely—their nearly identical features seeming both perfectly young and unnaturally old. The woman's eyes glowed, ever so slightly, and the sight of her evoked an odd fear in Dietrich's gut. He held up his dagger, preparing himself for the battle that was sure to come.

The dark-haired man snickered in response.

"You are Xia's son," the woman said, walking closer to him. He threw his knife out toward her, more a threat to halt her advance than an effort to hurt her, but she stopped the dagger with the slightest lift of hand.

It fell to the ground with a thud.

The woman smiled, an uncomfortable, sinister smile. Her blood-red lips peeled back to expose white, perfectly human teeth.

Dietrich had half expected them to be pointed.

"Perhaps it might be better to let things be," she said, analyzing him with subdued excitement. Her twin's amusement faded, his displeasure obvious.

"Better to take him now," he said, *calling* a dark element. Before he could cast it, Seera flew in, landing between them. The man grunted in frustration, but the woman's smile widened.

"You. You are Zoran's girl." She pointed at Seera. "Well it seems I can't kill either of you."

She gave them another grin before turning away, knowing full well they wouldn't risk provoking her. She beckoned her brother to follow, the man still glaring, but he too joined in her retreat.

The two faded back into the forest, gone as quickly as they'd come.

Dietrich held his breath, not wanting to believe he was safe only to have them suddenly return. He swallowed, trying to unravel the strange words the woman had spoken.

They're gone, Seera said.

Dietrich looked up at her uneasily, beads of sweat dripping down his face. He exhaled, knowing the dragon was right, then sheathed his weapon and walked back into the cold water of the creek. He waded in until his torso was fully submerged, the few burns he still had searing with pain. He grimaced and closed his eyes, his aching muscles finally telling him just how tired they were.

He stayed there, letting the moment stretch, not wanting to think of all those who had likely died that day.

Is she safe? he asked, watching as his fingertips began to texture. Seera didn't respond, instead walking a short way into the forest and breathing flames onto a small stack of branches. She coiled her legs and laid down, curling up as close as she could to the fire's warmth.

Seera and Savine, they're very susceptible to the cold, Dietrich remembered, recalling the sad truth Zoran had revealed. He looked up, the twinkling of stars finally coming forth as the moon brightened. *It makes them weak.*

Yes, Seera finally answered, her slit eyes opening and closing heavily. She watched the flames, the reflection of them glowing dully in her gaze. *The princess is safe. For now.*

Dietrich nodded, glancing back sorrowfully at his dragon. He knew how fatigued he felt, his mind registering the weary nature of his own body, but that was all he knew. He could sense Seera's pain, but he couldn't feel it, couldn't comprehend her sensitivity to the cold. He walked out of the icy water and grabbed what was left of his clothes, then walked over to her and grabbed a red *aurora* in his mind. He pushed the element's warmth into his hands, kneeling down beside her and guiding his palms gently across her scales. She grumbled, a soft, throaty purr. Her lids shut as he put his strength into keeping her warm.

I won't let you freeze, he said, enjoying the way the crackling fire dried his wet skin. When the dragon didn't answer, he smiled, knowing his soothing warmth had put her to sleep.

Alone, Dietrich tensed at the sudden solitude of his thoughts. Try as he might to evade them, all he could see were the Elder Bloods, commanding more and more fiends to kill. He closed his eyes, trying to escape his musings, and eventually slipped into a cold and haunted slumber.

Despite selling wares of every kind, element shackles are still what we make the most profit on.

Fiona Collinson

Chapter 40

X'ODIA

"Let her go!" someone screamed. "Please, she's innocent! Let her go!"

X'odia panted, eyes opening wide. Everything around her was spinning and swirling and twisting. A sickening pound beat against her skull.

"X'odia!"

Her eyes focused in time to see Ravel being held back by two men. She winced as a strong hand latched onto her arm, pulling her up onto shaking feet.

It was the soldier with the blue cloak and grey-blue eyes. His armor was wet and bloody.

"Was she aiding you?" he asked someone. X'odia looked to see he was speaking to the man from the balcony, the one who'd looked to control the fiends. His wrists were pulled together by thick, glowing shackles.

"Yes," he answered, smiling. "She was."

X'odia opened her mouth, desperate to refute the man's lie, but her voice hadn't returned from the pull of her vision. She stood fearful, hardly able to stay upright, and trembled as the soldier surveyed her.

"Odin," he said, beckoning someone over. Another man stepped forward, significantly older than the first, and stood at attention.

"Sir?"

"Find a place for the other prisoners and interrogate them. Until Pierre gives the order, you and your men will stay stationed here in the city."

The older man—Odin—nodded.

I'm innocent! X'odia thought, wishing her lips could form the words. She tried to say them, opened her mouth and forced her tongue, but her voice still refused.

"What will you do with the girl?"

A wiry man, hardly taller than X'odia, sprung out from those around them.

"She'll come back to the Forest of Fiends with us," the soldier answered. "Bind her."

X'odia knew what would happen if the shackles clamped shut. They would block her from her elements, separate her from fire and air and water and lightning. She tried to shout again, to say something in her defense, but when the words wouldn't come, her only choice was to run.

Move, she told her quivering muscles. *Move!*

Before she could make it an inch, the soldier yanked her back. She grimaced at the pain, arm aching.

"You could kill them," the other prisoner whispered. "You know you can."

X'odia trembled, meeting the feral glance of the prisoner beside her. She could kill them, she realized, could kill all of them and save herself and the Evean sailors. Her muscles were weak and her body fragile, but the *auroras* inside her mind, the *auroras* with the strength of the Shield within them, raged excitedly. Even if her physical self was unstable, the *call* of her elements was not.

No, she told herself, tears forming in her eyes. She thought of her faith, of the warmth and the pureness in the Creator, and forced her elements down.

I can't.

She looked through her dark curls at the other prisoner, the corners of his mouth upturned, then watched as the clasps of her element shackles buckled shut.

PART THREE

MASKS OF MOURNING

I wait now for my next assignment.

I've not seen the sky so colorful since I served in the War of Fire.

Voradeen townsmen

CHAPTER 41

GWENIVERE

It was the day of the funeral march. Three days after the fiends had invaded.

The day the dead would ascend.

A hollowness rang in Gwenivere's chest. Her father spoke beside her, a poet instead of a king. He was trying to calm the qualms of his people.

She hardly heard him.

The first night had been fearful. Everyone stayed awake, aching for rest, but hardly a lid stayed closed. Knights and nobles circled the city, candles in hand, counting the fallen and aiding the wounded. Servants brought flowers from the royal gardens to the families whose loved ones had been lost.

There were few homes where petals need not reside.

The morning after, day came late, like the sun was too weary to rise. Rain trickled down in thin sheets of darkness.

The city was masked in shades of grey, brightening the pallor of the dead.

The second night came with a meek moon, a reflection of the people, but with the dawn they rallied. They lifted their lanterns. They cared, they wept, they mourned, and they loved.

But today was the third day. Today was the day of ascension.

Gwenivere stood silent, eyes stinging.

"People of Abra'am," Gerard called, looking over those who stared sorrowfully back at him. They were a sea of black, the only color that didn't rise with the other *auroras* and a perfectly blank canvas for the hues to come. No jewelry was adorned, no lavish charms or ornaments were flaunted. Only quivering lips and bloodshot eyes brought about any color.

"I address you today not as a king, not as a leader or nobleman or person of diplomacy, but simply as a man. I stand before you as your servant, as the hand that offers often, as the back that lifts upon it your burdens and carries them in your time of need.

"Join me, now, in honoring those who have fallen."

Silently the knights of Xenith lifted the slings of the dead, hoisting the heavy rods that held them over their shoulders. The corpses within lay with their arms crossed and their eyes closed, bouquets of flowers placed within their hands. Petals draped around their figures. Those whose bodies had been heavily mutilated were covered with sheer cloths, enough fabric to disguise their disfigurement, but not enough to hide their identities from their families.

Behind the Xen knights marched the leaders of each nation in attendance. All walked beside their guardsmen as their own fallen were carried. Not all the bodies of their dead were adorned the same. Flowers were often replaced by swords, soft fabrics traded for the skins of animals. Incense and small embers burned from some, the smoke drifting into the sky as the first *auroras* began to surface.

A new bustling among the people signaled the awakening of the lights. The silent tears of onlookers shifted to wailing cries.

Gwenivere led the death march to the river, the Golden Knight beside her, as the rest of the knights gently rested the slings into the steady waters.

She stood stoic alongside the river's edge, her face shaded by her veil. She listened to the breathless murmurs, the cold sighs that always came with the *auroras*. The sound was much like that of a fallen leaf descending from its home. It was strangely overwhelming, a sort of dim goodbye.

"Creator," Gerard said, standing near Gwenivere as the last of the bodies made their way to the waters. "We thank you for the lives of these men and women, for the wonderful happiness they gave while they resided among us. Let their passage into the afterlife be uninterrupted, that they may finally rest in peace in the glory of your dwelling."

Gwenivere listened to her father's voice, her eyes locked on the swirling *auroras* as they reflected from the water. Within one passing sling lay a young woman, her arms draped around the small body of a boy, a deep red scar laced across his neck.

Her jaw tightened as *auroras* drifted from them both.

"Although their deaths may be difficult," Gerard said, "we stand united because of it. Where once our quarrels would have rendered such a scene, we now come together, putting our differences aside to ensure this river not be filled with more of your children. We grieve for them; we mourn their loss. But we do so as one.

"Let us now reinvest the wealth of our future to celebrating the lives of those who return to you. We pray these times ahead be a true indication of our growth, that we may now be united by more than we once were before. Bless the masquerade when it comes, that it be filled with nothing but the happiness in knowing those who won't be here to dance with us will now be dancing with you.

"So be it."

"So be it."

Gwenivere said the words, her voice joining the mass of others as they echoed the prayers of her father. She would've been grateful he'd brought consolation to the troubled hearts that remained, but her thoughts were only focused on the oddly familiar face she saw floating past. Without thinking she found herself rushing toward it, the water of the river to her waist before she realized she breached its currents. People gasped around her, Garron only a few steps behind, but the hand of the king halted him. Gwenivere hardly heard their whispers, hardly saw their pointing fingers. Her gaze was only able to see the body of the elderly woman who lay within the sling she grasped.

She recognized her as the glassmaker from the market; the sweet, wrinkled face hardly there now as the *auroras* faded around her. She'd been so content to sell her wares just a few days before, so joyful to see the happiness her creations brought.

Gwenivere reached out to touch her, but her fingers met nothing. The body was only a mirage of who the old woman had been.

"We have to let them go," Gerard whispered, wrapping his hands around her shoulders. She released the rods that halted the sling's progress. Watching it go, she let her father guide her away.

The old woman's hands faded around a glass bouquet.

I've always found it peculiar that Riverdee—the land with no enemies—calls the Forest of Fiends its own. It seems a rather ominous place for such a cheery realm.

From a letter between Markeem the Mute and his wife

CHAPTER 42

X'ODIA

The warmth that filled Evean breezes didn't exist on
Riverdee's shores.

Everything about the northern continent seemed consumed with bulk and solidity. The trees were mighty, their
leaves darker than the vibrant ones that speckled Eve's coast.
The wood of them was darker too, and the waters they resided
by, the blue so murky it was impossible to see the sands below.
The waves, harsh as they broke apart along the ocean's edge,
were all X'odia could hear from her small prison.

The place the soldiers kept her in was small, a rotting shack
that seemed about to collapse come the next storm. It had small,
rectangular windows near an alcove with a sitting area, along
with an attached room X'odia had been told was for relieving
herself. The wood was splintered and poked her when she tried
to lean against it, so she kept near the shack's center, where

the floor had either been torn out or never existed at all. Cool sand was what she lay on, then, which was more like mud from the constant foggy weather. It made the room feel wet, even at noonday, and it kept bodily smells embarrassingly present.

If it weren't for the guards constantly stationed nearby, X'odia might've thought about chancing a good kick at the wood to see if she could escape. As it was, there were always blue-cloaked soldiers standing just outside.

She trembled as she tried to pat sand onto her skin and create a barrier between herself and the wind that howled through the cracks in the walls. Her tattered clothes and dark hair were the only things she had to combat the cold, and even those felt damp. The blood from the fiends she'd battled against should have crusted and dried by now, but instead the Riverdian climate kept it constantly dank. Curling her knees against her chest, she huddled on the floor and tried not to think of fire.

She looked down at her wrists. The elemental bearings didn't seem very strong, but she didn't test them. She knew any attempts to *call* elements would only make it more difficult to accept she no longer could. Not while the shackles still bound her.

Her body ached from the trials of her battle with the fiends, any scrapes or gashes she'd accrued stinging and itching regardless of how she positioned herself. The growling in her stomach seemed a vocalization of her weakened state. Days went by without food. The soldiers nearby walked past her shack and looked into her window to ensure she was still there, but none offered her anything. No food, no words. Just the condemning glares deserving of a murderer.

Outside her door, X'odia could hear the shifting of sand. She didn't react at first, expecting it to be one of the soldiers checking in, but the sound of her door unlocking sent her to her feet. She pressed herself against the wall, afraid of what the person entering might do to her. As the door opened, her fear escalated. The tall, dark-haired soldier from her visions walked in.

He said nothing. He simply stared, grey-blue eyes cold.

X'odia's hands shook. She placed them behind her back, hoping to conceal her terror. Her first glimpse of the man—of the beating he'd ordered in her vision aboard the *Seagull*—all came rushing back to her. She inhaled sharply and kept silent as he mounted a torch against the wall.

"What's your name?" he asked. He sat down at the benches opposite her, one leg crossing over the other. He placed his hands atop where his ankle rested on his knee.

X'odia stood for a moment, caught off guard by the simplicity of his query. She feared the juxtaposition between it and his weathered composure.

"X'odia," she said. He nodded, his scarred hand motioning for her to sit against the other bench in front of him. She looked at the seat's proximity to his own, fearful of how close it was to his reach. He was a large man. If she answered him in a way he didn't find pleasing, he wouldn't have to move far to strike her.

She kept her eyes on him and cautiously made her way to the bench.

"How old are you?" he asked. "Nineteen winters? Twenty?"

"No . . . I'm thirty-five."

He stared, then coughed into his shoulder.

"And where are you from, X'odia of thirty-five winters? Eve?"

There was an inflection in his voice, a strange, almost kind quality. X'odia released some of the tension in her grasp and nodded.

"Good," he said simply. "I believe you."

He said nothing more, only leaning back further against the wall of the shack. He no longer wore the armor as he had before, the light metal now replaced by a leather-padded vest. The blue cloak remained.

X'odia sat quietly, uncertain what to do. She'd felt herself care for him in her vision as she would a friend, felt a sort of bond with him only to have him order her beaten. He had yet to command that, and she had yet to understand why such feelings would develop, but she knew the morbid disposition was there.

I must cast out such peculiar notions, she thought, furrowing her brow. *How could I ever befriend him when he holds me prisoner?*

"Who am I?" he asked suddenly. "And not just my name." He sat forward, slowly, his hands inching closer to her. She couldn't help but see they were still bloody from striking someone else. "I want you to tell me why you looked at me the way you did just now. Why you look at me as if we've already met."

She broke his pressing stare, knowing he'd sensed the feelings she'd tried to hide. She squeezed at her skirts and took a breath.

"Your name is Dravian Valcor," she said hurriedly. "You're the leader of King Pierre's Elite. You've been residing in Riverdee because Pierre caught word from Duke Bernard VII that the Duchess Yvaine knew of an attack that was to take place here." She swallowed, eyes flickering back to his. "I know this because I've Seen it. In a vision. I had one before my ship brought me here, and I had another when I saw you—"

Dravian didn't let her finish. He snatched her arm, grip tight, and *called* ice.

Her skin instantly numbed. The damp fabric of her sleeve turned cold, her arm losing motion. She watched helplessly, opening her mouth to say something, but Dravian's other hand was making its way toward her. She flinched. She expected him to hit her, but his fingers never met her face. Instead they grabbed her neck and clenched, firm, but loose enough to let her breathe.

"To See something doesn't explain how you know so much. Who gave you this information? Yvaine? Bernard?"

Any compassion in his voice was gone. X'odia shivered, the bones in her neck aching.

"The Sight doesn't just show me things!" she managed, grimacing as the ice spread. "I often come away from it knowing things I would've known in that moment. Only the Light has given me this information—no one else!"

Dravian stood from his crouched position and thrust her against the wall.

"Prince Roland wrote to us of a woman like you. A woman whose eyes glowed after visions."

He stared at her, searching, then abruptly released her.

X'odia thanked the Creator as he backed away, grabbed the torch off the wall, and left.

When she heard him lock the door and bark orders to his soldiers, she let herself collapse to the floor. She put her right hand to her neck, the left gaining back movement as the ice melted away. Not certain if Dravian would return, she stayed where she was, too afraid to move, and embraced the hot tears that flooded down her cheeks.

X'odia was dreadful the day following her encounter with Dravian. Each time a soldier came to her post, she feared it was him, her hand unknowingly reaching to her side.

She was surprised to find that they at last fed her, though it was only a few scraps from whatever the rest of the soldiers had left uneaten. More surprising yet was that none of the soldiers were Dravian. None of them questioned her. None of them beat her. They walked to the window, looked through, and left.

The night's events didn't deviate much from the day's. One

of the soldiers brought her another meal, this one slightly more than the one before it, and a thick cloak along with it. X'odia thanked him profusely, grateful for his kindness, but he immediately thrust his hands to his ears and rushed from the shack. X'odia might've pondered the act if not for the smell of the food and the warmth of the cloak.

As she ate, she prayed Ravel and Bronal and the rest of the Evean sailors were safe. She tossed the bowl of scraps aside when she was through and curled up on the floor, wondering what had become of them.

She hoped it was nothing like this.

The series of days after were similar. She was fed two meals and was even accompanied outside to relieve herself rather than forced to use the small room within the shack. She'd stood awhile the first time, not wanting to be so immodest in front of anyone, but that was soon forgotten the more she did it. It was better than the adjacent room of the shack. At least now, at a reasonable distance away, she wouldn't have to worry about insects following the smells to her.

She thought about fleeing when they let her relieve herself. The thick wood of the coastal trees would serve as a decent place to hide her, and she was used to living on her own. The idea of solitude within the forest didn't frighten her, nor did the fiends she might encounter, so long as they didn't think her their enemy.

The howls of the soldiers' dogs did frighten her, though. She wouldn't get far with their tracking.

Sleep resisted her those first nights, but weariness and a familiarization eventually granted her rest. Her stomach became accustomed to the small portions, and any aches and pains gradually began to heal, though at a much slower rate than she was used to. Even the night breeze became somewhat pleasant. The salt and the sea reminded her of her cottage back in Eve.

Despite the subtle pleasantries, the solitude of the wrist

bearings was never something she could ignore. She'd heard stories of how the people of Abra'am had used the metals to keep their enemies from *calling* elements and shields and weapons. It was certainly tempting to *call* something herself, especially when nights became cold or her muscles ached, but she knew better than to try. The metal would simply absorb them back up.

As much as she fought to ignore their absence, her elements were always there when she closed her eyes. It was so empty not to feel them, like her soul was hovering just outside her body. She imagined this was what stories meant when they described heartache, or betrayal or sorrow. It wasn't tangible, nor was it a wound, but it was painful.

Not knowing what else to do, she prayed, then she let herself cry. At least then, as the quiet sobs took her, she could tire herself out enough to sleep.

"Hello there, pretty thing," someone whispered, nudging X'odia's side. "Time to wake up."

X'odia did nothing, thinking it a dream. She gasped when she was kicked, the boot proving an effective means to wake her. She clutched her stomach and made to rise, sucking in the saliva that had dripped while she'd slept.

She expected the soldier to let her up. Instead, he waited for her sleep-filled vision to clear, seized her hair, and slapped her across the face.

A silent scream rested in her throat. The soldier snickered, pulling at her hair again. When she cried out and reached up for it, he yanked her head back and thrust his forehead against her.

Frantic, X'odia tried to back away. Her scalp burned, and

her vision speckled and blurred. She made to blink away the water in her eyes, hoping to chance a look at her attacker, but his head was already making its way toward hers again.

"Enough!" someone shouted.

The soldier halted. X'odia looked through her tangled hair, recognizing the man holding her as the one who'd been eager to bind her back in Riverdee's city.

"Enough, Rellor. Let her go." It was Dravian's voice. He stepped forward, dragging the man away. "Wait outside. I'll call you in if you're needed."

The man—Rellor—scratched his jaw, spit, then walked out.

Dravian crouched by X'odia and grabbed her arm. She winced, afraid he'd *call* more ice, but his touch was gentle. Reluctant, she let him guide her to the creaky benches they'd sat at before.

When he lifted his hand, she instinctively backed away. She stopped when she realized he was only pushing aside her curls to examine the wound.

"Although I'm sure you don't believe me, it was best he hit you here." He pointed a finger toward her temple. "Had he hit your nose or cheekbones, he might have broken them. At least this way you'll only have to endure a bad headache."

He leaned back and resumed the position he'd had during their last encounter. When he didn't say anything more, X'odia eyed him, head indeed aching.

Looking out the window, he didn't appear as fearsome as he had before. The stubble that'd darkened his face had been trimmed to nothing, though the shadow of it lingered against his jaw. His hair wasn't as disheveled as it had been, and it seemed shorter, or at least combed back. Against the dawn, his eyes looked lighter.

"My cloak has kept you warm, I presume?" he asked. His voice was still husky from the morning. "There's not much of you."

She sat still, staring at him blankly as she realized he wore no cloak of his own.

She didn't know if she should feel grateful or disgusted.

"It has," she answered. She leaned back in her own seat, deciding there was no use holding herself with fear. If he was going to strike her or lash out at her again, there was nothing she could do to stop him. "Would you like it back?"

He chuckled. "No—you keep it."

He didn't say anything else. She sat uneasily.

I have to get out of here. I have to keep to the mission the Council assigned . . .

She sat up a bit taller, pushed her shoulders back, and cleared her throat.

"Last time you came," she started carefully, "you asked me how I knew things about you. I want to reiterate that I was telling the truth. I didn't come to Abra'am for anything pertaining to you. I have no control over what the Sight shows me."

Dravian's eyes turned back to her. "Why did you come to Abra'am, then?"

"I came because the Sight showed me an Evean prophecy being fulfilled that would lead to war. I told the council of my people, and they ordered me to come here to try and stop it."

Dravian held out a hand, motioning broadly. "Why you? You aren't particularly strong in stature. And even if you're gifted with elements, I know Eveans are reluctant to use their elements against other humans."

"Not reluctant," she corrected. "At least not I. I refuse to use my elements against humans."

"Even if your life depends on it?"

"Even then."

Dravian pursed his lips, suspicious, but nodded.

"And my other query? About why you were chosen?"

"I was chosen because I heal—when these aren't on at least." She lifted her arms, pulling them taut to snap the chain of the element shackles. "My council also thought it wise to send me because my visions have shown me what people look like."

"I see." Dravian rose from the bench. "You've been very helpful, X'odia. Now if you'll excuse me, King Pierre has ordered that both Rellor and I have a go at conversing with you. Be as responsive to him as you were with me, and no harm shall come to you." He paused, holding his palms up submissively. "No additional harm, at least."

Despite herself, X'odia found herself tempted to smile at his sudden camaraderie.

She didn't.

There are four Artifacts: The Ring, the Shield, the Dagger, and the Amulet.

The powers vary. It says in books from the Age of Old that the Shield grants invincibility and the Dagger immortality. Why the difference? I'm not sure, but there's a clear distinction in the original text.

The Ring is said to be an extreme version of a wedding band. It allows the wearer to bond themselves to another so if they die, the person they've bonded themselves to will die as well, and vice versa.

The Amulet is known to reverse the effects of "magic." It's assumed that means the powers of the other Artifacts, though that point does not translate clearly in modern tongues.

Legend says the Shield was used by an Evean man to save his home from invaders. The Dagger and the Amulet were found in the Dividing Wall's mountains. It's believed the effects of their stones are what's caused the caves and mines to be so filled with elemental metals.

No one knows what happened to the Ring.

Artifact researcher

CHAPTER 43

PIERRE

Beneath Stonewall castle, in labyrinths known to few, Yvaine Barie screamed.

It was a guttural sound, not a fearful one evoked by something frightening or unexpected. The duchess of Mesidia knew exactly what was coming to her, when it was coming to her, and for how long it would be upon her. It wasn't work Pierre was proud of, but it was what needed to be done.

The only regret he had was that standing beside him, outside the dungeon Yvaine was being tortured in, stood his son.

"She has to be close to breaking," Roland muttered. He chewed his lip, pulling up the bandaged skin along his jaw. Pierre swallowed, knowing if Yvaine's knife had just been a few inches lower when she'd held Roland in the forest . . .

"She'll break when she breaks," he answered.

Roland stopped biting his lip, but his hand rose to scratch at his bandage. The Dagger glowed dimly from his side, casting an eerie light on the hall.

"Do you think Dravian would've gotten her to break already? Or Rellor?"

"Knowing how manic Rellor is, Yvaine would've probably fancied him and found a way to make him her next husband."

They both laughed at that, though it was a nervous laugh that died quickly.

"Dravian, then?" Roland asked. He seemed to grow irritated that he couldn't quite scratch his wound, so he settled on rubbing the back of his head. "He is the Inquisitor, after all."

A loud scream erupted from Yvaine's dungeon. Roland and Pierre both perked, hoping it meant she'd broken, but when the Elite didn't come fetch them, they resumed their tense stances.

"He's doing good work in Riverdee," Pierre answered. "They think they've caught the woman you said killed Merlin. She has visions, and her eyes glow."

Roland lifted his head.

"I didn't know that. That's good."

"Indeed."

A screeching sounded from the door beside them. Pierre and Roland stood tall from the walls they leaned on, each facing the Elite before them.

"Giane," Pierre said, nodding to the woman. She nodded back respectfully.

"Milord, the prisoner has said she will now answer any questions you have for her."

Pierre relaxed, then glanced at Roland. The boy was doing a poor job of hiding his shock, his blue eyes wide as he stared at the Elite. Pierre turned back to Giane, noticing her how his son might—sweaty, weary, and covered in blood.

"Go back to the queen. The word is this: Lilacs."

Giane nodded.

"Tell her that, and she'll bring some servants in to prepare you a bath. We're on full guard right now, so fail to say the word before anything else and Rosalie will make sure you drift. Understood?"

"Understood."

Pierre gave the Elite a salute, which was crisply reciprocated, though lacked the woman's usual valor. When she retreated back toward the castle's upper levels, Pierre turned to Roland, patting him gently on the shoulder.

Roland winced, but fought to hide it. Pierre immediately felt a pang of guilt, already forgetting that Roland had come back from his mission with a busted shoulder, burns, and bites from fiends. Most of it his elemental garb had absorbed or defended for him, but there'd been a few places he'd still been hit. Sighing, Pierre released his hand and made his way into the dungeon.

Dankness was common in underground levels of the castle. In Yvaine's cell, it was accompanied by the coppery scent of blood. Pierre had to fight the urge to cover his mouth.

He nodded to the Elite still in the room. None looked particularly proud, despite knowing it was their enemy who lay on the ground before them. Pierre wasn't proud either, never one who relished the act of torture, or the act of commanding it. Still, he was Mesidia's king, and he needed to ensure what had happened with the fiends didn't happen again.

That thought faltered as Roland crossed into the room. Pierre let his eyes flicker to his son, watching as Roland's skin visibly paled. Sweat beaded across his forehead and along his neck, and his brows furrowed deeply. It pained Pierre to see him that way, so disgusted and disturbed. He'd been in the battle with the fiends though; he'd seen Bernard's head roll and Merlin's gut split open. If there was anyone who needed to understand this, to see Yvaine so bloody and beaten, it was him.

"Sit her up," he ordered. The next highest in command after Giane, a woman with bright red hair and shoulders to rival a man's, stepped forward and complied. Yvaine didn't make a sound or protest as the red-headed Elite propped her up. If not for the way her icy eyes rolled over him, Pierre might've thought her already dead.

"My dear king," she said slowly. "Have you come at last to dirty your own hands?"

Taking a breath to steady himself, Pierre lifted a finger to signal Roland stay put and walked toward the duchess.

"I want to know everything, Yvaine. Everything."

She chuckled. When her lips pulled back, blood laced her teeth and gums.

"All right, love. Shall I start at the beginning?"

The beginning, it seemed, started centuries ago.

Pierre thought it some cruel jest Yvaine thought amusing to tell. She spoke of the High Council of Eve, and of an immortal group called the Ageless or the Elder Bloods, insisting she'd been one of them and had the ability to control fiends. He'd listened and ordered his Elite scribe to record all of it, despite the look of skepticism the woman had given him. He was skeptical himself, but one glance at Roland and he knew he needed to see it through. Whoever those twins were—the strange, dark-haired individuals Roland had seen kill Bernard and Merlin—they'd not been entirely mortal.

"The Eveans were weak when the people of Abra'am brought war against them," Yvaine said. The element shackles binding her clinked against the floor. "They didn't understand war—they could hardly comprehend its intent. They fell the second a sword was placed at their throats.

"We in the High Council fought with one another on how to handle the invaders. We fell into two ideologies: those who felt it was not our place to interfere with the plights of mortals, and those who felt it was our obligation to protect them. Xia, the strongest voice in favor of aiding mankind, decided our quarrels were wasting countless lives. She broke our unity by persuading Alkane, the Guardian of the Shield, to call upon the Shield's power. He did, using the invincibility it granted to defeat Eve's opposition."

The duchess paused, her features twisting as she brought her head up. Blood from her wounds emerged where her cheek had rested against the wall. Her legs extended out in front of her, hands limp atop her lap.

"Alkane's actions had been forbidden under the oaths he'd taken as the Shield's Guardian. The punishment was death, but the High Council couldn't order such a sentence when the entire nation of Eve saw him as their savior. Ordering his death would lead to retaliation, and thus couldn't be considered. We were immortal, but not entirely invincible. An uprising from the nation could lead to our end, so we had to ensure we went about his sentence with caution."

Pierre held up a hand to silence her, needing to take it all in. The scribe used the moment to frantically catch up.

"So this Alkane," Roland said, stepping forward, "he used the Shield to protect Eve from Abra'am?"

Pierre lifted his head, not liking his son asking the questions.

"Yes," the duchess answered.

"And the High Council of the time—which you say you were a part of—they didn't approve of this action?"

"Correct."

"What verdict did your High Council come to for him?"

Yvaine smiled, showing her crimson grin.

"A member of our Council—Vahd'eel—ordered immediate reversal of Alkane's powers by way of the Amulet. It was a fair punishment, and when held to a vote, the majority of the Council agreed to it."

Vahd'eel. That was the name of the other prisoner Dravian was holding captive.

Folding his arms across his chest, Pierre decided Dravian would need to keep his captives held indefinitely. If they were still capable of doing what they'd done during the fiends' attacks, they couldn't afford to have them be freed.

"And did you?" Roland continued. "Reverse the Shield's power?"

Yvaine shook her head.

"No. Alkane refused his punishment."

"Is he still alive, then?"

"Yes. That's why my allies attacked Xenith. To get the Amulet."

A growl reverberated in Roland's throat. Pierre knew all of what'd happened the day of the attacks had been disturbing for his son, but the idea that someone had put their sights directly on Gwenivere and her Amulet made the battle all the more personal for him.

"Why weren't you after the Amulet with them?" Pierre asked, ending Roland's questioning. "Why did you come for the Dagger if you're supposedly immortal?"

"Immortal? Come now, Pierre, you've surely noticed me age over the years."

"You said yourself the Ageless were immortal," Roland countered. "And you said you were one of them. Are you now saying that's not true?"

"No, child, I'm saying that I'm not immortal *anymore*. Giving birth to Natalia robbed me of that."

Roland grunted, as if to say he didn't quite believe it.

"And what of Riverdee?" Pierre asked. "Why did your allies attack there?"

Yvaine shut her eyes.

"Vahd'eel has a personal vendetta. It doesn't matter to me."

He stared at her intently, wishing he had Dravian there to

tell him if she were lying. Even knowing her as long as he had, he couldn't tell.

She opened and shut her eyes again before slumping back against the wall. The red-headed Elite hurried over, checking Yvaine's pulse and opening her lids. A thick tension held in the room. The scribe's hurried writing ceased.

"She's alive, milord, but not by much. I'm sorry, I'm afraid we need to cease the interrogation."

Cursing, Pierre agreed. Roland opened his mouth as if to protest the decision but quickly shut it. As eager as he was for justice, he was smart enough to know they needed Yvaine alive if they were going to get more answers out of her. And, based on everything she'd told them so far, they would need a lot more of them.

Gwenivere and Prince Dietrich at the masquerade.

From the sketchbook of Elizabeth al'Murtagh

CHAPTER 44

ᴳWENIVERE

The masquerade had come. Shouts of merriment took the place of the mournful cries and prayers from the funeral march. The dark shades that had adorned every person were now substituted for an array of colors, some deep and lush, others bright and vibrant. Sequins and jewels shined from masks and gowns.

Gwenivere saw none of it. Through her masked eyes, she barely even saw the ground she walked on.

As much as she'd tried to move past the evil that had ambushed her city, there'd always been a reminder of what it had done. The moment she felt herself recovering from its lesions, she'd see where one of her favorite buildings had stood or overhear discussions of how to go about funding the city's repairs, and once more the cuts were opened.

Everyone was calling it the Attack of Fiends. It seemed too

recent to already have a name.

The funeral march had been a painful but beautiful moment for Abra'am, a time when centurial rivals had come together to respect and honor the fallen. It wouldn't last. Already arguments were beginning to come about that the attack was somehow a trap, or that Voradeen was poorly constructed for such a large gathering of nobles. Such accusations were thankfully frowned upon by the majority, but the mere fact they existed was disconcerting.

The gossip among the servants was far worse than among the royals. While most proclaimed Gwenivere a hero, it'd been brought to her attention by Becca that some believed her involved with whoever had led the attack. Dietrich Haroldson had, after all, allied with a dragon, and that same dragon had last been sighted with her, departing her balcony. Perhaps they'd been using the fiends but ended up losing control of them, thus having to fight the Behemoth themselves.

Becca had to pick up the glass Gwenivere had thrown at the wall when she'd relayed those rumors. She'd been her servant for years, though; she'd grabbed a broom before the glass had been thrown.

As for Dietrich, speculation of him and his dragon was a popular topic of discussion. Since being seen with him Gwenivere had been flooded with inquiries, both polite and unnecessarily accusatory, but she had nothing to tell her questioners except that she'd had an opportunity to help protect her people and she'd taken it. She didn't know Dietrich's whereabouts now, nor had she any affiliation with him before the attack. The latter was essentially true, as she didn't consider their encounter the one night in her chambers to be anything more than conversation. Nevertheless, she didn't know where he was. Whoever had come for him after they'd defeated the Behemoth had likely captured or killed him.

No. She didn't want to think like that.

He was alive. He had to be.

"The palace is very full," Garron said, stealing Gwenivere's focus. "It feels unsafe."

She looked to him lazily. Where most were intricately dressed, he was plain, and where most flaunted the finest of fabrics, he wore the simplest of elemental armor. He'd refused to don a mask, so his trimmed beard and strong features were easily visibly. It was almost comical how he managed to stand out by dressing as his usual self. She couldn't help smiling as he scowled at the crowded ballroom.

"What? What is it? What's wrong?"

She said nothing, only grabbing his arm and leaning her head against it. With all the commotion that'd surrounded her since the attack, he'd remained a constant calm.

"Would it be so strange if I just lived here with you forever?" she asked. "No husband, no children? Just you and I?"

"Yes, milady, I believe most everyone would find that strange."

Laughing, she patted his arm and lifted her head back up. She continued to cling to him, not wanting to let go as she gazed at the plethora of people nearby.

She didn't mind watching them—she enjoyed their different costumes and masks—yet the idea of engaging with them seemed a daunting task. She didn't know how to speak with them about their cultures or their countries, and even worse, she was unsure who she could speak with. How embarrassing it would be to walk up to the leader of another nation, babbling on about something only to discover he or she didn't speak Common.

Perhaps Garron would know; she could ask him. And if he didn't, then she could stand with him until someone approached her. That seemed a good idea. She was the one who they were supposed to win over after all, not the other way around. Let them do the work if they so desired her hand. She would just stay put with her knight until they did.

Her heart sputtered when she noticed Aden dancing with a group of small children. Maximus, more protective of her brother now than he'd ever been, loomed over the little gowns and vests that clumsily spun and stomped with what they thought were proper waltz steps.

The night after the Attack of Fiends, Gwenivere had stayed at Aden's side, brushing her hand across his hair and kissing his forehead until he'd fallen asleep. Already his youthful mind was getting over everything he'd seen, though his sleep was haunted by night terrors, and he'd had to admit to his servants from time to time, with great shame, that he needed new sheets. Those incidents were decreasing, something Gwenivere thanked the Creator for, and she thought that might be in part because his knight had survived.

She'd thought she'd lost Maximus that day—she'd been sure of it. Looking at him now, a boy in a bear's body, she could still feel the warmth of his blood on her hands, could still see his skin paling. When Aden had fallen asleep after the attacks, she'd pulled the knight aside and demanded to see his wounds and know how he'd healed. His cheeks had beamed red as he'd stripped off his shirt and showed his scars. *The Eastern prince, Dietrich Haroldson, used an elixir on me,* he'd told her. *It hurt immensely, but I'm grateful to him. And to you. If you hadn't tried to bind my wounds, I might not have lived for him to aid me.*

That had been her cue to redden. She'd insisted then that he put his shirt back on and returned to her brother's bedside, more sure than ever that Dietrich Haroldson wasn't the person some of the rumors were making him out to be.

"Your father mentioned you playing your harp for the guests earlier," Garron said. Gwenivere looked away from Aden and Maximus and looked to her knight, trying to determine if he was jesting. Not surprisingly, she couldn't tell.

"Are you being serious?"

"Yes. He said he thought it might be a good way to showcase your talents to your suitors."

She scoffed. She hadn't wanted to think about those matters, but the pressure of wedlock was as pressing as it had ever been. It was not unusual for a father to be concerned for his daughter, and Gwenivere couldn't really be mad with her own father's logic. He only wanted her to be safe and cared for. But Light, that didn't justify the suggestion of placing her on a platform for all to consider. The idea of it sickened her.

"I'm not a dog that rolls over to be pet. Go on, tell him I said that."

"I can't leave you unaccompanied. You'll have to tell him yourself."

"No, it's fine. He'll figure it out."

"If you insist."

Annoyed, Gwenivere went to rub her eyes, then remembered all the creams and shadows Becca had placed along her lids. She settled for readjusting her mask, a simple thing she hardly noticed was there, but grew annoyed at it too.

She needed some of the wine the servers were carrying around.

"Gwen, darling, is that you?" someone asked. Gwenivere cocked her head, recognizing the overly charismatic voice. She took a step away from Garron, her spirits lifting as she caught sight of who'd called.

"Vel!"

She beamed and hugged her cousin, who wore a pearled mask that bumped against her own. Her dress was tight around the waist and loose at the skirts, the length just short enough to reveal more pearls and jewels along her feet. The neckline was low, enough that she could rival Natalia Barie in scandal, but her face, round and dimpled, was far less conniving than the Mesidian duchess-heir. When she pulled away, she took Gwenivere's arms and looked her over with bright eyes.

"My goodness, Gwen, look at this figure. You're so lean—

so strong! You certainly grew into those gangly limbs of yours, wouldn't you agree . . ." she turned to Garron, forehead wrinkling. "What's your name again?"

"Garron Hillborne. And yes, she has grown since childhood."

Vel sneered, the expression visible even through her mask.

"Ah, yes, I remember you now. You're the big brute who is as dull as the Sadiyan desert is long. Go on, go join the rest of the armored statues along the walls. You'll feel more at home with them than with us interesting people."

"I will do no such thing," Garron answered, hovering behind Gwenivere. She kept her lips sealed, knowing it better to stay quiet until the standoff passed.

Vel puffed out her chest, defiant and revealing. "And why exactly won't you leave her with me? Do you think she's unsafe in my care? Do you think women are incapable of protecting one another? That we need some muscled man constantly looking after us?"

"No." Garron spoke through tightened lips. "I have trained Gwenivere for many years; I know how capable she is of protecting herself. Had she been trained by you, though, I'm sure she would be very good at other things."

Vel peered at the knight, nose crinkling.

"If you meant that as an insult, you failed. You implying I know how to use my body for more than just whacking sharp sticks at things—it's a compliment really. You make soldiers out of men. I make *men* out of men." She stopped, nudging Gwenivere out of the way and stepping closer to Garron. "If you ever let go of that pride and care to let me show you—"

"All right!" Gwenivere said, grabbing her cousin. "I think maybe we need some time to chat, just us girls!"

Garron lifted his arm to protest, his eyes no longer focused on the winking Vel, but Gwenivere waved him off dismissively.

"We'll only be a short while. I won't leave your sight, I promise."

Vel laughed as Gwenivere led them just barely out of Garron's earshot. He was still following a close distance behind but gave them space.

"My, my," Vel said, snatching wine from a nearby server. "That was fun."

Gwenivere shook her head, her cheeks no doubt as red as her knight's. She glared at her cousin.

"Oh please, Gwenie. I was only playing!"

"You two might have your differences, but you shouldn't say such things to him. It's embarrassing and degrading."

"Degrading? And it wasn't degrading that he was saying I've been with lots of men?"

"You have been with lots of men."

The woman stood still for a moment, glancing around at the people around her. Then she smiled coyly and took a sip of her wine.

"I really have."

Gwenivere tried to hold her composure, but Vel's wicked grin and batting eyes finally forced a laugh.

"That's the reason Garron doesn't like you and I spending so much time together. And my father, for that matter."

"Well I'm not the heir. I don't have to be good. You, though, you do have to be good. And I respect that. If you have been, that is . . . "

The princess glowered again, not liking the expectant stare Vel gave or the query she implied.

"I have been good, if you must know, though it's really not any of your business."

"Really? Even with Roland?"

"Yes, even with Roland!"

Gwenivere glanced back at Garron, then the other royals nearby, afraid their conversation would be overheard. Her romance with Roland was no secret, especially with other gossip-driven people like Vel, but it was not something anyone needed to hear details about. She leaned nearer to her cousin, the smell of her floral perfume almost overwhelming, and carried on in a hushed whisper.

"I haven't been with anyone, and I intend to keep it that way until I'm married. No insult to you, it's just what I believe is right for me."

Vel smiled and nodded, lacing her arm through Gwenivere's and tapping it gently.

"I'm happy for you for that. I wouldn't want my little cousin to be talked about the way people talk about me. But honestly, if I had the heir to Mesidia on one arm, and that tall, strong knight on the other—"

"It was almost endearing, Vel, almost."

The woman harrumphed in a very unladylike way. Then drank more wine.

"Say, speaking of men, do you know what's happened with the Sadiyan prince?"

"No!" Gwenivere answered, holding back a stomping foot. She blew air out of her cheeks and gave Vel an apologetic shrug. "I apologize, I've just been asked that a great lot. All I can tell you is he helped me when the earthquakes started, and then I helped him defeat the Behemoth. I haven't seen or heard from him since."

Vel's playful expression turned pondering. Behind her wine glass, Gwenivere thought there was a hint of something more.

"Do you know something? Have you heard from someone?"

"Gwen, darling, I don't know any more of the man's current whereabouts than you. All I can say is be careful—if you do see him. Supposedly others are out there who bear a striking resemblance to him."

Gwenivere fought back a shudder. Her cousin's tone was serious, and it was never serious.

"Enough with your gossip. If you know something, say it."

Vel finished her glass and held it to her chest, surveying

Gwenivere calmly.

"Do you remember at the Peace Gathering, the way the one Prianthian brother—Nicolai—had that little outburst? He claimed the assassin who killed his brother might be in the Assembly Hall."

"I remember."

"Well." Vel leaned in, so close her breath grazed Gwenivere's skin. "I was naturally concerned, what with you and Aden being heirs, so I looked into it. According to them, the assassination attempt was on Alanna, the one in line to the Prianthian throne, but her brother Pasha saved her and was killed in her stead. One of the assassins escaped, but the other they captured and . . . interrogated."

Tortured, Gwenivere thought. After how the Prianthians had spoken of Sadie, as if the country was still enslaved to them, she didn't expect much else. Barbaric people took barbaric measures.

"They gleaned quite a lot from it," Vel continued. "Though how much is fabrication and how much is truth is hard to say. But they're claiming the Redeemers were responsible for their brother's death. The assassin who'd escaped was a shapeshifter, a Sc'ahl, known as Victor of the Black. If you can believe such things."

Vel looked into her glass, seeming disappointed that it was now empty. Her long nails clinked against its edge.

Gwenivere stood quietly, taking in what her cousin had said. Shapeshifters were legends, nightmares older siblings told the younger ones to scare them into giving up sweets. They weren't real; someone had invented the idea of them long ago. Even the anthology *Fire and Fiends*, the Holy Book for fiend hunters and analysts, noted that Sc'ahl were likely just stories. After what'd happened with the fiends, though, after taking down a Behemoth from the Age of Old atop the back of a dragon, perhaps there was some validity to the claim.

"So this Victor," Gwenivere started, "do you think he's acting as Dietrich now?"

Vel shrugged. "Who's to say? But that's what the Prianthians claim. They say Victor was planning to use a poison a Redeemer girl named Brelain had concocted and do it in Dietrich's form. The Redeemers believe all nations west of the Dividing Wall are filled with heathens, and that we've tainted Sadie and Prianthia. So, by having their assassin kill people pretending to be Dietrich—"

"Then we'd be forced to cut ties with them."

Vel nodded.

"That's absurd! I thought the Redeemers were just a small group. A cult. Are they really capable of something like this?"

She eyed the empty glass Vel held, suddenly fearful. Her cousin caught her stare and rubbed her arm consolingly.

"Don't worry, dear, the Prianthians made sure to tell your father all of this. The food tasters have been surveying the ingredients in everything for days, and no one has turned up sick."

Gwenivere sighed, relieved. Even if that was true, though, it still seemed quite the risk to keep such a rumor quiet. Then again, others were claiming her responsible for the Attack of Fiends, and there she stood, a free woman among them. Perhaps her cousin's words were just that—words.

If she did see Dietrich again, she'd have to warn him. It was the least she could do after all he'd risked for them.

"If you don't mind, Vel, I'd like to change the subject." Gwenivere linked arms with her cousin and walked her to the window, pulling her out of earshot from the other nobles. Garron followed in the distance.

Gwenivere's exchange with the Yendorian man Edifor the day outside her chambers continued to worry her, even if it hadn't been much of a concern as of late. It was still troubling, though, the things he'd implied and the hints he'd made.

Perhaps the conclusion then is not that Mesidia needn't have a Yendorian on the throne, but that it needn't have a Victorian.

What had he meant? She knew Mesidia's capital Stonewall had been attacked as well, but that thankfully Roland and his family had lived and Yvaine had been captured. Despite that, it seemed Edifor might have known of the attack, or had been hoping to somehow put Yvaine or Natalia on the throne over Roland. Gwenivere couldn't make that accusation of course. Not when the only proof she had was an awkward conversation with him outside her bedroom.

"Edifor of Yendor," Gwenivere said. "What do you know of him?"

Vel's forehead wrinkled.

"Not much, to be honest. He's normally a quiet man. Yendor itself doesn't have the most convenient place on the map, so their economy relies a great deal on trade routes between Prianthia and the Arctic. Which, not surprisingly, he seems to be speaking with the representatives of those nations the most. Although . . . " Vel's wrinkles deepened. "Come to think of it, I did see him speaking to the Commandant of Theatia recently."

"Theatia?" Gwenivere pinched her nose. Maybe her conversation with Edifor hadn't meant anything, and he was simply a man who wanted to converse with others. Theatia wasn't even a significant political nation.

She let go of her nose and waved her suspicions away. No need to spread more rumors unjustly. She'd be better to let the odd conversation go.

"Perhaps you should dance with him," Vel suggested. "They say you can tell a lot from dancing with a man."

Gwenivere narrowed her eyes.

"For one"—Vel continued, holding up a finger—"you can see if he has good hygiene and if he bathes often. Two, you can tell whether his breath will be atrocious or somewhat bearable. Which is, of course, good to know for many reasons. Most importantly, though, you can tell how well he moves his body."

"Vel." Gwenivere could feel her cheeks flushing. "Those things have nothing to do with anything."

"Maybe not for you. Men will ask you to dance tonight, doll, but it will be me they ask to bed. If you aren't going to make good use of that information, at least pass it on to me."

Gwenivere snorted and released her cousin's arm. Though Vel jested, Gwenivere couldn't very well stand by her all night. It was her obligation to speak to her suitors, and her father would be upset if he knew she chose to speak only with Garron and her cousin. He was still giving her the freedom to pick her own spouse, which was more freedom than other heirs had. She planned to make good use of it while she still had the chance.

She kissed her cousin on the cheek just below her mask, whispered, "I love you," then made her way toward a handsome group of nobles.

Please, Light, have mercy.

Hours of dancing had gone by. Gwenivere politely declined the next man who asked her to waltz, looking instead for a server with water.

"In a minute, perhaps," she managed to the suitor. "I just need a moment to catch my breath."

The man seemed let down, but Gwenivere didn't find that particularly concerning. If being declined a dance was so upsetting, even after being promised one only the slightest bit later, then she'd never be able to handle him as a spouse.

Light, where is there some water? She dabbed at her neck, feeling the chain of the Amulet resting just beneath the lace of her gown. Although she was relieved she wasn't as exposed as most of the other noblewomen, she envied them for the coolness their chests must feel. She couldn't wait until the masquerade was over, when she could at last retire to her chambers and be rid of her warm clothes.

"Are you all right? You look faint."

She ignored the query, at last finding a server whose tray didn't contain wine. She snatched two glasses from him and drank all of one and some of the other before turning to respond.

"Yes, really, I—"

She froze, breath catching.

The man standing next to her was Dietrich Haroldson.

He bowed dramatically, then stood tall and smiled. His teeth were a stark white against his skin, and his face was covered by the same plain mask she'd first seen him with. He was elegantly garbed, with black sleeves covering any of the possible burns left on his arms and a vest pressing his shirt's collar down to hide any burns there. Surprisingly, he looked perfectly well.

Gwenivere wasn't sure how to proceed, both pleased and shocked at his presence—and, if she was being honest, a bit apprehensive after hearing Vel's talk of shapeshifters. Still, the smile he gave was knowing, familiar, the kind of smile someone gave a friend. She'd only seen him twice, but after all he'd done, after almost dying to save her capital, she felt more connected to him than most of the nobles in the room.

"Would you like me to get you more?" he asked, gesturing toward her glasses. She shook her head, the motion no longer making her queasy, and set the two cups down on the nearest table.

"Everyone has been looking for you," she said. It was a dull thing to say, she knew, but she wasn't sure how else to start.

"Have you been?" he asked, grin widening. She glared at him, angry that he felt he could act so casually after disappearing from such a monumental event.

"I'm not some foolish girl you can charm your way around. And, more importantly, you can't just abandon a nation when it lies in partial ruin. Everyone is seeking truth, looking to understand what in the Light's name happened, and the one man who saved us, who might possibly have some answers, is nowhere to be found. So why, why now, do you suddenly show up?"

Dietrich stood silent. His lips parted as though to find an explanation, but whatever he was considering was lost. He pulled his lips closed, the music around them subsiding from its current song.

"Princess," someone called. "Are you feeling better? Shall we have that dance now?"

Gwenivere broke her gaze from Dietrich and turned toward the man she'd declined earlier. Before she could answer, Dietrich walked forward, grabbed her hand, and waved the suitor away.

"I apologize, good sir, but I'm afraid I must steal her away first."

The man began to protest, upset at having been robbed of his chance again, but Gwenivere didn't dispute the prince as he guided her to the ballroom floor.

The music started once more, and the melodies of the strings resonated beautifully off the tiles and walls. The Creator loved music; that was what Queen Rose had always told Gwenivere. She'd insisted music was the only thing besides prayer that connected people to the divine. Musicians were like the Light's servants, working their whole lives to perfect the sounds of purity, pulling colorful notes from their instruments and sharing them with the rest of humankind. The princess felt it, heard it echo through her as the new piece began. The powerful energy seeped through her fingers as they joined Dietrich's.

With faultless unity, the ballroom began to move to the

sounds, their bodies responding elegantly to vibrations that pulsed through the hair of the performers' bows. As a whole, the guidance of men's hands and the sweeping of women's feet created an illustrious vision, a whirl of striking colors that seemed to float across the room. Gwenivere hadn't felt it with the other men, hadn't truly heard the wondrous harmonies the music created. Something in Dietrich's touch made it come to life.

The dance wasn't sensual. It wasn't cause for provoking thought or unsettling nerve. It was just what it was: tranquil, invigorating, full of breath yet breathless all the same. It was light, as though they were tiptoeing on air or floating on the currents of a river. It was heavy, when the downbeats came, their feet feeling as connected to the ground as if it were nothing but natural earth and soil. Within their joined hands was an energy, the pulsing of internal lights.

It was the *auroras*, Gwenivere realized, inside her and him and everyone around them. They weren't being *called* upon, they were just moving. They were dancing. They, like the notes around them, were connecting and transcending to something beyond.

And, just as the music began and their feet trotted their graceful path, they stopped, and the magnificent sensation was over.

Gwenivere looked to Dietrich, letting him go as the dancers around them began to exchange partners. He swallowed and exhaled lightly.

"There is much I need to discuss with you," he said. "And I'm afraid your eager friend will be robbing me of my chance."

Gwenivere followed his gaze to the approaching suitor.

"Meet me in my chambers," she whispered, "while the night still covers the sky and the dawn has yet to come."

Dietrich nodded, then gently pulled her toward him and kissed her forehead. She didn't reject his touch, didn't tense or try to pull away. Instead she welcomed it, accepting every instant his lips met her skin.

Despite there being so many people around, it felt as if it were just the two of them there. It wasn't of course, and kissing her forehead was inappropriate for anyone to do but perhaps her own family. The pudgy-faced suitor, who now stood beside them, had his mouth open and his hand held to his chest.

"Here she is," Dietrich said, backing away with a grin. He nodded to the nobleman and winked as he held up Gwenivere's hand.

"I shall see you in your chambers, Princess. Until then."

Gwenivere said nothing as Dietrich bowed and walked away. She looked to the suitor, trying to act as though she were deeply upset, but it was hard when the man appeared so overly stunned.

"He's foreign," she said, forcing a laugh. The suitor's expression shifted from shocked to offended, his hand thumping roughly against his chest.

"*I'm* foreign!"

"Light above, do you want to dance or not?"

The man shook his head theatrically, but grumpily took her hand and waist. Once the music returned, he guided her along, clumsily but sufficiently, then passed her off to the next suitor when the song was done.

The *auroras* didn't dance again.

I've always been curious about the Dagger. If called *upon, it's said it grants immortality. Does this mean it will cure ailments? It must. In order to be immortal, one must constantly be in a state of healing.*

Forgive me for such inappropriate musings. As someone who specializes in elixirs, the concept of eternal healing fascinates me.

From a letter between Abaddon Haroldson and Dorian Cliffborne

CHAPTER 45

GWENIVERE

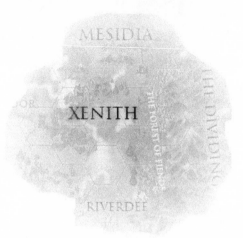

Gwenivere paced about her chambers, the sounds of the masquerade still echoing outside her walls. It would last throughout the night and well into the morning, the guests growing less and less competent as the hours went on. It'd been difficult pretending to be interested in any of the suitors while queries of Dietrich went unanswered, but she'd not been allowed to leave. With the masquerade now representing more than just peacetime and alliances, her father would've been displeased if she'd retired early.

After countless dances and suitors, though, and a decent amount of wine, it'd eventually ended. Now she simply grew impatient in her chambers, waiting for Dietrich to arrive.

Despite all the gossip, she knew the rumors about him weren't true. Not the ones about him controlling the fiends at least. She'd felt it, the desire for the Amulet; there'd been someone, something, that wanted it, but it hadn't been Dietrich. But what did *he* want? What reason did he have to interest himself with her? She knew he wasn't responsible for the fiends' attack, but that didn't mean he wasn't still dangerous. He was the Assassin Prince.

Suddenly anxious, Gwenivere wiped the sweat from her forehead. Her gown was hot, and tight, and her head was starting to spin. She attempted to undo its back, wanting to change into something lighter, but her hands were clammy and her muscles shaky. Steadying herself, she *called* a knife and split the dress open, then shimmied out of it and tossed it to the ground. She *vanished* the knife and took a deep breath, savoring the feeling of air against her skin.

"Well this is not how I expected to find you."

Gwenivere spun around, the Sadiyan prince veiled in the shadows near her balcony's windows. She yelped, hurriedly lifting the dress back up.

"How long have you been here?" she demanded, hands trembling. She still had her undergarments on, and her Amulet, but that was far more than any other man had seen. The prince looked to the floor, a grin on his face as he held his hands up.

"I only just arrived," he assured, tapping against the window's glass. "It was just coincidental timing."

"It was bad timing!"

"I'll agree to disagree."

Gwenivere sneered and attempted to put her dress back on. The feat proved impossible, though, especially with the rips she'd made. She felt helpless.

"Turn around or I'll bring back the burns your elixir cured."

Dietrich chuckled and walked to the wardrobe by her vanity, bringing back her lace robe. She looked at him suspiciously as he held it out.

"Thank you," she managed, still eyeing him.

He nodded and turned around for her to make the switch.

"Close your eyes, too. There's a mirror over there."

"They're closed."

She stood for a moment, unsure whether he was telling the truth. He had, after all, not been the slightest bit hesitant to kiss her temple in front of everyone at the masquerade. It wouldn't hurt to make sure she lined herself up with where he stood, just in case he thought it clever to peek.

"All right, I'm decent."

He turned around, gesturing toward the chairs in her study. She nodded and walked to them, her bare feet making more noise than his covered ones. She glanced over to the light coming through her chamber door, noting the shadow of two knights standing guard outside it. With as swift and silent as Dietrich was, she doubted they would be able to save her if the meeting was not to his liking.

"What do you want?" she asked.

Dietrich looked up with wide eyes, his bottom barely having met his chair. When he didn't say anything, she cursed, then held her hands out demandingly.

"You were all charms earlier this evening. Regain some confidence and spit it out."

He squirmed in his seat, looked behind him, and turned back to face her.

"I want to give you a way to marry Prince Roland. I know you care for him, and my mother is dying, and I need the Dagger to keep her alive."

Gwenivere blinked. She sat perfectly still, arms heavy against her chair.

"I see." She leaned forward, crossing one leg atop the other and brushing a strand of hair behind her ear. "I'm afraid you've come to the wrong person. Roland isn't here, and even if he was, he wouldn't turn over his birthright for my hand."

"Even if you had good reason to ask him?"

"Losing your mother isn't good reason!"

Dietrich rose from his chair and held his hand against her mouth, green eyes glaring. The two shadows outside the chamber door continued to hold still, the masquerade's gaiety and glee covering the outburst. When it was obvious they hadn't heard, Dietrich slowly brought his hand down.

"I'm sorry," Gwenivere said. "I lost my mother nearly six springs ago. Forgive me if I don't seem sympathetic to your need."

"I wouldn't ask such a thing if it was so simple a matter." He returned to his seat but didn't sit, instead standing at its side. "Do you know much of Sadie? Of its history?"

"I know some. I know it was enslaved by Prianthia, and that your father freed it."

"And its recent history? Do you know of it? Of the Redeemers?"

She shook her head. She thought she'd known some, but after her discussion with Vel, she likely didn't know much at all.

"Not a lot, unfortunately. That's the most recent knowledge I have."

"It's more than many, I'm sure." Dietrich chanced at a smile. "I know it's unlikely you'll agree to any ploy for the Dagger, but if you'll allow it, I would appreciate the opportunity to speak on my country's behalf."

Gwenivere forced a smile of her own. She bowed her head and motioned him to speak.

"Thank you." He swallowed, shoulders tense and stance rigid. She wanted to offer him a chair again, to give him some kind of comfort, but he leaned against the wall, clearing his throat.

"My home hasn't thrived the way yours has. Unrest here has come from disputes over resources and lands and rivers. Barbarians have come about, as is inevitable for any nation, but allies have always come to aid you. There is unity in your struggles, present in the battle I fought in against the fiends, and while power may shift, the lives of your people are still fortunate.

"The same cannot be said for Sadie. We do not live in illustrious buildings but rather the ruins of what our nation was before enslavement. We have nothing: no abundance of crop, no inflow of goods, no academies or libraries. We only have the few things freedom has allowed us. My father has dedicated his life to making Sadie better, but we have enemies, and ones that wish to take away our chances at prosperity.

"The Prianthians have continuously tried to enslave us. Numerous attempts have been made on my family's lives, and they continue to come, though not as often as they did before.

"Where they falter, the Redeemers rise. They hate my father, and the Prianthian royal family, and they seek to take over our lands and ally the East.

"The first time my father traveled here, when I was barely more than a boy, the Redeemers sent assassins after my mother and brother and me. Their threats haven't ceased since. Now my father loses fervor as my mother grows sicker. My brother fights to keep her alive, but he has yet to find her a cure. If she passes, my father's spirit will falter and his leadership will weaken. My brother and I would do what we could to aid him, but I don't believe either of us are ready to take his throne . . ."

Dietrich trailed off at the mention of heirdom. Gwenivere knew that fear, that worry, having heard it numerous times from Roland. He'd at least grown up near royalty, though, and while he'd not initially been groomed for the throne, he'd learned from being near Dorian and Pierre. What would it be like for Dietrich, spending so much time among the peasants, to then be asked to rule them?

He started to speak again, but Gwenivere held up a hand.

"I am a Guardian," she said. "I want to save your nation, to restore balance to you, but I could never give up my responsibilities to my nation, and I'm not sure Roland could either. What if, rather than risking his refusal, you instead asked for my hand?"

Dietrich squinted at her, then stood from his place against

the wall and pointed between them.

"Your hand? You, the heir to Xenith?"

"Yes. I think it makes sense. You'd inherit my wealth and my allies, and you'd gain better access to rivers across the Far West." She rose from her seat, stepping toward him. "You wouldn't have to fear the Prianthians either, as their armies are far inferior to ours."

"What about the terrain?" he asked. "Even if your armies are strong, there's still the issue of getting them across the Dividing Wall and through the desert. And if they're there fighting my enemies, who's to keep your enemies from attacking here?"

Gwenivere opened her mouth to reply, but quickly closed it. She didn't have an answer.

"And what about the Redeemers?" he continued. "Have you ever known what it is to be hunted? To constantly fear for your family? I'd welcome you as my wife, but you love your father and brother dearly, as shown by how you fought against the fiends. Could you live with yourself, knowing you'd put them in danger?"

The question hung in the air, thick and palpable. Gwenivere felt it tightening against her heart. Her *auroras* grew dimmer, less willing to be *called*, dissuaded at the very thought of her family threatened.

"No," she admitted shamefully. "But you saved my home, and my people. For that you deserve my aid."

She turned to her desk and reached for the pen and parchment in its corner.

Gwenivere walked Dietrich to her balcony, surprised to see his dragon outside. She pondered how no one had seen her fly to the balcony but let the thought pass, more concerned with the letter to Roland now tucked in Dietrich's vest.

"Before you go"—she started, opening the balcony's door—"how did you escape those who sought my Amulet?"

Dietrich shrugged and shook his head. "I'm . . . I'm not sure. They came to Seera and me, but they didn't harm us. They said they couldn't."

Couldn't harm you? Gwenivere thought, wrinkling her nose. That didn't make sense. They'd somehow sent fiends after the entire capital of Xenith but couldn't cause harm to one more man and fiend?

There was no use pushing the issue. If Dietrich didn't know he didn't know. If he did know and was choosing not to tell her then she wasn't sure she could do anything about that.

"All right, well I'm grateful they didn't harm you. I rather fancy you alive."

He smiled at that, though it was more smug than humble, as though he was accustomed to women being fond of him.

It made her wish she could take the words back.

"Oh! One more thing." She followed him out onto her balcony, wrapping her arms around herself as the chill of night seeped through her lace robe. "You should know there were rumors of a man named Victor planning to assassinate someone disguised as you. The Prianthians told my father he was going to use a poison a woman named Brelain had given him to kill westerners during the masquerade." She paused, fearful of the sudden stillness in Dietrich's frame.

"Do you know them? Have you heard of them before?"

His jaw twitched.

"I've only ever heard of Victor, but Brelain . . . Thank you, Gwenivere, for telling me. And for everything else. If the Light exists, I hope it illumines your path."

She gave him a hesitant smile, wishing she could console him.

"And I hope it illumines yours."

She watched him go to his dragon, wondering if it was the last time their paths would cross. With a quick prayer, and a twisting feeling in her gut, she closed her door and listened to the dragon's wings. When there was nothing left but the sounds of the masquerade, she locked her door's latch, walked to her vanity, and examined the glass rose Dietrich had gifted her the night they'd met, the one he'd tried to use to insist he didn't mean her harm.

The burn marks from her fingers, from when she'd unintentionally *called* fire at his presence in her chambers, still warped its stem.

Eyes like the sky on a dreary day
Soul like a body left to decay
No auroras come
Animal, not man
Dravian Valcor
Kills again, kills again

Mesidian nursery rhyme

Chapter 46

DRAVIAN

Something was wrong.

Dravian Valcor, leader of the Elite, could feel when things were amiss. He could feel a person's lies, or their shame, and he could feel when someone was innocent or guilty. It was a gift in his king's eyes.

It was a curse in his own.

In his camp, on the outskirts of the Forest of Fiends, men and women practiced *calling* weapons and elements. His Elite never stopped honing their skills, and the Attack of Fiends hadn't disrupted their daily practices. The only ones who didn't partake were those who had been wounded, of which Dravian felt the need to occupy himself with now. He needed the distraction, as his prisoners weren't the kind of people he'd ever encountered before.

The distraction was lasting too long, though. Rellor Bordinsua, his second in command, still hadn't returned from questioning X'odia.

Dravian gave his wounded soldiers words of encouragement before heading back to the shack X'odia was being kept in. The other prisoner—Vahd'eel—was being kept apart from her, currently tied up against a tree in the camp.

A woman with glowing eyes, Dravian thought, recalling the description Pierre had sent him. The message had come just after the Attack of Fiends, and in it Pierre had informed him of Prince Roland's encounter with the people Duke Bernard had warned them of. Roland had managed to escape with a few burns and wounds, along with a badly injured shoulder, but was otherwise fine.

His guardsman Merlin, though . . .

Roland described the woman as tall, with dark hair, the message had read. *And pale.*

Pale. That was the only part of the description that didn't match X'odia's appearance. She had dark skin, not quite the shade of those from the Arctic, but darker than the Prianthians and Sadiyans. Aside from that, the description matched her perfectly.

If her eyes glowed from time to time, she could have other abilities. It didn't seem likely that she could change her flesh, but what did he know? Some of his soldiers were gossiping about a shapeshifter, a man who'd supposedly killed Pasha of Prianthia. The rumor had come from the Peace Gathering held in Xenith, the same day as the Attack of Fiends.

None of it added up. Or rather, all of it added up, and pointed directly at the young woman, X'odia, that Dravian held captive.

"Soldiers," Dravian said, calling to the Elite he approached. The two, a man and a woman, immediately stood up taller.

"Sir!" they said, lifting their hands in salute. Behind them, where the small, isolated shack stood, Rellor's laughter rang.

"What's been happening?" Dravian demanded. "I ordered you to come to me when Rellor had retrieved more information from our captive."

The soldiers glanced at each other, neither seeming sure who should answer.

"He's been in there the whole time," the woman said.

"And he never told us if he'd found anything out," the man added.

Dravian pulled his fingers into fists. He must have worn a scowl, too, as both the Elite shifted uncomfortably.

"What have you heard then? Surely you heard something—I can hear Rellor laughing from here."

"Nothing, sir!" the man answered hurriedly. "That's all we've heard!"

Dravian looked to the woman, expecting her to provide elaboration.

She only nodded.

"Return to your post," Dravian ordered. He pushed past them and made his way for the shack, panic jolting through his bones.

He didn't knock as he came up. He didn't call out to let Rellor know he was entering. He stormed through the shack's entrance, *auroras* at the ready, and met Rellor's feral eyes.

He was crouched, like a wolf with its prey, over X'odia's still body.

"You were meant to question her, not kill her!" Dravian shouted. He yanked Rellor up and shoved him against the wall. The man's tunic was covered in blood, the smell of it coppery and the air thick. Dravian ground his teeth, cursing, and rushed over to their motionless captive.

Her features were hardly recognizable. Her dark skin was bruised and discolored, her hair sticky from blood.

How had the two outside not heard her cry out in pain? How had they not heard her say anything?

Rellor must have threatened her. Or done something to her that made screaming too painful.

"She murdered people," Rellor said, stretching. "I did what you should've the second we captured her."

Dravian set X'odia down, then stalked toward his subordinate.

"Come now, Dravian," Rellor said, backing away and holding up his palms. "You know you won't be able to harm her. Look at her. Look! She's too young, too pretty, too interesting." He grinned, his eyes bloodshot. "It'll be me who breaks her."

He didn't look at Dravian as he said the words. He stared at X'odia, lips curling.

Dravian ordered him to leave. He did, without protest, his stroll too cheery for the act he'd committed.

Dravian locked his attention back on X'odia. Her clothes were bloodier than when they'd first come across her during the fiends' invasion. Cuts and gashes ran along her body, blood dripping from them and into the sand. He checked her neck for a pulse, relieved to find there still was one.

"Let's hope you were telling the truth," he said, pulling the key to X'odia's element shackles from his tunic pocket. She'd said she could heal, when the shackles weren't on. He slipped the key into the lock, twisted, and released them from her wrists.

As soon as the chains fell, she writhed. She bent back sharply, gasped, and burst her swollen eyes open.

Dravian could feel every muscle in her body tighten. Her bare feet extended out, and her fingers squeezed around his arms. The pressure of them was startling, but more startling was how her wounds began to vanish. The openings Rellor's knife had made closed, the purple marks on her arms and face replaced by the smooth, healthy color of her skin.

She breathed quickly and heavily, the last of her wounds

closing shut. Her eyes, swirling from one color to the next, stared blankly. Dravian's own were watery from not having blinked, so he closed them for a moment, letting out a breath.

Shakily, X'odia pushed herself away. She met Dravian's stare before letting her fingers slip away from his arms. Leaning over, she groaned lightly and reached for her shackles.

"What're you doing?" he asked. He lashed out and snatched her wrist, thinking she might try to put the shackles on him.

"You'll put them back on me, won't you? I might as well do it myself."

He grunted. "Why wouldn't you try to fight me? If you're as strong as you say, why wouldn't you try to kill me?"

"I told you: I won't hurt anyone."

Dravian released her, watching as she sat up on her knees. Rips were everywhere in her skirts, some small, some large, all soaked red.

"You're doing what you must, to protect a people you cherish," she continued. "My freedom will come in the afterlife. I'm not willing to risk such peace for the temporary freedom killing all of you would bring."

With that, she slid her wrists back into the element shackles and buckled them shut.

Dravian stood afar from his camp. He was still too enraged at Rellor and disturbed by X'odia's compliance to make his presence known. His soldiers sat calmly around a campfire, some grooming the horses and feeding the hounds, others sitting quietly among one another. They all hated making camp in the forest, especially the Forest of Fiends, but Dravian had decided it was too dangerous to keep the two main prisoners in Riverdee's city. He'd ordered his fourth in command, Odin Iceborne, to stay there, help rebuild the homes and shops that'd been destroyed, and try to glean insight from the Evean sailors they'd captured. There'd been the one, with braided hair, who had shouted that X'odia was innocent before they'd bound her.

Let her go! he'd screamed, *let her go!*

Dravian folded his arms across his chest and spat. He didn't like thinking of the man, a boy really, or any of the other Evean sailors. Eveans were a peaceful people, and he'd only heard truth in the man's voice. He'd almost thought to free X'odia then on instinct alone, his instincts rarely wrong, but too many feared the frail woman with the glowing eyes. Then the reports came in from Pierre and Roland, reports that Merlin had been killed.

Ah, my friend, why did you have to die?

Looking back to the camp, Dravian forced himself to watch Rellor. He sat among the other soldiers, head against a log and feet out in front of him. Most soldiers were sickened at the idea of hurting people, but Rellor relished it, embraced every instant he was able to crush the bones and spill the blood of those who threatened the good of the world. He loved when their prisoners were the ones no one else wanted to touch.

What a perfect prey this X'odia had made for him.

"How was she?" someone asked Rellor. It was the other prisoner, Vahd'eel, who sat with a smile on his face.

"I didn't force myself on her," Rellor answered. "If that's what you mean."

Vahd'eel's smile widened, the orange blaze of the fire reflecting in his eyes.

"She heals," he said. "Even if she's been with a man, it wouldn't matter. Every time for her would feel like the first. Every time would bring her pain. Is that not your dream, Rellor?"

As he spoke, another soldier rushed forward. With his

element resistant gloves, he picked up a stone from the fire and held it to Vahd'eel's cheek. Vahd'eel grimaced, his face contorted with pain, but the only sound that escaped his lips was laughter. The soldier threw the stone back into the fire, shoulders heaving.

Dravian wondered if he should finally step in, make himself known, but he stayed back. The soldier, Markeem, was his third in command, and he didn't feel like reprimanding him. Especially when he was doing what he himself had wanted to do for days.

"Calm down, Markeem!" Rellor said, lacing his fingers atop his chest. "It was just a bit of jesting."

Markeem fumed. Even if he'd wanted to, he wouldn't be able to reply. He was mute.

"Markeem," Dravian called, at last standing tall and walking through the camp. Markeem stood at attention, loyally waiting for whatever order was commanded. As Dravian walked toward him, his eyes flickered to Vahd'eel's burned face, the shape of the stone embedded in his cheek.

Vahd'eel had already admitted his guilt. He'd confessed, without prompting, that he'd been the one to send fiends after the people of Riverdee.

Dravian had to keep from smiling as he saw his burn up close.

"What happened here?" he asked, feigning ignorance. Markeem stepped forward and pointed to the fire, then to Vahd'eel, then back at himself.

"Come now, Dravian," Rellor laughed. "You know he can't answer."

Markeem looked to the ground. Dravian scowled and took the mute man by the shoulder, walking him away from Vahd'eel and the camp. Rellor sprung to his feet and followed behind, despite the glares Dravian shot him, until all three of them were out of the camp's earshot.

"Any word from Pierre?" Dravian asked. Markeem headed to a pack horse and brought back a crinkled envelope. Dravian opened it, turning slightly to make sure Rellor couldn't read it over his shoulder.

I don't care if you think the girl innocent, or if you have doubts of her guilt. You say her eyes glowed and she was taken by a vision? Then keep her bound, and keep the interrogations going. Don't come home with either of them. Once you've beaten every last bit of truth from them, kill them, and leave their corpses for the fiends. Their auroras *don't deserve to drift.*

Pierre Laighless

Dravian finished reading the message and placed it in his pocket. Markeem looked up expectantly. He had a wife back in Mesidia, a pregnant wife, and when this mission was over, he was planning to leave the Elite.

"I'm sorry," Dravian told him, "but it looks like we're going to be here for a while."

He lifted his arm and patted the young man comfortingly. Markeem nodded, but his shoulders sank beneath his blue cloak. Next to him, Rellor looked relieved.

Glowing-eyed woman

There were rumors during the masquerade that two individuals were captured in Riverdee. It's believed they're the ones who caused the attacks there. People say the woman prisoner has eyes that glow.

I pray it isn't sinful to be curious of what such a woman looks like. I just couldn't resist trying to depict her.

From the sketchbook of Elizabeth al'Murtagh

CHAPTER 47

X'ODIA

X'odia rolled over, her muscles stiff and her lids weary. She inhaled, grimacing slightly as she sat upright. The night was beginning to remain for longer now, the sun seeming to take its time bringing the light of morning.

That didn't seem to keep the Inquisitor from his routine.

"Who is Alkane?" he asked. By the firm tone of his voice, it seemed it wasn't the first time he'd asked the question.

X'odia looked up at him, nervous. He'd come to her daily since Rellor had tortured her, and he'd always come with questions. To her surprise, he hadn't struck her or harmed her, and he hadn't been overly forceful with his questions. Still, she didn't want to test her luck. He was still a dangerous man, and she was still his prisoner.

Thankfully, though, he'd not let Rellor back.

She swatted away the flies that buzzed around her, which

seemed to take the blood along her clothes as signs of death. Dravian leaned down beside her, gently grabbing her arms and helping her over to the bench by the window. It was a kind act, but its destination dismissed any hopes of sympathy.

"Who is Alkane?" he asked again.

X'odia's stomach turned at the sound of her father's name. She didn't know how Dravian had heard it. Her father's existence was only known to her and the people of the High Council. And, she realized, the other prisoner, the one she'd heard them call Vahd'eel.

"The Keeper of the Shield," she answered. "He's a hero in Eve. It's said he saved Eve with the Shield's power, used it to defeat our enemies when war came to our shores."

Dravian's expression didn't change as he took in her words. He looked down at his hands, casually rolling up the sleeves of his shirt until they rested above his forearms.

X'odia's mouth went dry. That seemed something a brute would do if he didn't want to get his clothes bloody.

He's not a bad man, she told herself. *He only follows the orders of his king.*

It was a lie, but it was one she had to tell herself. She'd told herself many since her beating at Rellor's hands.

"What else do you know of him?" Dravian asked, folding his arms over his chest. "You must know more than stories."

"Yes, I do," she said, licking her lips. "Have you . . . have you heard of Neveah? The City in the Sky?"

Dravian nodded.

"It exists. And many of my people believe that it's because of him. They believe years of the Shield's power have made his elements strong, and that it's given him the ability to cast our capital where no threat could ever come."

"Then do they believe he's still alive? Your capital still rests in the sky, doesn't it?"

"It does, yes. And some Eveans believe he still lives, but

many believe it is the will of the Creator that keeps our city in the sky."

"And what do you believe?"

X'odia tilted her head, surprised. Her palms were growing wet, but she kept herself from wiping them on her skirts.

"There is something in Eve called Knowledge—an idea, or a concept, rather, that people possess. The more Knowledge one has, the more he or she must guard it, protect it from being placed in the wrong hands. Knowledge, to some extent, is as powerful as the Artifacts the Guardians have been entrusted. More powerful, some believe.

"I, in the visions the Creator gives me, have gained much of this Knowledge, not by any choice of my own, but by fate. So I have a more informed perspective than most others."

Dravian sat still, eyes drifting from X'odia to the view outside her window. His shoulders rose and fell with steady breaths, his dark eyes surveying the landscape with a cold indifference.

X'odia's own shoulders eased as he let the silence linger. She was pushing her luck, dodging questions like this, but she didn't have a choice. If she willingly gave up her Knowledge, especially Knowledge that didn't pertain to keeping Dravian's people safe, she could never forgive herself. She closed her eyes, listening to the ocean's waves outside, and tried to steady her nerves.

There was a strange sensation then, in the way her body began to fall into synchrony with the sea. It was as though she'd been in that moment before, felt that same connection with the water's call. No, not a connection—a binding, an awakening of the powers that lay dormant inside her. She opened her eyes and tried to fight the sudden sensation, her muscles numbing and her bones aching. Her hands began to tremble. Her throat went dry.

Then her shackles started glowing.

"Dravian!" she managed. She collapsed from the bench,

the sudden glow of her eyes visible against the floor. The Elite was instantly at her side, holding her firmly. She tried to ask him, beg him, to take the shackles from her wrists, but she couldn't. She couldn't utter a word.

Everything around her—the shack, the sandy floor, the grey-blue of Dravian's eyes—turned into a blur. Then she saw nothing but black.

I worry for Roland. Where my sons drink loudly, he drinks quietly. There is always something to be said of that.

From the journal of Joel al'Murtagh

CHAPTER 48

ROLAND

MESIDIA

Waking was always the worst part of the day. The pain that'd begun to fade with the night was always more present in the morning. How cruel of the body, to fool one into believing the healing process had taken over, only to reveal its trickery come sunrise. Roland took in a sharp breath, his uninjured arm grabbing at his aching shoulder as he rose from his bed.

"What happened to you?"

Roland turned, casting a bolt of lightning at the speaker and grabbing the sword at his bedside. The intruder was clad in black, everything but a small slit around his eyes covered. He was tall and lean of build, *touched* blades strapped to his calves and thighs. He stepped aside gracefully from the bolt of lightning, the element striking the window beside him.

"Well aren't we glad that window was closed," he said. "Unlike the one I climbed through. You really ought to be more cautious, you know, being a future king and all."

Roland fumed. "Who are you?" He held his sword toward the intruder. The man smiled, entertained it seemed by his attempts at intimidation. After everything that happened to Stonewall, after everything Yvaine had revealed, Roland was in no mood for jests. Especially not with a cloaked intruder.

"I can see why Gwenivere is so charmed by you." The man gestured toward Roland's shirtless chest. "You're quite the strapping young lad."

No, Roland thought, hearing Gwenivere's name. He growled, tightening the grip on his sword.

"If you've harmed her, if you've laid a finger on her—"

"Light above, I've done no such thing!" The man reached into his vest and pulled out an envelope, tossing it to the ground. "It's a letter, from the lady herself. She asked that I personally deliver it, and that I involve no one else in its journey to you. She's demanding, that one, and surprisingly frightening. You can understand why I was forced to come to you in such a manner."

Roland glared, still refusing to put down his sword. He looked between the stranger and the intriguing parchment on the floor, the Xen seal of a rose without thorns clearly visible from its front. He stared at it for a moment, questioning the authenticity of the seal. He'd seen it dozens of times, though. He knew it was real.

Eyes never leaving the cloaked messenger, Roland inched forward and picked up the envelope.

"Just to be clear," the man said, "if my intentions were to harm you, I would have done it while you slept."

"There is no honor in killing a man like that," Roland spat. "Only a coward would do such a thing."

"Or someone who appreciates silence and efficiency. Which I do, so if you don't mind, I would ask that you complete the task the Lady Gwenivere has entrusted me with and read the letter."

Roland stormed toward the man, shoving the envelope against him and lifting his sword in warning. The action was meant to evoke fear, but the intruder simply rolled his eyes.

"Really? You're going to make me read it?"

When Roland nodded, the messenger split the seal from the parchment's fold and mumbled to himself that it seemed "a bit personal" to be read aloud.

Roland ignored him.

"'To my dearest Roland'—that's sweet."

"Read the bloody letter!"

The messenger furrowed his brows, cleared his throat, and started again.

"'To my dearest Roland. First, I must apologize for the way in which you'll receive this letter. I ask that you dismiss any informalities my chosen messenger portrays. He's foreign, and he's not very accustomed to our sense of 'proper.'"

Roland snatched the letter from the man's hands, quickly skimming the first few lines. After a brief moment, he looked up and handed the letter back.

"What was that for?" the man asked innocently.

Roland swallowed, fighting the urge to cast another bolt the man's way.

"I thought you made that first part up," he admitted. "Keep reading!"

"Yes, yes, all right, where were we? Ah yes: 'When I received your letter from Elizabeth, I too felt unable to accept my role. I couldn't believe the day had come when I'd be forced to choose another man after so many years of believing fate would some-how allow me to be yours. It's all I've ever wanted, wishing so terribly that I could trade every bit of wealth and power and stature just to be called your queen, and you my king.

"'Despite these desires, I knew our roles as Guardians to be a task neither of us could forfeit. But as you've stated, if there was some way in which this fate could be justly passed on to another, I too would want nothing more than to make it so.

"'As I know is the same in Mesidia, Xenith was recently attacked. Many of my people died that day. It was a tragic and haunting moment, one that has left a great deal of apprehension and fear in what each tomorrow brings. It is because of this that I present my current proposition.

"'My capital, had it not been for Prince Dietrich of Sadie, would have perished. My life and my kingdom is indebted to him and his people, and if I possessed anything worthy of gifting him for such an act, it would be his. But alas, not my hand in marriage, nor the prospect of being Xenith's future king, would suffice.

"'There is, however, a possession that would indeed nullify mine and my people's debt to him. The Dagger of Eve, your birthright, would grant his nation the power it needs. It would ensure that, when the nation of Prianthia tries to once again bind his people in chains, evil would be cast back and forced to retreat. It would ensure that when the rebel movement in the East tries to slay the king and queen of Sadie, they would fail. And it would allow us to marry. Any threat—whether it be a political rival, the rebel nations from the War of Fire, or the ever-present existence of those who attacked so many an innocent people—could be crushed under our unity.

"'Never again, for as long as I remained a Guardian and you remained my king, would our people fear the violence of those who wish to destroy us. And albeit a less grand and just a reason, we would never again have to speak of the day when my throne and my name would belong to another.

"'Whatever path you choose, let the Creator be with you. I love you dearly, Roland. Your faithful friend, Gwenivere.'"

So far the Evean sailors haven't told us anything useful. They're a Lightless waste of time. You're lucky you've got the girl as your prisoner. I would've had fun with her.

A letter between Odin Iceborne and Rellor Bordinsua

CHAPTER 49

X'ODIA

X'odia awoke with a gasp. Her body's convulsions final-ly calmed as the healing in her blood began to pulse new life. She breathed heavily, her weakened fingers clutching tightly to the strong hands that held her. She could hear her soother shushing her softly, feel as calloused hands swept the hair away from her face. As her vision cleared, the glowing of her eyes eased.

In that instance, Dravian didn't look at her with regret or scrutiny. He didn't study her or wait for her to reveal some-thing of importance. He merely held her. She buried her head against his chest and clung to him, knowing the moment of sincerity would fade.

"What did you See?"

She didn't answer at first, couldn't, the pain of healing more than she could bear. As she waited, she realized it was only without her chains that she'd been able to See. She wanted to believe that some part of Dravian had acted on his own, that he'd given her a moment of freedom to ease her suffering. In truth, he'd likely just done it so he could keep gleaning information from her.

"I Saw Prince Roland," she started, catching her breath as the fatigue faded. "I Saw him forfeit the Dagger of Eve to Dietrich Haroldson. And it wasn't a vision of what was to come. It was a vision of something that'd just transpired."

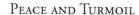

The patients Prince Abaddon ordered quarantined seem to be making a full recovery after being administered the elixir he gave us. I'd have thought he'd be happy with these results, but he seems surprisingly indifferent.

From the journal of Samuel Sandborne

CHAPTER 50

ABADDON

SADIE

Abaddon watched as his mother lay asleep. Her eyes fluttered beneath her lids and her fingers twitched against her sides, proof perhaps that there were still thoughts in her mind. Yet she couldn't rise, couldn't waken. The elixirs he'd been giving her were unable to combat the strange coma she now lay in.

"Why won't she wake up?" his father asked.

King Harold, the most vicious man Abaddon had ever known, leaned down at Lenore's bedside. He was broken, as Abaddon knew he'd be, his bear-like shoulders hunched and his eyes heavy. Even his hands, scarred from the lashings he'd received as a slave, were shaking.

"Her *auroras* are gone," Deladrine answered. The girl was an oracle from one of the temples, the oranges of her veils bright and silky. It was common garb for priestesses, but to

Abaddon it seemed ill-fitting. She should be wearing black, a more appropriate thing to wear for the dying.

"How can her *auroras* be gone?" Harold asked. "*Auroras* are a part of us—they don't simply vanish. Even when we use them, we only draw from them. It's not as though we only have so many to cast about."

Abaddon opened his mouth to say something but refrained. He didn't really know the answer. It was just common for him to give them.

"How such a thing can be is simply not an answer we know," Deladrine said. "The Creator doesn't grant us understanding in all things. We're merely bestowed pieces of grace. The *auroras* are glimpses of such."

"Does she suffer?" Harold asked, looking back to Lenore. Abaddon curled his lips, angered as he stood helpless beside his parents. He wished it was him in his mother's place.

"I don't know," Deladrine said. "I pray she doesn't."

The king nodded, his brows furrowed and his posture rigid. Abaddon knew he wanted to see Lenore freed from her condition, wanted to rid her of this coma, but to liberate her would be to end her life. His father would do no such thing when his prayers still called for her return.

How long has it been since Dietrich left for the Dagger? he thought. He rubbed his head, not wanting to think back on their last visit. It'd been so many moons ago that he was starting to think Dietrich wasn't coming back.

But this condition their mother was in—it shouldn't have happened. All the patients he'd tested on never had these results.

I could've healed her. He reached for the pocket of his vest, the cure to his mother's illness—the way it had been before this coma—resting in a small vile.

The cause of her illness rested in another.

"How long can she live like this?" he asked. It was the thing he knew they needed answered, the question that would perhaps give peace to his father's troubled mind.

"She was weak before, so it's hard to say. The body needs food and water. That fact is no different now that she rests like this."

"And if her *auroras* are gone, how will we know when she ceases her rest?"

The oracle blinked. She looked from Abaddon to Harold, the king's shoulders still slumped as he sat protectively over Lenore. He seemed too lost in his watch to pay Deladrine any mind.

"The usual signs will occur," she answered. "Her heart and her breathing will stop. But the remaining *auroras*, the ones that drift, are still a part of her body. Not every *aurora* serves the purpose of being *called*. So, if such a thing is to happen, those remaining *auroras* will appear."

"What of these?" Harold asked. Lifting the sleeves of Lenore's shirt, he pointed to black, burn-like markings.

Abaddon narrowed his eyes, perplexed. He hadn't seen those before. They hadn't been there the last time he'd come to treat her.

"They look like the wounds from a fiend," Deladrine guessed.

"They run up to her neck," Harold pressed. "If a fiend was able to do this, why wouldn't it just kill her?"

The oracle bit her lip. "I don't know fiends well, sire. Perhaps Yeltaire Veen would know."

Abaddon grimaced. How ironic, after spending months poisoning their mother and convincing Dietrich their only chance was the Dagger, it was now he who might be able to help them.

Abaddon ran his fingers through his hair. He'd done all of this for Dietrich and his parents. He'd wanted to let them live without fear, to let the Prianthians and the Redeemers know they shouldn't take them for enemies. Immortality from the Dagger meant constant and eternal healing, and if they had that, they wouldn't need to reign from such a fragile throne.

Dietrich wouldn't have to live as he did, cast out on the streets. Their mother wouldn't have to cry for her assassin son. And their father, mighty as he was, wouldn't have to rule with constant fear for his family.

"Thank you, Lady Oracle," Harold said. He rose and gestured toward the door. "Culter will escort you out."

"Good fortune to you, sire," she said, resting a comforting hand on his arm. She nodded to him and said a quick prayer of condolence before making to leave.

Harold followed her and closed the door when she'd left.

"The Redeemers will find her," he said quietly. He walked to one of the room's windows and peered through it, waiting until his second, Culter, appeared in view. The watchman walked the oracle through the streets, guiding her among the shouting merchants and pushing crowds.

"Will our men protect her then?" Abaddon asked. He followed where her and Culter walked, careful to store the path in his mind. "I didn't sense she belonged to our enemies."

"Nor did I," Harold said. "But they will find her nonetheless. They mustn't know what she knows. If word reaches them that Lenore is as she is, they will likely attack."

Abaddon breathed in heavily, nodding as the oracle turned a corner and vanished from his sight.

"Culter will tell you where she lives," Harold continued. "And then you will kill her."

The alleys of Sovereignty had always been shadowed and narrow. Working hands and bending backs worked tirelessly from the rise of the Day Star till its descent. So little of the sun managed to creep into the streets, the heights of each clay building housing passersby from the reflections against the temples and the gleams of the palace's glass. If not for the heat, it was easy to forget one strode outside.

Abaddon watched his people, his cloak pulled high. He dreaded the fading light as the moon took its place in the clouds.

It was a cold night, colder than most, the chill of dusk giving way to darkness. The prince stretched his fingers in their gloves, his green eyes lost in how the leather formed and moved so perfectly with them. He tore his gaze away, trying not to think of the deed his hands would soon commit. He glanced instead to the sky, the stars just starting to show. He rose from where he sat, vendors at last ceasing their shouts, and fingered where his *touched* blade lay.

The oracle's home wasn't far from the temple grounds— that's what Culter had told him. She dwelled alone, without a lover or child. Besides a few elderly neighbors and families residing in the homes nearby, she was isolated.

Culter had been detailed in his description, even noting the hanging plants outside her window and the occasional stray animal she felt compelled to feed. The watchman clearly liked the girl, admired her sympathetic spirit. He hadn't realized his account would aid in her death.

Why me? Abaddon had asked, making sure his tone was neutral. His father would be furious if there was any protest or whine in the query. *Culter is already escorting her back.*

Culter's loyalty is not endless, Harold had answered. *Do you think men would follow their kings with such zeal if they knew all the atrocities they'd ordered?*

The question had sentenced Abaddon to silence. Given all he'd done for the betterment of their family and kingdom, he couldn't argue.

Taking a breath, he gauged the distance from where he

stood and a smaller building below him, then leaped down from his place. After descending a series of rooftops, the loose rocks of the ground were beneath his boots. His steps were careful and silent. He hugged his body to the cooling clay of a wall, turning from its cover to look into the street.

A few boys played, each kicking a ball back to the other. No others remained, not a single adult or parent. Children were observant, though, and curious, too much so to risk being heard or seen. Abaddon crouched down, resting in the shadows as something rubbed against his calves.

Quickly he unsheathed his dagger, the black of fur bolting away from him. He watched as the creature darted into the streets, the boys giggling as they saw it. Abaddon grunted, shaking his head and cursing his pounding heart.

A cat, he thought, glancing back over the alley's cover. A woman appeared from the house behind the boys, calling for them in a pleasant voice to wash up and come inside. They did as they were told, if at a delay, neither wanting to abandon the stray. Abaddon took a deep breath, knowing the streets around the temple wouldn't remain empty for long, and hurried for the oracle's door.

I've done this before, he told himself, remembering with regret the night he'd slit another woman's throat. It'd been necessary to his plan, to set everything in motion, but it didn't change the fact that his stomach twisted when he thought of it.

Would Dietrich hesitate at all, if their father had given him this demand?

The door to the oracle's home creaked as it opened abruptly, the young woman gasping as the prince stood before her. Whatever she'd been holding fell and shattered on the ground.

Abaddon backed away, not having expected her to walk out. Instinctively he reached for the thing she'd dropped.

"I'm very sorry, good man, I hadn't realized you were there." The oracle's voice was kind, her small frame bending down to join him on the ground. She clearly didn't know who he was, not with his cloak wrapped around his face. He handed her back the thing she'd dropped—a shattered bowl with milk meant to feed the stray—and stood back up.

"Go inside," he demanded quietly, pulling the cloth down from his face. She nodded, closing the door shut as he followed her into her home.

"The watchman Culter said someone would come to protect me." She smiled and reached for the towel atop her table. She walked over to him, eyeing him warmly as she reached for his hand. "I hadn't expected it would be the prince himself, though."

Abaddon winced as she pressed the fabric to his skin. The broken glass from the bowl had sliced through his gloves. He cursed as she smiled at him again, her fingers dabbing the towel gently before throwing it into a washbasin.

"I'm no healer," she muttered. "I suppose it's a bit silly for me to try tending to your wounds."

He said nothing. He watched as she walked back to her cupboards and reached for another bowl.

"I do beg your pardon, but I'm not sure how this whole protection thing is to go about. Am I allowed to walk outside? The neighbors and I, we take turns feeding the strays." She lifted a hand to her chest. "Today is my turn."

Abaddon sighed and grabbed the new bowl, taking it from her and walking toward the door. He pulled the cover back over his face, just for that brief moment, nervous of any who might spot him as he placed the milk a few feet from her home. He set it down, noting a few priests perusing through the street, and hurried back inside.

"How long will you stay?" the oracle asked, sitting down at her table. She took a sip from a cup. "Shall I make us both supper?"

She pushed out a chair beside her and beckoned Abaddon to sit. He shook his head. Looking around the room, he noticed her window curtains lay open.

"All right, that's just as well," she said. "I have little to eat, and certainly nothing as grand as you have in the palace. And, if I'm being honest, I don't rather feel like cooking."

Abbadon held back a grimace. Deladrine was kind, and painfully innocent. He walked back to the windows, not wanting to look at her, and pulled the curtains shut.

Behind him, Deladrine cleared her throat.

"I know you're a man of studies," she said, voice uncertain. "I know you believe in what you can hold, what you can see. I know you think little of my work."

Abaddon turned back to her. The smile she'd worn was gone.

"When I touched your father's arm earlier," she continued, "when I said a parting prayer, I sensed what he intended. I'm no Watcher, not like the ones in the prophecies, but I know what I feel is real. You aren't here to protect me." She stopped, her lips beginning to quiver. "You're here to kill me, aren't you?"

She sat still, her back pressing itself further against her chair. Her hand trembled as it held to her mouth.

"Yes," he whispered. He pulled the blade back out from its sheath, his mind laden as he felt its weight. The oracle choked back a sob, wrapping her arms around herself.

Paralyzed, Abaddon stood where he was, looking at his reflection in the knife. It showed a distorted image of himself, twisted and dark. He knew it was just a trick of the light, but he thought it looked like what he really was. A monster. A fiend. A killer.

He tossed the blade aside, letting it clatter against the table. He pulled out the chair Deladrine had offered, letting out a breath and sitting down.

"I'm not going to though," he said. He met her eyes, wide and tear-filled, and decided he never wanted to make someone look like that again.

Well Henry never wants to go outside anymore. He's constantly afraid fiends are going to attack. I managed to get him out of the house once, just to help me hunt some rabbits, and can you guess what happened? A dragon flew over us. What luck.

A Mesidian countrywoman

CHAPTER 51

DIETRICH

The air in the sky was notably warmer near the Dividing Wall. After days of flight, with hardly any rest, Dietrich and Seera were almost home.

And the Dagger of Eve was with them.

Dietrich hadn't really believed his brother's plan would work. With so many years living with such little hope, he'd just accepted his life would always be what it was. Now he was almost too shocked to believe it might actually change. He knew he should test the Dagger, ensure it was the real thing, but he couldn't bring himself to do it. It didn't feel right without Abaddon.

I'll call *on it once I'm home,* he decided. Until then, he was content with its place among his other knives.

At the thought of the capital, a grimness emitted from Seera. The fervor in her wings lagged, her speed almost dependent on the momentum of the wind. Dietrich leaned against her and clutched her quills, trying to listen or see what was wrong.

Something's happened, she managed to him. *Something's happened to Savine and Zoran.*

Dietrich held her comfortingly, about to ask if they should go faster. She bellowed a somber sound, sensing his query. Her answer came in the dismayed image of sunlight.

Realization settled. Dietrich felt a fool, forgetting her aversion to the cold. It wouldn't be affecting her so strongly if they'd been able to complete their quest hastily, but they'd fought in the Attack of Fiends, battled against the Behemoth, and flown through the rainy hills of Mesidia. She'd gone too long without heat.

We should rest, he said, patting her side. He hadn't noticed it before, but her scales were dulling.

No! She began to beat her wings with more force, her will to defend Zoran and Savine pressing her onward. Dietrich felt it, the connection between them. His body filled with the same angst and hopelessness that enveloped her.

She flew nearer and nearer to the Path of Dragons. Her strength waned as she finally crashed to the ground. Dietrich braced himself for the collision, his arms tensing when he caught sight of smoke escaping from beyond where they fell. He quickly dismounted, his muscles aching, but Seera's urgency willed him onward. She stayed where she was, feeble but alive, and soaked up what she could of the desert heat.

I'll find them, he assured. He made his way through the cliffs they'd hunted in together, remembering the way he'd warily guided Zar as she'd flown overhead. She'd been hateful of him then, fearful, wondering what his presence meant for Zoran and Savine. Now she relied on him, waiting in desperation for what he found.

Thoughts flooded his mind, her thoughts, flowing from one nervous query to the next. Why wasn't Zoran answering her when she reached for him? Why wasn't Savine? Why had she gotten a sickening twist in her gut, as if something dreadful had occurred?

"Oh no," Dietrich whispered, halting as he made his way to Zoran's lands. Everything he'd built—his cottage, his shed, his workhouse—had fallen to ash. A trail of blood was stained along the dirt, leading out from the road Dietrich had first traveled. He reached out to Seera in his mind, knowing she could sense his distress, and attempted to show her what he saw.

Find him! she begged. *Find him!*

He raced along the bloodied path, his feet hardly touching the ground as he ran. He'd barely known Zoran, barely shared more than a few words and meals with him, but Seera loved him dearly. Her affection overwhelmed him.

He hurried through the canyon, retracing the steps he'd taken moons ago. He hardly noted the place where he'd first struck Savine down with his bolts. He was almost to the signs now, the ones that had marked the footpaths to all the different nations.

He stopped, eyes widening. Ahead of him, where the sign for the Path of Dragons lay . . .

What is it? Seera asked, her voice faint. She still lay lengths apart from him, her words hardly there in his mind, but she sensed his grief. She rallied herself through her fatigue, pressing her thoughts back to him. *What's happened?*

Dietrich panted heavily, his body numb as he slowly walked up to the scene. He didn't want to believe it was real, but still he sauntered forward, praying somehow his eyes deceived him. He stopped where the trail of blood ended, collapsing to the ground.

Zoran, he managed, looking up at the man. The Keeper's body lay limply against a wooden cross, his hands stretched to its sides as strips of a cloth hung mockingly from his arms. They were meant to look like wings, the sign spelling PATH OF DRAGONS only a short distance ahead. Savine lay at his feet, her wings nailed to the ground, their flesh torn to pieces and her horns severed from her head.

Their *auroras* hadn't drifted yet. They'd only just been killed.

Don't try to look, Seera, Dietrich said, fighting to keep what he saw from her. *Don't look.*

He could feel her tearing through his skull, prying what she could from his mind's eye. He clung to his head, desperate to cast the thoughts out. She moved then. Her muscles stirred as if they were his own, and the sun of the desert mountains gave her just enough strength to bring her back to flight.

Please, Seera, he pleaded, trying to keep her back. *Please, stay where you are!*

His words were useless. Seera was already casting herself to where she felt him kneel. She was there in moments. Her wings batted with panic as she fell beside him. When she saw Zoran and Savine she opened her jaws, craned her neck toward the sky, and roared.

The night came with dreadful mockery. A fire had been needed to combat the cold, as well as to replenish Seera's strength, but it'd also brought flickering shadows. It made Savine and Zoran's corpses look a thing of horror, more so than they already did. Dietrich glanced over at them, forcing himself to take the sight in.

Who would do this? he wondered, looking back at their campfire. Seera had laid silent for hours, still weak as she absorbed the heat of the flames. She lay by the bodies of her fallen, who now rested on the ground beside her. She'd been insistent Dietrich rid them of their nails so they didn't have to rest so theatrically.

Who would do this? he thought again, directing the query to her. The lids of her eyes lifted and closed, visibly dismayed.

He should let her rest, he knew, let her grieve for as long as she required, but the guilt he felt pushed him to take action. He looked to his thigh, cursing the Dagger of Eve as it rested against him. He tore a strip of cloth from his cloak and hurriedly tied it around the glowing hilt.

When I first came here, he started, *Zoran told me Savine thought I was another. One of the Ageless. Could it have been one of them who did this? Did they have any reason to take up arms against him?*

Seera opened her lids again, this time keeping them lifted awhile before pulling herself from her curled position. Her scales had begun to deepen again. They shifted to their former gleam as they took in the blaze.

Zoran feared them, but they wouldn't have done this. She looked back to Savine. *They respected Zoran, understood he was the son of their own. He was neither their enemy nor their friend, but he was one of them all the same. They honored that.*

She extended her wings out toward the other dragon, nestling beside her. She looked to Dietrich with a sense of loathing.

He understood then, knowing what he feared was true. It was his enemies who had taken the Keeper's life, his enemies who had slaughtered them, eager to make a statement before his return. Seera didn't want to hate him. She felt and understood every emotion and every thought he had, yet her heart couldn't help detesting him for the violence he'd wrought.

He met her fury. As she began to turn away, the first of Zoran's and Savine's *auroras* surfaced.

The colorful streaks emerged quietly and whisked into the air. Dietrich grimaced as he heard their strange whispers, watching sadly as Seera bolted from her place. She peered down at Savine, her throat releasing a woeful bellow, her wings trying to shield the *auroras* from leaving the corpse. The lights did nothing to appease her attempts, only seeping through her as they ascended to the sky. She cried out again, her eyes darting fearfully as she looked to Zoran. She lifted her wings and did the same to him, trying in vain to press the lights back down. Dietrich's heart tore as he watched. He rose and made his way toward her.

"Seera," he whispered. He tried to put his hand on her to console her, but she only replied with snapping jaws.

"Seera."

His voice was firmer this time, his arms wrapping around her as he tried to force her to look elsewhere. She resisted. She tried again and again to save Zoran and Savine, to keep them there with them, but their *auroras* kept drifting. Dietrich continued to hold her, wincing as her talons scraped against his skin. He wouldn't release, though. He was all she had now, and he wouldn't abandon her in her sorrows.

Let them go, Seera, he said, grinding his teeth as her thrashes cut deeper. Zoran and Savine's bodies were fading, their corpses a dull facade of what they'd once been. *They will drift, no matter how much you want them to stay. You must accept this. Don't let their deaths fill your life with woe. You must press on. You must avenge them.*

The dragon at last ceased her resistance. Her slit eyes stayed on her family, watching as their *auroras* lifted from what remained of their bodies. She looked back to Dietrich, consumed with misery, and nestled her neck against his stomach. He tightened his hold, then brought forth fire in his touch and pressed it to her scales.

"*We* will avenge them," he said, correcting himself. He could feel Seera's response, her talons opening and her throat pulsing with a subdued cry. She opened her wings again, slowly and deliberately, then folded them around him.

Please keep our children safe. With all that's happened, we don't wish for them to return home yet.

From a letter between Catherine al'Murtagh and Gerard Verigrad

CHAPTER 52

ELIZABETH

"Greetings, milord," the quintet stated. The al'Murtaghs, Natalia, and Dorian fell to their feet and bowed, Peter the last to shuffle beside them. The King of Peace beckoned them to rise. The hall was empty save the knights at his side. He turned toward his men and commanded them to leave.

Elizabeth watched as the knights left. Kings didn't leave themselves vulnerable—not any kings of wisdom, at least. Whatever Gerard wanted to say to them, he intended it for their ears and their ears alone.

"Ambassador," he said, his voice booming. "Duchess, al'Murtaghs."

William and Dorian hardly moved, their necks only creasing slightly. Peter nodded his head dramatically, disgracefully so, his actions conveying he was neither concerned nor curious of the words to come. Natalia, not moving at all, simply lifted her eyes.

Elizabeth couldn't help noting that Gerard had called her duchess. Not duchess-heir.

"The attacks that came to Xenith's lands came to others as well," he started. "Ravens have reached us from the north, as well as the south, ambushes of similar types present throughout. Riverdee has captured those who led the attacks there: a young woman named X'odia, and a man named Vahd'eel."

Riverdee, Elizabeth thought, remembering the stern face and deep voice of the soldier Dravian. Riverdee had been where he and his troops had been headed. Had it been them who'd captured the people in the south?

"King Pierre has been questioning people he believes may have insight to the attacks in Stonewall, Mesidia," Gerard continued. "From what we know, there is a strong connection between all of them.

"Ambassador—Pierre and Rosalie wish to inform you that Roland was injured but is recovering well. As he's in relatively good health, the king has asked that you stay here in Xenith and continue representing them."

"Thank you, your majesty," Dorian said, returning the king's nod, "I shall."

Gerard inhaled deeply. He eased into his throne before lifting his hand and pointing to the door. "You may leave."

Dorian's poise faltered, obviously surprised at his swift dismissal. He met the eyes of the other Mesidians, resting a moment longer on Natalia, then walked out.

A pang of jealously struck through Elizabeth. She shoved it down and stood at attention as Gerard looked to them.

"Al'Murtaghs—Joel and Catherine wish for you to go back to Mesidia, but they fear what may happen to you upon your travels. They send their regards, but prefer you wait to return. They don't trust the roads without a band of knights or Elite to protect you.

"Know that I would give you a troop of my most trusted

men if I could, but as Xenith has suffered from the attacks, I fear I cannot aid you in this regard. When my ranks have recovered to their former strength, I will do what I can to help you home."

"Thank you, milord," William said, with more gallantry than Elizabeth thought necessary. "We appreciate the words you've relayed to us and thank you for your hospitality. We are indebted to your goodwill." He leaned forward and bowed, his body rising tall as Peter clumsily followed suit. Elizabeth curtsied. She was unsure if such a response was needed, but decided it was best to err on the side of respect.

"You hold no debt to me," Gerard answered. He gave a slight smile and pointed again to the door. "You may leave."

The siblings turned without word, Elizabeth standing back as she followed her brothers. It would just be Natalia now, and as much as Elizabeth despised the woman, she couldn't help pitying her. Nothing good could come of speaking alone with the King of Peace. Especially when he'd failed to call her heir.

Based on the hardened expression lining Natalia's face, Elizabeth guessed she thought the same.

The Baptism of Blood usually occurs when someone marries into a noble family from a different nation. The most notable individual to have done this in present day would be Gerard Verigrad, as he was originally born in Mesidia.

This can also occur when soldiers agree to serve in the army of a nation that is not their own, such as the Elite commander Odin Iceborne. Ironically Odin is of Mesidian blood, but he was born in the Arctic.

I myself have never partaken in the Baptism of Blood as I was too young when I was adopted into the Laighless's home. Why the interest, my friend? Are you looking to become a Mesidian man?

From a letter between Dorian Cliffborne and Abaddon Haroldson

CHAPTER 53

GERARD

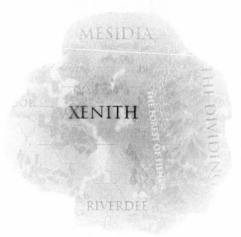

"**A**m I a Duchess now?" Natalia asked. She inhaled deeply, icy eyes glaring as the al'Murtagh's left and the chamber door shut behind her.

Gerard rose from where he sat and took a few steps forward. Natalia looked back up to him, a glisten in her eyes.

"Your father is dead," he said.

He let the words linger. Natalia licked her lips, her fingers curling and uncurling at her sides.

He remembered her as a child, when she'd been more vulnerable and prone to outbursts, as all children were. He'd watched begrudgingly over the years as her mother had transformed her into the woman she was now, a calloused creature comparable to fiends.

Clasping his hands behind his back, he took another step forward. "Your mother is alive, but she was captured by Pierre's men. They found her, in the forests outside of Stonewall, guiding the fiends that made the attack there."

A bitter laugh escape Natalia's throat. She put a finger to her nose, as if to stifle back a sob.

"Pierre and Rosalie have always hated my mother."

"That is true."

"But my father—he wanted Mesidia to thrive. He was a good man."

"That is true as well."

Gerard offered Natalia a seat, but she gave a gentle wave to dismiss it. He stood there, quiet, uncertain what to say. He was a king; he gave people consolation from podiums. He wasn't accustomed to giving consolation in chambers.

"Mesidia is a broken land," he finally said. "It's not without its roots, the lust of men present within its borders. Goodness resides in few.

"Bernard was certainly among those few. He believed in dignity. He believed in justice. But Pierre and Rosalie believe in such things too. As is the world in all its quarrels, so is the feud among them. It's not cruelness that tears apart, but plights, sparked by the differing views of what is and is not righteous."

It was a kingly thing to say. It had grandeur. Truth. Understanding. Gerard didn't think it particularly sympathetic, but it seemed to pull at Natalia. The glistening in her eyes deepened.

"I know some people rally for your mother's death while others rally for her freedom. Pierre believes her guilty, as do many in his ranks, but those who hold faith in her believe as you've stated. I don't come to convince you she's innocent, nor do I come to condemn her ways. I merely wish to grant you a choice now that the state of your family is as it is."

Gerard took a breath. He had no reservations about what he was going to offer, but he knew others would. There were issues at play he'd have to face because of it.

"Gwenivere is strong," he said. "But she's very alone in this world. When I die, there will be no one save whomever she marries to help guide her. I'd like to offer you a position here, then, as a sort of second queen."

Natalia stared suspiciously, eyes narrowed.

He held up a hand.

"I wouldn't name you as such, mind you, but I would give you a great deal of influence. You'd act on Xenith's behalf when Gwenivere couldn't, and you'd counsel her and aid in commanding her knights. You'd still get to marry whomever you choose, and you'd get to bear children without pressing a throne on them to declare."

Gerard pressed purposefully toward her. He smiled kindly, one hand behind his back, the other gesturing to the city outside his window for her to survey. She did so wordlessly.

Before having his own daughter, he'd thought often of her. He'd wished terribly there was something he could do to free her from her mother's grasp, to let her live within the care of his home. His wife, Rose, had been a kind and loving woman, and she'd have made a far better mother to Natalia than Yvaine ever would.

This was his chance now, to do for her what he'd not been able to then. With moons of healthy breath still in his lungs, and Yvaine trapped in Stonewall's dungeons, this was his chance to give Natalia a new home.

"You're a Mesidian by birth," she said quietly. "Tell me, do you regret becoming a son of Xenith?"

Gerard's smile widened as he held up his palm, exposing his pledging scar.

"No. I don't."

Natalia didn't smile back, but she did nod. She pulled a sapphire-hilted knife from a sheath beneath her skirts and sliced it across her palm.

"Then I accept your offer." She opened her hand, now dripping with blood, and pressed it to the ground.

Bernard and Merlin are dead. Yvaine was leading the attacks on Stonewall, controlling the fiends somehow, and is being held in our dungeons. Despite this, the rebels are starting to demand her freedom.

I wish you were still one of my Elite, Gerard. It feels like all of Mesidia is collapsing.

From a letter between Pierre Laighless and Gerard Verigrad

CHAPTER 54

GERARD

"**I** don't believe it!" the commandant of Theatia spat. He blew the smoke from his pipe aggressively. The smell of it wafted across the council table. Gerard kept his palm from rising, his features still as the pungent scent filled his nose.

"It's true," he said, waiting for the smoke to clear. "Natalia vowed her allegiance to Xenith this morning with the Baptism of Blood. The mark of her pledging is still fresh."

He looked between the four individuals at the table: Vanessa of the Artic, Hedford of Theatia, Alanna of Prianthia, and Edifor of Yendor. They were all of influence and power, and Gerard knew they'd all had their sights on Natalia.

Across from him, Vanessa chuckled, amused as the commandant continued to suck on his pipe. Gerard glanced at her with careful eyes. She'd abandoned the heavy furs of her usual attire for string and cloth. It would seem Xenith's coming winter was still too warm to warrant her modesty.

"You're clever," she said, waving her finger. "You knew Natalia was important to us."

"It's of no matter now," Edifor cut in, pushing his spectacles up. He crossed his legs and glared at Commandant Hedford, who looked at him nervously before setting his pipe aside and blowing smoke at his belly.

"It is of matter, Edifor," Vanessa hissed. "If Pierre were to kill Yvaine, then Natalia would take her place as the Victorians' leader. And she's accustomed to being used. We would've had complete control of her."

Gerard listened intently. He had eyes and ears that answered to him, men and women who claimed to be no more than humble servants or curious minds, and all had been attentive to who seemed to be allying with whom, and for what purpose. After hearing what news they brought him and looking at a map, he knew what Vanessa's Arctic, Edifor's Yendor, and Hedford's Theatia all had in common: a border with Mesidia.

Though Alanna of Prianthia is certainly an uncertain, he thought, glancing at the dark-haired girl to his side. What business she had with the others, when she was so far removed from the quarrels of the West, he didn't know.

"We'll find someone else to replace Natalia," Edifor said. "Women can be influenced easily by men. Flatter them, and they'll spread their legs for you. Provide for them, and they'll bear your children. Give them power"—he paused, glancing at Gerard before looking back to the baroness—"and they'll worship you. I applaud your offer to the girl, Gerard. Too much so to condemn it."

Gerard looked back to the women at the table. Alanna's nostrils flared. Vanessa's chest rose and fell.

"The baroness is a woman," he said. He glanced over at the other girl beside him, her dark eyes looking to him with reserve. "As is Alanna. I doubt either cares for your portrayal."

"I don't need you to speak on my behalf," Vanessa said. "No Arctic women do."

"Nor do Prianthians," Alanna added.

Commandant Hedford chuckled, picking up his pipe again. "Turn off the lights and you all feel the same."

His laugh cut off abruptly as the women scowled.

Edifor ignored them all and pulled out a parchment from his satchel. He scooted his chair closer to Gerard, unrolling the parchment until it stayed open on its own.

"My dear friend," he said, crossing his legs again. "We need you to know we've done all we can to avoid interfering with Mesidia's conflicts. We haven't pledged allegiances to either bloodline, nor have we extended a favorable hand to the Laighlesses or the Victorians. We've only ever held peaceful negotiations, and with whoever has held the throne.

"With their current plights, however, and with civil war looming, it would seem it's now impractical not to intervene. We hold peace as strongly as you do, but it would be a shame if that peace were broken because we were too afraid to act."

Gerard sat calmly, only his eyes moving as he looked over the parchment before him. The four guests had already signed at the bottom, a fifth space left blank for him to fill. He smiled to the man beside him, returning his feigned amity.

"Internal skirmishes are far from war. Pierre's Elite are among the highest trained soldiers in Abra'am. The Victorians are without a leader, and their heiress has just pledged her life to Xenith. I don't see anything worth intervening in."

"Do you take us for fools, Gerard?" Commandant Hedford asked, coughing slightly as he grasped at his pipe. "Pierre's best Elite are dabbling in Riverdee, while the rest are wondering why they don't wear armor into battle. They're divided and weak, and they'll fall to Yvaine's followers if the bastards are smart enough to rally."

"Commandant Hedford is . . . right," Alanna admitted,

turning to Gerard. She looked at him with saddened, almost pitying eyes.

"Civil unrest in Mesidia means starving people in other nations," she said. "Yendor is the only land between the East and West that isn't disrupted by the Dividing Wall's mountains. Thus it's the only practical means of transport and trade among my people and all of yours. Even if we wanted to go through the Dividing Wall, we would have to go through Sadiyan land, and you know as well as I that those wounds have yet to heal."

"Prianthia isn't the only nation that would suffer," Edifor added. "Yendor, as the daughter-heir has put it, is the only kingdom between both lands. It is also trapped by both. The Dividing Wall is to the south, Prianthia to the east, and Mesidia to the west. If Mesidia is ravaged by war, Yendor will be forced to alienate itself to the East, and that would only increase the hostility the two sides have toward each other."

"Not to mention the growth the Redeemers have had," Alanna interrupted. "Their ranks are continuing to rise in Prianthia and Sadie. They preach the West is a war-torn land, that it sucks my people into its quarrels and then rapes us of our wealth and riches. War in Mesidia will only prove this—"

Gerard held up his hand to silence them. Alanna looked annoyed but sat back in her chair and kept quiet.

"War in Mesidia," he said, fighting to keep his voice even, "isn't certain. As Commandant Hedford stated, Yvaine's followers would have to unite quickly, and with strength. Pierre's Elite may be divided and weakened, but they're still trained. That's more than can be said of the rebels.

"With that, in the event they do manage to put an army together, why aid them? Why not pledge your allegiance to Pierre?"

The guests looked to one another. Hedford perked up, drinking from his glass and wiping his mouth with his sleeve.

"We believe your past with the Laighless family has influenced you too much," he said. "We were all born as heirs and nobles to our nations. You were born a peasant. You made your name as an Elite, and a fine one at that, but a soldier is not a king. You never should've been anything but what you are, certainly not when men of more worthy blood stood to gain what you have. If Pierre hadn't called you his friend, he would never have introduced you to the Lady Rose. You would never have wed Xenith's heir, and you would never have become the leader of a nation you weren't born to. You owe what you are to Pierre." He paused, sucking on his pipe and blowing the smoke before clearing it with wine. He looked to the rest of his treaty mates, then back to Gerard.

"The throne belongs to Natalia, though we likely can't persuade her to take it now. You offered her a nation of peace and power. We could only offer her the latter. As much as we've tried not to meddle, the Victorian bloodline has a rightful claim to Mesidia's throne, and Pierre hasn't done his duty as its king to rid himself of the uprising. Yvaine has proven herself heartless when it comes to her enemies, which ultimately serves other nations well. We can't continue to sit on our hands and pray for peace as Mesidia continues to piss on itself. Sooner or later, the rest of us need to ensure they prosper. *Without* revolts."

Gerard nodded and took another breath before pointing to Alanna.

"I'd think Prianthia could sympathize with Mesidia. You do have quite the imposing uprising of your own."

Alanna's hands drew into fists. "The Redeemers are different. They slaughtered my brother without mercy, came for us while we slept. They are cowards who wish not to show their faces. The Victorians make clear who they are."

"As you say." Gerard took a sip from his cup, peering down at the girl as she contemplated his words. When her temper calmed, he knew she would reflect on them.

"So I understand Yendor and Prianthia's feelings toward

the manner, but what role does the Arctic and Theatia play? Alienation is certainly not a fear for either of you."

"Theatia builds its wealth on the trade it brings through Mesidia," Hedford answered. "Prianthia is our largest buyer of spice and incense. We'd lose a great deal of coin if our trade routes were ravaged by beggars and bandits in Mesidia's lands."

"I see." He glanced back at Alanna. "Coin *is* important for a nation's well-being."

The Prianthian swallowed.

"And what of you, Vanessa? What business does the Arctic have in Mesidia's quarrels?"

"Coin as well," she answered shamelessly. "Many pay us to house their prisoners, and many by way of Mesidia's roads. We would lose a great deal of profit if those roads were tampered with."

"Understood. I hadn't realized there was so much to buy in your dungeons." He examined the treaty before him, Edifor casually beckoning for a feather and ink to be brought forth. When a servant handed Gerard the feather, he thanked them and crushed the feather in his hand.

"I command the most powerful army in Abra'am," he said quietly. "I command these loyal knights surrounding us, and as Hedford stated earlier, I made my name among the highest-ranking soldiers in the West. Do not think you hold jurisdiction over me, Edifor. You are nothing but a petty scholar."

He grabbed the ink that'd been placed beside him and lifted it over Edifor's head. The man sat motionless, his body rigid as he waited for the ink to fall.

"I suppose I shouldn't do such a savage thing," Gerard said, slowly setting the ink back down. "Your attire looks to be worth a great deal. And I know how much wealth means to you now."

He sat tall in his seat and waved his knights to leave. They did so without protest. Once gone, he unsheathed the *touched* sword at his side and placed it on the table. His guests looked between him and the blade, eyes darting.

"Not a single one of you could grasp that and plunge it into my neck before it'd be in your stomach. If I had to put my bets on who would come closest, I would say Vanessa, though she is perhaps not as spry as the young Alanna."

They said nothing. Gerard smiled, lifting his hands to his lap and lacing them together.

"If your plan is to assemble an army and aid the Victorians, thus overwhelming Pierre and his Elite into submission before battles have even been fought, then you're all traitors. The people of Mesidia fight with righteous hearts, not lustful eyes. Shame be on all who deem themselves worthy of naming a nation's leader. Especially a nation that's not their own.

"If you think I fear my name being smeared by broken peace, you're mistaken. I'll fight beside those who I've sworn to protect, not because of what they've done for me, but because of what they do for others. Pierre is a good man and a fine king. I will not betray him."

The Baroness leaned back in her chair and laughed. "Those are empty words, King of Peace. You think the power you hold over your own sword represents the power of your nation? Foolish. You are weak. The Arctic holds an army of grateful soldiers who love the women that command them. Xenith's knights are soft-handed farmers."

Hedford scooted his chair forward, riled by his treaty mate, and pointed between them. "We'd split your armies if you tried to fight us. Unless you tried to fight us with Mesidia as the battleground. If you did that, you'd be surrounded."

"And Xenith would be unprotected," Edifor added. "You may be a powerful nation, but power attracts the greedy. With your men so invested in a foreign war, who's to say others wouldn't strike you while you were weak? Concord and Tiador certainly have a bitter taste for you after you defeated them in the War of Fire. I'd think them eager to strike again."

Gerard's gut turned. He looked back to the sword lying on the table, aching to feel the grip of its hilt and the weight of its blade. He could kill them all, he knew, even in his sickened state, slit their throats and take their heads. They had him trapped, by words and parchment, and he needed to protect Mesidia. He needed to protect Pierre.

He brought his gaze to Alanna, the girl hardly older than his own daughter, and felt shame for his violent musings. The men and the baroness were smart to bring the Prianthian heir along. He was weak as her brown eyes watched him.

"And who is to be named Guardian, if I comply?" he asked, shoulders heaving. "Who is to take the Dagger of Eve from Roland?"

Edifor lifted the broken feather, its tip still intact, and slowly pushed it and the jar of ink forward.

"Sign the treaty," he said, settling himself comfortably in his chair. "You've been told everything you need to know."

It's done, Gwen. I'm no longer a Guardian of Eve.

From a letter between Roland Laighless and Gwenivere
Verigrad

CHAPTER 55

GWENIVERE

"Milady? Milady, what's wrong?"

Becca threw her items aside, her small legs rushing forward as a raven flew from the window. Gwenivere looked up at her, eyes wet with tears, and slowly let herself smile.

"It's a letter, from Roland," she managed, her voice cracking. It was a happy sound, not a pained one, and her smile widened.

"He's given up the Dagger." She handed the letter to Becca, letting her look it over. "He gave it to Dietrich of Sadie and . . . and asked me to be his betrothed."

Part Four

Fraying Edges

Will I always be bound this way?

Abaddon is rarely at the palace these days. I've tried to follow him, but if he's not working on his elixirs, he seems to vanish. He has his brother's elusiveness.

I miss when they were boys and the world didn't press at them so cruelly. Are the lives they live much better than ours were as slaves?

From the journal of Culter Sandborne, watchman of Sadie

CHAPTER 56

ABADDON

SADIE

A baddon resisted the urge to yawn. He wiped his sleep-less eyes, forcing himself to sit straighter in his chair. De-ladrine bustled about her kitchen, her hands clumsy as she searched through her things. They weren't her things—not re-ally. They were just the possessions an old man had left behind when he'd died.

Abaddon hadn't wanted to force Deladrine into the aban-doned house, but he doubted his father would give him the task of killing her without having at least three watchmen confirm she'd disappeared. The king trusted nothing and no one, not even his own son, and he certainly wasn't going to leave the knowledge of his wife's condition with the girl. Abaddon watched her, then, remorseful that he'd changed her life so drastically. He should've slipped something in her drink, poisoned her when she slept. At least that would've been quick and merciful.

Now Deladrine could hardly step outside. All the kind people she'd known could no longer be talked to, and the stray cats that followed her to her new residence had to be ignored. Abaddon could hear them meowing in the night.

He came frequently, sitting watch beyond her door to ensure no one had discovered she still lived. He told himself it was to protect her, to make certain she was safe and well-guarded.

He wasn't convinced.

She can sense things, he thought, reminding himself of her gift as an oracle. Perhaps if he let her feel the skin of his hand or his arm, she'd know he wasn't worth treating as well as she did. She'd know he poisoned his mother to convince Dietrich to go after the Dagger. She'd know he'd been testing the poison on innocent patients.

She'd know he'd killed someone to set the whole plan in motion.

"Are you hungry?" she asked, knocking something over. She picked it up quickly, then tossed her thick braid over her shoulder. "I'm quite hungry."

"Yes, but I really must go." He squinted as she moved the flour sacks she used for curtains from her window. She quickly realized her mistake and closed them back shut.

"Stay," she said, gesturing to a seat at her table. "Please."

Forcing a smile, Abaddon nodded.

"I made this, last night, before you came," she continued, grabbing a basket of bread and sitting down beside him. "I'd hoped I could give you some as soon as you'd arrived, but I'd sensed something."

"I assumed it'd already been eaten."

She looked at him, brows raised. He laughed and waved his hand.

"I mean I smelled it," he clarified, "before I even came in.

I suppose assuming it was gone was to assume you would've given me some. Being who I am, I just expect things."

"I don't think that's true." She grabbed a piece of bread, her cheeks flushed. "I'm sorry. I speak to you like you're a common man. I should humble myself more than I do."

"No, please." Abaddon stopped chewing the bread and swallowed, dabbing his mouth. "This is delicious, by the way. And don't fret—everyone treats me with respect and I deserve none of it. I didn't free any slaves from the Prianthians. I haven't killed as many Redeemers—"

He paused, fearful he'd been too forward. He didn't like the idea of Deladrine thinking of him as an assassin, despite it having been he who'd been assigned to murder her.

"I'm not my brother," he corrected. "And Sadie, it is what it is because of them. I'm not a man who should merit shame when the wrong title is used or forgotten."

Deladrine sat quietly. Abaddon had intended to make her feel better, to lighten her mood rather than dampen it, but he felt instead that he'd somehow scolded her.

"Thank you, for the meal," he said finally, standing awkwardly. Deladrine stood with him, round eyes expectant.

He smiled at her and walked to the door, about to turn its knob, but she rushed over and held it shut.

"I-I'm sorry," she said, meeting his stare. She brought her hand back down from the door to her side. "When I said I sensed something, I meant that something is amiss. I know you don't believe in what I do, not fully, but I must know. Please, will you let me?"

Abaddon leaned back from her raised hands, nervous to let her fingers touch him. He did believe in what she did, believed the Creator gave her some semblance of the Sight, but he'd preferred to let her think he found her abilities nothing more than tricks. He didn't want to let her know of the guilt he suppressed.

"Please," she begged, hands inching closer. "Abaddon."

He released the breath he held, meeting her eyes. He didn't want to do this, didn't want whatever she felt to alter what she thought of him. She seemed to find him a good man, or, if not that, at least a decent one. He didn't want that to change.

But he could use foresight. Especially if it entailed his family.

Giving her a nod, Deladrine put her hands against his face. She closed her eyes and took in a breath.

Abaddon waited. His throat suddenly felt dry, and his lip sweaty, but he didn't move. He only swallowed, watching the small bits of motion beneath her lids.

She abruptly released him. When she opened her eyes, they were wide and dazed, as though she'd seen every bit of evil he'd done. He reached out, instincts telling him not to let her go, but he was afraid touching her again would only tell her more.

He could explain what he'd done. He could make her see. He could explain why Dietrich had needed to believe their mother was sick—

"Don't leave," she whispered, stepping toward him. "Don't leave."

She wrapped her arms around his torso and clung to him tightly. He stood aback, too relieved to force her away, but too shocked to move. Finally, when he felt his shirt dampen from her tears, he allowed himself to return her embrace.

"What was it?" he asked, resting his head against her veil. He was careful not to let his skin touch hers again. "What did you feel?"

She sniffled loudly, wiping at her cheeks. Pulling away, she wrapped her arms around herself and looked to the ground.

"I felt death," she answered, body shivering. "And I felt *auroras* ascending."

In some ways, the occupation of Redeemers has been good for business. Most of their members are men, and they seem eager for the talents of my girls.

Some of my girls have gone missing, though. Seeing as it's only ever the western ones, I can't imagine it was by choice.

From the journal of Josie Sand, owner of The Merry
Lady brothel

CHAPTER 57

DIETRICH

Days had gone by since Zoran's and Savine's drifting. The cold of winter was coming even where the desert sun fell on the Dividing Wall's mountains. Their towns were cooler than the rest of the Sadiyan kingdom, and daylight didn't reign for long.

Dietrich watched his breath cloud in front of him, lifting his cloth above his nose as he welcomed the black.

Only two people had known of his intentions to discover the now-dead mountain man. Brelain had been the first, and she'd been the one to suggest he seek Zoran out. She'd been eager to help, unjustly so, her eagerness perhaps proof of what Gwenivere had confessed to him after Xenith's masquerade. But the idea of a man—a shapeshifter—going in his stead to the western lands seemed too beyond the Redeemers' capabilities.

He had no reason to doubt the princess told the truth of

what she knew, yet he also had no reason to believe the words were anything more than rumors.

Not until he returned to the Dividing Wall's towns.

He'd been furious to find the Redeemers now claimed the land. Their presence was no longer reduced to the weakest of the towns, but instead had spread through all of them. Prianthia's harsh tongue seemed to be spoken more than any other. The lilt of the westerner's words and the smoothness of the Sadiyans' speech were only careless whispers compared to the cruel growls of the northeastern lands. The eyes of the speakers were green as often as they were brown, and the irony of seeing former slaves talking in the language of their captors was more chilling now than when it had occurred before. At least then, when Dietrich had cautiously guided Zar through the streets, it only happened on occasion. Now it seemed as natural as an infant crying for its mother.

He listened intently to the betraying sounds, interpreted what he could from where he hid, then escaped from his place. He slipped about silently, from one shadow to the next, and continued toward his destination.

There was another who could have aided his enemies besides Brelain. The wealthy western woman he'd dined with to gain knowledge about the West.

Fiona Collinson.

He glanced at where the Dagger of Eve lay against his thigh. The strips of cloth he'd tied around its hilt had held up, the jewel's annoying glow still suppressed. Deciding it didn't look any more noticeable than a regular blade, he lifted his fist, carefully surveyed the area around him, and approached the door to Fiona's house.

With a few aggressive knocks, the door opened. A burly man with a well-trimmed beard stood inside. He'd just awoken, it seemed, his hairy chest exposed from the nightwear he adorned. Dietrich had him by the throat before he could blink, shutting the door with his foot.

"Where's your wife?" he asked, voice low. The man clung to his arms in panic. His feet dangled from the ground. Dietrich shoved him against the wall.

"Where's your wife?"

The man released one arm and hurriedly pointed up the grand steps behind him. Dietrich released him, wincing slightly when the man's legs locked and sent him to the ground. Sighing, Dietrich grabbed him by the arm and hoisted him up, pushing him toward the stairs and gesturing him to lead.

The man coughed and looked him over. His eyes fell to the blade pointed at his chest. He didn't take another look before starting up the steps.

When they reached the top, he walked over to a door and jerked his head toward it. Dietrich gestured with his dagger, not bothering to put the man at ease as he ushered him onward. With shaking fingers, the man turned the knob and slowly opened the door, a long, drawn-out creak sounding.

Just inside the room, Fiona lay sleeping in her bed, undisturbed by their entrance. Dietrich stood for a moment, allowing his eyes to take in the details of the room, ensuring there were no *touched* swords or antique crossbows hanging. When he was certain the room was safe, he closed the door behind him and whispered, "Fiona."

The man, still shaking beside him, had a look of puzzlement at hearing his wife named. Based on her invitation to discuss things through pillow talk during their previous encounter, Dietrich doubted it was peculiar for her to wake from another man's voice. If anything, she might be woken by other men more often than her husband.

"Fiona!" he said again, this time with more force. She sighed loudly, her hand leaning against her bed as she sat up. She wore no clothes, her breasts exposed in what little moonlight crept through her windows, her skin pale and her body full from a life without struggle. She caught sight of her husband, the older man standing nervously in the corner, then caught sight of Dietrich.

"What do you want?" she asked coolly, rising from her bed. She strode across the room and grabbed her robe, knotting the ties around her waist and pulling her hair from the collar.

Dietrich watched her, intrigued at how little she seemed to fear him. "The Redeemers," he said, holding his blade up. The *called* weapon disappeared as he released his hold.

Despite how he'd entered, he needed them to know he was only there to talk.

"Have the Redeemers come to question you? Have they threatened you in any way?"

Fiona looked to her husband, but the man seemed oblivious to the query. He sat down in a chair, rubbing at where Dietrich had held his throat, and hunched his shoulders.

"They've come to us, yes," Fiona answered. There was a hint of disgust in her voice, more it seemed for her husband than for Dietrich. "Why? What business do you have to ask such a thing?"

Dietrich was grateful for the cover of his cloak, as he didn't want Fiona to see his brows lifting. She'd been forward when he'd met her before, enough so for ten women, but that'd been in the comforts of knowing she was safe. He wouldn't have expected her to be so steadfast after being confronted by an intruder.

"You're a westerner," he said. "What reason would the Redeemers have with you other than to want you dead?"

She shrugged and shifted her weight irritably. "We're known for our success in trade," she said, waving her hand. "Rather than kill us, they decided to extract our talents for their benefit. We continue our trade with the West, and our profits are being used to fund their cause."

"And what of the miners?" he asked. "Do the Redeemers allot enough money for them to get by on? And what of the miners that aren't from the East? What've they done with them?"

"Any with blue eyes . . . " Fiona paused, looking out her window as her shoulders tensed. "Any with blue eyes were shown 'compassion.' They were told that despite their wickedness, they were allowed to live and continue working the mines. They're given enough to get by on, which truthfully isn't much less than they got before. It's not enough of an injustice for them to rebel. They're simple folk, with little education to aid them. As long as they can eat and sleep in peace, they don't seem to mind."

Dietrich held back a scoff. Even if they weren't educated, would people really be so submissive?

He thought about the stories of his father's and Culter's youth, of the cracks of the whips and the shouts that ordered them beaten. That'd been far worse, yet how many generations had endured that before they'd finally rebelled?

"Did they ever contact you about Yeltaire Veen?" he asked, pushing the thoughts down. "Did they ask you anything about a man named Zoran?"

Fiona thought for a moment, holding her hand to her chin, but eventually shook her head.

Dietrich said nothing. He'd found often that the guilty interpreted ceased questioning as an indication that they'd been caught in a lie, that the questioner didn't believe what they said and was running through holes in their confessions.

The silence stretched. Fiona began tapping her foot, more annoyed it seemed than deceitful.

"Forgive my intrusion," Dietrich finally said, nodding his apology to her before turning to her husband. "Know that I'm greatly sorry for any fear or pain I've caused you. The Redeemers are my enemies, as I believe they'll be for you someday. When the mines have nothing left for the miners, and you have no one left to manage, they'll have no use for you. I'll protect you when such a day comes, as payment for how I came to you this night.

"Right now though, sir, your presence here is no longer needed. I have other things to discuss with you wife—things you'd be safer not knowing. Would you allow us to speak in private?"

The man groaned, but his hands pressed firmly to his knees as he rose. Fiona was there, helping him up, whispering reassurance in his ear and kissing him gently on the cheek. He nodded as he let her convince him, then peered through the dark with heated eyes.

"If you harm her, I'll have your head!" he proclaimed dramatically, pointing a finger. Dietrich nodded, deciding it best to give him what dignity he could as Fiona guided him out.

Once he was gone, Fiona spun back around and held her hands out with grandeur. "Must we remain in the dark?" she asked, *calling* a weak sphere of fire. Dietrich said nothing, not bothering to stop her as she set blazes to the sconces along the walls. She breathed heavily at the effort, obviously not skilled at using elements for more than household conveniences, then wiped at the small bead of sweat at her forehead.

The newfound light did little to detract from the slimness of her robe. Dietrich forced himself to stay focused on her face, noting that she appeared younger than when he'd seen her before.

"The Redeemers aren't allowing anyone out of the city without their command," he started. "They aren't allowing falcons to reach the capital bearing letters, either. They seem to fear what will happen if the leaders of Prianthia or Sadie discover their stronghold here before they've truly established themselves. Clever, but unfortunately for me, it's very inconvenient."

Fiona walked to a lounge chair beside a fireplace near her bed, falling into its embrace and crossing her legs against the leather.

"My husband and I would be publicly beaten if we tried to

deliver something from here to Sovereignty that the Redeemers didn't approve of. I don't believe it's possible."

"I'm not asking you to deliver an object, only a letter."

He pulled out a scroll bound by a small ring from beneath his vest. Fiona narrowed her eyes, her curiosity outweighing any rightful fear as she snatched the scroll from him.

The ring was precious to Dietrich, something his and Abaddon's watchman Culter had passed down to them. Dietrich had worn it the length of his journey, promising he'd send any message with it so Abaddon would know it truly came from him.

He didn't like watching Fiona survey its worth.

"You're the prince of Sadie, Dietrich Haroldson, aren't you?" she asked. She watched his eyes as she undid the serpent seal within the ring's scroll. She didn't break his gaze. Instead she waited for him to try and take the scroll back as she undid its folds.

"Yes," he answered finally, pulling his cloak down. Fiona stared at him. Her mouth hung open as she took in his face. It was only a moment before she recalled who he was, her shock quickly morphing to excitement.

"So *you're* the prince?"

Dietrich nodded slightly, gesturing toward the paper she held before she lost focus. She sat up then, her posture more serious, and read over the letter.

He knew she wouldn't be fond of it. It told Abaddon of the Redeemers' hold on the border and of his inability to escape and return home.

When Fiona finished reading it, she set it down, pushing it away from her as if it held a plague.

"Why would I send this? I'll be dead if it's discovered."

Dietrich stepped closer to her. He found a spot on her wall not covered in paintings and leaned against it.

"You'll send it because I know you feel guilt for aiding the insurgence," he said. "You'll send it because if you aid me in this, you won't have to live in fear. You won't have to worry about the day the Redeemers decide the color of your eyes and the blood in your veins isn't worthy of their compassion." He said the words with disdain, then reached for the Artifact strapped to his thigh. He unsheathed it and unwrapped the cloth around its hilt, holding it up for her to see.

"And because the letter is a much safer thing to deliver than the Dagger of Eve itself."

This is no ordinary fiend. If seen, warn everyone in nearby towns and villages.

From a torn-out page of *Fire and Fiends*

Chapter 58

X'ODIA

The forest rustled with tempting whispers. The falling leaves and bustling branches beckoned X'odia to run toward them. She looked out blankly, the hanging moss and twisted limbs less menacing than the stare she knew held to her back. She shook her head to the trees, refusing their eerie offer, and sighed in pained acceptance as she lifted her skirts and bent to the ground.

She wished terribly it was not Rellor Bordinsua who'd been assigned to her watch again. The wiry man seemed to take great pleasure in her misery, finding every small opening he could to cause her humiliation. When she was allowed a bath, he made her do it in front of Vahd'eel, the other prisoner, knowing full well how much her modesty meant to her. She'd tried to hide her thin frame, her body growing slimmer as the days in the camp passed, but the other captive seemed as eager to tear at her reserve as the Elite. He'd smiled at her with crazed eyes, not seeming at all bothered by his own naked frame. She shuddered as she tried to forget the thought. She was unsure whether the memory was worse than what she experienced now.

The bath, she decided, grateful when she'd finished relieving herself. *At least this way, only one man is looking at me, and not in a yearning way . . . I hope.*

Before she could stand up fully, Rellor's hand was there, shoving her to the ground. The soil had done well to soak up what it could, but the smell of her urine would settle in her clothes. She grimaced as Rellor laughed to himself. The more she suffered, the more he seemed to grow merry, and she'd had her fill of giving him such satisfaction. With a penetrating glare, she balanced herself on her forearms and pulled herself up, her legs weak but able.

Rellor's grin slowly trickled away. Behind him, X'odia could see Markeem, the mute man she remembered saving her from Vahd'eel after Dravian had been attacked. She hadn't known his inability to speak at the time, but she'd heard Rellor and some of the other soldiers make remarks his way.

Markeem's eyes, even from the distance he stood now, seemed to convey a sense of pity. She was their prisoner, but not all thought her guilty. Swiftly she took her eyes from his, not wanting to clue Rellor in on the shared glance. He'd likely only harass the youth for his bleeding heart.

X'odia stumbled behind Rellor. He always tied her with a rope, like a dog to a leash. She did her best to stay afoot, knowing he'd only hoist the tie over his shoulder and drag her if she fell. She was surprised how accustomed her hands grew to being bound, how capable her balance had become when her wrists lay clamped together. Her feet thudded with uneven steps, Rellor whipping the rope from one spot to the next, but she did well to keep her shoulders up. It was a small conquest over him, but it was a conquest all the same.

He spat again as they entered the camp, slowly walking behind her and kicking the back of her knee, forcing her down. She winced, but kept her jaw clamped, grateful at least for the warmth of the fire to distract her.

Rellor untied the rope and walked away, whistling as another man brought her a meal. She nodded and thanked him. The soldier nodded weakly back as he kept his eyes away. Rellor delighted in her dismay, and the mute man Markeem seemed to wish her escape, but most of the Elite lay somewhere in between. Based on the way this one avoided her swirling eyes, she guessed he feared her.

"Has he forced himself on you yet?" someone asked. X'odia gasped as she looked up, the dark eyes of Vahd'eel staring back at her. He wore a smirk, deep lines crinkling his face.

She said nothing, hardly able to piece together his morbid statement with his grin. Slowly she raised her chained wrists up and wiped her hands against her collar, knowing her skirts were too unsanitary to use for that now, and began eating.

"He will eventually," Vahd'eel continued, picking up a piece of bread and dipping it into his food. He chewed loudly, his mouth thankfully closed, but the sounds of his jaw moving seemed more like an animal's than a man's. At least his wrists were bound by the same element shackles as her own.

"When he does, will you wish it were Dravian Valcor?"

X'odia did her best to keep her head down. She hoped her muddied hair would keep from revealing the red in her cheeks. She had no reason to blush or to think of Dravian so, but she'd indeed found herself wishing it was he who'd come to watch over her again. Not for anything immoral, not for anything like what Vahd'eel was implying. Rellor was just so much worse.

When she refused to reply, Vahd'eel laughed. He sunk his teeth into the stale bread and ripped it apart. From the corner of her eye, X'odia thought he looked like a wolf tearing open the flesh of its kill. She shuddered.

"He longs for you too," Vahd'eel continued. "Though not like Rellor. Rellor wants to rip you open, hear you scream as he takes your purity. He knows how much you cherish it."

She kept eating. It took every bit of strength not to drop her food.

"Dravian, though . . . " Vahd'eel lifted his bowl, flicking his tongue at it repeatedly. X'odia furrowed her brows, a small element igniting. Her bindings swallowed it back up.

"I'm not your prisoner," she snapped. "Why do you speak to me so?"

Vahd'eel laughed again, more heartily this time. He'd thinned as she had since she'd first encountered him in Riverdee's coast, but he didn't seem to mind as some of his food escaped his lips. It smeared across his jaw and neck, the image of an animal feasting only growing stronger.

Not a wolf, though, she decided, watching him more intently. *A vulture.*

"How much do you know about your father?" he asked. X'odia opened her mouth before quickly closing it, deciding her curiosity wasn't merited. Vahd'eel had known who she was the moment he'd seen her swirling gaze. That was why he'd looked at the women on the balconies during the attacks— why he'd only cared what he'd seen in their eyes. He was dangerous, likely more than all the men in the camp. She'd be smart not to let her tongue slip in front of him.

"Fiends!" someone shouted, hoisting a *called* spear above their shoulder. X'odia started, tossing aside her bowl and springing to her feet.

The soldiers around her cast elements and hurled daggers in a second's time, creatures sprinting into the camp and lunging at them. With her wrists bound and no *touched* blades in sight, X'odia stood helpless, watching in horror as the camp erupted into mayhem.

She looked down at Vahd'eel. It'd been him who had controlled the fiends before, the day she and the sailors had come to Riverdee. But now, with his wrists bound in chains . . .

Vahd'eel still sat smiling, hardly fazed as the battle began around them. His eyes stayed locked onto X'odia, the strange shadow of something slowly creeping out from behind him. X'odia felt her breathing cease, her feet locked as the shadow began to reveal itself.

It looked like a kind of panther, but with horns extending back from its head and tentacle-like whiskers. The tips of them pulsed a bluish hue, its eyes a cold, icy shade. When its lips pulled back hungrily, blood dripped down from sharp teeth.

"Paenah, my love," Vahd'eel said, at last rising. His hand extended toward the thing, his skin drifting into the dark fur as he pet its neck. The fiend purred, a low, growling sound, its icy eyes looking eagerly at X'odia.

Vahd'eel's own eyes narrowed. "We've found her."

With a flash, the creature was atop her. Its long claws pinned her to the ground, its horned head leaning forward. X'odia screamed as its whiskers stroked along her neck and face. Their touch was agony—fiery and freezing and stinging all at once. X'odia's lungs burned as she yelled.

Then the pain was gone. The fiend retreated, several daggers pierced into its back. It howled. The sound nearly forced blood from X'odia's ears. She wasted no time getting to her feet as the strong grasp of someone grabbed her arm.

She was quickly pulled onto the back of a horse. The howls of the fiend grew dimmer behind them, X'odia's fingers clasping firmly to the waist of her aider. He called more blades, throwing them at the fiends surrounding them.

The soldier's heightened position atop his horse gave him an advantage. Not all were as lucky, and most would join their comrades' deaths if they didn't run from the slaughter.

No armor lined their bodies, only light elemental tunics and coats. X'odia wished their customs weren't so susceptible and exposed. The creations of the mind were useless if a talon pierced their hearts.

"I can help you!" she yelled, clinging to the soldier's back. Beneath his clothes, she could feel him perspiring. "Please, you have to unbind me!"

The man continued to make his marks, her words seemingly lost to the chaos. He turned for just a moment, enough for X'odia to see his face.

It was Markeem. Even if he'd heard her, a mute man couldn't reply. And she doubted he had the keys to her chains.

With a deep breath, she let go of his back, pushed against him, and threw her leg over the horse. Markeem looked back with wide eyes, his head whirling as he tried to guide his mount back to her. A fiend came between them though, cutting him off.

X'odia sprinted away, praying Markeem would survive. She had to help him and the men and women still ensnared in the onslaught.

She had to find Dravian.

With a panicked glance, she looked past the dying soldiers around her until she caught sight of Dravian's armor. It hardly seemed like him then, the dancing blades she'd seen him wield before now slow and clumsy.

"Dravian!" she screamed. The wounds along her face from Vahd'eel's fiend tore, but she pressed through the pain. If she didn't reach Dravian soon, she wouldn't be able to heal or use her elements. She needed him to free her.

"Dravian!"

The Inquisitor hurled one blade into the jaws of a charging fiend, another spinning around and piercing through its neck. The blow cut through bone, the fiend's head falling to the ground and rolling forward. Dravian slew another beast quickly after, his armor splattered with blood. It was not his full outfit, much of the metal resting somewhere in the camp as only thin chainmail covered his chest. X'odia hoped none of the red that soaked through its chinks was his own.

"Dravian, you have to unbind me!" she yelled. He turned to her with surprise, his face dirty and his chest heaving. He looked at the skin along her cheeks, his eyes peering at whatever wounds the shadowy creature had left. *Vanishing* his swords, he pushed her toward the thick cover of a tree.

"You have to stay here," he ordered. His words were forced between breaths. X'odia shook her head and grabbed his chainmail, the slight motion revealing the damage to it.

It was torn apart, a heavy gash piercing through its links and into his chest. The cut was too deep to warrant his return to battle. She looked at him with distress, unsure how he was standing.

"Unbind me," she said, holding her wrists up. "I can end this."

Dravian winced as his hand fell against the tree's bark, the other rising up to hold his wounded chest. She held him up in support, her hands wetting with blood.

"Where is it?" she asked hurriedly, the screams of a dying soldier sounding not far from where they stood. She fingered through his pockets, but he quickly thrust her away. She thought for a moment he wasn't going to heed her advice, but he'd only cast her aside to grab the key from a pouch on his leg. When he had it, he yanked her arms up, fingers fumbling, and unfastened the chains.

The healing started as soon as the bindings opened. X'odia cried out as her skin mended back together. She fell to the ground beside where Dravian too collapsed, her muscles trembling.

Despite the pain, her elements had returned.

She shut her eyes, the searing light of her *auroras* rippling through her. They consumed her senses, filled her lungs, each small semblance of breath invigorating her. When she opened her eyes again, she sent the elements out like arrows.

The first wave of fiends fell instantly. A pain tore through X'odia with each heart she stopped, her own sputtering until she thought it would burst. A nausea took her, her skin cold and clammy, but she pushed through, continuing to *call* her elements. She wouldn't stop until the soldiers were safe, until every last fiend had fallen or fled. She'd make sure the bloodshed she'd encountered along the shore and in Riverdee's city wouldn't be these men and women. They were husbands, wives, sons, daughters. They were people. They deserved to keep living.

After scores of fiends were dead, X'odia's elements finally ran out. Even without the bearings to prevent her healing, her body yielded to fatigue, and she fell to the embrace of darkness.

A gentle shaking woke her.

The flames of a campfire nearly blinded her as she slowly peeled her lids open. Voices whispered around her, their words low and solaced, a sense of grimness evident in their tones. X'odia tried to make out what they were saying, but her head felt too clouded to focus on anything. She lifted her hands to her face, wiping at the tears the fire's smoke evoked, and looked up as the gentle shaking continued.

The kind eyes of Markeem looked down at her. His face was somewhat hidden under a thick cloak. He reached one hand to her back, easing her up to a sitting position as the other held her arm.

She winced at the heaviness beneath her breast. One of her hands rose to press back against it. Only after a moment did she realize her arm had lifted alone, no longer pulling the other with it.

The shackles were gone, then. X'odia looked to Markeem, but he didn't meet her eyes. She looked out to the camp, finally able to take in what she already knew.

They'd been attacked.

She understood then why her heart twisted so terribly in her chest. She'd hoped it'd all been a nightmare, a bad dream, but it clearly hadn't been. Turning back to the mute man at her side, she shook her head in consolation.

"I'm sorry," she said. She squeezed his hand, feeling a thin ring of silver that marked him a wedded man. Markeem seemed to take no note of her discovery, only lifting her to her feet.

She followed where he led, taking in the sight of all the soldiers who had fallen. Their *auroras* would drift eventually, in a few days' time, but for now their bodies were simply lifeless reminders of the men and women they'd once been. She lifted a hand up to her neck and cheeks, already knowing there'd be no blood or scars where the shadowy panther-fiend had touched her.

Why should she live, why should she heal, when so many people had to crumble to the weakness of flesh? Why, when they mattered to so many, should they fall to death instead of her?

She hung her head, hoping they didn't loathe her.

The mute man pointed his finger toward a small circle of soldiers, their backs without cloaks and their hands stained red. She nodded and headed where Markeem motioned, walking up cautiously to the group as the young Elite followed. One of them caught sight of her after a moment, all clearing from her view to reveal the injured man before them.

It was Dravian Valcor, wounded and bleeding on the forest floor.

"Both our medics were killed," a stout woman said. "And

the only other medic we have is stationed in the city, with Odin's forces."

A large, blistering bubble lay against the woman's neck, her flesh still black and red from where fire had sealed a wound. "Dravian needs stitching," she said, "but none of us knows how to do it."

A man, the only one in the group, added, "he ordered us to bring you."

X'odia nodded and surveyed Dravian's wounds. The soldiers had done as fine a job as they could, certainly without the counsel of their healers, but their efforts wouldn't save Dravian if she didn't act.

"Unwrap his bandages," she said. "And fetch whatever your medics used to clean and sew wounds. I'll need the sharpest blade you have, too. I can't sew the flesh if it's too jagged. Infection is more likely to settle that way."

The group all looked to one another, each seeming to ask the other an unvoiced query.

"What're you doing?" she pressed, looking between each of them. "Make haste!"

"We don't carry weapons," the man said. "You'll have to *call* your own if you wish to cut the wound's edges."

X'odia grunted. She pushed passed the group, kneeling down beside Dravian.

She'd never *called* a weapon before. Using the black *auroras* to create weapons was forbidden in Eve. She wasn't about to let the soldiers know that, though, and she certainly wasn't going try for the first time on Dravian. She put her hand to his forehead, his skin wet with sweat, then glanced back up and pointed.

"The medics' things!"

The group turned to Markeem. He nodded.

X'odia looked down, astonished when she found Dravian's grey-blue eyes staring at her. She hadn't realized he was still conscious. She rested her hand on his arm, examining him for a moment and thinking on the irony of their predicament. He held no power over her now, and the mute man certainly had far weaker elements than hers. She could kill them both in an instant, send a quick bolt their way and escape her forest prison.

What was there to stop her? Who was there to stop her? She was innocent; she'd told them the truth when they'd come to her with questions. Why not kill them now? Why not escape?

She knew she wouldn't do it. As much as freedom called out to her, her morality always fought against lethal thoughts. It was the same reason she hadn't refused being bound in the beginning, the same reason she hadn't taken her chance when Dravian had released her chains before. Still, perhaps she could flee, try to outrun Markeem and fall under the darkness of the night without committing any acts of violence. She didn't think he would kill her, but his loyalty would certainly try to stop her, and she doubted he would miss if he sent one of his *called* knives her way.

She took a deep breath, abandoned her liberating fantasies, and began her work on Dravian's wounds.

Despite the soldiers' denials, the medics' kits did indeed have sharp utensil for cutting. X'odia took some clean bandages and wet them with icy water, making sure her element was cold before placing the cloths atop Dravian's head. She removed his bandages as best she could, careful not to leave any of the fabric inside his flesh.

Three gashes total lined his stomach and chest, though only one seemed fatal. It was deepest just above the top of his ribs. She took a cleaning fluid from the kit and spread it across each item she planned to use, then grabbed the cutting tool and took another breath.

Carefully she evened out the skin on the gash's edges. She only cut what she needed to ensure the stitching would heal the skin well. Dravian groaned from time to time, his legs moving or his toes clenching in his boots, but he was good not to writhe too much.

The other soldiers left after delivering her the supplies, but Markeem studied intently. The fact that he was trusted alone with her and their leader—without her element shackles—solidified her acceptance of his lethality. She would never have escaped under his watch without committing violence.

"Tell me of yourself," Dravian whispered suddenly. X'odia turned, almost not having heard his request through her concentration. His head moved from side to side, his throat bobbing as he swallowed.

"Not like in the shack," he said. He opened his lids a little wider and looked at her with dark eyes, their grey-blue hardly noticeable with the orange of the campfires reflecting off of them.

"I'm not the Inquisitor now," he continued. He breathed deeply as X'odia grabbed the cloth atop his head and wet it down again. "I'm just curious of you, and your life in Eve."

X'odia nodded and glanced back over at Markeem for approval. He shrugged, then smiled as he gestured that Dravian had drunk a great deal earlier.

She smiled, then placed the cloth back atop Dravian's head.

"I was born in Neveah, the Sky City of Eve," she said. "When I was a very little girl, I used to go to school with the other children in the High Temple, where my mother was a member of the High Council, and I began my studies as a priestess. That's actually where I learned to do this, when I got older." She gestured toward her sewing hands. She smiled, more to herself than to Dravian.

He smiled back anyway.

"When I was young, my body aged normally, and my eyes didn't shift colors as they do now. I was born with green eyes—like my mother's—but they slowly became blue as I grew older. My parents thought nothing of it; children's eyes change from the time they're babes.

"As I grew older still they started to change to a dark purple, and within half a year they became almost lavender. When they started turning red, I had to wear a veil to class, and I could only take off my veil once I returned home. Within a month they turned again from red to orange, and in about another two months they'd gone from golden back to green. I stopped sleeping almost entirely, and I started to recover quickly from scrapes and bruises.

"The visions started then too, though they weren't as painful when I was a girl. I saw King Pierre of Mesidia in them—your king—when he was the Guardian of the Dagger, and Queen Rose of Xenith, before she gave the Amulet to Princess Gwenivere.

"I told my mother of the visions, of the strange blue-eyed people I'd never met that kept appearing in my head. I started studying Abra'am then, learning about the Guardians, trying to understand more about the things I Saw. If I'd just had a vision, my eyes would glow like they do directly after my visions now. If I had a vision just before school, my eyes would be too bright to hide behind a veil, so my mother began teaching me mostly from our home.

"I don't remember much of her. I do remember her reading me my favorite book, though, every night before I slept. I liked the paintings, mostly, because I didn't understand the stories, but now, sometimes, when I go to sleep, I can still picture the pages."

X'odia grew silent then, continuing on with her task. Dravian's eyes had drifted shut, his chest rising and falling with such even breaths that he almost seemed asleep.

"What happened to her?" he asked, reaching his hand out toward a water skin. X'odia would have served him the skin herself, but her hands were too occupied, and she didn't want to risk dirtying them again.

"She left, when I was nearly six," she answered. "I would see her in my visions, on occasion, but I haven't seen her in person since."

She felt a small tear fall down her cheek, not bothering to wipe it away as she kept her hands steady. She needn't tell the Elite that she'd seen a glimpse of her mother's death, had watched as her *auroras* drifted and faded to nothing in her visions. She only needed to keep sewing his wound, and then she could pray she didn't see the haunting images later.

Dravian's hand reached out and brushed against her cheek. His fingers were rough and calloused as he pushed her curls behind her ear. X'odia was taken aback by the gesture, and she tried not to look his way as his hand continued to linger. He gently wiped the tear from her face, then dropped his hand back to his side.

"I had a wife, and a son and daughter."

X'odia finally looked back over to him, glancing at his hand for the ring she'd never seen.

There wasn't one.

"Are they in Mesidia?" she asked, realizing she'd stopped her task. She made sure her vision was clear before going on, grateful only a little more of his wound still needed mending.

"My boy died when he was young," he said, looking to the stars. "My wife and I, we didn't have the wealth to take care of him when he got sick. He died of a fever, when he was only three.

"I joined the Elite after that, promised my wife I'd send her coin. I told her I'd visit, that I'd come back to see them when I had the chance. I never did. I just stayed with the Elite and kept giving her every bit of coin I could. If I went back, I'd be reminded of my son's death, and there is no greater mourning in a man's life than the death of his child.

"I still loved my wife, though. I told her that in every letter I sent. She'd write back, tell me how big Milian was getting, even send me little paintings she'd done. She was only a baby when I left for the Elite; she didn't know who I was, but she started writing her name on the bottom of the letters as she got older. I wanted to go back home every time I got one. I wanted to see my wife and girl, but every time that want came, another opportunity came in Pierre's ranks. I was always afraid if I didn't take them, the Creator would punish me for abandoning my calling, and something would happen to my girl as it had my son.

"Three years passed without me coming home. Caileen, my wife, stopped writing she loved me at the bottom of her letters. She stopped letting my daughter write her name.

"Five years passed. Caileen told me she'd met another. She said for so long she prayed I'd come home, that I'd come back to them and give up serving my king, and when I never did, she started to pray that I'd died so she wouldn't feel guilty for no longer loving me. She married another man after that, gave Milian a proper father. And I just . . . kept going."

X'odia sat quietly beside Dravian. His tale had taken some time to tell, his words slow through laden breaths. She'd finished mending his wound long before he was done.

She had no purpose to linger; the warmth of a blanket tempted her chilled bones, and the realization that this man held her captive berated her sympathizing spirit. Yet still she remained, fingers laced in her lap, ears and eyes patient as she listened to the sad story he told.

As he finally fell to the calls of slumber, she leaned forward and removed the cold cloth from his head. She stroked his hair for a moment, then let her fingers drift to the stubble of his jaw.

She pulled her hand back quickly when she realized what she was doing.

Unsure whether she should leave or stay, she looked to Markeem. The soldier made no gesture to indicate a preference toward either. Deciding she might be needed to aid Dravian again, she leaned against the stump of a nearby tree and folded her arms around herself.

Markeem strode over, seeming to note she was cold, and gave her a cloak. She accepted it with thanks before realizing it was the same one Dravian had given her before.

This time, despite knowing it was his, she didn't mind wrapping it around her shoulders.

It's true that I was once betrothed to the Natalia Barie, despite her being of the Victorian line. It was that very betrothal that prompted Pierre to give heirdom to Roland instead of me. At the time I felt I was losing nothing, as I loved Natalia dearly. It wasn't until she called off the betrothal, just after my status was revealed, that I felt the consequences of loving her.

From a letter between Dorian Cliffborne and Abaddon
Haroldson

CHAPTER 59

NATALIA

Dorian stood with his weight rocking from the back of his heels to the tips of his toes, his hands together in front of him. Natalia knew he loathed her, at least assumed he did, but he'd always been the one man she couldn't entirely read. Her past with him had made her ignorant to his thoughts, and she hated that he skewed her judgment.

One thing she could sense was his displeasure at being called to her chambers. Solitude with her, his former betrothed, made him appear susceptible to the desires of the flesh. People would gossip about their meeting, make insinuations and improper implications.

Good. Let them.

"My knight tells me you refused at first when I requested you come to my chambers," she said, leaning from her lax position and setting her wineglass down. Her bodice hadn't been very modest as it was, but it left less to imagine when she bent forward and stood. She noted Dorian doing his best to ignore it.

"I don't much like being ordered by a boy," he said.

"Oh? Do I sense a bit of jealously, Ambassador?"

"Sir Nicolas is as fine a knight as any. He's just young is all."

"Young and attractive, you mean."

She offered a glass to him, but he shook his head. She shrugged and sat down.

"I hadn't realized men with such soft features were what you fancied these days, but I suppose I never really knew what you wanted."

Natalia fought back a wince. The silent tapping of her fingers along her wineglass halted for a moment before picking up their pace again. It was barely a second, if even that, but it'd been enough.

"He's loyal, and I admire loyalty," she said simply. She gestured to the chair beside her. "Would you like to sit?"

He did want to sit. She could sense it in the way he shifted his weight, his feet likely tired from his endless meetings throughout the palace. Even then, after appearing to think it over, he refused.

He always thinks I'm trying to trick people, she thought. It wasn't an unmerited assumption, but it bothered her that Dorian thought of her that way. Didn't he remember the nights they'd been with each other? Didn't he remember her confessing her love for him?

It didn't matter if he did.

She took another sip of wine.

"Gerard has signed a treaty with the nations surrounding Mesidia," she said. "It says they'll aid the Victorians if Pierre doesn't agree to surrender his hold on the throne."

She looked up, watching for Dorian's response. He was fixating on her, likely trying to figure out if she was telling the truth. She knew how the words sounded, how terrible they must seem to him. The King of Peace was Pierre's greatest ally, the one man who'd always stood by Pierre when civil war had seemed all but certain. He couldn't suddenly sway. Not after the suffering Mesidia had endured during the Attack of Fiends.

"Gerard is the King of Peace," Dorian said slowly. "He doesn't threaten any nation with violence. Certainly not the nation of his own birth."

"I thought the same. But that doesn't make it untrue."

Dorian chuckled. He ran his hands through his hair and looked up, first to the lavish room, then to the elegant furniture filling it. He eyed the door he'd come through as well, likely cursing her beautiful knight Nicolas just outside, then eyed the aged bottle of wine beside her.

She swallowed when he peered out her window, out at the kingdom that extended beyond her balcony. She knew how it all must seem. Xenith was the Realm of Scholars, the most prestigious nation in all Abra'am. And now she was suddenly its daughter.

She glanced back at Dorian, hardly realizing she'd started staring into the red of her wine. The ambassador's chest heaved, up and down and up again, his fists clenched tightly at his side.

He wasn't chuckling anymore. He wasn't looking about.

He was staring straight at her.

"You whore," he whispered. He crossed the room, stopping just shy of her chair. She stayed still, eyeing him flatly, daring him to act.

What could he possibly do? Call her more foul names? He certainly couldn't harm her, not with Nicolas just outside her door.

She stood up, close enough to feel his breath, then made her way to her window.

"It wasn't me who convinced him to do such a thing," she

said softly. Her blue dress glistened under the sunlight, and her silver-blond hair was almost metallic under its warmth. She wondered if Dorian hated how her newfound wealth bathed her so derisively.

"You'd become Mesidia's queen if the Victorians rule," he said. "You'll become a Guardian of Eve. How can I believe that's not what you wanted?"

Natalia turned, the jewels in her hair casting small reflections on the ceiling. She laughed, the sound surprisingly hopeless, and shook her head.

"I never asked you to believe I didn't want those things. But even if I did, it wouldn't matter. I belong to Xenith now."

She lifted up her palm and displayed the pledging scar across her skin. To die for one nation and live again in another, to be born with living blood into a new land. The Baptism of Blood.

Natalia thought herself fierce and cruel and ruthless, but she was loyal too. She'd sacrificed her own body and her own wants and desires when it meant gaining what her mother Yvaine deemed worthy of knowing.

And if she'd bled with intent for Xenith, she'd forever be a daughter of Xenith. She was not one to break her vows.

"Gerard informed me that my father was killed," she continued, "and that my mother has been captured. Pierre is holding her in Stonewall's dungeons. Gerard has been told she was aiding the fiend attacks that came to Mesidia.

"He offered me a home here, said he wanted me to help guide Gwenivere after he dies. He wanted to keep me safe—that's what he made me believe at least. He signed the treaty later that day, when my blood still stained the carpet beside his throne. He knew what was to happen, at least had some idea. I believe he did have my best interest in mind, though. And Mesidia's.

"Yendor, Theatia, The Arctic, and Prianthia—they all

seemed to have found a way to convince him to sign against the Laighless bloodline, even without me to lead the Victorians and gain back the throne. They thought they could use and manipulate me if Pierre surrenders. I certainly don't believe they'd have been able to, but if they can convince the King of Peace to turn his back on his birth nation, then perhaps I too would've fallen under their influence."

Natalia stood quietly then, her body tense.

Dorian's breathing shifted, more pondering than angry. She'd listened to him breathe like that so many times, as he wondered how to appease foreign diplomats or how to convey Mesidia's interests. He wasn't just an ambassador because Pierre had decided to make Roland the heir instead of him; he was truly good at what he did. He cared about people—about everyone—borders and bloodlines meaning little to him when it came to what was fair. It was why she'd loved him.

"I suppose we're not unlike Gerard," she said. Her wineglass had gone empty, so she set it down, not bothering to refill it.

"How so?" he asked.

"All three of us are now devoted to a nation that's not our own." She ran a finger along her collarbone, gentle and meandering. "He was born to Mesidia; now he rules in the interest of Xenith. I was born to Mesidia, and now I too must conduct myself with Xenith in mind. And then there's you, the orphan from Yendor. An olive tint in your skin, golden eyes and black hair. Even Gerard's and Aden's hair is brown, when they stand in the sun. But yours"—she paused, walking back to him and running her fingers through his hair—"Yours is like a raven's feathers. You can't even try to hide what you are."

Dorian's jaw locked, but he said nothing. Natalia took that as permission to go on. Her fingers turned from gentle to stern, her nails gliding against the back of his neck before stroking into his hair and back again. Her perfume was subtle, only a single spray against her neck, but she could see his eyes searching for the exact spot it'd soaked her skin. It was the same scent she'd always worn, the same scent he'd loved so much when she'd rested in his arms. Lily blossom, a scent only made in Yendor. He'd always told her it reminded him of home.

"What's your point?" he finally asked.

She pulled her hand back, forcing a smile.

"Pierre is a stubborn man. He believes his bloodline deserves the throne, so much so that he was willing to ruin his own son's future to ensure it didn't end up in my hands.

"Gerard signed the treaty because he knows that if he hadn't, Mesidia would fall into the wraths of war, and blood would soak its lands more than the rains. He loves Pierre, views him as his own brother, but he won't allow such feelings to impede on what a king must do. One doesn't earn the title King of Peace by making choices that fit whatever he desires.

"In his perfect world, his treaty mates would have aided the Laighless family and not the Victorians. But he did what he thought best for Mesidia, and for Xenith. It may seem he's demolished his devotion, but I don't see it as that. And I don't begrudge him.

"I do, however, question the loyalty you bear so proudly." She cocked her head, surveying him. "Mesidia is not your birth nation, Pierre is not your father, and the throne you thought to be yours was taken because you wanted to marry me. You have no reason to hold allegiance to Mesidia, and you have no reason to die for either mine or Roland's lines. You're an orphan of Yendor; you're a wanderer who ended up in the care of royals. But you can walk away. You can go wherever you please. You have no reason to hold an alliance with anyone, and no one will condemn you if you leave."

She let her statement linger, then eased herself back into her chair. She propped one leg atop the other, the slits of her skirts exposing skin.

Dorian looked to the ground. Natalia knew he battled with feelings of contempt toward Pierre and Rosalie, knew he still begrudged them for dangling Mesidia's throne and taking it away. They'd told him time and time again that it was not blood that made him their son but love, and the throne and the Dagger would be his when the time came.

But they'd gone back on their word. They'd given the Dagger to Roland, named him heir, all because Dorian had fallen in love with her. It was easy to blame her with the reputation she held, and it was certainly easy to blame someone of the Victorian blood. Victorians had, after all, always been enemies with the Laighless family.

But beneath all that hatred Dorian directed her way, she knew he didn't entirely blame her. There was disdain in his heart for the inheritance Pierre had alluded to, and there was disdain for the man Pierre called his son. Roland Laighless had done nothing but be born from Rosalie's womb. What'd he ever done to deserve Mesidia's throne?

"Make your point, if you have one," Dorian repeated.

Natalia flashed another smile, if only to hide the desire she had to console him.

"Pierre won't surrender," she said. "Even with the devastation of having Gerard's name on the treaty, Pierre will still force the Elite to fight. He'll take war before he'll raise the white flag, especially if he believes I'll break my Baptism of Blood and lead the Victorians.

"You don't owe anything to anyone, though. You're your own man. But you're a man who is destined for greatness, and a man who was meant to mend a nation where others cannot."

She stood then, pulling a small knife from a drawer beside her and looking up at him. Slowly she came back to where he stood, gently grabbing his hand and placing the sheathed blade in it.

"A Mesidian blade, an heirloom of Queen Victoria herself,"

she said. "It was one of the few things my ancestors were able to keep after the Great Castle was destroyed."

Dorian examined the hilt. It was a twisted work of glass, a slender sapphire running through its center. Natalia knew he'd seen it before, knew he'd watched her untie its strap from beneath her skirts before lying down to share his bed. He'd loved it, loved knowing her secret, but she hadn't ever thought he'd paid much mind to it until he'd proposed. The ring he'd given her, the one she'd worn so happily for so short a time, had been made of glass with a sapphire as its stone.

"I know what it is, Natalia," Dorian said. "I can't take it."

Despite herself, Natalia had to force back tears. She shook her head, her grasp on his fingers tightening.

"Please," she choked, backing away from him. He shook his head as he attempted to refuse but stopped when he looked to her again.

"Gerard's name on the treaty won't be enough for Pierre," she repeated. She reached up, her arm extending as her fingers brushed against his cheek. "Go back to Mesidia. Use the blade to name yourself its son. Lead the Victorians; you've lived as one of the Laighlesses, but you were once betrothed to me. You are a man who can rally both bloods. You can mend our nation—"

Her words were cut short as Dorian forced her lips to his. She didn't fight his touch or refuse his fervent grasp. She accepted it, knowing she should not.

His grasp shifted from her neck down to her waist, every small distance he traced forcing her pulse faster. With all the strength she possessed, she pulled away, burying her head in his chest as they both stood breathless. He wrapped his arms around her, kissing the top of her head.

"You can't ask me to do this alone," he whispered, clasping her tighter. Natalia clenched her eyes shut to keep from crying, hoping he didn't sense her weakness as she clung to him.

"I'm a daughter of Xenith now," she whispered back. "Pierre will never surrender if I have any part of Mesidia's rule."

She felt Dorian sigh, imagining he might perhaps share the same pain she did. She held him for a time, contemplating the consequences of Mesidia's unrest and imagining a life without him in sight. Even when she'd taken others, she'd never forgotten the love of their youth. She would always love him.

At last she stepped away, her scabbed palm burning as it pressed against Dorian's chest. Her heart ached as his fingers lingered on her own, refusing to let her go.

"Go to Mesidia," she said, casting aside the yearning in her chest. She held the sapphire-hilted knife out to him again, the piercing of her gaze softened as she silently pleaded him to take it.

He kissed her lightly once more, then took the knife.

Natalia Barie

As someone who cares dearly for those I'm close to, I find it difficult to depict Natalia. She's been cruel to my family, and she's manipulated people who've been kind to her.

But alas, I am an artist, and cannot deny that she makes for a fine model. Perhaps someday she will no longer bear the mind her mother shaped.

From the sketchbook of Elizabeth al'Murtagh

CHAPTER 60

GWENIVERE

Gwenivere abandoned the thought of sleep when the morning was still dark. She watched her people from her balcony's windows as they gathered for a good place to marvel. She shivered, the cold air of the coming winter seeping through the lace in her clothes.

It was Natalia's name day, the day she'd formally be born into Xenith. It was rare that such an event occurred, the ceremony considered a blessing from the Light. Many great kings and queens in Xenith's history had been brought under the fall's cascading into the palace's lakes, the water of the land poured over them and cleansing them of their previous selves.

Gerard himself had undergone the ceremony, and Gwenivere's grandmother before him, generations and generations of men and women having vowed to serve Xenith. Queen Rose had told Gwenivere of how beautiful the ceremony was when

Gerard had undergone it, how much hope it gave people. It had always seemed a turning point in the War of Fire, a moment of strength and assurance when the harmony of the world had threatened to shake.

"Milady," a rough voice called. Gwenivere tore her gaze from the gathering people, shutting her windows as she walked to her chamber door. Garron waited patiently as she opened it, the large, blue eyes of a chambermaid waiting behind him.

"Sir Garron," she said formally, glancing at the girl. "Maiden."

The dark-haired servant curtsied clumsily, her nose nearly to the floor as she pulled at her skirts. Gwenivere watched her, holding the door ajar and beckoning her in. She did so swiftly, scampering in and looking for a task.

"Fetch me a gown for the ceremony," Gwenivere ordered. "A white one, and modest." She thought about the cold outside, about how it would be amplified from the mist of the falls, and added, "And warm!"

Garron stood attentively, waiting for the girl to do as she'd been bid. He likely would've left if Gwenivere wasn't leaning against the door's frame, waiting for the chambermaid to disappear. When she did, Gwenivere turned her attention back to him, peering down the hall.

"Where's Becca?" she whispered. "Why hasn't she been returned to my service?"

"She was requested by the Prianthian sisters," Garron answered. "And Natalia."

Gwenivere groaned. Becca was the only one who knew she'd accepted Roland's hand, that he'd given up the Dagger of Eve to Dietrich of Sadie. If Natalia found out somehow, if she knew . . .

Gwenivere didn't want to think what would happen if she knew.

"All right, thank you Garron. I'll see you soon."

The rest of the morning went by as Gwenivere imagined

it would. The new chamber girl did her best to dress her, and then Garron, along with a small band of knights, accompanied her through the palace's halls. Maximus was there as well, leading another troop with Aden.

As they made their way to the gardens, Gwenivere took a moment to look through the trees and petals. What little hadn't yet died in the autumn's air had fallen during the Attack of Fiends. She clutched her Amulet, remembering vividly when she'd leaped from the palace and onto the garden's grounds. She looked up to the windows, noting the one she'd jumped through after killing the teradacts. When she blinked, she could still see the city the way it had been that day, the pillars of smoke from the fiends' flames and the bolts and arrows that'd launched into the sky.

The cries she heard in her head morphed into the ringing of the city bells. She forced her lids back open.

"It'll be my birthday soon," Aden whispered. Gwenivere squinted, then looked down at her small brother. He was right; it would be his birthday soon. But if that was true, then that meant hers had already passed. How many moons had it been since the Attack of Fiends?

The large expanse of the lake they approached was surrounded by a sea of white, the people dressed in the very simplest and chic of garb. They needed this day, something besides the past masquerade to help cheer their spirits. Repairs to the city—and their livelihoods—were still in disarray.

The heavy mist of the falls was felt even from where Gwenivere and Aden eventually stood. The princess was grateful then that her new chambermaid had listened to her request for thick clothing. She glanced out at the lake, the waters tranquil save where the falls crashed. She wondered if she was the only one who remembered it was from the lake's depths the Behemoth had awoken.

The crowd stirred as they caught sight of Gerard. A simple

silver crown sat atop his dark hair, and a white cloak whipped gently behind his back. With him stood the guard of Sir Charles and Sir Nicolas, the two men clothed in the same light armor as Garron and Maximus beside her. Nicolas looked as beautiful as any man could, the white complementing the tan of his skin and the blue of his eyes. It was almost comical seeing him next to Charles, the old man nearly as pale as his garb. Even his hair, what little there was, matched the white of his cloak.

The bustles from the crowd heightened when Natalia emerged from behind the king. She wore a radiant white dress, which flowed freely against her body, and her hair looked more silver than gold as it fell in loose waves to her waist. She smiled and looked out at the people. The king took her hand and walked her closer to the water.

Gwenivere had half expected Natalia's dress to be the shift she slept in. She was glad the woman had dressed appropriately.

Gerard lifted Natalia's hand, guiding her through the dark rocks along the lake's shore and to the river's falls. When they were feet away from it, Gerard released her, accepting a silver chalice from Charles and walking closer to the waters.

He filled the chalice until it overflowed, returning to where the duchess stood. When he stood just a pace away, he nodded. Natalia carefully lifted her skirts as she kneeled to the ground. She closed her eyes. Her chest and shoulders rose as she took a deep breath. Then her neck fell back, awaiting the formal cleansing.

Gerard lifted the chalice high, the crystal waters slipping from its curves and running against Natalia's forehead. The crowds cheered. When the last droplet had been poured, Natalia brought her head back up and smiled brightly.

"Your first name day ceremony. What did you think?"

Gerard said the words to Gwenivere from back in his throne room, seeming cheerful as he drained honey-colored liquid from his cup and filled it again. He looked happier than he had in days, the heavy bags under his eyes gone and the slight hunch in his weary stance straightened.

Gwenivere didn't know how to answer him. She didn't want to dampen his mood, especially when she was preparing to tell him her intentions for marriage. But, if she were being truthful, she hated that Natalia was now formally a Xen.

"It was grand."

Gerard chuckled. "Grand indeed. You know your mother said when I became a son of Xenith, she remembered that day more than the day we married." He paused, beaming. "She said it wasn't my marrying her that made me a king, but my vowing to serve this kingdom. She said she'd never seen a more just ruler, even if I was born a peasant."

Gerard's expression shifted then, as if saddened at the thought of Rose.

"Speaking of . . . marriage," Gwenivere started, not wanting him to dwell. Her father glanced back up, the cheer in his face returned.

"Yes?"

She opened her mouth to answer, but a heavy tapping at the door cut her off. Gerard quickly called the person in. Sir Nicolas entered and, behind him, Natalia.

"May I join?" she asked.

Gwenivere turned to her father, who was already looking at her coolly. He had to know she wouldn't want Natalia there when she revealed her marriage acceptance to him, but Natalia would know of her decision soon enough. She supposed there was no harm in her knowing now.

"Yes, join us," Gwenivere said. Natalia came forward as Nicolas left. The door shut loudly behind him. Gwenivere and her father returned to their thrones, Natalia not bothering to sit in a simpler one as she stood against a pillar at Gerard's side.

"Gwenivere was just going to tell me who she's chosen to marry," he said.

Natalia gave a contrived, "Ah, I see." Gwenivere made to start again, but her mouth was suddenly dry. She knew there was no fault in her decision, not when Roland no longer held the title of Guardian, yet she couldn't seem to settle the unease that twisted in her stomach.

"Roland gave up the Dagger," she blurted. "I-I've chosen him to marry."

The room was silent. Gwenivere gritted her teeth, chancing a look at her father.

Any joy in his face was gone. His lips were tight beneath his beard, his eyes slim and glaring. Behind him, Natalia stood with raised brows.

"I forbade you, Gwenivere," Gerard said quietly. He stood, nostrils flaring, and leaned in toward her. "I *forbade* you."

"Because he held the Dagger," she said, rising with him. "Because he was a Guardian of Eve—"

"Because he's our enemy!"

The shout echoed through the chamber. Gwenivere stepped back, the words hitting her like a strike to the stomach. She swallowed, then glanced over at Natalia, who'd managed to recover her shock. She now stood with knowing pity.

"Because of you?" Gwenivere asked.

Natalia shook her head. "No. My being here hasn't altered this. I pledged my life to Xenith before the Laighless family lost your alliance. I played no part in it."

"In what?"

Gerard put up his hand, his anger now coalesced with remorse. He grabbed the side of his throne, clenched, rather, to the ornate extensions that continued past either side of its back, and sighed.

"The civil unrest in Mesidia has placed a burden on the economies of its neighboring nations. They began drafting a treaty to renounce their support to Pierre and Rosalie, due to what they felt was a lack of necessary leadership. Yendor reached out to me, some time ago, explaining that the flow of goods from the West to the East has suffered immensely since the Victorians have been causing such turmoil.

"I refused to be a part of anything that went against Pierre, especially since Yendor didn't pose a threat to us. They're far, and as they were already facing strife, I didn't believe they could support or provide for an army. I told them we would address the issues during the Peace Gathering and dismissed it as nothing more than a political obstacle.

"By the time the Masquerade was underway and the Attack of Fiends occurred, Theatia, Prianthia, and the Arctic had unified with Yendor's cause. An attack stemming from the northeast hadn't seemed a considerable risk, but coming in against nearly every one of Mesidia's borders was something I couldn't ignore."

Gwenivere stood motionless, concentrating as much on her father's words as she did on her effort to stand. She felt lightheaded, her weight drifting into nothingness as she reminded herself what her feet felt like beneath her. She licked her lips, biting the lower one as it passed under her tongue.

"So you . . . abandoned them?" she asked. "You turned your back on Mesidia?"

Natalia scoffed, stepping away from the pillar she leaned on. "He's not turning his back on all of Mesidia. The Laighlesses are just one family."

Gwenivere shook her head, feeling as her *auroras* began to brighten in her mind. She tried to force even breaths through her nose, fearful she'd burn the entire room to the ground.

"She's right," Gerard said, walking toward Gwenivere. "Justice and peace are joined, but there is no justice in allying with Pierre's men. Keeping people alive—innocent, helpless people—that's justice."

"That's an excuse," Gwenivere said. "That's fear. That's being a coward." Her voice began to rise, her finger pointing in accusation. "Yvaine has flooded the Mesidian people with lies, led fiends against the people of Stonewall—"

"That's not true," Natalia interrupted. "Pierre has lost the faith of his people, and he'll make any claims he can to gain it back."

"An entire legion of Elite saw it happen!" Gwenivere yelled. "Your mother has been desperate for power her entire life, so much so that she forced you to bed Dorian because she thought he'd inherit the throne."

Gerard stepped forward, stopping beside Natalia. Gwenivere froze, a coldness sinking into her, and watched as he lay a steadfast hand on Natalia's shoulder.

"That doesn't explain how she could've been controlling the fiends, Gwenivere. Nothing explains that claim."

"But I felt it!" she said pleadingly. "I felt the way someone, something, controlled the fiends in Xenith's attack. I felt the way they came for me, the desire they had for my Amulet. It was no different with Yvaine and the Dagger. Do you not believe Roland and Pierre? Do you not believe me?"

Gerard stood quietly, his refusal to speak more of an answer than any words he might mutter. Gwenivere put a hand on her stomach, the smug reassurance in Natalia's stance making her sick. The king was becoming more the Mesidian's father than he was her own.

"Many people saw the Cloaked Prince, Gwenivere," Natalia said. "They saw his dragon, and they saw you with him. But I wouldn't accuse you of leading an attack against your own city, just as I wouldn't accuse my mother of attacking Stonewall."

Gwenivere struggled to breathe, overpowered and outnumbered. How could her father not hear Natalia? How could he stand so resolutely beside her?

"That was different," she insisted. "Dietrich and I almost died fighting to protect Voradeen. Not once did we raise a sword against it."

"And Yvaine was never seen with a sword before Pierre's claims either," Gerard countered. "Neither of us is insisting that you had any part in what happened. We simply feel it's unlikely that Yvaine—a woman who's fought to do what she believes is right for her kingdom—would lead a slaughter against it."

Gwenivere looked between the two of them. Her sight spun. She raised her palms to her head, trying to ease the sickness that filled her skull.

"Was that what changed your mind then?" she pressed. "Pierre's claims? About Yvaine? Even if they weren't true, how would that be any different than the things she's said about him?"

"Are you mad?" Natalia quipped. "Have you even been listening? It—"

"Silence!" Gwenivere yelled. "I wasn't speaking to you! I wasn't asking your opinion! As my inferior, I order that you be silent. If cutting your hand and sprinkling water over your head makes you a Xen, then heed my command: Do not speak unless spoken to. Do not think your words are of any value. Do not mistake your nights spent with a former heir as anything that warrants worth to your being. You. Are. Nothing."

A hand snatched Gwenivere's arm, pulling her away roughly and thrusting her aside. She nearly fell to the floor, the tall stance of her father casting a shadow over her. The flare of her *auroras* burned out, her heart twisting at the condemnation in his eyes.

"Mesidia was your home once," she said. "Pierre was your king. You served him."

Any sympathy Gerard had shown was gone, only a cold stone seeming to lie in the confines of his chest. He turned his back to her, returning to his throne and resting himself in its seat.

It had never appeared so unfitting.

"Served," he repeated. He put emphasis on its end, stressing the implied tense of the past. "I serve Xenith now."

Gwenivere looked at him, the pounding of her heart and the strain of her breath the only thing she seemed to hear. She followed where he sat, standing before his throne, and leaned in toward him.

"You are no Xen," she spat. "You only serve your name."

She saw him sitting, his back to the chair's, and she saw him lunging, but she never saw his fist as it rose to strike her.

The Golden Knight came into my tavern today. He drank until he was nearly drunk, which is saying something as he's a large man. I didn't mind. I've needed the coin ever since the Attack of Fiends damaged my tavern's roof.

He did let slip some of his quarrels. He said something about questioning the actions of King Gerard. From what I caught, it sounded like he called his sword on him.

Good thing he's the Golden Knight. Most men would be sent to the Arctic's dungeons for such transgressions.

A Xen tavern owner

CHAPTER 61

GWENIVERE

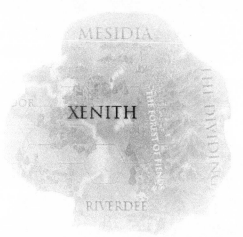

"You said you thought the Prianthians might know?"
Gwenivere heard the question. She heard it through
the throbbing in her skull. She groaned, trying to make out
the view of her surroundings, but her blurred sight made it
too difficult. She kept to the ground, grateful for the cool tile
against her face.

She'd never really thought she could see her lids when she
closed her eyes, but she seemed to see them now. Even her
lashes seemed to cast little shadows when she tried to force her
lids open.

"She tells Becca everything," Natalia answered. Her voice
was quiet, but also far too loud. "And the sisters are known for
making people talk."

"If Alanna knows, and she tells the others, they may take
this as a sign that we're trying to aid the Laighlesses."

The Laighlesses? How could he say that? How could he refer to them like that? Not Pierre, not Rosalie, not Roland. Just the Laighlesses.

"Get the girl quickly, and Alanna. We must find out if the Verkevs know."

Footsteps sounded after that, banging like a blacksmith's hammer on the inside of Gwenivere's head. She managed to force herself up, her arms somehow finding a way to prop her off the floor. The chamber door opened, and more footsteps followed, these ones heavier than the last. They came toward her with urgency. When they were there, she felt strong hands—Garron's hands—lift her up and back into her throne.

"Did Natalia do this?" he asked. Gwenivere smiled, forcing her lids open again. It still made her dizzy, the smeared way her sight appeared, but she could try to see. She would do anything for him, for her perfect knight. She loved him so much.

"No," Gerard said, "I did."

Gwenivere blinked a few more times, each time seeming like a small frame of a moving painting, like the little birds that flew in the corners of her books when she shuffled the pages quickly. Only this time, instead of a bird, it was a sword, the strange swirl of *auroras* forming into existence.

"*Vanish* your sword, Garron," Gerard demanded, waving his hand. "I don't need your defiance to know I've done wrong."

The Golden Knight stood silent, his eyes peering as he looked upon his king. Slowly he did as he was commanded, releasing his *called* blade. Gwenivere forced her eyes to stay open, her blurred sight at last shifting into focus. Garron had done what he was ordered, but his stance hinted that he wasn't leaving her side.

"Let me tell you what's about to happen," Gerard said, kindness present in his voice again. Gwenivere didn't mean to pour salt in the wound that was his shame, but her hand couldn't help rising to her temple. It still pounded where he'd struck. Especially when he spoke.

"Natalia believes your serving girl may have told the Prianthian sisters about your betrothal to Roland. According to her, the girl already let it slip when she was bringing Natalia her bathing towels, but she hadn't thought anything of it at the time. Hence why she didn't tell me. She thought the girl was just gossiping."

Gwenivere winced as she felt the bump on her head, another wave of nausea beginning to envelop her. She sat still for a time, waiting for the moment to pass, unsure whether she should hold her head or her stomach.

Serving girl? Becca? Becca was the only one who knew. But she wouldn't have said anything. She wouldn't have let it slip, as if it was some good bit of gossip between maids. If she'd said anything, it was because Natalia forced her to, not because she'd had a careless tongue.

"Did you tell her?"

Gwenivere opened her eyes again, realizing her father had asked the question twice. She tried to nod, but the motion seemed too difficult, so she managed a hoarse yes. He sighed heavily, leaning back in his throne.

"Did you send a parchment back in reply?" he asked. "Did you sign it? Did you seal it with Xenith's seal?"

Gwenivere hardly had to think, the image of the seal, of the rose without thorns, embedded into her mind.

Regretfully, she answered again.

"Yes."

The chamber doors opened. The Prianthian sisters stormed in. The fullest figured of the three, Anastasia, clung tightly to Becca, the girl's hair tangled and her dress torn. Bruises lined her face and arms, her lips swollen and red from being struck. Natalia stood behind them all, a strange air of knowing emitting from her. As shocking as it was to see Becca so battered and beaten, it was more startling to see how unsurprised the rest of the women seemed. Gwenivere couldn't resist reaching for her *auroras*.

"What have you done to her?" she spat.

Anastasia raised a single brow, shoving Becca forward with indifference. The servant ran to Gwenivere and collapsed at her feet.

"So you're to wed the Laighless prince?" the heiress, Alanna, asked. She strode forward, her thin frame lined with muscle beneath her clothes. Garron stepped forward, a giant standing over a girl.

"No," Gwenivere answered, shaking her head. All the pain and self-pity she'd felt for herself evaporated as she held her sobbing servant. "I was going to, but no."

"How do you expect us to trust you?" Alanna asked, turning toward Gerard. "You can't even trust your own daughter."

"First the fiends and the dragon with the Sadiyan prince," Anastasia added, nearly spitting as she said Dietrich's title. "And now this. The treachery within a man's daughter shows the treachery in a man's heart."

Gerard sat calmly, turning away from the Prianthians' glowers as he gestured to his knight.

"Sir Garron, please escort Becca to her chambers, and bring however many girls she asks for to aid her. Speak to Charles afterward; make sure she's given compensation for her leave. She's not to work until the next half moon."

Garron nodded, leaning down beside Gwenivere and gently holding Becca's arms. He helped her to her feet, walking her up the Assembly Hall's steps and back through the chamber's doors. Her legs wobbled as she walked, more marks visible where her dress's hem was torn. As she ascended the stairs, Gwenivere could see blood spotting near her bottom, the Prianthians forcing shame upon her as the blood of her youth stained through her clothes. Garron didn't seem to see it, but he removed his cloak out of benevolence, wrapping it around her tiny shoulders as he closed the doors behind him.

Gwenivere forced her legs from under her and stood. She'd never wanted to kill another person more than she did then.

"You signed the treaty," Alanna continued. "But I will ensure my treaty mates know what's been happening behind closed doors." She walked forward again, confidently, smiling as she met Gwenivere's glare. Gwenivere's lips twitched, the *auroras* in her mind blinding.

"Do you want to attack me?" Alanna asked, turning her head back toward her sisters. They snickered. Behind them, Natalia stood with a grimace. For once she seemed to be on Gwenivere's side.

"Attack you?" Gwenivere asked, holding her chin high. "Why would I do that? Your people are starving in the streets because your parents can't feed them without the aid of Sadiyan slaves. Sadie itself has risen to a state of growing prosperity after having regained its stronghold over you. And if I'm not mistaken, your brother Pasha was killed by a man of the Redeemers, an insurgence started by your own people." She took her turn to grin, stepping forward what little distance still existed between them.

"Why would a lion eat what's already dead and rotting?"

Alexandria, the youngest of the sisters, barely grabbed Alanna's arm as it rose to strike. The heiress shoved her sister away and shrugged her outburst off, staring at Gwenivere with hatred.

From beyond them, Gwenivere could see a rare smirk of camaraderie on Natalia's face. At her back, she could feel her father's disapproval.

"As punishment for her treachery," Alanna started, looking to Gerard. "I demand your daughter be held in confinement. If she can't be trusted with the affairs of nations, then she shouldn't be trusted outside her chamber's walls."

Gwenivere ground her teeth, turning to her father. With a sinking heart, she watched him meet Alanna's gaze, close his eyes, and answer, "So be it."

Fear the Forest
Fear its might
Fear the fiends
That cause great fright
Men can go
But dead they'll be
Slain by beasts
You'll see, you'll see

Riverdian nursery rhyme of the Forest of Fiends

CHAPTER 62

ROLAND

Roland bolted upright from a nightmare, grabbing at his neck and gasping for air. It sharply filled his lungs, his throat tickling and forcing shallow coughs.

Once it ebbed, he sat wincing. The quick motions of waking reminded him of the pain still present in his shoulder. He rubbed it with his opposite hand, knowing the pain would soften soon.

The fire he'd made still burned strong, but the cold of night lingered. It wouldn't be morning for some time.

He toyed with the idea of returning to sleep, knowing it'd still be a while yet before he reached the Elite's camp in Riverdee. The vivid images of his dreams—of Yvaine bloody, of her screams, of the fiends she'd commanded—made him reconsider.

He reached for his satchel, finding a piece of dried bread

and a small sliver of cheese to eat. Then he grabbed his wine-skin and took a drink.

As he did, he thought of his parents, their faces disappointed and scornful. He'd told them he'd given up the Dagger, hoping that, after everything Yvaine had revealed, it might make them relieved.

It hadn't.

Roland wanted to fault the Sadiyan prince Dietrich Haroldson, wanted to hate the man for coming into his life, but how could he? Temptations had been presented and indulged in time and time again, and the thought of wedding Gwenivere had seemed too sweet an offer to pass. Strangely, though he never thought he would, he found himself blaming her for his decision.

You made the choice, he told himself, poking a stick at the fire. It crackled loudly, small embers flicking about. *She didn't make it for you.*

He remembered seeing the letter of her acceptance, sealed by Xenith's rose without thorns. Days later, the same seal had thrust Mesidia to its knees, revealing war was soon to come.

Roland wondered if Gerard had played a role in Gwenivere's acceptance of his proposal. She was the successor to the greatest nation in Abra'am, and any man she desired would be her king. Why then would she pick him to love, a man she could never have, who was the heir to a rebel-filled kingdom? Surely there were others who wanted her hand, others better suited than he.

Some said Gwenivere had allied with Prince Dietrich for the Attack of Fiends. They claimed that she, and Dietrich and his dragon, had controlled the fiends in Xenith the way Yvaine had in Mesidia. Roland didn't think it possible, not his Gwenivere, but he wasn't sure of anything anymore.

He hadn't been since Gerard's betrayal.

Five nations to one, he thought, scratching the stubble along his jaw. Mesidia stood no chance, not when half the Elite were still protecting their allies in Riverdee. Pierre had been insistent though, as had Rosalie, that they wouldn't surrender Mesidia over without a fight. If it was war Gerard wanted, it was war they would get. Roland just needed to meet with the rest of their men and bring them home in time.

I pray this X'odia is as strong as Dravian claims, he thought, lying back down. His father had wanted the prisoner dead, along with the other prisoner named Vahd'eel, but Dravian had insisted the woman could be of use. He wrote to them that she'd slain an entire legion of fiends, and that she'd done so in a matter of seconds. And, more importantly, she'd done it to protect the very soldiers holding her captive.

I hope Dravian is right about her, he thought, closing his eyes. *If he is, perhaps we have a chance at winning this war.*

If she refuses the offer, have her beaten until she accepts. If that fails, hang her, and let the ravens have her flesh. Her auroras *can drift from bones.*

From a letter between Pierre Laighless and Dravian Valcor

Chapter 63

X'ODIA

X'odia sat on the bench in her shack, her body shivering as the ocean breeze crept through the cracks in the walls. She tried to wrap Dravian's cloak around her, hoping the blue fabrics would warm her, but they proved useless. Nothing but flames, or perhaps a bath, could get the cold out.

She'd been shackled again, by Markeem this time, when she'd fallen asleep after mending Dravian's wounds. She glanced down at her bindings, tempted to try casting a tiny blaze, but she knew nothing would happen if she did.

Curling up in a ball, she pulled the hood of the cloak up, and breathed against her palms.

She hadn't expected the door of her shack to open. The silhouette of a man came through with two torches in his hands. X'odia was curious but stayed wrapped up, too frozen to bother acknowledging the stranger with a stand of respect. She was grateful for the torches he brought, though, and she watched their small inferno until he propped them against the wall.

She held back a gasp when she saw Dravian enter behind the soldier, his light armor abandoned for a thick coat. She hadn't seen him since the night of the attack, fearful he hadn't survived his wounds. Yet there he stood, shoulders broad and back straight, nothing in his stance or walk revealing the new scars that rested beneath his clothes.

She thought she remembered looking at him like that before.

I have, she thought, her chest tightening. *I've certainly seen this. But where . . .*

Aboard the *Seagull,* she realized, before docking on Riverdee's coast. She'd sat on the same bench in the vision that she did now, with the same soldier standing at Dravian's side.

Just before she'd been ordered beaten.

"X'odia," Dravian said, bringing his eyes to hers. They were cold, militaristic, the flames of the torches reflecting off them.

She remained silent. She was too afraid to speak.

"Mesidia is going to war," he said grimly. "Prince Roland has been sent to meet us and bring us home, crossing back through the Forest of Fiends. We can't go through Xenith's lands; they're our enemy now, so we must take extreme measures once Roland arrives. You'll be traveling with us, as . . . one of us."

X'odia breathed in heavily, unsure of Dravian's meaning. This part of her vision hadn't occurred, but that wasn't uncommon. The Sight often only gave her fragments of the future.

"Pierre has been informed of your abilities to heal," he continued, "as well as your strength. Though you're our prisoner here, you'll be a free woman there, so long as you pledge your life to serving as an Elite. Markeem and a few others of high command gave their word that you aided us against the fiends. Pierre wishes to give you freedom as one of his soldiers."

X'odia's stomach tightened. She didn't think she'd heard

him right. He couldn't possibly be asking her to be an Elite—
to be a killer of people. She was a priestess, a follower of the
Light and a servant to the High Temple of Eve. How could she
possibly fight in a battle, use her powers to kill other people?
Her heart still ached from the lives of the fiends she'd taken.

"I can't," she whispered, shaking her head. "Dravian . . .
I can't."

She felt tears settle in her eyes, knowing it wasn't a request
she'd been given. After all the times she hadn't tried to harm
them to escape, after compliantly accepting her shackles over
violence, Dravian had to know her strife. And he did, based on
the remorse in his eyes, but it slipped away quickly.

She knew then what was to come. Her will needed changing, and the Inquisitor would be forced to break it. Even having foresight, she still felt a stab of betrayal. She'd thought
after that night outside her shack, after mending his wounds
and hearing his tale, that maybe—

It didn't matter what she thought. He was her captor, and
she his prisoner. And his king had ordered him to make her
comply.

She held up her palms, inching back as the other soldier,
the one who'd brought the torches, came toward her. He lowered the fist he'd started to raise, looking from her submissive
stance back over to Dravian.

The Inquisitor let out a breath, then ordered the man to
leave. He nodded, his face visibly relieved, and made his way
out.

X'odia lowered her arms, realizing they still held defensively in the air. She met Dravian's eyes, grateful he'd sent his
man away.

"I'll do it," she whispered. She hated herself, hated how the
cold and hunger and fear made her weak. Yet she also felt an
air of shameful relief knowing she wouldn't be made to bruise
or break.

Dravian didn't say anything. He didn't move or do anything that indicated he had any reason to stay. He stood, tall and looming, watching as she weighed her sins.

"I'll send word to the king," he said finally, moving forward. He crossed the small distance between them with a few steps, then reached a hand out and placed it on her shoulder.

"You did a brave thing, saving my soldiers the way you did. I want you to know you have my gratitude, and that . . . that I'm sorry."

He squeezed her shoulder tightly, desperate almost, then pulled it back. This time, when she finally began to let her tears fall, he took the torches and left.

The Lady Gwenivere will make a fine queen someday. She is compassionate at times, like when she wept openly at the funeral march. But she is also cunning, and just as capable at the game of politics as other nobles.

Becca Hill, servant to Gwenivere Verigrad

CHAPTER 64

GWENIVERE

Gwenivere enjoyed watching the bird outside her window. There seemed to be a rush of adrenaline in its movements, an excitement for the changing heights and whirling views.

If not for the Behemoth that had pursued so dangerously behind, she wondered if flight atop Dietrich's dragon would've been as wonderful as the bird made it seem. It certainly looked cheery, its head tilting and its beak opening to sing—

An arrow struck it to the palace wall. It wouldn't take further examination to know it was dead.

Sighing, Gwenivere stepped away from the window. She pitied the ravens, and the pigeons and the crows. Any birds that came near her rooms were now struck down by a sharp eye and a keen shot.

Ever since her revealed betrothal to Roland she'd been forced—as Alanna had demanded—to stay confined to her rooms. Nearby birds were killed in fear that she might be using them to relay messages to Mesidia, despite the fact that none of the birds had been found carrying notes. It was a pity, then, to look out over her balcony, where small, feathered corpses littered the floor.

Palace confinement hadn't left her without her ways, though. Years of solitude had made her adept at gaining knowledge where others might not think it there. Especially with the palace servants. She couldn't believe she'd still been permitted to have them, not when birds couldn't take flight nearby. Yet there the servants were, coming and going with clean sheets and dry towels. The nobility clearly thought nothing of them, likely believing Gwenivere was too regal to belittle herself with their gossip. She knew better. Her royal blood wasn't going to stand in the way of common sense.

The servants of Voradeen's palace encountered every person in every way. They saw women sneaking out from the chambers of patrons and men hiding their rings to swoon. They saw the noblest of scholars having affairs, and the wealthiest of diplomats naked before their baths. It didn't matter if the people they encountered were old or young—they saw everyone, and they saw everyone daily.

Natalia and Dorian, as luck would have it, were the recent topic of the palace's servants.

"I hear they've been visiting with each other," one chambermaid said. "That handsome knight Nicolas was telling me when they visit, they do so for a *long* time."

"I never understood what she sees in him," another said. "Those Yendorians are nothing but bandits and thieves. We'd be better off if the Arctic just put all of 'em in their prisons."

That bit wasn't helpful. Not all the gossip was.

"I think Dorian is going to war," a dark-haired girl said. Gwenivere recognized her as the one who'd replaced Becca on Natalia's name day, the one who'd come most often since

Becca had been given leave.

"For the Laighlesses?" Gwenivere asked, feigning casual interest. The girl shook her head and folded some blankets, too occupied in her task to realize Gwenivere was hanging on her every word.

"Not for the Laighlesses," she said, setting the blankets in a chest. "For the Victorians."

After several days hearing similar rumors, Gwenivere had significant information to mull over: Natalia and Dorian were indeed seeing each other again. Perhaps not romantically, but at least as allies. Natalia had done nothing to show she'd be leaving Xenith, and Dorian had been seen speaking with all the members involved in Treaty of Five. He was an ambassador, but still, if he was continuing to serve Pierre, he should consider the Treaty's members his enemies. By talking to them so frequently, Gwenivere suspected he didn't.

What could she do with that knowledge? She hadn't wanted to believe her new chambermaid was right, but all the rumors did seem to prove that Dorian was going to war. And that he was going on Natalia's behalf.

As much as everyone insisted Pierre would eventually surrender, the Mesidian king hadn't done anything thus far to indicate he would. It was likely believed that having to face his own adopted son would change his mind, but Gwenivere knew Pierre better than that. He wouldn't surrender—he'd only fight harder. She thought her father knew that too, but without having the chance to speak with him, she had no way of conversing that point.

Regardless, she couldn't let Dorian fight for the Victorians. For one, it would give the rebels a chance. They were currently disjointed, and if Dorian rallied them together, they'd be shaped under his leadership.

Two, Dorian was her friend. As much as she hated him for possibly betraying the Laighlesses, he was still someone she cared for greatly. She didn't want to see him go to war. Especially against his own family.

And three, if Dorian succeeded in making Pierre surrender, the Treaty of Five would likely make him the new king. Dorian had political savvy, but he was also a man who'd spent much of his time pleasing foreign nations. If he ruled Mesidia, he'd likely be doing so with the instinct to appease other kingdoms. That, or he'd do whatever Natalia commanded him to.

None of those outcomes could happen. The Laighlesses deserved to have a fair chance at war, and without the interference of dirty politicking.

"Milady," Garron said, opening the door. She'd requested he bring her a certain guest after she'd crafted a plan. That guest now stood next to him with scruffy hair and puffy eyes.

William al'Murtagh.

Gwenivere smiled at her friend. She wasn't allowed to cross the threshold of her door, so she beckoned him forward, surprised when he came toward her eagerly. Unbeknownst to Garron's glare, he wrapped his arms around her, lifting her up off the ground. She hugged him back, albeit less forcefully, and waved off the bolt of lightning Garron *called* to his hand.

"Hello, William," Gwenivere said. The burly Mesidian set her back down, his fingers lingering on her waist for a moment before settling them back at his sides.

"Am I allowed in?" he asked. "Or do we have to chat in the hall with this fellow?"

He gave an ornery smile to Garron and pointed his thumb. Garron didn't smile back.

"My father has permitted me some visitors," Gwenivere said. "And thankfully you're considered innocent enough."

"I see," he said, retracting his thumb. "Shall we, then?"

Gwenivere stepped aside and let him in, holding up a hand to Garron as he made to enter behind them.

"I'd like some privacy with the al'Murtagh, if you please,"

she said quietly. She called to William to make himself comfortable, then leaned back toward her knight. "I'm not going to bed the man, Garron, I just want to chat with him for a bit."

"I'd prefer you chat with Elizabeth."

"Well then take that up with my father."

The two eyed each other, both narrowing their eyes. Garron grunted but eventually took a step back, grabbing the chamber's door handle and closing it shut.

"Seems a bit protective of you," William said. He'd chosen a seat by her desk, the chair almost too small for his bulky frame. Gwenivere blushed and shrugged as she made her way to join him.

"He is," she said. "More than my father in some ways. He's more *like* a father in some ways, if I'm being honest."

William chuckled. "Well, that's nice. My family doesn't exactly think the best of Gerard right now, so I'm glad you've got yourself another father figure looking after you. Makes me feel a little better for you."

Gwenivere wasn't sure what to say to that, so she took a seat beside him and said nothing.

William had never been a particularly well-groomed man, his messy mop of hair and stubbled face an intentional look of his, but he'd always been presentable. Staring at him now, Gwenivere couldn't help noticing his appearance seemed more disheveled than relaxed, his cheery nature dampened.

"How're you handling things?" she asked. "I can't imagine what you're going through."

"I'm not doing well," he admitted. He wrinkled his nose as she handed him a cup of water, but he took a drink anyway.

"My parents and Pierre and Rosalie aren't in Stonewall anymore; they went into hiding. I know where they are though. I've not told any of the Treaty of Five, but your father seems aware. Not of where they are—just of the fact that I know.

He doesn't question me about it—thank the Light—because I think he's too honorable. It still weighs on me though, every time I see him."

He took another drink of water. He stared at it disappointingly, as it wasn't ale or mead or wine, but Gwenivere wasn't about to give him any of that. It wasn't even noonday and he already smelled as though he'd been drinking.

"The worst of it, Gwen, is pretending everything's going to be all right, for Peter and Elizabeth." He sniffed, then cleared his throat, as if to cover the delicate noise with something gruffer. "I don't know how long I can keep up the act."

Gwenivere's stomach twisted. She rose from her chair and crouched in front of him, taking his hand.

"William, I want you to know I've . . . I've heard rumors recently, about the Treaty of Five. I don't know anything for certain, but it seems they're planning to use Dorian to—"

"I know."

She met his eyes. There was fury in them. And pain.

"I'm sorry," she said softly, squeezing his hand tighter. "I know Dorian is like family to you."

He nodded, readjusting their hands. Now it was his fingers wrapping over hers, his thumb stroking along the bones of her wrist.

"Natalia's putting him up to it," he said. "I know she is."

"Do you have any proof?"

"No. But you know how she is."

He didn't say anything for a while after that, only continuing to look at her hand. She became aware then of how close they were, of how easily she could hear his breathing and see his bloodshot eyes. Swallowing, she gently pulled herself back, not wanting him to think her consolations were anything more than they were.

"I have an idea," she said, breaking their silence. William cleared his throat again and sat up, emptying what was left of his cup before setting it atop her desk.

"Do you now? What is it?"

She reached up and grabbed her Amulet, fingering the smooth metal. "It's nothing grand, but at best, it might give your family a chance."

William started, holding out his palms. "And at worst?"

"At worst . . ." She released a breath, feeling her heart beating aggressively beneath her chest. "At worst, it might make Elizabeth a queen."

Would I ever consider marriage again after what happened with Natalia?

Men in Mesidia aren't meant to unveil their heartache, but as you're a Sadiyan I know you don't hold as strongly to such restrictive beliefs for male emotions. I can thus admit to you that I would.

From a letter between Dorian Cliffborne and Abaddon Haroldson

CHAPTER 65

ELIZABETH

The clock ticked loudly. It was maddening, the perfection of it, constantly reminding its listener of the time. Elizabeth tapped her feet, trying to ignore it, but every few minutes her eyes were drawn back to it.

"William?"

Her brother turned toward her quickly.

"Yes?"

She swallowed. She'd not actually had anything to say—she'd just wished for his comforts.

"Sorry. Never mind."

He pursed his lips but didn't press her.

An hour ago he'd come back to their quarters revealing an idea Gwenivere had shared with him. Elizabeth had listened to it in its entirety, shocked—and a little fearful—when she'd learned it involved her.

Nothing ever involved her. She was Elizabeth al'Murtagh. She was no one.

A light knocking sounded at the door. Elizabeth started and William grumbled, despite both knowing who it was.

"Shall I get it, Will?"

"No, I'll get it."

"Are you certain? I don't mind."

"I said I'll get it."

William stood with hunched shoulders, walking the distance of the room. He cursed under his breath. Then, straightening to his full height, he opened the door.

Dorian Cliffborne, elegant and garbed in black, stood just beyond it.

Despite herself, Elizabeth's breath caught. She was supposed to loathe Dorian, hate him for siding with the rebels, but her heart beat a little faster as he stepped inside.

"Will, thank you for seeing me," he said. He looked slightly withered, distressed, but his voiced sounded relieved. "After all the rumors and lies going around, I hadn't thought you'd want to speak."

William crossed his arms and slammed the door.

"Piss off, whoreson."

Dorian's mouth hung open, but he didn't say anything. He sighed and nodded, as if he'd expected the retort.

"Um, hello," Elizabeth said. Dorian's head shot up at her voice, his defeated expression lifting.

"Elizabeth. I hadn't realized you'd be here."

He pulled at his shirtsleeves—a habit she'd noticed he did most often when he was embarrassed—then looked back at her brother.

"If the lady remains, I ask that this exchange be civil. If it's fighting you crave, let it be done elsewhere, and at a later time."

William let out a mocking laugh.

"You're a real bastard, Dorian. I didn't call you here to fight."

"No? Then why have you called me here? I thought it might be to talk, perhaps as old friends, but it's apparent you have no desire to do that."

"I'm not friends with traitors."

Dampening, Dorian said nothing. Elizabeth grimaced and wished she could console him, but she couldn't very well cross her brother. He had every right to be cruel.

"Forgive us, Ambassador," she said, breaking the standstill. "Tensions have been high as of late. You understand."

"I do. Though I hadn't realized I'd become just *Ambassador*. Especially with you."

Her cheeks flushed; there was nothing to say to that. She'd always been the magnanimous one, and now she'd been distant. The thought made her queasy.

"We know the strategies the Treaty of Five have in play," she said, forcing her chin up. "And we know the role they've made for you. But we don't believe it'll be enough to make Pierre surrender. We still want the Laighlesses in power over the Victorians—we're not attempting to hide that—but if fate would have it some other way, we'd at least prefer it be with them alive. We don't want our family to be part of the bloodshed."

"They're my family too," Dorian countered. He stepped forward, looking as though he wanted to take her hands and beg her to believe him, but he didn't. William was still glaring beside him.

"I know what you think," he continued carefully, "I know you deem me greedy for a crown and desperate for power. But you must believe I pray for the same things as you. Roland is my brother, Pierre is my father, and Rosalie is my mother. I want this war no more than you two, and certainly not any more than they do.

"It's coming, though, despite what we want. And you have to know the Victorians will be merciless when they take the throne."

He paused, turning back to William.

"Call me a bastard if you want, call me a traitor, but you can't tell me you wouldn't do the same thing I'm doing if it meant keeping your family alive. Our family, I mean. They're one in the same."

Elizabeth remained silent, not knowing what to say. It'd been easy to place blame on Dorian's shoulders, to think that if only he refused the Treaty of Five, their uncle might have a chance. They knew he didn't. He was outnumbered, and his armies were split. Even without Dorian's help, Pierre's strongest chance of living was to surrender. No amount of denial could change that.

There was Gwenivere's idea, though. It wasn't completely fleshed out, but it was something.

"Brother, could you leave for a bit?" Elizabeth asked. William inhaled deeply, looking between them with nervous stares.

"Just for a bit," he said quietly, kissing her temple. She smiled at him reassuringly, then watched him walk out.

"I'm sorry, for all this," she started, fumbling through her words. She laced her fingers together, if only to hide their shaking, and shifted her weight.

"You've not spat at my feet," Dorian said, referencing the drunken act her younger brother Peter had committed. "And you've not come at me with threats. The only thing you've done is . . . nothing."

Elizabeth smiled. Her breathing came a little easier knowing he didn't hold her accountable for her brothers.

"I'm sorry all the same," she said. Her voice caught, which she found surprising, as she'd thought she was holding herself together well. Evidently she wasn't. Her face grew hot and her eyes welled with tears. Embarrassed, she lifted a hand to her nose, looking away.

"Elizabeth."

Dorian reached out to her, pulling her toward him. He

rubbed his hand against her hair and shushed her softly.

"They want me to go with you," she whispered. "As your betrothed."

He pulled away abruptly, staring. He likely thought he'd misheard or that she'd elaborate, but when she didn't he pulled a kerchief from his pocket and handed it over. She accepted it, pressing it to the corners of her eyes.

"I believe some explanation is in order," she said. "It was Gwenivere's idea, not mine. She thinks that if Natalia knew you were going to Mesidia with me as your betrothed, she might try to make you stay. And if you stay, the rebels won't have a leader, and Pierre will have a better chance in the war."

She paused, waiting to see if he'd respond.

He didn't.

"Gwen knows Natalia likely still loves you," she continued. "And she knows the idea of us being betrothed might make her force you to stay here.

"If she does let you go, she might try to manipulate you. You've never ruled before, and you're not—in some people's opinions—truly a Mesidian. It would be considered wise for you to seek advice from Natalia, since that's who the Victorians wish to rule.

"But to put it rather bluntly, none of us wants that to happen. Gwen has suggested that, if I'm your wife, perhaps you might be otherwise occupied. She thinks my being a queen might give you more approval from the people, and most importantly convince my uncle to surrender before the battle even starts."

She looked up, embarrassed and uncertain. It was a daring idea she'd revealed, and one she didn't think Dorian would truly consider.

"Gwenivere's a clever girl," he said. "Pierre might surrender to the Treaty's terms if he knows he'd be battling against not only me, but you as well." He smiled, almost shyly, and rubbed comfortingly at her arm "You've always been the good one—the sweet one. I can't imagine he'd want to risk hurting you."

Elizabeth bit her lip. It was hard to feel at ease when his gold eyes held her fondly.

"I do have a question, though," he said. He lifted his hand to her cheek, pulling an errant strand of hair from it. "Is this what you want?"

Yes, she thought instantly. Ashamed, she broke his gaze, patting her hands against his chest.

"It is," she whispered. "It's not what I'm supposed to want. I'm supposed to want you to give in to Natalia, to stay here in Xenith with her. That's what Will thinks I want, what he expects me to want. He doesn't think I'm capable of wanting to wed you."

Dorian nodded, moving his fingers to her neck. "I won't be meeting with the Treaty of Five again for a while. Take your time in this decision. We all want what's best for Mesidia, and I don't want you feeling guilty for whatever path you choose."

He leaned in, both hands falling to the back of her neck as he kissed her head. The scent of him, alluring and sweet, was all consuming, almost enough to convince her then and there to say yes. But he was right; she needed to think about this and the consequences it would mean for her and her family.

She squeezed his arms tightly, her lids clamped shut. She hoped, no matter what decision she came to, they'd find a way to keep Mesidia safe.

Today our instructor told us to think of two women of import and imagine who between them would win in a battle of wits. I chose to consider Rose Verigrad of Xenith and Yvaine Barie of Mesidia; one is known for being lovely and kind, and the other is known for being cunning. I think it's quite obvious who would come out victorious between the two, despite the statures they possess.

From the school notes of Fiona Collinson

CHAPTER 66

GWENIVERE

G wenivere sat in her quarters, trying to calm herself with the words on her book's pages. Garron had told her that with all the time she had locked away in her bedroom, it might be good for her to study up on *The Art of Calling*. It was his Holy Book for elements and *auroras*, and, seeing as they couldn't train in the palace arena, he thought it might be wise for her to keep her senses sharp. She could take her rage out by burning the curtains and the rugs throughout the room. They were hers, after all, and no one would really mind.

She'd snickered at his logic, but ultimately took it to heart. It was rather alleviating to let her elements out.

In that moment, though, *The Art of Calling* was doing little to distract her. She'd read the same paragraph at least three times, and her lack of interest was nearly palpable. She stood from her chair and shoved the book back in her shelf, not caring if it stayed in order.

Elizabeth isn't mad, she thought, wrinkling her nose at the shelf's dust. *That's more important than what Natalia ends up doing.*

As much as she tried to convince herself she'd plotted in Mesidia's favor, she couldn't help feeling selfish. There wasn't a part of her plan that was rooted in deceit, but she still questioned her motivations for it. Was she doing this for Mesidia, or for the chance to still marry Roland?

She exhaled. She was doing this for Mesidia.

"Milady," Garron called, tapping her door. She jumped, cursing, then quickly composed herself.

"Yes, let her in."

Garron opened the door and Natalia entered. She wore a well-fitted dress, and her hair, woven in intricate plaits, rested perfectly atop her head.

"Hello," Gwenivere said, stepping away from her shelf. She waved Garron back out to the hall before motioning Natalia further inside.

"Thank you for calling me," she said, voice pleasant. "It's quite the surprise."

Painfully aware of how much shorter she was, Gwenivere forced her chin up higher. Holding herself in such a way was difficult, though, as blatant disdain was easier than feigned respect.

"There are things I'd like to discuss with you," she said, lacing her hands together. They buzzed with anticipation as if her *auroras* wanted to burst out from inside them. If she wasn't careful, or if she let her temper rise, she might do to Natalia what she'd done to her rugs. "I think it best we converse now, before the upcoming meeting with the Treaty of Five."

"I see," Natalia answered. "Discussion sounds grand."

There was an elitist tone to her voice—as if Gwenivere was a just girl playing princess. It was infuriating, but ultimately expected. Gwenivere pushed down her rising annoyance and straightened.

"I'm going to be forthright with you: I don't want Dorian going to Mesidia."

Natalia gave a small laugh and shrugged. Licking her lips, she leaned her weight to one hip, nestling her hands in front of her. "I assumed you wouldn't, especially given your relationship to the Laighless family. But the ploy being set forth with Dorian is a good one. If you care for Mesidia's wellbeing, you'll see that soon."

Gwenivere clenched her fists. They were growing warm with flecks of fire.

"He won't be a good king," she said firmly. "He's never ruled, he's not thought he'd rule for the last several years, and he's Pierre's son in all but blood. Even if he has the capabilities to reign, he won't after having to fight his own family. Would you, if you had to kill your own mother?"

Natalia gave another noncommittal gesture. She looked more a statue than a woman, all stillness and poise, her body blending with the elegant fixtures around the room.

"You raise valid points, but those points are moot. Dorian is stronger than you think. And he has allies, Xenith being one of them."

"By Xenith, do you mean my father and I, or do you mean you?"

"I mean the entire nation. I don't think a select few represent the whole."

It was a dig at Gwenivere, at her stance with the Laighlesses. They were a family of three—Mesidia was an entire kingdom. She didn't hide the grimace that took her.

"The Laighlesses are a good people, and just." She leaned forward and pointed forcefully in Natalia's direction. Feeling a fool, she pulled her hand back, taking a breath to calm herself.

"They deserve a fair fight," she continued. "You convincing

Dorian to fight alongside the rebels isn't anything more than a pretense for you to rule. You know he'll hang on your words; you said so yourself. He has allies here, in Xenith, but those allies don't include me. And I'm the heir to this kingdom.

"Now as for better solutions, one is that Dorian stays here. This allows the Laighlesses a chance to fight against their enemies rather than their family. If they still end up defeated, at least someone more fit to rule—someone all the Treaty of Five decides on—will be given the throne.

"If Dorian refutes this idea and does still choose to go, I believe it's wise he goes with someone to counsel him. Someone who also has Mesidia's best interest in mind." She lifted her palm, gesturing toward Natalia's. "Unfortunately for you, you can't be that person."

Smirking, Natalia opened her own palm and rubbed at its scar. "I never intended to go with him. I take the Baptism of Blood quite seriously."

"I know." Gwenivere took her turn to grin. "Elizabeth al'Murtagh, though, is still free to do as she pleases."

Tilting her head, Natalia looked up from her hand and stared. There was skepticism in her eyes, and amusement, but Gwenivere noted a slight twitching in her neck.

"Are you trying to spite me, Princess? Are you punishing me for being there when your father struck you?"

"No," Gwenivere answered, jaw locked. She felt an animal as her lips curled and her nostrils flared, but she kept herself contained. "If I wanted to spite you, I'd have you clean the chamber pots. Be clear-headed and see this as truth: Elizabeth going with him is a good idea."

Natalia shook her head, poise faltering. "I know you're aware of my former relationship with Dorian. If you claim this isn't for spite, why not have Peter or William go? William is the eldest between them."

"William doesn't wish to go," Gwenivere said simply. "And

I'm not going to consider your mention of Peter. We both know he's too young, and too much of a drunkard.

"It has to be Elizabeth. She's kind and sympathetic, and she has the blood of the Laighless family. You know as well as I that even if Pierre surrenders, there may still be revolts. Much of the nation still hates the Victorians, and Elizabeth could be what Mesidia needs to ease any additional tensions that arise. She'd make a good ally at Dorian's side."

She let the implication lie. She'd yet to say Elizabeth would be going as Dorian's betrothed, but by the visible dismay of Natalia's features, it seemed obvious.

"Those are your suggestions, then?" Natalia asked, voice quiet. "Make Dorian stay, or let him go with Elizabeth?"

"Yes," she answered, holding her hand toward the door. "If you need no further clarification on them, you may leave."

Natalia stood silent for a moment, more stiff than still, then gave her formal niceties and left.

Once she'd gone, Gwenivere let out a curse. Her *auroras* burst out from her hands, held back for too long, and dripped onto the carpets. Despite feeling so fervent before, so bustling and anxious, they were now only cold.

There are rumors that Dorian Cliffborne and Elizabeth al'Murtagh are to announce a betrothal before he serves as the leader for the Victorians.

If this is true, I can only imagine Pierre will surrender. I doubt he'd fight against both his niece and his adopted son.

Do not fret. I have made deals that will help combat these things if they come to pass.

A letter between Anastasia Verkev and an unknown party

CHAPTER 67

GWENIVERE

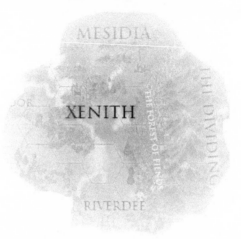

The Treaty of Five convened. The al'Murtagh siblings had joined as well, all three sitting with heads down and knuckles white.

Opposite them was Alanna of Prianthia and her four siblings. She'd insisted that her bear of a brother, Rokinoff, was needed, as he was the next leader of Prianthia's army, and explained that he might prove insightful on the coming war. The other three—Alexandria, Anastasia, and Nicolai—had no purpose to come, yet there they were, tall and domineering. No one suggested they stay out.

Natalia, seated beside Alanna, faced the baroness of the Arctic. The women looked an odd, inverted image of the other, both in hues of blue, both with nearly white hair. The only difference was their skin, Vanessa's dark and rich and Natalia's light.

Ambassador Dorian sat at the divide of his blood and

mind—between the Mesidians and the Yendorian. Edifor looked pleased to be sitting by him, but the al'Murtaghs looked anxious.

Commandant Hedford sat off to the side beneath a cracked open window smoking a pipe. It would seem he cared more about inhaling its contents than sitting at the table.

Gerard and Gwenivere were the last royals in attendance. Gwenivere's lips were ordered sealed for the entirety of the meeting, her input confined to her head. The only purpose for her presence was to carry out any decisions made by her father in the event something happened to him.

"Thank you all for convening," he said. "The war to claim the Mesidian throne under the Victorian cause has begun.

"Despite not having a leader, the rebels have started leading their men against Pierre's followers. Due to the number of Elite still stationed in Riverdee, the Laighlesses are no longer dwelling in Stonewall Castle. As our wishes to avoid bloodshed are among the highest priority, I ask that each of you take a moment to reflect on what you know. If you've an idea of where they've gone, or where they may be going, please consider sharing this information. Our purpose is not to kill them, but to keep them safe."

Hedford of Theatia looked to the al'Murtagh siblings. Others joined, necks craned and eyes peering, each trying to pressure the three into revealing what they knew. Gwenivere wished them strength, not envying their predicament.

To her surprise, Elizabeth sat tall, her hands laced courteously in front of her. William and Peter sat similarly. They both wore looks of serenity.

"Moving on, then."

Gerard held his hand out and accepted a parchment from Sir Charles.

"I'd like to formally announce that Ambassador Dorian is interested in going back to Mesidia. He's been closely aligned with both the Victorians and the Laighlesses in the past, having once been betrothed to Natalia here, and having been raised by King Pierre and Queen Rosalie. After much discussion, we believe he may prove useful in mending the tensions between the two families.

"As someone who considers herself a representative of the Victorian people, Natalia believes her followers will listen to his command, especially if she makes it known she supports him."

Gwenivere lifted her hand to her Amulet. She tried to catch Natalia's eye, but the woman was looking straight ahead.

"We have something to suggest," Peter cut in, holding up a finger. Gerard turned to him, mouth agape, clearly taken aback that—of all the people there—Peter was the one who'd spoken.

"All right. Go on."

Peter coughed into his shoulder, clearing his throat.

"If it's agreed on by your council, we believe it would aid the cause to propose a betrothal between Dorian . . . and my sister."

The room fell silent. Peter retracted his finger, returning it to his lap.

"If I may," Dorian said, standing from his chair. He walked toward Elizabeth, placing one hand on her shoulder and the other out toward the nobles.

"Despite what Peter has proposed, it's not his place to decide the fate of his sister. It's also not my decision, nor is it any of yours. That said, if Elizabeth agrees to this, I'll gladly accept her as my betrothed."

It was a brave thing to say. He was sticking up for Elizabeth, while still giving her a chance to change her mind. Gwenivere commended him, noting the supportive way he held Elizabeth's shoulder.

It was silent for a painfully long while. Natalia had clearly not spoken to Dorian, or if she had, Dorian had decided on going back to Mesidia anyway. Gwenivere gripped the sides of her throne with tense hands, angry at both of them for ruining her plan.

Not ruining, necessarily, but not doing what she'd expected. She'd thought for certain Natalia would break if knowing she'd lose Dorian for good, and he the same.

Had she misjudged them so severely?

You don't have to go along with this, she thought, willing the unspoken words across the room to Elizabeth. *You don't have to do this; you don't have to declare yourself against your own family.*

But the pleading would do no good; she knew how Elizabeth felt about Dorian.

Perhaps it wasn't that she'd misjudged Dorian and Natalia, but that she'd misjudged her dearest friend.

"I accept," Elizabeth finally whispered. Gwenivere shut her eyes, pained she'd forced this burden on her friend. She listened to her say the words again.

"I accept."

It is believed by many in Sadie that suicide prevents one from resting with the Light. Such a belief is derived from passages in the Holy Book, though such passages are vague and up for interpretation.

It is my personal belief that this mind-set was forced into my people by the Prianthians during enslavement. If every slave felt death would be their freedom, then it would make sense for their captors to ensure they believed damnation awaited those who took their lives.

As a priestess and an oracle, I cannot preach this belief, as I do not know it as fact and I do not wish to spread false teachings.

From the studies of Deladrine, the Lady Oracle

CHAPTER 68

ABADDON

SADIE

Abaddon was grateful for his family's palace, of the old, still intact ruins that had awaited his people when they'd freed themselves from slavery. There seemed to be a constant bead of sweat trickling down his back, a little reminder of Sadie's incessant heat, and the desert sun felt more unbearable than normal despite the coming winter. He thanked the mild cold the palace offered as he chatted with the watchmen standing outside his mother's chambers.

He'd come to see her often since Deladrine had warned him she'd felt death. Each time he dreaded the frail form that awaited him, the lifeless body he'd see, knowing he'd eventually feel at her neck and not find a pulse.

You did this to her, a voice said, plaguing his thoughts. A different voice comforted and commended him, insisting he'd done what was needed.

You did this for *her,* the second voice said. *You did this for all of your family. You saw the way your mother wept. You saw the way your brother fell to sin. This was a way out for them. This was their escape.*

He battled the voices, forcing out enough useless chatter to his watchmen in front of him as he pondered what lay in his mind. He knew he'd initially made his mother sick, given her vials and vials disguised as cures to keep her subdued, but he'd not initiated the strange coma that'd surfaced. What had caused that he still wasn't sure. It was likely a side effect of the poison he'd been using, but when patient after patient hadn't shown the same results, it seemed too isolated to be connected.

That was the optimistic voice insisting such a thing. The other made it clear it was his fault.

"My lord!" a voice called. Abaddon ended his musings and looked to his side, surprised to find Culter coming toward him. He excused himself from the conversation with his guards and regarded the older watchman, noting as he wheezed for breaths.

"Culter, my good man, have you been running?" He took a vial from a belt at his robes and handed it over. Culter was certainly in shape, more so than Abaddon himself, but the elixir would help. All men grew weary.

"Thank you," Culter managed, accepting the vial. He downed it quickly, his muscles visibly relaxing. Abaddon waited impatiently, knowing the older man wouldn't be bothering him if he'd not had reason to, but he made sure not to show his anxiousness. Culter was a loyal man, and a good one. He didn't deserve the disrespect of the youth he'd practically raised.

"My apologies, my lord," he said finally. His voice was hushed, as it often was when speaking outside private quarters. He leaned in and pulled a parchment from beneath his uniform, handing it over.

"It was sent to me directly," he whispered. "The cord around it is Mesidian, but the ring in its center was my brother's. It's the one I gave you boys, years ago—I can tell by the engraving on the inside."

He pointed toward the modest ring looped through the parchment's center. Abaddon slid the parchment from it and held the ring up, reading the inscription *for my brother* on the inside. It was indeed the ring Culter had given them, the one they'd often used to confirm messages were from each other. Abaddon smiled and put the ring in his pocket, then unrolled the small parchment that'd been folded inside.

A Pillar in Vines,

The border has been conquered by the insurgence. A legion is needed to end their power. I carry the cure for death at my side. Come to the Dividing Wall. Find the Path of Dragons. Meet me there. Alone.

The prince swallowed, rereading the letter over and over. His mind seemed to lose its will to command, his body numb as his pulse pounded in his skull. He could feel Culter there, waiting, asking him questions, but his words were an indecipherable mesh of noise. All Abaddon could hear were the letters on the page, the ones that said Dietrich carried the cure for death.

Giving Culter his thanks, Abaddon clutched the parchment in his hand and made his way to his mother's quarters. His father would be there at her side praying for an answer to her illness. And Abaddon finally had it.

The Dagger was theirs.

Once they brought it home, they'd have a chance at saving Lenore. At the very least, they could save themselves. No more living in the streets for Dietrich. No more fearing the Redeemers' assassins or the Prianthians' armies. They'd be immortal, and they'd be free.

His hasty steps became frantic. He hardly glanced at the

watchmen he'd been speaking to moments before. The men stepped aside as he crossed into his mother's antechamber. No other guards stood beyond that point, just another set of doors.

Abaddon pressed his hands to them, stepping inside.

"Father?" he asked, looking around. He repeated himself, louder this time, but his call went unanswered.

The room was empty.

Alert, he grabbed the *touched* knife at his side. The bed his mother had rested in held nothing but scattered sheets. The imprint of her body was still visible on the cushions. Harold should've been there, sitting at her bedside.

He wasn't.

Abaddon stepped forward and looked through the windows, wondering if his parents were on the balcony. No one was there, though, save a lonely falcon, watching over Sovereignty.

Then he heard it. The quiet whispers. The eerie singing.

The *auroras*.

Tightening his grip on his knife, Abaddon followed the sounds. They led to an adjacent room, a bathing room, which lay just a few steps away from the balcony. Swallowing, he made his way over, crossing into it.

Heightened from the floor of the room was a deep, tiled tub. Its copper color was magnified by the sun outside, which shone down from the slits of glass running along the top of the walls. Inside the tub was Lenore, legs extended in front of her, head resting to the side.

Emitting from her body, colorful and bright, were her *auroras*.

It wasn't real. It couldn't be. The *auroras* only came when someone was dead, and Lenore couldn't be dead. They finally had the Dagger.

It took a moment for Abaddon to realize his father was there too. He sat on the ground in front of the tub, head hanging low. He held a *touched* sword in his hand, hilt gripped loosely.

"Close the door," Harold whispered. His eyes were stuck to his blade.

When Abaddon didn't obey, his father lifted his head and slammed the door shut with a gust of air.

Abaddon flinched. In his hand, Dietrich's note crumpled.

"The Immortality Dagger," he managed, licking his lips. He took a step forward, trying to ignore the dancing *auroras*, and looked to his father. "Dietrich has it."

Harold grazed his finger along his sword's edge, drawing a thick line of blood. It smeared onto the blade, red and bright, but his expression remained hard.

"Use it then, on yourselves," he said. "Your mother's illness has taken her."

Slowly he turned the sword's tip to his ribs, holding the hilt out. He watched Abaddon, eyes steady, nodding for him to take it.

"I can't do that," Abaddon whispered, shaking his head. "I can't."

Harold didn't falter. "Either you do, or I do. But you know what happens if I take my own life. I'll be with the Fallen One, instead of with the Light."

He leaned forward, only a bit, enough that he could reach the sword's handle from where he sat. Abaddon watched as his father wrapped his fingers around the hilt, nodding for him to come along and do the deed himself.

"Don't do this," Abaddon urged, rushing forward. The king hefted the blade up, ready to strike it into his stomach.

"No!"

Abaddon caught his father's hands, halting them. The *auroras* danced around them, empty and lifeless.

Tears blurred Abaddon's sight. He lifted a hand to his face to wipe them away. His other hand, still holding his father's sword, trembled violently.

"Don't weep for me, son," Harold whispered. He smiled then, letting his head fall back against the tub. "I'll be dead with her. I'll be happy."

Abaddon didn't listen. He cried harder. He cried until he couldn't see, until his sobs blocked out the *auroras'* singing.

Then he pierced the sword into his father's stomach, and held him until he was dead.

I will be home soon, my love. I fear that I am no longer a patriot, though, as I've lost faith in my king. Our prisoner X'odia is innocent, which both Dravian and I have sworn, yet Pierre refuses to grant her freedom. The letters we've received from him have not called for Rellor's punishment, either. After nearly killing her that one day—despite her cooperation—I'd thought he'd be sent to hang.

I hope not to worry you with these words. I know you are close to delivering our child. When I return to Mesidia, I will make sure we escape and go somewhere peaceful. Pierre will not honor my request to leave the Elite now that war is coming. You come first though, you and our baby. I will protect you both.

From a letter between Markeem the Mute and his wife

CHAPTER 69

X'ODIA

The hooves of horses cantered about, steady and slow. The city within Riverdee hadn't taken long to get to, but the poise in the saddle made X'odia's back ache. She accepted it— anything was better than what she'd endured in her shack. At least out here the air was free, untainted and unconfined.

The shores of Abra'am were everything she'd ever expected, the waters nearly black and the trunks of coastal trees dark. It was a marvelous view, so unlike the brilliance of her own back home. It was vastly different from the narrow palms and the bright, white sands. Yet within every plant and every animal, within every pebble and shell and grain of earth, life still breathed with a darkened air. Branches still quivered when the wind howled.

The Riverdian city itself was not as X'odia had imagined. She'd seen it, yet she hadn't, her time during the Attack of

Fiends too engrossed in combat to remember what she'd looked upon.

Now her eyes saw stones, large and grey, their color meshing with the pillars of smoke that rose from rigid chimneys. The clouds were grey too, thin and undefined, rarely white and puffy as she thought they'd be. They left dew drops in her hair, when they came toward the ground, the eerie fog laden enough to descend upon them. When she licked her lips, she could almost parch her thirst from all the moisture that settled.

A pang of guilt was a constant in her stomach, though, ruining her time outside. She was to become a soldier—a murderer. She didn't deserve joy.

"Why stones?" she asked the soldier riding next to her. She hadn't noticed him before, but she needed someone to distract her, and he was the closest person around.

"What?"

"Why are all the buildings made of stones?" she repeated. "And why so far from shore? In Eve, we build out onto the water, with straw and leaves and grass. If the tropic rains come, we build again, but it's easy, and our laborers stay near where they work. Why build such heavy fortresses, and so far from where your profits come? Riverdee's cities are known for trade; why not be closer to where such things occur?"

The soldier stared at her blankly, his features youthful but already hardened. He looked past her, out toward Markeem, questioning the man wordlessly as he awaited permission to respond. The mute glanced at the two, uninterestedly, before giving a slight nod.

"The tropic storms—I've heard of such things," the soldier started. "They bring winds, narrow and fast, like the Creator was trying to blow out the flames of a candle. But it is easy, as you said, to put the flames back when the rains subside. Here in Abra'am, our storms are not as strong, but they are common, and cruel, and they leave little behind that we can use. Besides, it's not just the sky that attacks, but the ground as well. It shakes, rattles everything until even the trees fall to their trembles. Would you not want stones to keep you safe from such ravaging?"

X'odia watched as the young man looked away, his horse eased onward and away from where she rode. Few knew of her purpose with them—of the Mesidian king's intention to have her in their ranks—none save Dravian, Markeem, Rellor, and the man who'd been about to strike her before she'd complied. That man wasn't there, though, riding alongside her now, not that she could see at least. He was back at the camp, as was Dravian and the rest of the forest troops, guarding Vahd'eel and awaiting Prince Roland's arrival.

The first she'd seen of Vahd'eel since the ambush in the forest was as she'd departed on her current venture. Ropes had tied him taut against a tree. His shirt was gone, and his boots taken, only his trousers left to keep him from the cold. Red had lined where bark and bugs had gotten his skin, but he'd still smiled when she'd passed.

After agreeing that she'd join their forces, Dravian had unbound her and let her heal any small infections or cuts she'd incurred. There'd been regret in his touch when he'd undone her shackles, and regret again when he'd put them back on, but there'd been no words exchanged between them. That was the last she'd seen of him before Rellor had come and fetched her from her shack. She needed new clothes, he'd said, and they hadn't had any of that lying around the camp. She'd have to go with them when they fetched the other soldiers left stationed in Riverdee—Odin Iceborne's troops. From there they'd make their way back to the Forest of Fiends, then on northward to Mesidia.

War would come after that.

"We stop here," Rellor called, echoing back through the

lines. Voices of approval sounded, the soldiers nodding gladly as they took a look around. Inns were all around them, their walls built from rotting wood rather than the hard stones of the other buildings. X'odia had taken note of the other places they'd passed, most far grander than these. The smells from their kitchens had been pleasant, and the sounds of their bards had filled her ears. Their mission hadn't been one of niceties, though, but efficiency. Perhaps the rank smells of these inns and the emptied chamber pots in the streets were to make the soldiers want to keep moving. Why else would Rellor choose to stop here?

"That one, right there," a man said. "The girls there'll do whatever you want."

The man wasn't familiar to X'odia; he must have joined them with the rest of Odin's troops. The other forces had only joined Rellor and Markeem a short time ago, but X'odia had developed an uneasy feeling about them. The only person who'd given her disturbing glances in Dravian's troops had been Rellor. Most of the soldiers in Odin's troops—all happening to be men—eyed her hungrily.

X'odia followed where the soldier had pointed. A smiling woman came forward from one of the inns, heavy amounts of powders and creams exaggerating her features. Despite the cold, she wore little clothing. She beckoned the soldier inside with a curled finger, the man slumping behind as he handed her coins.

"Haven't you ever seen a brothel?" someone asked. X'odia flinched, her ears acute to the mocking lilt of Rellor's voice.

"No," she answered. She grimaced as she watched other men tying up their horses, most accompanying their comrade into the surrounding buildings. "We don't have such things in Eve."

"No brothels in Eve?" Rellor laughed, bringing his horse up beside her. "What do bored men eat?"

He pulled off his riding glove with his teeth, flicking his tongue through two upheld fingers. He barked a laugh when he met X'odia's glare. Though she pitied the girl the manic man would choose, she was grateful when he dismounted from his stallion and left.

If not for the new boots she'd been equipped, she might've been afraid to follow suit and take to the ground. As it was, her new shoes laced high up her legs, and her long skirts had been replaced by thick riding pants. She'd been wise to tuck them in, the boots keeping the warmth in and the wetness out. None of the repugnance of the streets seeped onto her skin.

Her bodice had been changed too. It was dark, black like the rest of her attire, with laces up the front. Markeem had guarded her while the woman at the shop had helped her put it all on, the Elite not allowing her freedom from her chains even to let her change. It wasn't that he didn't want it; he likely knew her to be innocent by then, but he couldn't show her sympathy while she still remained their captive. Some still blamed her for the attacks, especially the rest of the troops they'd met up with in the city. It wouldn't do his rank well to be seen giving her temporary freedom.

Dravian had made it clear that her bindings needed hiding. The soldiers might've known who she was, but it would've been dangerous if the common people did, some likely wanting revenge for those who'd fallen. Her shackles would give her away, make it too obvious who she was, and he couldn't have her stoned to death when King Pierre needed her alive. A new cloak, then, one with buttons to keep the front closed and a hood to shield her features, and a pair of gloves, were added to her ensemble. The chains were barely visible now, and only if one looked closely.

Another few bits of similar clothing lay in her new mare's saddle pack, all of the attire swaddled in the dark-blue fabrics of Dravian's cloak. Try as she might, she couldn't find it in her to burn the cloak alongside her other clothes, to destroy it and cast it to the flames. She told herself it was because it had kept her warm during the nights, and that it proved there was good even in seemingly-evil men.

As the men cleared out, answering to the calls of women and slumber, X'odia followed dutifully behind Markeem's lead. He was entrusted with her care, but she doubted he would have been tempted by the damsels regardless. He was loyal, to his men and to his nation; such loyalty likely extended to the girl he was married to. It made X'odia smile when Markeem picked the one inn that seemed disjoined from the brothels.

The inside was nicer than she expected, the smell of wood burning and the warmth of a fire making her sweat within her clothes. She could do nothing of it; her cloak and hood had to stay on, and her hands had to stay laced together as she walked. Markeem noticed the inn keep, and she noticed him. The stout woman dropped the cloth she held and headed toward them.

Markeem glanced back at X'odia suddenly, covering his eyes and then looking at the ground. She nodded her understanding. With the constant attempts to keep her chains hidden, she'd nearly forgotten the swirling, shifting colors of her gaze. She wasted no time looking to the floor.

"One room?" the innkeeper asked, her voice high and kind. From where her sight fell, X'odia could see Markeem nod, watching as he slipped some coins in the woman's hands. With anyone else, a single room would make X'odia stir. With the mute, despite the accuracy of his knives and the constant attention of his watch, she felt some semblance of security. Though it was foolish to think such a thing, she considered him a friend.

No one bothered them as they went, and the innkeeper asked nothing more of Markeem that could not be answered by a simple shake or nod of head. He closed the door behind him and threw his satchel on the ground, not bothering to claim the bed as he settled for an old, torn-apart chair. X'odia stood silently, unsure what to do.

Markeem slowly untied his boots and kicked them off his feet. He noticed after a moment how she stood, then reached for a container of ink and parchment on a desk and wrote something down. When he was done, he beckoned her over, holding the paper up for her to see.

You deserve the bed.

X'odia smiled. Markeem smiled in return as he set his message down. He didn't bother writing more, only leaning his neck back against his chair and sinking into its embrace. After a moment, seeing her find her way back to the bed, he lifted his hand, and the flames in the candles around them ceased. It didn't take long before X'odia noted his breaths falling to the evenness of sleep.

Silence was far from expectant with the Elites' chosen resting place. The constant bustle of drunkards and the overly ecstatic moans of women echoed through the night. So much desire for liquid and flesh, so much enticement toward sin, was almost enough to make X'odia wish she were back in the forest camp, praying the tiny patters she heard along her floor weren't from the legs of bugs and rodents. She did pray still, but not for those things. Now she prayed for forgiveness, for her heavy heart to be lifted. It still ate at her that she'd sacrificed her ideals to avoid being struck and beaten.

She didn't normally need sleep, not when her body healed itself so often, but with the shackles still tight around her wrists she grew as weary as any mortal. Her aching muscles thanked her for the rest, unhealed after days along the back of a horse. She succumbed to her insatiable comforts, to simple dreams without the Sight, dreams of home, of her cottage, of the books she'd lost on her voyage to Eve. She dreamed of Ravel and Captain Bronal, and the rest of the Evean sailors, and of the peaceful breezes of the Evean shore. And then she dreamed of Dravian, his hands no longer calloused, his eyes no longer burdened. He was being reunited with the daughter he'd told her of, the girl he'd called Milian.

His touch with his daughter was kind. He was firm, pulling her into an embrace. He brushed his hand along her cheek, forcing her hair back from her eyes. Then Milian grew tall, and her skin darkened, and suddenly it was X'odia standing there instead of her. Dravian's hand went from her cheek to her jaw, unfazed by the change. Slowly, tenderly, his fingers drifted down, uncurling from their laxed state to close around her neck. His grey-blue eyes went from joyful to hungry. His grasp tightened.

It wasn't until X'odia opened her eyes, gasping for breath, that she realized it wasn't just in her dreams that she was being choked. Rellor Bordinsua was there, straddling her sides. His fingers were wrapped at her throat.

My sister is dead because of that woman. Why didn't the Elite kill her when they had the chance?

Riverdian townsman

Chapter 70

X'ODIA

X'odia thrashed. Rellor kneeled upon her, forcing her quiet. He held his hands to her neck and a cloth to her mouth. It absorbed her attempts to scream.

He took one hand from her neck and pulled her arms above her head. It was easy for him with both her wrists still bound together.

Tears flooded her cheeks. Rellor laughed and took his hand from her throat, fumbling at her clothes. She screamed louder, her throat burning as she prayed Markeem would return. Where was he that he couldn't keep his watch? Why had he abandoned her?

Rellor began *calling* a knife. X'odia's shackles glowed brightly as she tried to use her elements. It was useless. Rellor laughed again as he saw it, then leaned down with ale-filled breath and licked his tongue against her face. She took the moment to force her head to his own, pounding it again and again until blood fell from his nose. He cursed loudly, then squeezed his hand back around her neck.

The pressure made X'odia's vision speckle. Desperate, she lifted her legs and curled them around his head, yanking him down and ripping away his grip. He fell off the bed and onto the floor. X'odia rose quickly and spat out the cloth.

It was then, at last free from her captor, that she saw Markeem still seated in his chair. His eyes were wide and lifeless as blood spilled from his gut.

A bolt of lightning struck toward her, just barely missing where she stood. She ran, grateful for the drinks that had distorted Rellor's aim, and sprinted from the room. Rellor stumbled after her. He shouted at her to return, but she kept running. She tried to pry off her chains and force them from her hands, but the metal was too strong for her to break. She gave up and focused on getting away.

The innkeeper yelled after her when she came into the main room. The stout woman followed her as she burst outside, trying to see if she was all right, but her concerned shouts were cut off as a blade struck her throat.

X'odia screamed. The woman collapsed to the ground, blood soaking into the ground. Rellor followed behind her, face contorted as the knife he'd *called* vanished from the woman's neck.

X'odia wanted to go back and help the poor woman, but there was nothing she could do in chains. She kept going, running to her mare tied up across from the inn. She fumbled with its reins, fingers shaking violently, but managed to get it freed. She hastily placed her boot in the stirrup and her body in the saddle. Urging the mare forward, she ducked down against it. She blocked out the image of the dead woman and Markeem and fled.

Dravian Valcor

I was only near the man once, but I still remember him vividly. I was afraid when I first met him, as I'd heard the rumors of his reputation, but I found him to be a different man than I suspected. He is what he is—the Inquisitor—but does that negate any good in him? People always speak of the trials placed on kings, but what of the executioner who's ordered to do the killing? What of his morality?

That is how I think of Dravian. A loyal man, and a good soldier. I hope that does not cost him the Creator's grace.

From the sketchbook of Elizabeth al'Murtagh

Chapter 71

DRAVIAN

The trees stood silent. A single owl cooed, lost amid the trees' heights. It was morning, an unusual time for such a thing, but Dravian released his book, indulging in the sound.

He wondered what reason the owl had for calling out. Most likely it was claiming its land. The Elite had been residing in its home for some time now, and it probably just wanted them gone. That was too somber a reason, though. Dravian wanted to believe it was for something better the owl cooed. A companion, perhaps? A mate? That was a cheerier thought.

"Perhaps it's looking for its owlets," Vahd'eel said, noting Dravian's musing. He was tied to a tree, his lips split with a grin.

"They do that," he continued, "when their owlets have fallen to the ground. Wouldn't that be dreadful, Valcor? Losing a child?"

Dravian sat motionless. Vahd'eel laughed, then cooed

along with the owl.

It wasn't pleasant anymore. It was sickening.

Dravian licked his finger, flipping his book's page.

"Commander!" a soldier called, rushing over. "Commander, I bring news!"

The soldier approached with panting breaths, clutching his knees. He stood at attention when Dravian set his book down and rose, then gave him a crisp salute.

"Speak," Dravian ordered.

"Sir?"

"Go on."

The soldier looked to Vahd'eel, who sat with a feigned expression of expectance.

"In front of him?"

"Is it confidential?"

"No."

"Then yes. In front of him."

Nodding, the soldier straightened, trying to avoid Vahd'eel's stare.

"The troops stationed in the city—they've made their return. Odin Iceborne leads them, and says he has urgent news."

Dravian nodded and thanked the soldier. He bent down to gather his things, wincing at the pain of it. The wounds along his chest and stomach still stung. Not as badly as they had before, but enough. He envied X'odia's abilities to heal.

"Would you like me to assist you, sir?" the soldier asked, noticing Dravian's expression. "I used to be a squire for a Xen knight, so I'm used to fetching things."

"I'm no knight, boy, but thank you for the offer." Dravian smiled, then cocked his head to Vahd'eel. "I will have you watch him for me, though."

The soldier's mouth fell open. He tried to hide it with an obedient nod, but he'd already given himself away. He wasn't particularly good at hiding his emotions.

"Don't fret," Dravian said, pointing to the burn mark on Vahd'eel's face. "If he provokes you, consider it a test of will not to burn him. You'll have bested your superior Markeem if you can do that."

He gave him a reassuring pat on the shoulder, then went off to meet the others.

Odin Iceborne stood at the western point of the camp. He was tall, with white hair and weathered skin, and had an air of elitism that only came with age. A flask was in his hand, and an array of soldiers surrounded him, the men and women carrying out various tasks Odin could've done himself.

"Hello, Valcor," he said, saluting. "I'll be forthright with you, and not waste your time—one of our soldiers is dead."

Dravian started but didn't say anything. Odin grimaced.

"It was Markeem. I'm sorry. I know you were close."

Markeem? No, Markeem couldn't be dead. Markeem was the best of them. Markeem was gentle, and kind, and had a wife back in Mesidia. He was going to leave the Elite soon, to be with her, and his new child—

"We tried to bring his body back," Odin continued, "but his *auroras* drifted before we could get it here in time."

"How?"

Odin blinked, putting his hand out. "What?"

"How can he be dead?"

"Light, Dravian, by losing too much blood. Same as any other man. That X'odia woman killed him, last night we were in the city. Took a knife to his gut. Rellor's tracking her now."

Dravian snarled, grabbing Odin's collar. The older man held up his hands, trying to press him away.

"Were you whoring again?" he asked.

"What? Dravian—"

"Were you?"

Dravian shoved him to the ground, *calling* a sword and holding it to Odin's throat. Nearby soldiers watched in shock, some rushing forward, others shouting cautionary warnings.

"You were in the brothels, weren't you?" Dravian asked. "Drinking and whoring, like you always do."

"Burn in darkness, Valcor!"

"Weren't you?"

"Yes," a timid voice said. Dravian looked up, a short, blond-haired soldier stepping forward.

"We were in the taverns and brothels the night Markeem died," the soldier confessed. "None of us saw the prisoner escape save Rellor, sir."

Dravian swallowed. Beneath him, Odin's face was red, his eye twitching.

"Thank you soldier. Your honesty is appreciated."

He stood then, *vanishing* his sword. The soldiers around him were a blur, a silent, guilty mass.

She didn't do it, he told himself. He remembered how X'odia's hands had been when she'd mended him, how her time unbound had been spent fighting to save them.

She wouldn't have killed Markeem.

"You're a disgrace, Odin," Dravian said quietly. He turned and pointed to the soldier who'd come forward, beckoning him closer.

"If I'm not back by the time Prince Roland arrives, make sure he knows it's because Odin let our prisoner escape."

The soldier nodded. Dravian left Odin on the ground, anxious to find X'odia before Rellor did.

Some wounds are too fatal to heal with elixirs.

A note to the healers of Sadie, from Abaddon Haroldson

CHAPTER 72

DIETRICH

The shadows felt tangible. They were familiar, like a roof over one's head. They were dark, and confining and cold, but they were home.

Dietrich clutched the knife in his hand, breathing silently. He was shrouded in the shadows, crouched in the corner of one of the Dividing Wall's shops. It'd been a bookstore, at least from what it advertised, but it hadn't taken him long to discover it belonged to the Redeemers.

That wasn't surprising. Everything in the Dividing Wall belonged to them now.

Still, it seemed this particular shop had always been a front. With so many members out in the open now, it was hard to discern which Redeemers were worthy of Dietrich's pursuit. He'd kill them all if he had the means, but as it was, he needed to find those who might have insight on Brelain.

The first place he'd started with was the home she'd healed his wounds in. Not surprisingly she didn't live there anymore. Dietrich assumed the man she must have mistaken him for upon their first meeting—Victor of the black—had eventually returned. When that happened, a very unfortunate misunderstanding had likely been revealed.

He had no way of knowing for sure, but Dietrich had an idea now of why Brelain had been so helpful to him before. He remembered trying to tell her his alias' name when she'd asked it of him, remembered trying to tell her *Veen*. The full name had never come out though, and if she'd already been expecting to meet with the Redeemer's supposed shapeshifter, then she'd thought she'd been helping an ally. A fellow follower of the Redeemer's cause.

And he'd never mentioned his real name was Dietrich.

For a while he wondered if Brelain was already dead. If the Redeemers had discovered she'd mended the wounds of their enemy, it was possible they'd killed her themselves.

He didn't think that was likely. With as capable of a healer as she was, they'd be foolish to murder her.

Beyond that suspicion, there was also the fact that Zoran and Savine were dead. Dietrich doubted Brelain would've disclosed information about him seeking their help if she hadn't been bent on righting her blunder. Otherwise, what reason would the Redeemers have had to kill Zoran and Savine?

With Fiona Collinson as an ally, Dietrich was provided easy access to significant men in the Redeemers' ranks. They came to her often to check the mines, and to take their cut of her and her husband's wealth. Dietrich wasn't proud of what he'd done to some of them, but he'd gotten answers he'd been looking for.

And now he stood silent, as he had for hours, waiting for Brelain to show herself in the abandoned shop.

Seera still hadn't been strong enough to leave the Path of

Dragons, so Dietrich had to come alone. It was for the best—it'd be too challenging trying to get around unnoticed with her at his side. She'd not liked the outcome, but she'd accepted it, trusting him to do the deed himself.

She'd initially demanded that he bring back Brelain's body. She'd wanted to look upon the woman responsible for her family's deaths, and she'd wanted to watch her *auroras* drift. Dietrich had fervently refused. He wasn't about to make a mockery of the woman, not like the Redeemers had with Zoran and Savine. Besides, Seera and he could share thoughts with one another. Next he saw her, he'd let her pry through the images of him—

Something sounded from the shop's front. Dietrich tightened the grip on his knife, listening.

From where he crouched, he couldn't see the shop's entrance. The feet that walked across the floor were light, though, and the audible sigh that escaped the person was undoubtedly feminine. And undoubtedly Brelain.

Dietrich hated remembering he'd shared her bed after everything that'd happened, but he recognized the voice behind the sigh because of it. It was no different than differentiating a person by their cough, or their sneeze. He'd just discovered the sound through a more intimate means.

When Brelain stepped closer, Dietrich let an emptiness take him. It made him numb enough to carry out his task, but not so numb that he couldn't feel his blades.

"Brelain."

The woman gasped. She dropped what she'd been holding—a satchel filled with elixirs—and lifted a hand to her chest.

"You. You're back."

Her words were expectant. She lowered her hand, noticing too late the open window across from her.

"I knew you would be," she continued, licking her lips.

"When I heard of the Redeemers that'd been killed recently, I knew I'd be next."

Her hand settled on her stomach.

He closed the window.

"Please," she whispered, lips quivering. "Please, I'm—"

She couldn't finish. Dietrich had crossed the room, lifted his knife, and slit her throat.

The red line across her neck thickened quickly. Her breaths became gargles, shallow and choked. Blood, dark without the moon or candlelight to illumine it, spurted onto him.

That was it then. Zoran and Savine were avenged.

Dietrich made to turn but Brelain, still clinging to life, reached out her hand. When he didn't take it, tears flooded her cheeks. She opened her mouth to speak. She gasped, a fish without water, trying to say something. With no words sounding, she let her hand return to her stomach, joining it with the other.

That was when he saw it. Beneath the flow of her dress, stretched and rounded, was her swollen belly.

His mind raced. It hadn't seemed so long ago. It wasn't so long ago.

It couldn't have been.

He caught her instinctively as she fell. Her blood poured onto him, her muscles weak. He collapsed to the floor with her, holding her in one arm, frantically searching with the other. She'd dropped a satchel—had her cures been in it? Could he undo what he'd done?

He had no idea which vial held what. They were all different colors, and Brelain had gone limp.

"Which one do I use?" he asked.

She didn't answer.

"Which one, Brelain? Which one?"

He was shouting now. And crying. He cut his fingers on the broken vials on the ground, mixing his blood with hers.

"I'm sorry," he whispered, rocking her in his arms. He moaned and looked down at her pregnant belly, so noticeable now, and let his hand fall against it.

"I'm sorry."

PART FIVE

THE CURTAIN AND THE STAGE

I've killed a prince, a sentient fiend, and a descendent of the Ageless.

I've never had to kill a king.

Harold was my dearest friend. I loved him since the time we were boys. He took beatings for me. He endured the whip for me when he knew I could not.

Yet now he's dead. Slavery did not break him. He feared no man. He feared no assassin. He simply feared a life without Lenore beside him.

My friend, why did you have to take your life?

From the journal of Culter Sandborne, watchman of Sadie

CHAPTER 73

ABADDON

Abaddon wiped his head before reaching for another *touched* dagger to sharpen. His current watchmen—Zelhada and Sehan—had insisted on building a fire, saying it would keep the fiends away and warm them once the desert night came. Abaddon knew they were right. Still, he hated the way the blaze made him sweat.

"I can't tell which is harder to see in out here," Zelhada mused, pulling down the cover of his cloak. "The day, or the night."

He licked his lips, the skin a bubbled brown from where they'd bled and dried, and turned to Sehan.

"What do you gather? I thought I saw Evog returning, but I can't see anything when it starts getting dark."

Sehan shrugged. "You've got better eyes than I do."

Abaddon slicked back his hair, setting his blade down.

"Out here, it's easier to see at night. As long as there's moonlight, that is."

He lifted his hand to shield his face. The sunlight, golden and bright, split into jagged beams from the Dividing Wall's mountains. He scanned the horizon nonetheless, pointing to a shadow no one else could see.

"Evog is there," he said, beckoning the men to look. "It'll be awhile before he gets here, but he's there. I'd be able to tell you more if the heat waves weren't so strong."

Zelhada leaned toward where Abaddon pointed, holding his palms out in defeat.

"I can't see a thing."

Abaddon rose from where he sat, retreating to his tent. After his parents' deaths, he and his small band of companions—three watchmen and the oracle Deladrine—had set out to find Dietrich in the Dividing Wall. They didn't know about the Dagger, nor that Lenore and Harold were dead, but they knew their mission required haste. Even then, having traversed the sands quickly, Abaddon was tired of the desert. His tent, thin as it was, granted him solace.

Deladrine stepped in after him. Her colorful veils had been traded for tan robes, the bulk of them already dirtied from hours of riding. Abaddon sat down on a blanket, acknowledging her with an expectant glance.

She kneeled beside him, tucking her feet beneath her.

"I know about your parents. Culter told me, before we left."

Abaddon took a breath, suddenly dizzy.

"I know. I asked him to."

She nodded, staring down at her fingers. There were no rings for her to tug on, no bands for her to turn. She found deterrence in them anyway.

"I'm sorry, Abaddon. I'm sorry I couldn't stop him."

Stop him. That was the newest lie he'd shared—that his father had taken his own life. That was the only explanation he'd been able to offer when Culter had found him holding his father's corpse.

Until now, only he and the watchman knew. And Deladrine. Everyone else thought the king was at Lenore's bedside, refusing to come out, and that Abaddon's absence from the hospital was because he was there with him.

"Would you have tried?" he asked quietly. "To stop him, I mean."

Deladrine swallowed. She met his eyes, her jaw tense.

"He was in pain," she said carefully. "He'd lost his wife. To say I would've tried implies I'm ignorant to his suffering."

"But you would have. It's a sin to take one's life, a sentence of damnation. That's what my father believed anyway. It would've been better for someone else to do it."

Deladrine didn't answer. She took his hand, clutching it firmly.

She wore gloves—riding gloves, she told the others, to keep from scraping her hands against her horse's reins. In truth she wore them to avoid sensing more than she intended. Her gift allowed her to know when something was amiss regardless of contact, but touching skin to skin always showed more. With the gloves on, she avoided that.

Abaddon was grateful. He didn't think he could handle her knowing what he'd done.

"The Light shows mercy," she said, squeezing his hand tighter. "It has no rules or limitations. We can't live our lives by a set of commands, nor can we judge the fate of others by them. We can only do good, guided by faith and devotion, and pray that such guidance is right."

Abaddon said nothing in response. He reached out and touched her cheek with his own gloved hand, brushing away her hair.

"And what of the man who takes life from another?" he whispered. "What mercy is there for him?"

Deladrine opened her mouth to answer, but excited shouts cut her off.

"Evog—you all right? Light above, you look exhausted."

The prince let out a breath. He took his hand from Deladrine's cheek, pressing it to the ground to rise. Before he could, she grabbed his arm and pulled him down.

"You hear that?" Zelhada continued. "You were right! Some eyes you've got, your majesty. Curse the Fallen One . . . "

"What?" Abaddon whispered, noting Deladrine's urgency. "What's happened?"

"Evog," she whispered. She swallowed, her eyes wide with fear. "I think he might've met with Redeemers!"

Abaddon started. He released her grip, crossing back outside.

"Your majesty," Evog said, bowing. He was a medium-height man, with hawkish features and a pointed nose. His cheeks and forearms were red from riding, and his lips were parted with panting breaths.

"Zelhada's right," Abaddon said, watching him warily. "You do look tired."

He sat down by the fire, motioning for Evog to join him. Evog took a clean cloth from Sehan and used it to wipe the sweat and sand from his brow. When he was through, he handed it back, then accepted Abaddon's offer.

"I'll sleep well tonight, I can say that much."

He chuckled and scratched at his face.

Abaddon said nothing.

"What news do you bring?" Zelhada asked. "How far are we from the border?"

"Not far. Barring a sandstorm, we should get there soon."

Abaddon studied the man. Any scout he sent should've mentioned the Redeemers' conquest over the Dividing Wall as Dietrich had in his letter.

Perhaps Deladrine was right.

"Are you thirsty?" he asked, motioning Deladrine over.

"I'm sure the lady wouldn't mind fetching you some water."

Evog nodded eagerly. When Zelhada said something to grab his attention, Abaddon met Deladrine's eye.

She returned a moment later. With her was a skin of water, held tightly by ungloved hands.

"Here, Evog," she said, sitting down beside him. She lifted the liquid to his lips. He drank greedily, unaware of her touch along his arm.

When he'd finished, she rose, turning her back to him. She gave Abaddon a single nod.

"Come for a moment, would you?" he said to her. "I'm quite thirsty myself."

She did, looking back for a moment before crouching beside him.

"Go back to the tent," he whispered, pretending to drink. He peered over her shoulder, unsheathing one of the *touched* blades he'd sharpened earlier. "Cover your ears. Don't let them go until I order you to do so."

I regret to inform you that your husband Markeem is dead. He was killed by one of our prisoners. My sincerest condolences. Markeem was a good man and loved dearly by all who knew him. May his auroras *rest in peace.*

From a letter between an Elite and Markeem the Mute's wife

CHAPTER 74

X'ODIA

X'odia used one cloak to warm herself, then rolled another into a ball until it resembled a cushion. The ground was moist from the wetness of the woods. Weeds drank in the dew drops that fell from the trees. X'odia felt her lids fall, trying to rest.

The howling of fiends stirred her awake.

Fearful, she scurried to her mare. The horse kicked beneath her touch, neighing loudly. She managed to get it calmed long enough to gather her things. It was a struggle, with her wrists bound, but she made do.

Every night had been like that. She'd settle herself and the mare somewhere, eager for rest, then be disrupted by nearby fiends.

Despite the fatigue it brought her, X'odia found the constant moving a blessing. It gave her mind something to focus on, something to occupy her thoughts. When she stopped, she saw Markeem dead, and the innkeeper, and Rellor crouching hungrily above her.

Still, the lack of rest had its flaws. Her body could only survive so long with little food and water. Her stomach was beginning to ache.

Determined, she pressed her mare back toward Riverdee's city. The Elite had likely left it by now, so she didn't fear running into them. And, if she kept her hood up and her chains hidden, she might be able pick through the scraps the taverns threw out. She'd get her strength back that way, and her mare's, then find Ravel and Bronal and the other Evean sailors she'd come to Abra'am with.

It was the only hope she had.

After a few hours of riding, she halted, listening. The forest always had some sounds—leaves rustling or branches shaking—but the howls were gone. She decided she'd stop, for a little while a least, and tethered her mare to a tree.

She was grateful she'd left her satchel with the saddlebags. If she'd brought it with her into the inn the night Rellor attacked, she would've been without supplies. As it was, the few items she had were the only things keeping her alive. She pulled out some berries and portioned them off, only allowing herself a few. They were sweet, and juicy, and she immediately wanted to eat the rest, but she forced herself to stop. She'd made do with little portions during her captivity. She could resist the temptation to eat more now.

After tending to the mare, she grabbed a stone from her satchel and settled against a tree. The stone was sharp, and sturdy, and she'd used it each moment she could to saw away at her chains. It'd seemed a hopeless endeavor at first, but a decent notch had indeed formed. She kept with it, hoping she'd eventually—

"Hello, girl," someone whispered.

She dropped the stone. She bolted upright, eyes wide.

Oh no. No no no no no.

Before her, wet and muddied, stood Rellor Bordinsua.

She picked the stone back up, scrambling to stand. Roots pulled at her, twisting around her ankles. She resisted, desperate, but weak as she was, she fell to the ground.

Rellor stood unmoving, watching. The roots he *called* spread to her arms, holding them back. She thrashed, trying to pry herself free, but it was useless. She was trapped.

"X'odia," he said quietly. He took a few steps forward, *calling* a small knife to his hand. Crouching in front of her, he lifted it up, gently dancing it along her cheek.

X'odia trembled, trying not to move. The blade wasn't cutting, but she knew Rellor's game. He'd draw blood eventually, when he was ready. For now, he wanted to see her fear.

"Do you remember when I had you in the shack?" he whispered. He leaned forward, pressing the knife harder. "Do you remember how you whimpered?"

X'odia locked her jaw. The knife split skin, slow and deep.

"Do you remember what I said I'd do to you, if you screamed?"

He clutched the back of her neck, pulling her face toward him. She growled in protest, trying to resist. A low, soft laugh escaped his throat.

Don't make a noise, she told herself, praying to the Light for strength. *Please, don't let me make noise!*

"That's not a scream," Rellor whispered, resting his forehead against hers. "I'll get your scream, though."

He turned her head sharply, pressing his lips to her wound.

X'odia gagged. A shudder ran through her, looping its way through her bones. She clenched her fists, struggling, but the roots wouldn't bend.

Rellor pulled away, smiling. Blood smeared his mouth and jaw. He brushed his hand across her cheek, stopping to press his thumb into her wound. A small cry built in her throat, but she kept it confined.

"I'll get that scream, X'odia," he said again. He stood, giving her a small window of relief from the pain, then walked behind her.

She knew what he planned to do. She might as well scream now. That'd make her suffering quick.

She couldn't, though. Wouldn't. She'd prove her will stronger than that. She'd prove, even in death, that the Creator bestowed grace to the righteous. She'd be strong.

She'd be strong.

Rellor's knife returned, this time dancing down her back. The feeling of it forced her shoulders up, her muscles tensing. The roots he *called* against her arms spread down to her neck and stomach, pushing her to the ground. Cool mud and grass rubbed against her face. She focused on the feeling of it rather than the blade.

She was crying now—and shaking. Rellor's knife was cutting into her again, this time near her thighs.

Take the pain away, she begged. *Please please please. I can't endure much more. I can't do this again . . .*

The pain kept. There was nothing she could do. There were no elements for her to *call*. She prayed, and she hoped, but she didn't fight. Rellor had her. Rellor would torture her—

A loud slicing sounded. The roots holding X'odia deadened. Something fell behind her, soft and thudding. Frozen, thinking it a trick, X'odia lay motionless.

It wasn't until Rellor's body fell onto her, bleeding and headless, that she let herself scream.

His blood was everywhere. It soaked into her clothes, slick and hot, clinging to her skin. She thrust the corpse off of her, bile rising. She tried to shimmy away, but the roots still held her feet, loose and ensnaring. She fought to pull free. Convulsions took her. She couldn't breathe. She couldn't move. She couldn't think.

"Shh, shh, shh, it's all right."

She was vaguely aware of someone grabbing beneath her shoulders, pulling her up.

"It's all right, X'odia. It's all right."

The voice was Dravian's. She hardly heard it. Adrenaline rippled through her. A raging *thump thump thump* pounded in her ears.

"It's all over me, Dravian. It's all over me . . . "

More words escaped her lips. She didn't know what she was saying.

Dravian lifted her up, holding her in his arms and carrying her away. He set her down for a moment, only to help hoist her into the saddle of his stallion. He grabbed her and Rellor's horses, tethering them to his own.

"I'm not going to hurt you," he said. He got up onto the stallion with her, gently grabbing the reins. "You're safe now, X'odia. I'm not going to hurt you."

X'odia heard and saw nothing. She kept feeling Rellor against her, kept feeling his knife. She collapsed forward, lids clamped shut, and welcomed unconsciousness.

She awoke to a deep voice. Rough palms lifted her head, bringing water to her lips. Her tongue and throat complied, greedy.

She opened her eyes to see Dravian beside her. He kept his hand against her shoulder, watching her with concern.

"You're sick," he said, pressing a cold cloth to her head. "You must eat, before fever sets in."

She nodded faintly. Nearby, the steady flow of a river sounded.

She managed to keep her eyes open long enough to look

around. They were still in the forest, but in an area more open, with less trees and a small campfire. There were only two horses nearby instead of three, her mare being the one missing. She rubbed her head, recalling something about the horse being too weak.

Above her, the sky was light but already darkening. It'd been that way once before, which meant an entire day had passed. Maybe even two.

She looked down at herself.

All that time. All that time, and she still wore Rellor's blood.

Swaying, she rose to her feet. She couldn't let the blood stay on her. It was cold now, and damp, like wearing something into the sea and never taking it off. It clung to her, sticky and smelling. The scent was almost enough to make her vomit.

She heard Dravian call out to her as she walked. She ignored him. She needed to get out of her clothes. She needed to wash the blood away.

She needed to get to the river.

It was only a short walk away, pretty and tranquil. It wasn't raging, and there were hardly any rocks, which made it seem more like a bathing pool or a lake. She sat down at its shore and pried off her boots. A change of clothes were in her saddle bag, but she didn't have a spare pair of shoes. If she ruined them, she'd have nothing to walk in.

She washed them first, scrubbing them using a stone she found nearby. The blood washed off easily. Relieved, she set them a few hand lengths back, hoping the setting sun was strong enough to dry them.

She dipped herself in the water next. It was shallow at the shore but quickly deepened, and she walked until it came to her ribs. It was freezing, more so than it'd seemed when she'd been cleaning her boots. Still, she greeted it eagerly. Rellor's blood would be washed away. She couldn't resist that.

Her fingers couldn't either. They shook uncontrollably. When she lifted them to her clothes, she couldn't make them loosen the ties.

She ground her teeth, determined, but they just chattered. It made her jaw numb, and her neck tense. Tears began blurring her eyes.

"X'odia," Dravian said softly. He was standing in the water now as well, a few feet to her side.

He studied her, his eyes falling over her partially open vest. He cast an element of fire around them, warming the water they stood in. Gently grabbing her arms, he lifted up her chains and unlocked them.

Elements roared back to life beneath her skin. The stiffness from sleeping faded, the kinks in her back and neck seeping away. The barrier between her and her *auroras* lifted like a window, the lights bright and welcoming as they came back.

It should've made her feel revived. It should've made her feel whole again. She had her elements back. She was free.

Instead she felt worse. She had all her power back, yet she couldn't shake the fear that plagued her. Her hands still trembled. Her tears still fell.

Dravian made to leave her, but she reached out to him. She clung to his arm, fingers weak, and silently pleaded him not to go. He stared at her blankly, surveying her, noting the constant shaking in her touch.

He *called* a dagger to his hand and pulled her close. He said nothing, offered no comforting words, only bringing the sharp metal down toward her tattered clothes.

He met her eyes, waiting.

She didn't need him to stay there with her. She didn't need his help. She had her elements back. She could do this on her own.

But she was so tired of being on her own. All her life she'd been in solitude, forced into hiding because of her eyes. Because of her visions. Because of her age-defying body.

For once she wanted help. She wanted a companion. A friend. Someone to care.

Swallowing, she gave a single tilt of her head.

Dravian started cutting.

The blade narrowly missed her skin. It made its way down from her chest to her waist, then on toward her hips.

Just before he made the last cut, Dravian brought his eyes back up to hers. When she nodded again, he cut what was left.

It felt liberating to have the clothing off. She crouched down, letting the water pull away the blood. She took a deep breath, closing her eyes. The water felt good now. Warm. It soothed away the fear in her bones.

Dravian stayed beside her. He grabbed her hair lightly in his hands and brushed it over her shoulder. She stayed still, grateful as he scrubbed the blood she couldn't reach.

When he'd finished, he rested his hands against her waist, turning her around. She looked up, meeting his eyes. They were as they'd always been: deep set. Grey-blue. Shrewd. They were warmer now, though, and softer.

Aware of how much they could see her, she wrapped her arms around her chest.

As if sensing her thoughts, he clutched a hand to the back of her head, pulling her into an embrace. She stood stunned for a moment, numb, uncertain, but eventually unwrapped her arms and embraced him too.

They stood that way for a time. Dravian's hold was tight and desperate, and X'odia's was weak. She was crying, she realized, harder than she'd been before. She didn't mind. She wasn't ashamed.

When the tears were gone, Dravian finally pulled away. He undid the clasp of his cloak—the cloak he'd given her before—and wrapped it around her shoulders. Once she'd situated it, he reached down and picked her up.

He walked her from the river and toward the camp, grabbing her boots along the way. When they were back by the fire, he stopped, slowly letting her down. She watched him as he reached through the belongings on his horse, grabbing the new, clean clothes from her satchel and some dry clothes for himself.

"We'll sleep here tonight," he said, setting her clothes beside her. "I know you didn't want it but using you as a soldier was the only way I could convince Pierre to let you live. He ordered me to kill you once you'd served your purpose, once I'd learned as much from you as I could, but . . . "

He stood for a time, like he'd continue speaking, but he never did. He pulled out the key to her chains, held it up, then set it down in front of her,

That was it then. She was free. She could go back home, having failed in her mission, but return to her life of solitude, safe and warm and content.

Dravian would likely do as he'd always done. He'd stay a soldier, too afraid to walk away and start a new life. He'd go to war for his king. He'd continue being the Inquisitor. He'd kill those he was ordered to kill.

Staring at the key, X'odia watched the reflection of the campfire's flames against it. Then, when she could stand no longer having only the cloak to cover her, she grabbed her new clothes and got up to change.

I miss my children. I hope that, whatever Pierre and Rosalie decide, I'll get to see them soon.

From the journal of Joel al'Murtagh

CHAPTER 75

PIERRE

Swallows chirped and sang from the trees surrounding the wheat-grass fields. The blades had taken on the yellow hue of autumn, the color dull and unobtrusive. Snow had fallen the night before, light and soft, and the white had started to fade to clear. It reminded Pierre of his youth, when he'd run through the fields with his sister, Catherine, both too small to be seen once they'd reach the tallest points of the grass. He could still remember the sound of her laughter. Her giggle had been the only thing he had to find her.

Catherine didn't laugh anymore, but the swallows seemed to. The birds had once been Mesidia's seal, before the civil disputes began, and they were now the symbol on the Victorian rebels' flags.

They, instead of the four-cleft leaf, were what Pierre saw when he'd read the letter from Elizabeth and Dorian.

I miss you uncle, it said, written in Elizabeth's perfect, artistic hand. *I don't know where you are—William and Peter won't tell me—but I miss you. Tell my parents I love them. Tell Rosalie and Roland I love them.*

By the time you receive this, Dorian and I will be betrothed and waiting to hear back from you within the Victorians' camp.

Please come to us. Please surrender.

Pierre glanced down at the letter in his hands, not needing to open it again to read the rest. Its words had stabbed at his heart, the weight of them encumbering his conscience. He'd known he had little chance of defeating the rebels, with five armies against his own, but he'd at least assumed the people he'd fight would be enemies. Gerard pledging to aid the other four surrounding nations was a surprise, and hurtful, but it'd made sense. Pierre couldn't hate his old friend for the decision; he knew how politics worked, and he knew Gerard was only doing what was best for Xenith.

But his own family . . .

Well that's that then, Rosalie had said. Pierre wasn't sure if his wife had been infuriated or about to weep when she'd read Elizabeth's letter. She'd just stared at nothing after reading it, her gaze lost. *Our own niece, and a man we raised as a son . . . Was your sister right to hate him all these years? Or are we the ones to blame?*

Pierre pictured his wife as he tucked the letter away. The youthful twinkle of Rosalie's eyes had gone dim by the burdens they shared. Wrinkles had started to show where they hadn't before, the concerned furrow of her brows now almost permanently embedded in her skin.

What had they done wrong? When had everything started to fall apart? The Duchess Yvaine had always been spiteful, but she'd been spiteful in a noble way. A *mortal* way.

Then things had begun to stir. The rumors had started.

Pierre thought he'd done enough to keep their home safe. He'd done what they thought was right, sending troops to

Riverdee when Bernard had told him of the possible attacks. And Bernard had been telling the truth, about that at least. How was Pierre to know that the dark-haired people he'd spoken of had been ancient, immortal beings? How was he to know that Yvaine had been one of them too?

Even now, even after having seen the way she'd led the Attack of Fiends on Stonewall, he didn't quite believe it. How could such things exist? How could the Creator make such terrible, powerful people?

And then the Treaty of Five had formed.

It had seemed absurd to concern oneself with such normal, kingly quarrels, but the Treaty was proving to be their downfall. Not Yvaine, or the fiends she'd somehow controlled. Not the dark-haired people who'd wounded Roland and killed Merlin.

It was a simple piece of paper filled with threats.

Elizabeth is a Laighless in all but name, his wife had said. *Dorian is as well. If we're to lose the throne to someone, I suppose they'd be the best people.*

He agreed with her. But he knew, deep down, Elizabeth and Dorian wouldn't rule with Yvaine still alive.

Pierre dismounted from his stallion, trying to push away the musings in his head. Rosalie had thought the same things as he and had contemplated the temptations of surrender. Both knew death would await them if they carried on with war.

The Treaty of Five had made it clear that mercy would be shown if a white flag was raised and Yvaine was handed over. But how could he, a defender of justice, hand his land over to someone who'd ended lives for the chance to reign? Yvaine was no descendent of Mesidia's throne; no blood of Queen Victoria flowed through her veins. Yet it'd be she the rebels cried out for.

Pierre rubbed his thighs and reached for the water skin tied to his horse. The ale he'd hidden inside it held little comfort, even less when its liquid drained down his throat. It burned at his tongue, his senses hazy, but at least it made him feel something besides disgrace.

If he killed Yvaine, the Treaty of Five would have him executed. He shouldn't kill Yvaine then, shouldn't end the wretched woman's life, but he wanted to. Light, how he wanted to.

He dismounted from his horse and walked up to the castle ruins he'd sent Roland to moons before. It was here that everything had changed. It was here Roland had seen Merlin and Bernard murdered.

Now his son was gone again, sent to bring back the Elite in Riverdee.

If they stood any chance at defeating the Treaty of Five and the Victorian rebels, they needed their army reunited. And that woman, the glowing-eyed X'odia his commanders had spoken of, might sway the tides. Pierre didn't trust her, but if Dravian did, he had to at least meet her. She might be their only chance.

Pierre looked around the castle ruins, finding the hatch beneath the vines. The hinges creaked loudly as he yanked on it and opened its door. The tunnel Roland had told him of was there, dark and murky.

Riding to the ruins had been risky, the land surrounding the old castle heavily occupied by the rebellion's men. But the southern reaches were the closest point of hiding to the Forest of Fiends, and the least expected place anyone would anticipate the king to be hiding. He needed to be somewhere the troops stationed in Riverdee could come to quickly, somewhere they didn't run the risk of being ambushed during their trek through Mesidia's realms. Stonewall had been too far north, too great a distance to not have a legion spotted along the way there. He couldn't risk losing men before they even reached him.

Elizabeth is my daughter, Pierre. Please, just surrender . . .

His sister's voice pounded in his skull. Years of adolescence as a princess had made her too bold for her current stature, too harsh in tongue. She'd never learned what it was to have him as her king, and she'd certainly never adhered to formalities. He could practically hear her shouts echoing out from his mind and off the walls of the dank tunnel.

Joel, his brother by law, had tried to ease Catherine's fury. He was a common man, clever when needed and roguish when not. He was every bit Peter and William, just with age to mature him.

Even he hadn't been able to calm Catherine down.

Dorian is the bastard they pretended to play parent with, she'd said. It hurt Pierre, even then, to think of the words she'd said next: *What a fine job they've done with that.*

He glanced around the tunnel, trying his best to ignore his recent memories. There was some merit to them, though it was none he wanted to think about.

He took a heavy breath, *calling* on an element of fire for light, and continued onward.

The smell of dew and rain vanished quickly. The scent of droppings in the tunnel took their place. Pierre held his arm to his nose, trying to breathe in the scent of his sleeve. Nothing seemed to block the odor out. His eyes stung, small streaks of tears falling down his cheeks. He stopped, holding his breath for a moment to wipe them away, then continued to press through. The rats themselves were quick to scurry.

The tunnel eventually revealed another set of stairs. Pierre's flames illuminated a handprint on the wall, large and smudged. It was Roland's handprint, Pierre realized. His son had sprinted down the steps and away from the strange people he'd described. It'd been his hand, pivoting him around the corner, desperately trying to escape to warn them of Yvaine's attack.

The visions of what Roland depicted, the nightmares that now plagued him, came to life against the tunnel's stones. Pierre pressed his own hand to where Roland's had been, feeling the urgency his son must have felt. He took a breath, still muffled against his sleeve, and began his climb up the new set of stairs.

It was as Roland had said: the steps led to an old wardrobe, furs still hanging from its poles. The doors were slightly ajar, burned from the outside, a last attempt as someone tried to halt his son's retreat. Pierre pressed gently against them, the old wood squeaking.

The opening gave way to the remnants of a startling scene.

A dark stain lay splattered across the floor and the far wall. Pierre stepped toward it, crouching down to examine its age. He didn't need to. He already knew it was a vestige of Duke Bernard's death.

He walked away, noting the spots where water had rotted out the floor. No, not water. Ice, where the dark-haired woman had trapped Roland in place.

He looked up, noting where dust had been disturbed along the wall. He headed toward it, realizing it was there Roland had been thrown. Where the bones in his shoulder had shattered.

Scorch marks emerged around the spot. Lightning, then, from Merlin. Roland had said the Elite had tried to save him.

Pierre turned to the last bloodstain. That was where Merlin had died.

It was just a small circle.

Taking it all in, Pierre leaned against the wall behind him and slid to the ground.

The light that came through the tiny ceiling windows shone down on him. They weren't really windows; the room was still underground, and covered outside by foliage, but the holes were wide enough to let light in.

He sat quietly and thought of Rosalie, his perfect, fervent wife. She questioned him, justly, always forcing him to reflect on his decisions and doubts. She loved Mesidia, she'd die to keep it from her enemies' hands, yet she wouldn't push her emotions on him to sway his judgment. If surrender was what he deemed best, she would fall to her knees and bow to her new leader. Even if Yvaine's feet were the ones she kneeled to.

If he didn't surrender, how many children would be orphaned for his cause? How many husbands and wives would he have to insist were widowed with reason? They wouldn't care if it were Victorian or Laighless they pledged to. They wouldn't care why it was honorable they fight. They'd only know they'd never hear or see or touch their loved ones again.

What king could do such a thing, sentence his people to death, solely for what he believed was right? What reason did he have to decide what was right at all?

"This," Pierre said aloud, facing the weakened light. He held his palms up around him, then let them fall back to his legs with a thud. "How can you ask me to forfeit my home to *this*?"

This was the product of Yvaine's deception. *This* was the proof that she was a monster—that she was heartless and cold. The stain of her own husband's death lay along the floor by Pierre's feet.

The king waited, feeling as though something in his solitude should warrant a response. It was just him and the Light, only him and the Creator there to fill the space. Why wasn't it answering?

"How?" he yelled, looking at the bloodstains throughout the room. What tiny difference could have ensued to have Roland's blood on the floor?

"How?"

His shout echoed around him, absorbing into the old carpets and walls before fading into nothing. Sobs took him then, just the motion first, then the tears. He pressed his palms against his lids, attempting to hold them back. He could do nothing to restrain them, though. They fell without restraint.

"I can't," Pierre choked, looking back up to the light. The muscles in his stomach burned from weeping. "I can't . . . "

The kingdom of Mesidia needn't have a Laighless to rule, nor a widow of the Victorian crown. He knew that, enveloped in his isolation—knew it for the truth it was. The Creator had whispered the thought into his mind, had created the path for him to amble. But he knew what would transpire if he took that path. He knew his footsteps wouldn't carry on.

"Yvaine must die," he whispered. "And I must surrender."

He took in a breath, a strange peace befalling his acceptance. Everything had been set in place; the noose in his mind had been tied around the duchess's neck. He just needed to order the floor ridden from her feet.

He rose from where he sat. The Treaty of Five would kill him if he killed Yvaine, but he knew he had to do it. For his kingdom, and for his family. It would be the last righteous thing he did as Mesidia's king.

Dusk had taken over the sky, any attempt for the sun to bring its illumination cast away for a new day. Pierre's stallion had been pressed onward with a steady pace. The king was in no hurry to acknowledge his fate.

His sister would mourn, but she would trade his life for the safety of her daughter's.

Rosalie would insist she take the fall with him. He wouldn't allow it. The Duchess Yvaine was his to kill—his evil to purge. He could only surrender knowing his queen would live, and the duchess wouldn't take their place.

After leaving the castle ruins and crossing back through the wheat-grass fields, a small shack stood weakly before him, its withering roof and damaged walls doing little to betray his family dwelling inside. He took his horse to a pen further down, tying it up and parting with it for the night. Alone and purposeful, he sauntered back to the cabin, ignoring the latch to the cellar a few feet away. Yvaine lay in its depths, bound and imprisoned, half alive in her new dungeon. He would go to her in the morning, a sword in hand, ready to bring her head with him alongside his white flag. He would only have a short while, her remains drifting before a few days' time, but it would be enough to find the camp Dorian and Elizabeth resided in.

He would take his turn as the prisoner then. He wondered what Dorian would do when the Treaty of Five ordered him executed.

With the sway of the breeze, the wheat-grass of the fields whipped against his thighs. He rid his fingers of his gloves, holding them in one hand as the other felt the grass' blades. They fluttered like a sea of faded gold.

He smiled, his body still as he admired the grasses' flow. He breathed in the air that forced them to dance. Turning, he walked toward the door of the shack, pressing down its handle and stepping inside.

Blood, wet and dark, soaked into his boots.

Pierre froze, not wanting to believe what he saw in front of him. His family, his beautiful wife, his little sister and his brother by law, all lay with empty gazes and slit throats. He wanted to rush out to them to hold them in his arms and force the blood to stop, but something in his stomach, something cold and sharp, kept him from going.

He looked down.

The blade of a sword was pierced through his gut.

It pulled back through him, the elements in his mind weak as a warm liquid spilled out from his stomach. A man in black circled around, his eyes green beneath the cloak he wore.

Rosalie, piled beside his sister's corpse, was the last thing Pierre saw before the metal of the man's sword met his neck.

I saw a corpse today, come back to life. It had to have been. No person could be so bloody and skinny and frail.

A Mesidian farmer

Chapter 76

Elizabeth

"Here, here, and here as well."

Elizabeth watched the general's hand along the map, distracted by the nubs of his missing fingers. There were three in all, one gone from his left hand and two from his right. She looked to Dorian and watched as he nodded, his eyes narrowed as he took in the rebel's words.

I wonder if he can even hold a stick of charcoal, she thought, itching to draw the Victorian general's harsh face. With everything that had happened, with all the sudden changes she'd been thrust into, her sketches had become her solace. She'd never drawn her brothers before—she'd always told them they'd make fun of her renditions of them—but now that she was here, with the Victorians, she couldn't stop thinking of them.

She wished they'd come with her.

"The men near Staughtentahl should be easy to reach," Dorian said to the general. He glanced at the others in the room, five in all, each varied in ages and heights. Element-re-sistant armor lined them, which was a strange sight. Elizabeth was accustomed to seeing the freeness of her uncle's Elite.

It was a relief, though, in its own way. The rebels' lack of custom gave Dorian a reason to wear armor of his own. He was a competent fighter, but he was more skilled in politicking than combat. He would've looked weak, shielded head to toe, if it were the Elite he'd been leading.

"Scouts have already been sent to find them," the general said, nodding dutifully. "As for the others, we've sent the ra-vens, but they travel through Laighless sky. They will likely be shot down before they make it."

Elizabeth could hear Dorian's quiet sigh as he placed both fists over the map.

Rallying the rebel troops had begun easily at first. Most of the Victorian-occupied land was closely aligned to the bor-der with the Xens. They'd come hesitantly in the beginning, doubtful and unsure, but persuasion swayed their minds as quickly as desperation did their men. Mesidia's winter was ap-proaching, and the cold and starving rebels were eager to fall behind the structure of a regal leader.

Not all could gather as quickly, though. Many were still stranded across the nation, struggling to stay afoot. Moving to where they dwelled was too risky; it'd been reported that the Laighlesses' followers had already prompted battles, and they likely wouldn't hesitate to do so again.

What little still remained of the Elite were already winning.

Elizabeth bit her nails. Pierre would surrender. He had to. With both Dorian and her aiding the rebels, betrothed and willing to ease tensions, he had to give in to reason.

"If the men in Staughtentahl can reach us before the Elite in Riverdee return, we should be able to make our ambush." Dorian leaned away from the map, holding his chin in his hand. "I believe this would eliminate a good portion of the Elite's men and buy us some time while we await the reinforcements from the Treaty of Five.

"The legions from the Arctic will likely be able to assist our northern troops, and those in the northwest reaches will be joined by Commandant Hedford's army upon his return. It will be some time before that'll all occur, but time is our ally in such an endeavor. Pray for your comrades' resilience and strength as the winter comes.

"You're dismissed."

The men all nodded, some muttering, "Yes, milord," as they slowly filed out. The same respect was not given to Elizabeth as she stood silently in the corner. Only cold stares emanated toward her.

She understood that. She was a Laighless in all but name. Her blood carried the lineage of Daniella Corrins and the bastard son.

She kept her head high, though, despite their revulsion. Beneath the heavy furs of her garb, her hands trembled.

"What're your thoughts?" Dorian asked. He stepped closer to her, crossing his arms over his chest.

Elizabeth pondered. "The Elite returning home from Riverdee wouldn't expect us rallied enough to implement an ambush. However, it may be wiser to allow them to seek out their intended destination, as it will likely give us some indication of where Pierre and my parents are hiding."

Dorian cocked his head. "You don't know where they are?"

"No. My brothers do, but they never told me. They thought I might tell someone."

She glanced at him for a moment before looking down.

"You're suggesting we not ambush the Elite, but instead have scouts follow them to see where Pierre is hiding? It is a fine suggestion, but—"

"It's war," she said simply. She shrugged, hoping Dorian couldn't sense her dismay. "We've given Pierre the chance to surrender, and my brothers sent him our letter. But he hasn't responded. It seems he's set on bloodshed."

The words were merciless. The manner in which she said them was not.

"Let us speak of something else," Dorian suggested. He stepped closer still, the heat of his body making her warm. "Have you thought of where we'll marry?"

Her mouth fell open. "Where we'll marry? Oh, um, no. I hadn't."

"I have." Dorian pointed to his chest, his lips pulling back. "Would you like to hear where?"

Elizabeth smiled. Her heart lurched in her chest, but she welcomed the feeling. She nodded eagerly.

"All right, it might not be what you'd expect, but hear me out." He turned around and grabbed the map the rebels had been looking over, holding it against his chest. "I thought perhaps in the gardens, outside the Church of Disciples." He pointed to the place. "There's an old building there, where the gardens meet the fields. It's where people would go to pray for prosperity and good fortune. I used to go there often as a boy and ask the Light to grant me strong faith and guidance. I thought it a fitting place to marry then, as the Creator would be giving me you for a wife."

Elizabeth looked down, trying to hide her cheer. She didn't want him to know just how ecstatic he'd made her. She feared it'd make her seem as if she were a love-sick girl.

"You could wear the flowers of spring in your hair," he continued, brushing her hair from her cheek. "If those are considered appropriate for such ceremonies. I'm afraid I know little of such things."

Elizabeth's laugh was stolen as a rebel came running back into the tent. Dorian's hand pulled away quickly.

"Milord," the rebel managed, gasping. "Milord . . . the Duchess . . . is here!"

Elizabeth and Dorian looked to each other. Then they pushed past the rebel, hurrying out of the tent.

A circle of men and women had formed. Elizabeth couldn't see who or what they surrounded, but she guessed by the shouts it was Yvaine. How could that be, though? If she were there, that meant Pierre had let her go.

Did that mean he'd surrendered?

With Dorian tugging her hand, they managed to push their way through the rebels. A few returned scouts stood in the circle's center, two crouched on the ground with what looked to be a starved corpse. Dried blood covered its skin. Its hair was a mangled mess and its dress was torn and splattered. Element shackles bound its arms together.

Dorian beckoned the rebels out of his way. He walked to the corpse, kneeling beside it.

It wasn't a corpse, but a barely living Duchess Yvaine. She had wounds on her chest and back, which had been sewn poorly and healed into disfigured lumps. Her dress hardly fit her, her body nothing but bone and muscle. When Dorian offered her his water skin, she took it, clenching to it like a babe at milk.

"Where's my daughter?" she asked. "Where's Natalia?"

"She's in Xenith," Dorian said. He ordered a few rebels to find a medic, then offered Yvaine more water. She declined.

"A man came," she said. She looked to Dorian, eyes wide.

"What man?"

"I saw him leave."

"Who?"

"The man. The one who killed the Laighlesses."

Elizabeth blinked. Her fingers tingled. Her body numbed. The rebels around them stood silent.

"What?" Dorian whispered. "They're . . .they're dead?"

Yvaine looked to him. Her eyes were less frantic now. More lucid.

"The man killed them. The man in black. He had a dragon . . ."

A dragon? The only person she'd ever heard of with a dragon was Dietrich Haroldson. He rode it like a common man rode a horse.

Elizabeth was dizzy suddenly. Lightheaded. She reached out, searching for something to hold, but there was nothing. Panting, she put her hand to her head. Then she squeezed her eyes shut, stumbled forward, and fell to the ground.

Gerard Verigrad,

It is with a heavy heart that I am writing to you today.

Chapter 77

Gwenivere

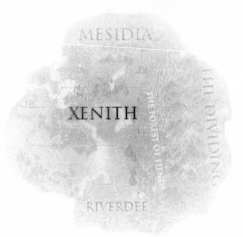

Gwenivere watched as her father tossed a letter on the table in front of him. A seal of a Mesidian swallow bubbled from its cover. It was the emblem of the rebels—of the Victorians.

It made her gut wrench to see it instead of the four-cleft leaf of the Laighless family.

"Tell me, Daughter," Gerard started. His hands were laced behind his back, his brow furrowed. "What relations, aside from the Attack of Fiends, have you had with Dietrich Haroldson?"

Gwenivere's heart pounded. What was this? She felt like she was on trial, with Natalia, the al'Murtagh brothers, Becca, Sir Garron, Sir Nicolas, and every member of the Treaty of Five as her jurors.

She glanced again at the swallow-sealed letter.

*Catherine and Joel al'Murtagh, and Pierre and Rosalie
Laighless, are dead.*

Chapter 78

ELIZABETH

MESIDIA

"Yvaine told me where it happened."

Elizabeth nodded to Dorian then looked at herself in the mirror. Her lids were swollen beneath her brows, her eyes consumed with red.

"If it would give solace, I can arrange to take you there."

Take her there. To where her family had been murdered.

Where they'd been slaughtered.

Dorian stepped closer, reaching out to console her. She should accept it, and console him too, as Pierre and Rosalie were his parents. They would both need each other's support. The rest of the rebels thought the Laighlesses' deaths a victory.

But to see where they'd been killed? To see the places where their bodies had lain, undiscovered and bleeding until their ascension?

She wasn't strong enough.

"Thank you," she said, her voice rasped from weeping,

"but I don't think I can bear it."

Dorian nodded. He eventually lowered himself beside her and kneeled at her feet, taking her hand in his.

"I'll find the man who did this," he assured, stroking her fingers. "I'll make him pay for what he's done."

The man who did this. Wasn't it obvious?

It had to be the Assassin Prince. It had to be Dietrich.

"What if . . . what if it wasn't just that one man?" Elizabeth sniffed softly. "Would you make our allies pay, if one of them had aided him?"

They were hiding in the ruins along the southern edge of Mesidia, in Victorian occupied land. Yvaine Barie was being held captive there and saw the man who killed them.

We don't know why, but the assassin chose to let her live.

CHAPTER 79

GWENIVERE

"Prince Dietrich first found me when Garron and I were walking through Voradeen's streets," Gwenivere began. "He'd noticed me in the marketplace, saw me admiring a glass rose. He bought it for me, as a gift, and wrote me a note saying he would meet me again."

Gwenivere felt Garron beside her, his chest rising and falling with shallow breaths. She forced herself to keep from swallowing, nervous the people around her would think her statement a lie. It wasn't, but she'd kept it to herself for so long that it felt strange to speak it.

"And did he meet you again?" her father asked. "Before the Attack of Fiends?"

"Yes."

Gerard took a deep breath. The others in the room shared glances.

"What did he want? What did he say?"

"Nothing. He remembered a book his father had given me, on his first venture to the West."

"Was anything else said during this conversation?" Gerard pressed. He finally brought his hands from behind him, walking slowly to his throne and sitting down. "Did he present you with any proposals?"

Gwenivere sat quietly, running through the exchange in her head. They'd discussed proposals, in every manner of the word, but none during their first encounter. She wasn't lying to say as much.

"No," she answered. "Nothing of the sort was presented."

The king nodded, then turned toward Sir Nicolas and Sir Garron. With a wave of hand, he beckoned them forward.

"Sir Nicolas Field, Sir Garron Hillborne: Do you vow to speak only truth in your confessions to this council? Do you pledge on your names and the names of your ancestors that the Fallen One will not misguide you to speak lies and fabrications as you bring us your admittance?"

"Aye," the men answered. Gerard sat up taller in his throne, leaning toward the knights.

Gwenivere leaned too.

Yvaine is with us now. She could not see much of the assassin as he had most of himself covered, but she did see that he had the dark skin and green eyes of Sadie. And that he had a dragon.

CHAPTER 80

ELIZABETH

"What do you mean?" Dorian finally asked, reaching up to hold Elizabeth's cheek. "Who do you think aided the Laighlesses' killer?"

Elizabeth let her head rest against his touch, pondering.

This could all be a mistake. She could just be looking for someone to blame.

But if she was right, and there was more to this, she had to say something. Even if it damned her dearest friend.

"I'm not sure," she whispered. "In my head, I tell myself I only seek someone to fault. But the more I turn from such thinking, the more the thoughts begin to linger.

"Do you remember, during the Attack of Fiends, how Gwenivere returned to the palace on the back of a dragon?"

I'm not one to make assumptions; I feel it is important to survey all information before coming to any conclusions. However, I find it difficult to believe the killer could be anyone but Dietrich of Sadie.

CHAPTER 81

GWENIVERE

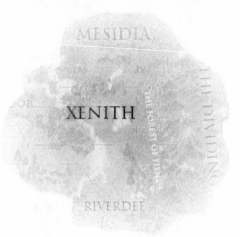

Nicolas stepped forward, for once not wearing his incessant smirk.

"During the Attack of fiends, you ordered Sir Garron and I to find Lady Gwenivere," he said. "While carrying out those orders, we saw her within a plaza, right as the quakes from the Behemoth's awakening began. The buildings surrounding her were about to collapse, and we didn't think we were going to make it to her in time.

"That's when Prince Dietrich and his dragon came."

I don't know what his motivations could have been. I've always had a good relationship with his brother Abaddon, and I will certainly reach out to him now, but a man cannot answer for his brother. He may not be able to provide us any further insight.

CHAPTER 82

ELIZABETH

"I thought it strange, at the time," Elizabeth continued. "I wondered what could've possibly made Gwenivere form an alliance with a dragon. With a fiend."

However, and know it brings me great pain to even suggest this, there may be someone else who can provide us insight.

Chapter 83

GWENIVERE

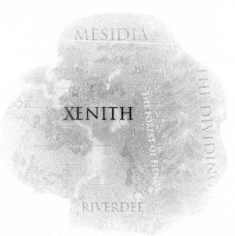

Nicolas looked to Garron, who gave a reluctant nod. "It was the same dragon that our men fought on the palace balconies," Nicolas said "Some of our knights had been trying to fight it off, but someone had drugged them all."

As was revealed, Gwenivere has been playing a role in Mesidian politics for quite some time.

Chapter 84

ELIZABETH

"Before we left for Xenith, Roland gave me a letter to relay to Gwenivere. When I gave it to her, before the attacks had happened, she was very angry with me, and told me not to tell anyone that she and Roland were still communicating. She said she didn't want to give the servants any more to talk about."

Mesidia has always believed the Creator has bestowed bless-ings onto it for guarding the Dagger of Eve. Now the Dagger has been given to Dietrich of Sadie, supposedly in exchange for his aid in the Attack of Fiends. This proposition was presented by Gwenivere herself.

CHAPTER 85

GWENIVERE

Nicolas stepped back as Sir Garron stepped forward.

"I saw them together at the masquerade," he said. "The Lady Vel asked that she and Lady Gwenivere have some time to themselves, but I never let them out of my sight.

"Once they'd finished conversing, Lady Gwenivere began attending to her suitors. From what I could tell, one of these men was Dietrich Haroldson.

"He and Lady Gwenivere shared in a single dance, and when their dance ended, he kissed her forehead."

"I saw it too," Alanna Verkev added. "As we'd mentioned during the Peace Gathering, my family and I had recently suffered the loss of our brother to an assassin, one we'd been told would be coming to the West as Dietrich's imposter. We'd been keeping a careful eye on Dietrich—or the man who might've been posing as Dietrich—every chance we could.

"We saw him riding a dragon while we were protecting Prince Aden. Eventually Lady Gwenivere returned to the palace riding that same dragon.

"Even though the battle had already been won, my sisters and I heard her whisper, 'Go save him' to the dragon."

Gwenivere listened intently, noting the implicative tone in Alanna's words. Nothing the Prianthian said was false, but she seemed to be saying it as if it were the damning words of a trial.

Please know that it is not an accusation of murder that I am placing on Gwenivere's shoulders. I am merely presenting that Gwenivere's chosen alliance with Dietrich may have contributed to this tragedy.

CHAPTER 86

ELIZABETH

"I hadn't thought much of it at the time," Elizabeth said, grateful for the hand Dorian placed on her knee. "But later, after hearing what the servants had to say about the battle—that they thought Dietrich and Gwenivere had somehow been controlling the fiends together—I thought perhaps Gwenivere had been warranted in her anger toward me.

"But then, as I am sure you heard, her chambermaid Becca revealed what she'd done."

I cannot comment further on Gwenivere's possible involvement in this, or why she might choose to be involved at all.

Chapter 87
GWENIVERE

"The servant can tell you herself of Gwenivere's plotting." Alanna reached for Becca's arm, the chambermaid flinching before Natalia quickly intervened. The two royals exchanged heated glares.

"It . . . it . . ." Becca looked over at Gwenivere, her lips quivering. Gwenivere felt a pang of sadness toward her servant. She wished she'd been able to keep her shielded from the schemes of nobles.

"It's true, milord," Becca finally managed. "The Lady Gwenivere told me she and the Eastern Prince—Prince Dietrich—had convinced Roland to give up the Dagger of Eve. She said the letter she'd sent Prince Roland hadn't forced him or threatened him in any way, but that it'd led him to believe Prince Dietrich was a suitable fit to replace him as Guardian. She told him that she thought this because Dietrich had been the one to save Xenith.

"Roland accepted her proposal and gave up the Dagger so Gwenivere could be his betrothed."

However, I must admit that my and Elizabeth's betrothal was neither her idea nor mine at its inception. It was Gwenivere's. She admitted that the betrothal was thought of in part to keep me from being influenced by and relying too heavily on Natalia Barie. Elizabeth has pointed out that she herself, once Gwenivere is queen, would likely turn to Xenith for guidance. She believes that in some ways this betrothal may have been formed so Gwenivere could have more influence over her, and thus Mesidia.

CHAPTER 88
ELIZABETH

"She'd manipulated Roland into giving up his Guardianship," Elizabeth said. "And she'd done it by insisting Dietrich had saved Xenith.

"While I know Roland loves her, I find it hard to believe he'd give up the Dagger on that alone. After all, he didn't . . ." Elizabeth met Dorian's stare, clearing her throat. "He didn't give up the Dagger to you. If he was to give it to someone, I'd think he would choose you over a stranger."

She waited to see if Dorian would say anything, but he kept quiet. She cleared her throat again and gestured between them.

"And then, of course, there was this." She laughed hopelessly as she wiped another tear, pained at how vulnerable and foolish she felt. "She convinced my brothers and me that it was imperative we keep Natalia from having any control over you.

"I never once considered myself the manipulated one, controlled by Gwenivere herself."

It is all very unclear. My family is dead, and Elizabeth's as well. We are grieving, and perhaps pulling at threads that do not exist, but I think it pertinent that as much information be found as possible. If you're able, question Gwenivere of these matters. She may not be guilty of these murders, but she is not innocent in all of this. She already schemed against the Treaty of Five. What else she's done may not be clear to us yet.

Dorian Cliffborne, Ambassador of Mesidia

Chapter 89

GWENIVERE

When Becca was done giving her account, Gwenivere felt her heart twist. She gave her a sympathetic glance, hoping she knew how sorry she was.

Then Natalia stepped forward.

Gwenivere tensed, seeing the dangerous look of serenity on the woman's face. The last time she'd been alone with her, she'd threatened to have Dorian marry Elizabeth if Natalia didn't try to keep him back in Xenith.

What vengeance had the woman thought of in return?

"I'm sure you're all aware by now that my father, Duke Bernard VII, is dead."

Her voice, like ominous music, pulled everyone in.

Gwenivere reminded herself to breathe.

"Before discovering what'd happened in Mesidia during the Attack of Fiends, I partook in a Baptism of Blood before his majesty."

Natalia paused, holding up the red scar slashed across her palm. Everyone already knew it was there; they'd all seen her made a daughter of Xenith at the formal ceremony.

They examined the scar anyway.

"This meant I couldn't be the leader for the Victorian rebels. With my father dead and me a daughter of Xenith, that left my mother. However, due to her captivity, I didn't anticipate I'd see her again. Peter al'Murtagh was kind enough to relay to me where his uncle was keeping her held so that I might be able to write to her one last time."

Gwenivere looked to Peter, his throat bobbing and his lips quivering. He seemed about to cry.

"Before we last convened to confirm Dorian and Elizabeth's betrothal, I met with Lady Gwenivere. Sir Garron can confirm this."

Begrudgingly, as Natalia held out an expectant hand, Garron nodded.

"During this meeting, Gwenivere ordered that if I knew where the Laighlesses were being held, I had to inform her. As my new position requires me to abide by both hers and Gerard's wills, I admitted the location."

Dumbfounded, Gwenivere stood from her chair and shook her head. Garron immediately ushered her back down, but she swatted him away.

"That's a lie," she hissed. "You never told me where they were."

Natalia stared at her blankly. "Then what did we discuss?"

Gwenivere opened her mouth to answer, but the words caught in her throat. What was she supposed to say? That she'd threatened Natalia? That she'd told her to convince Dorian to stay in Xenith?

That she'd gone behind the Treaty?

She couldn't say any of that. The silence was lasting too long, though—she needed to say something.

Lie, a voice in her mind said. *Natalia is lying. Lie back—*

"You discussed your plans for my sister."

The words came from William. Gwenivere turned toward him, alarmed by the hatred in his eyes. Even if she wanted to lie, he knew the truth.

"You convinced my sister that Natalia would try to control Dorian from here," he continued. "You manipulated her, put all these ideas in her head, so that you'd be the one to control her."

Gwenivere shook her head and tried to take a step forward, but Garron was there to stop her. This time, she didn't try to push him away.

"It wasn't like that," she said. It wasn't a denial though and she knew it. The whole room knew it.

"But it's true?" Natalia asked, pressing her to confess. Gwenivere felt herself scowling, unable to hold her hatred back. There was nothing she could say.

"You admit it, then?" she continued. "You admit that you convinced Elizabeth to go, knowing full well that if Yvaine had died alongside the Laighlesses, she'd become queen and *you'd* be the one she turned to for answers? *You'd* be the one who'd have influence over Mesidia?"

Gwenivere stood motionless. *If Yvaine had died alongside the Laighlesses?* The way Natalia spoke didn't sound as though she were being hypothetical. It sounded as though what she'd alluded to had already happened.

Swallowing, Gwenivere looked to her father.

"The Laighlesses are . . . dead?"

She didn't need him to answer, not with how obvious it was now that her father was in mourning, but he nodded anyway. Numb, she eased back into her chair, breathless and shaken. She didn't care anymore about the people in the room; she didn't care about their scheming and their accusations. All she cared about was Xenith's greatest allies, doomed to ascend too soon.

Wetting her lips, she forced out the only thing left to ask. "Was Roland with them?"

At a wave from her father's hand, Garron stepped forward and snapped something around her wrists. The *auroras* in her mind retreated, a broad, vast hollowness forming in her core, but she hardly noticed it. The only thing that mattered was that when her father finally answered her, he answered no.

After Dravian left to find the prisoner X'odia, Odin Iceborne killed the young man who had spoken against him. Then he demanded that any who wished to be free could leave with him. Any who wished to die fighting for a bewitched leader could wait until Dravian returned.

An account from a Mesidian Elite

CHAPTER 90

X'ODIA

X'odia's eyes blinked open, her dreams fading as wakefulness consumed her.

She was glad her newly unbound wrists let her heal again. Today was the first day in many she'd needed to sleep.

Dravian's stallion stood a pace behind her, the loyal steed requiring rest more often than she. When morning had come the day after she'd bathed in the river, the soldier had parted ways with her, his own horse cast behind as he'd traded it for Rellor's. A satchel of food was tied to its side, as well as a map of Abra'am's valleys, but nothing more, not even a note to advise her crossings. She wanted to be upset, to some extent, angered at his lack of farewell, but to want such a thing was useless. She was free now. That was all that mattered.

X'odia took the map from inside her pouch, unfolding it in front of her and scanning its roads. There was no need; she'd memorized it the first time she saw it, the blues of its rivers and the greens of its valleys like a painting against her skull.

She could see small turns in front of her, forks in the road, then trace them to the paper, knowing progress was made as she retreated back to the Riverdian coast. It would be a risk, going back to the stony city, especially after hearing the people thought her Markeem and the innkeeper's killer, but she had nowhere else to go. Her satchel only held so much, and even the healing of her ageless bones could not keep her from needing food. Or perhaps it could; she'd never truly tested it, but she certainly wasn't about to try. After everything she'd endured, it would be a fool's death to die from hunger.

Pulling the fabrics of Dravian's cloak over her shoulders, she rose from where she sat. The new clothing she wore was not so different from the last, her pants still fitted for riding and her vest still lined for warmth.

She took a step toward her horse and stumbled, one hand clinging to a tree as the other clung to her temple. Frustrated, she let out a groan, her legs wobbly.

What's happening? she thought, a sudden headache and bout of weakness taking hold. Everything around her was spinning.

And then she knew, with a blinding, painful reassurance.

The Sight was coming.

She cried out from the aching, the palm against her forehead pushing back her protruding veins. Sweat drenched her frame. Her muscles trembled in defiance. It made no difference, though—the vision would come no matter how hard she fought.

She grimaced and clenched her teeth, then fell into the Sight.

"Where is she?" Vahd'eel yelled. X'odia could see him clearly in the vision, his wrists no longer chained. The panther-fiend from the forest ambush stood with him, its shadowy body circling around Dravian. He stood panting, blood dripping down his hair, the hold on his *called* blade faltering. Corpses lay around him, some his allies, some his victims, all glowing under a brightened luster of light.

He said nothing in reply.

"So be it," Vahd'eel grumbled, casting forth the light. The panther lunged out beside it.

X'odia writhed with torment. She wanted to rise immediately, but her body wasn't yet in her control.

The Mesidian troops, beaten and broken under Vahd'eel's attack—that was what the Sight showed. How the prisoner managed to escape, X'odia didn't know, but the strange panther he'd called Paenah in the forest attack wasn't the only being aiding him. There were others, a man and a woman, their hair dark and their skin porcelain white.

They were all searching for her. Vahd'eel had somehow broken his bonds and ravaged what was left of the camp to find her. And there Dravian had stood, alone and defiant, refusing to expose where it was she dwelled.

He's going to die, X'odia thought, managing to lift herself back onto her feet. She tried to walk forward, wishing her healing would quicken, but her knees buckled beneath her. She fell back to the ground, tears falling down her cheeks, nothing but the thought of Dravian's death berating her weakness. She squeezed her hands. Her nails dug against her palms. The healing would be over soon.

When she had the strength, she climbed onto her horse and rallied it onward, praying she could stop the events her vision had shown.

While most fiends hunt alone, lupinfell are among the few that seem more comfortable in groups. They bear a striking resemblance to wolves and their pack-like nature seems derived of them, but they are clearly still fiends. They control elements easily and—though it is quite disturbing to inspect—the bulk of their bodies look to have the skin peeled off.

An excerpt from *Fire and Fiends*

CHAPTER 91

DRAVIAN

Dravian read the last few words of his book, anxious to occupy his mind with anything other than his thoughts. Any time he allotted for rest was spent engrossed in his book's story, the pages flipping one after the other until there were none left to study. He closed the binding, sighing heavily as it thudded shut. His mare nudged him on his side.

Rellor had never been a kind man, never given sympathy or kindness to his companions, but he'd been strangely sweet to his animals. People were evil, he'd said; animals were helpless and dumb. Blossom, as the mare had been named, was likely looking for the attention from Dravian that Rellor had always shown her.

Dravian stood from where he sat and rummaged through his things, pulling out a piece of dried food for Blossom to eat. She took it with chomping teeth, trotting in place as she indulged in her snack. Dravian smiled and patted against the side of her belly, deciding now would be a good time to continue with his trek. He gathered his things, putting out the fire he'd built with a wave of hand, and tucked his book back into his satchel.

I wonder if X'odia enjoys reading, he thought, grabbing a hold of his horse's reins. He guided her along, not eager to sit atop the saddle. His body and mind enjoyed the simplicity of walking on his own feet.

I'd imagine she likes reading, he decided, feeling a small drop of rain fall against his cheek. He chuckled as Blossom whinnied, the delicate mare not fond of the sprinkles. It was a shame the gentle creature had belonged to Rellor; X'odia would've probably been fond of her.

I should've given her a book of her own, made her journey more fulfilling. Light knows she's faced too much.

He imagined himself beside her then, her head nestled against his chest. In his mind, his arms were wrapped around her, eager to shield her from the world's cruelties as she helped cleanse him of his own.

He never wanted another hand to strike her. A pit of nausea grew in his stomach as he considered what he had once done; what Rellor had *almost* done. If not for the calling he'd been bestowed as an Elite, Dravian would have never left her, never parted from her side. In the end, he'd felt something for her. Maybe not what he'd once felt for his wife, but it had been something. A companionship, of sorts. A sense of being renewed.

A scurrying in the forest cast aside his thoughts. He halted and *called* a sword, searching.

A fiend crept into view. It looked like a wolf, but there was no fur to warm its body or skin to cover its flesh. It was merely muscles, which rippled as it walked. Dravian wasn't an expert on fiends, but he'd guess it was a lupinfell. The beasts were some of the few known for hunting in packs, with strong elemental capabilities. This one, currently alone, seemed entranced by something unseen up ahead.

Dravian watched it, perplexed by the eager way it continued forward. Had it been food it wanted it would've taken him for prey, yet the scent it followed didn't seem derived from instinct. It was too steadfast. Too certain.

Dravian pursued it, praying Blossom wouldn't make a sound. Not surprisingly, another lupinfell appeared, different than the first only in size. Its body had the same torn, fleshy look as the one it followed.

Two more emerged from further on, and another after that, one even coming from behind where Dravian stood.

The mare no longer stood silent. She stomped her hooves and neighed, Dravian quickly trying to force her steady. The lupinfell hardly seemed aware of them, though, their pointed ears not even twitching at Blossom's protests.

Swiftly Dravian got atop Blossom's back, urging her behind the fiends and off the broken path. The lupinfell were headed to his camp, propelled toward it by some unseen force. If it were anything like the attacks before, like the one on Riverdee's shores or the ambush in the forest, Dravian would need to ensure someone was there to ready his Elite. Markeem and Rellor were no longer able to help them.

The faster Blossom sprinted, the more fiends Dravian caught in his sights. They all still obeyed whatever ordered them on, and as he grew closer to his camp, their nostrils flared and their mouths dripped with saliva.

They'd noticed him.

Dravian held his breath, reaching for the *auroras* in his mind. Only several of the lupinfell had taken note of him, but several was enough. He found the green and brown lights of *auroras* in his mind, the colors of earth, and waited.

The fiends lunged.

Dravian *called* on the roots of the forest's trees, snatching the fiends and crushing their bones. Their howls and yelps died out as other lupinfell mimicked him, *calling* on their own elements and encircling him with the branches of trees. Dravian plummeted to the forest floor as his mare reeled back, then rolled away from her frantic steps as he tried to regain his own.

The foliage on the ground came to life. The lupinfell growled and roared as they tried to keep him confined. He *called* a sword quickly and coated the blade with fire. He seared through the roots and vines. A part of him felt the dull weakness that came with *calling*, the energy it stole and consumed, but another part, the part that trained rigorously to feed on that feeling, made him feel alive. He let out a yell, and he tore through the roots surrounding him. Then he turned and faced the charging lupinfell.

Dravian assessed the scene with haste. He *called* a shield of spiked ice as the first lupinfell dived toward him. Its body impaled against his defense.

He barely released the shield before thrusting his sword into the belly of a second beast. Two more came, jaws snapping, but they moved so quickly Dravian couldn't distinguish one from the other. *Calling* on the earth again, he forced up the roots he'd torn down and cast them out. Both fiends howled as their bodies were ensnared. Dravian lifted his sword and slit their throats.

He caught his breath, only for an instant, then rushed over to Blossom. He was back atop her saddle in a matter of seconds, leaning forward and squeezing his thighs against her sides.

Patrols from his camp eventually came into view. Some were already dead. The remaining fought to stay alive.

Dravian managed to swipe his sword in time to keep a fiend from puncturing one of his soldier's throats. The woman quickly stabbed a knife into the beast's side and thrust it off of her. Another fiend was there to take its place, though, bigger and stronger than the last. Dravian dismounted quickly from his mare, rushing to aid his comrade.

Together, he and the other Elite danced around the beast. One of them acted as the bait, the other making their advance. The creature was bulky and furry like a bear, but with scaled talons instead of paws and a beak-like snout. Dravian had never seen such a thing, didn't know its weakness or its strengths, but it was only a matter of minutes against him and his soldier before it was on its knees. When it had taken its last breath, he and the youth nodded to one another, then spun back into battle.

Further into the camp, the chaos heightened. Soldiers were tangled with fiends and bodies were piling. Not all the soldiers were present that should've been; many of the Riverdian troops stationed under Odin Iceborne were nowhere in sight. Dravian shouted as he killed another beast, yanking his blade from its gut as he pulled a random soldier aside. With a strong arm, he forced the man to the trunk of a tree.

"Where are the others?" he yelled, thrusting a bolt of lightning toward a nearing beast. He turned his gaze back to the soldier, urgently awaiting his answer. "Where are they?"

The man, no older than his twenty-fifth winter, lifted his hands in surrender.

"Odin Iceborne," he managed, gasping for breath. "He abandoned us, took his men with him!"

Dravian cursed loudly and released the soldier. Odin had never been a man he considered honorable, but he was a soldier, and the title of Elite should've bestowed him some dignity. How could he have abandoned their soldiers? Was that not the reason they'd come to Riverdee in the first place, to help protect innocent people from being killed?

He shouldn't have cursed him in front of all their soldiers. But Light forsake him, Odin let Markeem die. He let Rellor go after X'odia. He'd been too busy drinking and whoring to be a proper soldier.

Dravian stood tall and looked around, a newfound rage pulsing though his veins. Beyond him, within the cover of branches, a woman came into view, her gaze visibly glowing despite the distance she stood. Dravian let out a feral growl and ran toward her, thinking it to be X'odia after a vision. He halted when he took in how pale she was.

That was her. That was the woman Pierre had initially mistaken X'odia to be. The one who'd fit X'odia's description save the lightness of her skin.

The one who had killed Merlin.

The woman saw him, smiling darkly as she studied his face. She hoisted herself down from the place she stood and advanced toward him, fiends rushing out from the forest behind her. None hungered for her, none snapped at her or tried to tear apart her flesh. They simply continued on, as if her pale figure didn't even exist.

Behind her, a man with similar features emerged.

He didn't share her graceful movements, but he shared her face. He *called* a weapon, a massive, thick broadsword, then smiled slightly at something behind where Dravian stood.

Dravian's eyes followed where he saw the man's go. He barely ducked in time as Vahd'eel lunged toward him.

The prisoner had a sword of his own now. Dravian rolled to avoid it, noting that it was with unbound wrists that Vahd'eel now attacked.

Enraged, Dravian rushed toward Vahd'eel. Moons had passed since he'd last faced the man in combat. The day of Riverdee's attack flashed across his mind. Vahd'eel had fooled him, made him believe he was coming to X'odia's defense. Now Dravian knew the truth, that X'odia had been innocent all along. But the truth had come too late.

I should have killed him that day, he thought. *I should've cut off his head and left it for the fiends.*

At least now he had a second chance.

Vahd'eel pivoted and dodged with ease, evading Dravian's attacks with graceful feet. He made few advances of his own—only enough to catch Dravian off balance—laughing jovially as the Elite stumbled to stay standing. He took a risky swing and opened the skin along Dravian's side, right where X'odia had mended his previous wounds.

Dravian's own sword *vanished* from the pain. Momentarily weaponless, he ducked forward and snapped Vahd'eel's elbow, then pounded his fist against Vahd'eel's face. The man howled, the sound a pleasant ringing in Dravian's ears. Stepping back, he *called* the black *auroras* and regained focus on his sword. When he was certain it was steady, he made to strike again.

The burning ties of something snagged him back. His skin seared, and claws dug into his shoulders. He yelled, and his knees buckled beneath him. The jaws of whatever clung to him opened wide, saliva dripping onto his neck. Frantic, Dravian *called* ice and thrust a beam of it toward the creature.

The attack aimed true. It stabbed through the beast's throat, causing its claws to retract. As it fell from Dravian's back, Vahd'eel was there again, his sword abandoned as his broken arm hung loosely at his side. The other thrust a knife toward Dravian's gut.

Dravian ran, barely avoiding the sharp blade as he sprinted for better ground. Vahd'eel watched him for a moment before heading toward the injured fiend, blood dripping from its shadowy flesh.

Dravian thought the beast dead. Numbness filled him as he realized the beast, a panther looking creature, wasn't dead at all, but healing. The hole his dagger of ice had made was quickly closing shut.

Vahd'eel glanced back over to him, his lips peeling into a sinister smile. He lifted up his distorted arm, grabbed hold of it, and snapped it back into place. If not for the blood that dripped from his nose, there would be no sign he and

Dravian ever fought.

"Where is our dear X'odia, Inquisitor?" Vahd'eel asked, petting the fiend's back. It purred under his touch, its strange flesh-like whiskers pulsing a dull blue. Where they'd wrapped around Dravian now lay aching black marks, identical to the ones that'd marked X'odia's face in the forest ambush.

Calling a shield and readjusting the grip on his sword, Dravian stood silent.

A branch snapped. Dravian turned, casting up his shield just as the pale man, the glowing-eyed woman's twin from earlier, swung his broadsword.

Dravian's arm throbbed where the metal struck. The skin along the lacerations felt torn anew, but he counterattacked and lashed his blade across the giant's legs. The man yelled as his calf ripped open. Dravian ducked as the broadsword swung again. Narrowly he avoided its weight, leaning to his side as it swept past him. He took the moment to go on the offense, twisting around the man. The momentum of his attempt left the giant exposed.

Dravian's sword would have found flesh had the man not beckoned the wind around them. Dravian was thrown back, the air knocked out of him as he crashed into a tree. The bark scraped roughly against his head and neck, and the rain and sweat that dripped down his skin thickened with red. He lost the grip on his shield and sword, both instantly disappearing. He grimaced and forced himself up, hurrying to escape the trees he knew might spring to life and bind him.

As he stood, the woman with glowing eyes came into sight. Two lupinfell stood at her sides. She smiled, seemingly entertained by the theatrics of the battle, and lifted a finger at Dravian. The lupinfell rushed toward him.

Dravian tried to evade, but he was too slow. One fiend wrapped its jaws around his arm, its teeth sinking into his flesh as the other grabbed his leg.

He yelled in anguish. His body tensed as he fought to focus on the creation of a new blade. It came, and he stabbed again and again at one fiend until its jaws unclamped. He took the moment to hurl the knife through the skull of the other beast. Its attack ceased, and he pulled the blade back out.

The first was back again. It pounced on top of him, biting eagerly at his neck. Dravian lifted the dagger up, piercing through the lupinfell's throat and back out the other side. Every part of him was rattled with pain, but he couldn't rest, not even for a moment. He cast the beast's limp body aside and struggled to his feet.

The dark-haired woman was still there, her glowing eyes dimming. The smile she'd worn had shifted to an annoyed scowl.

Dravian *vanished* his dagger and replaced it with his sword. He took a tormented step toward the woman, the tattered, blackened skin from the panther-fiend's attack telling his mind to stop. Hundreds of other parts on his body joined in with their objections, each seeming eager for him to rest. He took another step, then another, only stopping when his eyes caught movement at his side.

Instinct told him to duck, and he was glad. He heard the sweeping of the twin's broadsword beside his head. The air *swooshed* past his ear.

Dravian kicked at his attacker's feet. The man fell to the ground, only to have the panther-fiend take his place.

Hurling himself back up, Dravian barely evaded the searing of the fiend's tentacle-like whiskers. Its shadowy form slipped in and out of his sight. One moment it was clear as night, the next flickering. The dark-haired woman returned too, and a blaze of fire spiraled from her pale hands. Dravian pressed it back weakly with a shield of air as her twin reemerged. His broadsword stuck where Dravian had stood seconds before.

Knowing he couldn't hold his element for long, Dravian

quickly bolted from his place and ran from the trio encircling him.

"Where is she?" Vahd'eel shouted, stepping into Dravian's path. The crazed man thrust his hand up toward the sky, a sphere of light forming in the space above him. It cackled loudly, bolts of lightning meshing with shards of ice. Dravian squinted as the element burned brightly. The grasp on his sword faltered, and his body gasped for breath. He wouldn't be able to escape the element if Vahd'eel cast it his way. His mind and body were too weary to endure much more.

Behind him, he heard the dark-haired man and woman step forward, both of them flanking his sides. The panther-like fiend circled around the space that remained. Dravian lifted his flickering sword up, his muscles straining, and braced himself for the attack to come.

No matter what they did, he wouldn't tell them about X'odia. He wouldn't tell them where he'd last seen her, where she was likely going; he wouldn't tell them anything. He owed her that much.

She has to live, he thought, remembering the way she'd felt as he'd lifted her from the river. She'd been so light, so broken.

She has to live.

"So be it," Vahd'eel growled. He lifted his arm, fingers outstretched, then cast the bright beam of light forward.

The prisoners broke free. The Elite in Riverdee have either fled or died.

A report from a Victorian spy

Chapter 92

X'ODIA

X'odia screamed. She'd finally found Dravian, after hours of tireless riding, only to find him surrounded by attackers. The panther-fiend she'd seen in the forest ambush wrapped its tentacle-like whiskers around his legs, holding him in place as Vahd'eel's beam of light pierced through his stomach.

She *called* her elements. Every *aurora* she could grasp released from her. Her attempt wasn't fast enough, though. It shattered through the beam of light, but only after it fell. Dravian was still struck, his stomach split open. He fell to the ground, the shadow of the panther-fiend retreating.

As X'odia forced her mare faster, a blond-haired man, likely another soldier, came into view. Several arrows escaped the man's bow and pierced through the body of the woman near Dravian's side.

The woman shouted as the arrow points sunk into her

flesh. Her twin caught her as she fell and carried her back into the forest.

The blond-haired archer vanished, as did Vahd'eel. X'odia leaped from her horse's back and rushed over to Dravian.

"Oh no," she whispered, collapsing beside him. "No, no, no, Dravian, please, *please.*"

She grabbed his hand in her own and squeezed it tightly. She pressed it to her lips, wanting to comfort him as he'd comforted her in the river.

"X'odia," he choked. Blood spurted from his mouth, his muscles convulsing.

"Shh," she urged, as if keeping him quiet might stop the blood from pouring out. She kissed his fingers, her tears falling onto his skin. Her other arm extended out and brushed his hair from his forehead. He pulled his hand free, lifting it weakly as he held it to her face.

"I'm . . . sorry," he whispered.

She shook her head, clinging tightly to his outstretched hand. His fingers shook against her, but still they tried to wipe the tears from her cheeks. It only made her cry harder.

X'odia leaned toward him, taking his face in her hands and kissing his forehead. What little strength he had left responded to her touch, his fingers clenching her hair as his other hand clung to hers. She pulled away for a moment, her lips quivering as she saw the life fading from his eyes. She kissed his forehead again before resting her head against his, willing him to stay alive, but his breath was lost, his body still.

Dravian Valcor was dead.

X'odia wept over his body, unable to let go. She didn't want to mourn him, didn't want to move or think or feel. She didn't want anything but for him to be alive.

"You're free now," a voice called. X'odia spun around, still clinging to Dravian's corpse. It was Vahd'eel who'd spoken.

"This is what your father did to me," he continued. "This

is what he did to all of us."

"Burn in darkness," X'odia whispered. She crouched protectively over Dravian's body, his blood soaking into her clothes.

"The blood of the Shield runs through you," Vahd'eel said, stepping closer, "as does the Elder Blood. Our blood. Within you is power you hardly know exists, power I can help you unleash. You are meant to free mankind—make it pure again—not fall victim to its plights. Let the mortal in you die. Cleanse your soul anew. Embrace what you are, daughter of Alkane, and join us in the Light."

As Vahd'eel extended his arm out to her, offered her his hand, an arrow sunk into his back. He yelled in fury and yanked it out, his eyes frantically searching for the archer. The blond man that had struck an arrow into the pale, dark-haired woman had returned. He guided his horse X'odia's way and held one hand steady to his reins, the other reaching out toward her.

She didn't want to leave Dravian, but she'd likely die if she stayed by his side. With a pang of remorse, she let him go and reached out, the archer locking arms with her. He lifted her up and she hoisted her leg over the saddle.

She didn't look to see if Vahd'eel followed.

Do you have to actually use the Dagger to draw on its immortality? I don't believe so. As far as I can tell, from the few times Pierre and Roland have let me hold it, it seems you just call *on its* auroras *as you would your own.*

From a letter between Dorian Cliffborne and Abaddon
Haroldson

CHAPTER 93

ABADDON

Abaddon trudged forward with heavy breaths. The air of the mountains was thinner, and the ground was littered with small stones. He kept losing his footing because of it, as his boots were meant for walking through sand. Eventually he learned how best to traverse through the terrain, but it left him weary. His legs were using muscles he wasn't accustomed to, and his back was hunched. He would've given up on the trek if it wasn't Dietrich he searched for.

After crossing into the Dividing Wall, Abaddon had ordered Sehan, Zelhada, and Deladrine to stay behind. Dietrich had been clear that he wished for Abaddon to come alone to the Path of Dragons, so alone Abaddon came. He didn't much care for the idea of leaving Deladrine behind, not after discovering Evog's deceit, but the oracle insisted Sehan and Zelhada could be trusted.

The sun began to fall over the mountain's edge. Birds cawed loudly and bugs chirped and buzzed. Abaddon lifted his cloak over his face, not wanting to get bitten or stung. Ahead of him, simple and ominous, stood a sign reading Path of Dragons.

Dietrich was nearby, then. The sooner Abaddon found him, the sooner they could go home. And he needed his brother back in Sovereignty—now more than ever. He didn't think he could rule their kingdom alone.

Stopping to take a drink of water, Abaddon leaned against the wall of the canyon. He was hungry, but he'd eaten his last scrap of food a while ago, and he'd not thought it wise to bring more. If he'd overpacked, he'd be cursing the weight, and the extra effort would've made him hungrier.

He had an elixir that helped with endurance. He could take that. But if he did, he wouldn't have it for his trek out of the Path of Dragons.

He took another drink from his water skin, deciding it best to save the elixir. He didn't think he had much further to go. Putting his hand over his eyes, he peered out, chancing a look down the narrow canyon.

It was then he saw him. He was covered in dust and held a *touched* spear in one hand. The other gripped the hilt of a dagger.

"Dietrich?" Abaddon called. He hurried forward, fearful it was the heat playing tricks on his eyes. But it wasn't as hot here, and the canyon cast heavy shadows. It was his brother, lids puffy and body slumped.

As he approached, Dietrich looked up. His gaze was hollow, and his breaths came through loud and slow. It was like he was decaying right there in the dirt, waiting to drift.

"Hello Abaddon," he said. There wasn't any emotion in his tone.

Concerned, Abaddon kept his distance.

"Are you . . . are you all right?"

Dietrich chuckled. He peeled his fingers back from the blade he held and tossed it at Abaddon's feet.

"There it is. The Dagger of Eve."

Abaddon leaned down and picked it up. There was cloth around its hilt, so he stripped it away, revealing the jewel. It glowed, dimly, and there was the faintest whisper emitting from it.

"Say, Brother, do you know why they call me the Shadow?" Dietrich asked.

Abaddon felt the coolness of the Dagger's metal, the pulse of its power. He didn't answer.

Dietrich's head slumped down, his eyes fixated on the dirt beside him. His palm lay upturned, empty.

Abaddon took a step forward. His pulse pounded against his head. His eyes stung, wanting to weep.

Dietrich looked so similar to how their father had. Just before he'd killed him.

"What of our parents?" Dietrich asked. "What of our mother?"

Abaddon stood silent, the Dagger growing heavy. He tried to wet his lips to speak, but his throat was dry, and no saliva came. He settled for shaking his head.

Dietrich nodded. Tears fell down his dirtied face, leaving thin, derisive lines.

"Father," Abaddon finally managed. His own eyes dampened, his heart crushed and broken at the sight of his brother crying. "Father is dead too."

Dietrich looked up.

"What?"

He took hold of the spear at his side, his vengeful vice awakened. Abaddon almost took a step back but stopped, trying to convince himself not to fear Dietrich. They were brothers after all. Dietrich would understand. He would listen.

He had to.

"He wanted to take his own life," Abaddon started. It felt right, to finally admit it. He fell to his knees.

"I couldn't let him. I couldn't let him take his life himself."

I suppose I don't know for sure though. I've never tried to call on the Dagger.

From a letter between Dorian Cliffborne and Abaddon Haroldson

CHAPTER 94

DIETRICH

Abaddon was lying. Or madness had taken him.
The cruelty of what he'd implied was too morbid to be true.

"Say you didn't kill him," Dietrich whispered. He rose, adjusting the grip on his spear. "Say you didn't kill him."

Abaddon looked up from where he kneeled. He took his turn to weep, his body racked with sobs.

"Please," he pleaded. "Please, Dietrich, don't do this. He wanted death—he begged me for it! If I hadn't taken his life, he would've taken it himself. And he wanted to go to the Light when he died. He wanted to rest with Mother—"

Dietrich yanked Abaddon's chin up with the point of the spear, its edge resting just above his throat.

"Why, Abaddon? Why, with all the enemies we share, would it be you to kill our father?"

He waited. Abaddon would give him an answer. He'd say

something to make this all clearer.

But he said nothing. He simply sat there, crying, letting the spear prick his skin.

This was Dietrich's fault somehow—it had to be. Abaddon was the good one, the faithful one. He wouldn't have killed their father if Dietrich had been there to stop him. He wouldn't have been so burdened—so astray—if he'd had his brother there for guidance.

Tossing his spear away, Dietrich kneeled to the ground, grabbing Abaddon's neck.

"Forgive me," he whispered. He shifted his grip to Abaddon's face, clutching it tightly. "Forgive me . . ."

His words faltered.

A pain stabbed at his gut.

Numb, Dietrich looked down. Abaddon's hand was there, pulling the Dagger of Eve from his stomach. Blood pooled around it, dark and wet and rapid.

Inching back, Abaddon stared, jaw twitching. He didn't want to do this—Dietrich could see it when he met his eyes—but he grabbed his shoulder again, thrusting the blade in. It twisted slightly, metal against flesh, then slipped back out.

The hilt of the Dagger brightened. A ringing started, haunting and sharp, like a harmony to drifting *auroras*.

"I'm sorry," Abaddon whispered. His voice sounded distant, hazy, as if it was miles away instead of inches. His veins traced black beneath his skin, his eyes darkening.

"I'm sorry."

Dietrich felt Abaddon's lips against his temple, and his arms around his body. Then he felt Abaddon lower him to the ground, whispering something before getting up and walking away.

With blood warming his skin, and pain in his gut, Dietrich closed his eyes, fighting the coming darkness.

To keep the bells from cracking, use a special coating made from the blood of a fiend common along our shoreline called a bellfish. Not a creative name, but it's easy enough to remember.

From a Riverdian manual for the town bells

CHAPTER 95

X'ODIA

Crickets chirped. They shouldn't have—night was already long past—yet somewhere, amid the other noises of the woods, they sounded. A raven cawed too, and rodents scampered. X'odia leaned her head against the rough bark of a tree and held her wrists to her ears as something thudded in front of her.

"This should be a fine enough supper," the blond archer said, holding the carcass up for her to see.

X'odia tried not to wrinkle her nose at it.

"What's the matter? You don't like rabbit?"

"I've never eaten meat."

"Never eaten meat?" He picked the rabbit back up, pressing against its joint. X'odia cringed, watching with disgust as he began separating the animal's hide.

"Explains why you're so thin," he said, gesturing toward

her. "I'd be too if all I ate was plants."

He attempted a grin, but it was halfhearted. X'odia didn't bother with a response.

The blond man, the archer who'd helped her escape Vahd'eel, was Roland Laighless. His stained clothing and unkempt appearance didn't convey his identity, but X'odia knew it was him from her visions. It was clear he'd been in disguise, hoping to pass himself off as a common traveler during his trek to Riverdee. He'd come to retrieve his Elite, lead them through the Forest of Fiends and back to Mesidia.

She'd been all that was left.

Roland was determined on riding back to Mesidia. He'd need to gather supplies from Riverdee's city before they left, but after that, he planned to head back home. X'odia requested they free Ravel and Bronal and the rest of the Evean sailors while they were in the city, in exchange for her help with Mesidia's war. She wasn't sure whether Roland had that much leverage in Riverdee, or that the sailors were even alive, but he'd agreed.

They sat in silence for a time. Roland prepared and cooked his meal, and X'odia listened to the crickets. Dravian's cloak lay around her shoulders, so she pulled it tight, wishing he hadn't died. Along its bottom, despite having tried to wash it off, his blood still remained.

The bells within Riverdee's city rang, but X'odia ignored them, thinking it nothing important. Roland sat up, head perked like a hound's.

"The bells only ring when tragedies occur." He stood from their campfire and began collecting their things. "We must make haste if we want to know what's happened. I'd say I'm sorry that we might miss some sleep, but you don't seem to sleep much anyway."

X'odia took a nervous breath and rose. Riverdee's citizens likely still thought her a criminal—and Markeem's killer. She'd have to keep her gaze down, and the hood of her cloak up, once they got there.

With only one horse, they rode together into the city. The closer they got to it the louder the bells became.

When they'd reached the outskirts of the city, Roland dismounted, then helped X'odia down. He cast up the hood of his cloak before nodding for her to do the same.

"Riverdee is its own nation," he said, "but it's a sister nation to both Mesidia and Xenith. Many of its people are northern born. There's a chance someone might recognize me."

X'odia nodded. She wasn't sure why Roland was telling her anything, but a small part of her was grateful. After being a prisoner for so long, it was nice to be treated as a person.

"What's happened?" Roland asked a passerby. His accent shifted, mimicking the Riverdian speech.

"The Laighlesses," the man said, shaking his head sadly. "Haven't ye heard?"

A muscle in Roland's jaw twitched.

"Nay, sir, we haven't."

The man, short and balding, ran his hand where hair used to be.

"Dietrich of Sadie," the man said. "That one they call the Cloaked Prince. He killed 'em, the whole lot. They're the ones who sent troops here, you know, before the fiends came. If it weren't for them, we'd all be dead."

X'odia stood in shock. She turned to Roland, watching for his reaction.

He narrowed his eyes, saying nothing.

The bells continued to ring.

Clouds opened up and rain began to pour. X'odia and Roland found their way to an inn's great room, eager to keep warm. A bard in the room's center sang songs of Mesidia, of its breaking and its heroes, already having added verses that included the Laighlesses's names.

"I don't know what to do," Roland said quietly. He clutched the hilt of a *touched* knife, spinning its blade against the wooden table they sat at. His eyes drifted to the people around them.

X'odia *called* air and forced his blade to still. He glared at her, but let it go.

"Perhaps you should go after Vahd'eel," she said. "And his allies."

Roland opened his mouth to answer, but a barmaid came to ask for orders. X'odia immediately looked away, hoping the woman hadn't seen her swirling eyes. Roland ordered for them both.

"I don't drink," she said, once the barmaid was gone. Roland pursed his lips and shrugged, looking about the room.

"I do."

They listened to the bard until the barmaid returned. The singer wasn't particularly gifted, but his lilting voice ensnared those around him.

"Do you have bards in Eve?" Roland asked. X'odia peeled her eyes from the man.

"Yes," she answered. "Most everyone in Eve sings."

Roland nodded and took a drink from his tankard. Some of the liquid dripped down his chin, but he wiped it away with his sleeve. He lifted it back up and drank again until the liquid was gone, then shoved it aside and grabbed the one meant for X'odia.

"I've seen them before, you know. Those twins. They killed someone close to me."

X'odia grabbed at the tankard, deciding she wished to try

it. Roland, about to drink more, pulled it down slowly, then handed it over.

She looked into the golden liquid, wondering what could be so wonderfully fulfilling about it. She'd never had it before, but she'd read stories of men who'd lose themselves in it. It must be delicious, and the drunkenness blissful, if so many found it intoxicating.

With Roland watching her, she lifted the tankard up and took a drink.

She immediately starting hacking.

"That's awful! How does anyone drink that?"

"Hush, woman. You'll make people stare."

The words were harsh, but a weary smile twitched at Roland's lips. When she kept coughing, he reached out and took the tankard back. He finished it and waved the barmaid over, ordering something else. When it arrived, he handed her the coin for it, then affably slid it to X'odia.

"That one's not as strong, and it has a sweet herb in it. It's a better one to start with."

She grimaced but gave it a chance. It was indeed sweet, almost overwhelmingly so, with a hint of spice mixed in. It went down much smoother than the last and didn't make her throat burn. It did still make her head swell a little, and her stomach warm, but the feeling quickly vanished.

"I heal," she said. Roland nodded that he already knew, but she waved her hand. "No, I mean I can't get drunk. At least I don't think."

"Well that's a shame. The getting drunk bit is the best part."

"Is it?"

"Yes. It's what helps you forget."

He sniffed then, and X'odia realized he was fighting back tears. He held them in well enough, but his hand still lifted to his forehead to shield them.

"You shouldn't forget," she said. "You should mourn, like

a proper person, instead of holding it all in. Then once you've done that, you should think, plan, and act." She paused, tilting her head and leaning in until he looked at her. "I'll help you. Whatever path you choose."

He chuckled, sitting up and tapping the table with his fingers.

"Mesidian men don't mourn. Perhaps your Evean men weep, but not us. And what path do I have? The Elite are gone. I don't have the Dagger. And that bard there is singing my name with my family's." He paused, gesturing toward the bard before shaking his head. "Besides, why would you help me? I doubt I can get your friends out of prison now, not with people thinking I'm dead."

X'odia clenched the tankard, letting the cold of it sink into her fingers. It was foolish to help him, the son of the man who'd ordered her captive, but she owed him her allegiance. He trusted her, when he had little reason to, and he'd helped her escape from Vahd'eel. And, if she were being honest with herself, she wanted an ally to fight beside.

"I don't know which path is right," she started. "But whatever is happening with those people—with the ones who led the attacks—it's more important than Abra'am's wars. With your family gone, and your title as Guardian forfeited, perhaps this is the Creator's way of assigning you the task of their defeat."

Roland snorted. "Why me and not you? You're the one who heals."

She nodded at the point, shrugging her agreement.

"Not you then. Us."

The prince's lips thinned, as though he might be considering the idea. X'odia wanted to say more, wanted to convince him not to dwell in his self-pity and drunkenness. She wasn't one to condone violence, per say, but she also wasn't one to let crimes go unpunished. Righteousness was something she believed in wholeheartedly. Vahd'eel and his allies needed to be stopped.

Despite wishing to say so, X'odia kept her words back. If she was going to ally herself with Roland, she needed him to want to act. She couldn't be the one to push him into it.

"All right," he said finally, giving her a firm stare. Before she could say anything in response, he held up a finger, pointing between them. "But besides you and me, is there anyone else? Anyone else besides your sailor friends who might be able to help us?"

X'odia let out a breath, then took another sip of her tankard.

She thought on the query. There was someone else, someone even more powerful than she. Someone who'd protected Eve for centuries. Someone she trusted.

Resolute, she opened her mouth to reply.

The Holy Book mentions people who can feel and see events to come. Do you think so much time around the Amulet gifts me this Sight? I wonder sometimes, as I swear I see things in the paintings along the palace walls. Perhaps we'll have to ask Pierre if he's noticed anything similar from his Dagger. Though, if I'm being honest, I doubt he spends much time around art.

From a letter between Rose and Gerard Verigrad

CHAPTER 96

GWENIVERE

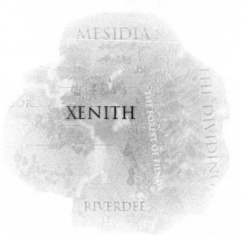

Gwenivere rested her forehead against the iron bars of her cell. The rods were smooth, and far enough apart that she could look out. Maximus and Aden sat cross-legged there, just outside her cell, each taking turns in their game finding matches to their cards. It looked to be a new deck from the last one she saw, the paintings now of people instead of fiends.

Aden flipped a card over, the first of his turn. On its face was a woman with brown eyes, pretty yet somewhat indistinguishable with a shadowy figure standing behind her. The figure was clearly a person, but only his—or her—eyes were visible, their lids heavy and coated with dark lashes. Aden sat a moment as he contemplated his choice, then picked up a card nearest his corner. He grunted when a man in black emerged, his green eyes mocking his failure.

"Dammit," he whispered. Gwenivere's brows rose, as did

the knight's, both sharing a strange smile at her brother's curse. She hadn't thought such a thing would make her happy, but with her hands in element chains and her quarters traded for a prison cell, she found it did. She wondered if somewhere, atop the dungeon's grounds, Sir Charles was chastising Maximus's careless tongue and its effect on the prince.

The knight took his turn and flipped over a card neither had touched yet. It revealed another green-eyed man, his body completely covered as he crouched on the spire of a domed roof. A *called* blade was visible in the man's grasp, its edges intricate and serrated as it swirled into creation.

Maximus stared at the card awhile before surveying the others. He settled on one beside where Aden had grabbed, flipping it over and revealing a woman. She was young, with pretty, colorful veils covering her body and face. She kneeled at the foot of someone's throne.

The knight shook his head, then returned each card face-down before gesturing for Aden to go.

Blue was all that seemed to occupy Aden's next turn. Each card he picked had a knife in it, and each knife's hilt had a sapphire inside. They almost looked like a match, the prince grabbing them excitedly before noticing the subtle differences in the hands that held the knives. The first had been a man's, with the blade to his palm, a thin line emerging where the slender metal cut. In the second was a woman's, her arm held out in the same manner, yet this time the streak of blood started across her wrist rather than her palm. Maximus was quick to point out the difference, smiling gratefully to himself.

Gwenivere sighed as she watched the next round, her gaze all but lost as a young blond woman with short hair and light eyes was revealed. She wore a torn shirt, her shoulders and back bare as her bound wrists rose to shield her. Behind her stood a man, a whip in his hand, ready to slice her skin. Gwenivere went cold as she looked at the card, the girl's eyes strangely familiar.

Maximus pulled his hand to his jaw in thought, remembering all the places he and Aden had already tried. He reached for his next card, barely sliding its edge up to see, then quickly slammed it down in triumph.

It was the girl's match.

The door to the dungeon's hallway opened and closed with a screech. Gwenivere and her visitors looked up, each sitting a little straighter as the King of Peace walked in.

Maximus and Aden quickly picked up their game. Maximus gave Gerard a slight bow, then a hesitant farewell to Gwenivere. Aden grabbed her hand, squeezing it tightly.

Praying Aden didn't understand or care why she was locked away, she watched them leave, heart burdened.

Gerard sighed before looking around the dungeon. The other cells weren't always empty, but after sentencing her to imprisonment, Gerard had ordered the other prisoners to the Arctic.

Gwenivere was grateful.

"You understand why you were put here, yes?" he asked her. "Why you weren't permitted to stay in your chambers like before?"

Gwenivere scoffed as she looked at her cell. The distance was small, and likely the size of her old bed. She wondered if the duchess Yvaine had been kept in a similar cell back in Stonewall, before the Laighlesses had been killed.

"I'm a prisoner," she answered simply. "Prisoners belong in cells."

Gerard curled his lips beneath his beard, his chest rising and falling with strain. He grabbed hold of one of the cell bars and lowered himself to the ground, leaning his back against hers.

"It should be me in there," he said quietly. "I've kept you in a cage all your life and expected you to be content with the view outside your window. There is little shame in a person wanting to be free."

Gwenivere stared at the ground. Duty had always been his

agenda, peace and prosperity had always been his faith. No person or thing had ever changed that about him.

It hadn't always made him the best father, but it had made him a mighty king. It felt strange to hear him denounce his ways.

"During the War of Fire," he continued, folding his hands atop his lap, "when I first took reign, the Tiadorians and the Concordians had taken from us the value of our lands. They burned the fields of wheat and grain with salt, made sure the ground would never reap value again. I didn't know what to do. I didn't know how to bring back our nation's wealth.

"I signed a treaty with Rimsky and Anya of Prianthia and allowed them to use Xenith's eastern roads to spread their goods. We gained a percentage of the profits in exchange, and we managed to keep ourselves afloat until Mesidia was able to back us in the war. We won, but at a price. Prianthia was extracting everything they had by way of Sadiyan slaves.

"I knew that. I knew the whole time, but I did it all the same. I saved one nation, only to reap the coin of another's suffering."

Gwenivere sat in silence. She wanted to tell him to stop, wanted to believe her father had only ever done what was right and just as a king, but she kept quiet.

"When the War of Fire was done and Xenith began to prosper, I went against my treaty with the Prianthians. Mesidia backed me. Prianthia lost a great deal of their influence after a time, and when they grew weak enough, the slave revolts started. Harold of Sadie was quick to lead his people. I encouraged other nations, as well as our own, to lend their support to his cause.

"I came away a diplomat—a hero—because everyone assumed I knew nothing of Prianthia's slaving before and condemned it once I did. I was a hypocrite. I *am* a hypocrite. I wear the name King of Peace as though it does me a deserved honor, but it's a façade. I am not that man."

He stopped for a moment, unlacing a hand and rubbing at his beard. It was more grey than black now, as though wishing to display the stress his withheld lies had caused.

"This is why," he began again, "when the Redeemers preach that the West uses the East for its own gains, people listen. Their leader isn't some madman who spreads hate among a cult. He's a scholar, a man who saw everything that happened and understood it for what it was. He knows no treaty of ours will ever uphold."

Gwenivere listened, numb and empty. Were it anyone else admitting such a thing, she would've condemned them. As her own father, she felt as though a piece of her, of her view of her life, of her past, was being torn apart.

"I remember," she started, easing herself up, "when I first began to learn my harp, you and Mother used to take me to the theater where the musicians played.

"I couldn't believe the sounds. They were so perfect. So profound. I'd never heard anything like them. So I practiced my harp as best I could because I wanted to be like those musicians. I wanted to be on that stage, seeing all those people watching me.

"And then I had a dream. I was trapped on the stage I sought. There were all these people—beneath me, above me, behind me—yet I couldn't see them. The curtain to the stage was closed.

"In the dream, no matter how hard I practiced, I knew it wouldn't be me on stage when the curtains opened back up. I knew somehow that I'd end up in the seats on the outside, looking at someone else who'd taken my place."

Gerard reached the cell bars, taking her hand in his. He turned toward her, kissing her cheek and leaning his head on hers.

"I never meant for anyone to die," she whispered. "You

must know that, Father. You must know . . . "

A tear dampened her cheek. She wasn't sure if it was hers or her father's. He stood tall, sudden but firm, and pulled his hand back.

She listened to his footsteps as he walked away. Then, when his key had locked the dungeon shut, she let her tears fall and wept.

Garron Hillborne,

There are none more loyal than the Golden Knight. I wonder, after all that has been revealed of Gwenivere, what he is going through. He always loved her as his own daughter.

From the sketchbook of Elizabeth al'Murtagh

Chapter 97

GARRON

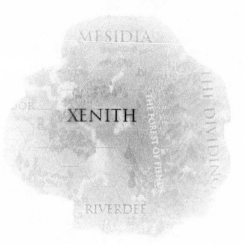

"Step forward, Garron."

The Golden Knight did as he was told. He stood at attention, politely folding his hands behind his back. He wondered if this was the day Gerard ordered his armor removed. He deserved it. He'd failed to keep his charge safe. It ate at his soul knowing she was in their dungeons, kept confined like a common thief or bandit.

It should be him in there. The Light knew she was far purer a soul than he. He was known for his reputation in the War of Fire. He'd earned honor by slaying men.

She'd earned a cell for trying to aid those she loved.

Garron faced the king, awaiting his judgment.

"Besides the moments you confessed before the Treaty of Five"—Gerard started— "had you ever seen Gwenivere allied with Prince Dietrich? Had you ever caught her speaking to him before all of this? Intercepted any letters sent her way?"

Garron's shoulders sank. Inside his chest, his heart twisted. "No, sire, I had not."

"Do you believe her innocent? Do you believe, in her own way, her alliances were meant to help?"

Garron held his chin high, proud to at least show dignity on Gwenivere's behalf. "Yes, sire. I believe nothing truer of the princess."

Gerard pursed his lips, nodding.

"For the failures you've incurred, you can no longer serve as a knight of Xenith. You shall have one last task before you leave the palace and Voradeen behind."

"Yes, sire," Garron said. Shame itself was a boulder on his shoulders, but he dropped his knee to the ground. "Anything you command, I'll fulfill."

The King of Peace took a deep breath, then sat down in his throne and waved toward the door of the chamber.

"Free Gwenivere from her cell. Get her as far from here as you can. Do this, the last order to your name, before the Treaty of Five and the Courts of Xenith put her on trial.

"You're dismissed."

The Golden Knight rummaged through the things in Gwenivere's room. He fumbled through her shelves, and drawers and desks, seeking out items for their escape.

If he was caught, it would be a noose to his neck.

When he'd finished collecting things, he headed for her cell. It was his turn to guard it, so getting there wasn't difficult. If anyone looked inside the satchel he'd packed, he could say the cloak was to warm her, the glass rose was to remind her of her mother, and the pepper tree leaves were for her to smell.

When he reached the dungeon, his fingers shook. He dismissed the knight who was currently on guard, wondering with a beating heart if he came across suspicious or uncharacteristic in any way.

Based on the knight's relief to have his shift end, it would seem he had not.

After being alone for a decent length of time, Garron turned to face the dungeon's entrance. The inside of its walls were melded and shaped with elemental rock to absorb any attempts to set them ablaze or cast a wind upon them. That wouldn't be a concern. He didn't need to *call* any elements from within the dungeon. It would be when he'd gotten Gwenivere out, forced to navigate through the palace without trying to harm any of his fellow knights, that he'd have something to overcome.

Taking a deep breath, he pressed the key into its slot, turned it, and opened the dungeon door.

Gwenivere looked up, her body garbed in the same clothing as the day she'd been chained. It pained Garron to see her as she was, eyes puffy and tired, nose red from crying, but he swallowed the emotion and made his way to her cell, tossing the satchel through its bars.

"Put the cloak on," he ordered, *calling* a blaze and setting it to her bars. "And be prepared to make haste. Your father has ordered me to help you escape."

I love you Gerard, but you have been a poor father to our daughter. She hardly knows you.

Promise me, when our son is born, that you will make more time for them.

From a letter between Rose and Gerard Verigrad

CHAPTER 98

GERARD

Gerard admired the portrait of his wife. He'd brought it with him from the Castle Fortress, and he'd looked on it often in times of stress. It gave him comfort. There were speckles of blood on it from his coughs, but Rose was still perfect.

He'd done many things she'd be ashamed of. Especially recently. But this ploy to free their daughter, to rid her of her plights, was hopefully one she'd condone.

"Rose was a fine queen," Natalia said, gesturing to the portrait. "It's a shame she died so young."

Gerard didn't say anything to that. He didn't really want company, but it was imperative Natalia be with him. If she discovered Garron was helping Gwenivere escape, she'd likely interfere. Nicolas, standing outside the room's door, was there as much to guard them as he was to keep her in.

"Do you think I believed you when you said you told

Gwenivere where your mother was being held?" Gerard asked, setting the portrait down. "Do you think I'd believe the tale you wove before the Treaty?"

Natalia's eyes narrowed.

"Are you accusing me of killing the Laighless family? You read what my mother reported; it was Dietrich of Sadie who killed them. I have no connection to that man."

"First," Gerard said, taking a step toward her. "Your mother didn't say it was Dietrich who killed them. If she had, I would've claimed her story completely falsified. Aside from his appearances here, Dietrich has never been seen on this side of the Dividing Wall."

"She said she saw a dragon." Natalia cocked her head. "How many assassins has Abra'am seen with dragons?"

"None," Gerard admitted. He smiled smugly and pointed a finger. "Which is why I said I'd have claimed her story *completely* falsified. As it stands, I think the dragon part of her story is untrue."

Natalia returned her arms to her side, unnaturally elegant and still. Even if his pressings weren't accurate, any person trialed by their king should be nervous. She was too steady to not be guilty.

"As you stated in your admittance," he went on, "I would find it logged that you'd visited Gwenivere before the Treaty of Five convened. However, I also found other logs interesting, ones in which you and the Verkevs were both noted. Prianthia is a nation that stands to gain much if we cut off our allegiance to Sadie. Without us as a means of income, Sadie would grow weak, and Prianthia could potentially take them back into slavery."

"I care little for Prianthian squabbles," Natalia said. "Or those of Sadie's."

Gerard took her hand in his, running his fingers along the scar across her palm. It'd healed smoothly, if a bit slow, but its discoloration was still prominent.

"Please, I cannot have this nation torn apart," he said softly. He let his tone grow sincerer, hoping she'd realize he only wished to mend what'd been broken. "I need to know everything that's—"

His throat tickled, interrupting him. He tried to ignore it, but the burning in his chest heightened. He pulled his hand from Natalia to shield his coughs, praying they'd subside after a moment and allow him some reprieve. She asked if he was all right, her bright eyes concerned, before rushing to get him a glass of water. It fell when she shakily tried to bring it back to him.

He held up a hand to ease her concerns, to tell her not to fret about him or the water or the broken glass, but his knees, growing weak, fell beneath him. More coughs came. Blood splattered against his sleeve, red and derisive.

"Nicolas!" Natalia shouted frantically. She returned to Gerard's side, placing a hand on his shoulder. "Nicolas!"

The knight burst into the room. It only took him a moment before he was on the ground beside them.

"Help him," she pleaded. Gerard tried to take the hand she held against him, assure her the coughing would pass, but he couldn't speak. He couldn't move.

Nicolas rose and ran to the cupboard. He knew of Gerard's ailment, and he knew which herbs would soothe his throat. Everything would be all right once he had those.

Even as the thought crossed his mind, Gerard knew this time was different. The coughs were too strong, too violent. They weren't going to leave him once he had the herbs. They weren't going to leave him at all.

He finally managed to grab Natalia's hand. He couldn't see her, not with his eyes squeezed shut, but he felt peace knowing he'd done what he could to save her and his daughter. They'd both be safe now—they'd both be free. Aden would be safe too. He was a good son.

Gerard took one last attempt at breath but failed. He thought of his queen, of her blood-splattered portrait, of her deep red hair and easy smile, and wondered if she'd be happy with the last things he'd done.

Is Natalia as cunning as people claim?
Yes.

From a letter between Dorian Cliffborne and Abaddon
Haroldson

CHAPTER 99

NATALIA

Gerard Verigrad was dead.

Natalia held back a sob. She peeled Gerard's lids back, not wanting it to be true. She looked at his eyes, blue, as they'd always been, but empty.

"Nicolas," she whispered, trying to keep her voice even. She shook her head, closing Gerard's lids back shut, and glanced at her knight. "Nicolas, what do we do?"

The knight swallowed loudly, then cleared his throat. He still held the herbs he'd fetched in his hand.

"We have to tell Sir Charles," he said. "He'll . . . he'll know what to do."

Natalia turned to him, forcing herself to gain back some semblance of control. She sniffed and rubbed her nose, hardly noticing when her hand came away wet.

"Yes, that's for the best. He'll have known this was coming.

Gerard's been sick for some time."

Nicolas let out a boyish sob, walking over to Gerard's body and kneeling with quivering lips.

"Charles didn't know," he said, voice choked. "Only I did."

Natalia blinked. Her fingers fumbled through Gerard's hair, her mind racing at the admission. Only him? Only her knight? That meant Sir Garron and Sir Maximus didn't know, or Gwenivere and Aden. Yet here she was, the woman everyone said craved power, the woman everyone accused of manipulation and deceit, holding the corpse of the King of Peace.

"No one else knows?" she asked. Desperation slipped through. She couldn't believe Nicolas was the only one. Someone else had to know. Someone besides her own knight—

"Only me," Nicolas answered. After a moment's thought, he added, "And . . . and the Laighlesses."

Natalia shut her eyes.

Her knight, and the family who'd just been slain.

Bells suddenly started ringing, loud and hard and mocking. Natalia thought them her own imagination, her own mind forcing mourning sounds to her ears. She held Gerard, at last accepting her dread, and began to quietly cry.

Nicolas stood. He walked around the corner of the room, opening the chamber door.

Someone shouted. Nicolas said something back. Sir Charles was called for.

I'm sorry Gerard, Natalia thought, kissing the king's forehead. *You deserved a better life. You deserved a better death.*

"Gwenivere . . ."

It was Sir Charles who spoke. He was at the door now, but still out of sight from Gerard's corpse. He was panting. And yelling.

"Gwenivere," he said again. "Gwenivere . . . escaped!"

Natalia froze. She understood now; she realized the bells for what they were. Not imaginings—warnings. Alarms.

The princess of Xenith had broken free.

This is my chance, she thought, opening her eyes and setting her jaw. She knew people would think her Gerard's killer, knew people would think her vying for Xenith's throne. She wasn't going to take that blame. She wasn't going to let people think she was so disloyal and unjust. Gerard had loved her like his own daughter, and she'd loved him. She refused to be deemed his murderer.

Grabbing the *touched* sword at his belt, she lifted it up, whispered her remorse, and plunged the blade into his gut.

"She killed him!" she yelled hysterically, scattering the now-pooling blood. She couldn't have it looking too fresh. It needed to look like she'd found him that way.

"Charles!" she shouted again. "Charles, she killed him! Gwenivere killed him!"

Nicolas and Charles rounded the corner. The old man stood motionless, stunned, then ran to Gerard's body.

Natalia looked up at Nicolas. She wept. She glared. She challenged him to deny her lie.

He only stood motionless. Whether out of loyalty to her, or shock or misperception, he didn't utter a word.

If found, please bring Gwenivere Verigrad to King Aden Verigrad and Queen Regent Natalia Barie. The former heir is wanted for the murder of her father, our mighty King of Peace.

From a note pinned in a Voradeen tavern

CHAPTER 100

GARRON

"Must the world always be in a state of mourning?"
The Golden Knight followed Gwenivere's gaze, taking in the mournful sea of black in Voradeen's streets. The bells hadn't stopped ringing since the day he had led Gwenivere to her escape. It would seem her father had been pronounced dead.

Banners proclaimed Gwenivere the killer. Hardly any two showed the same face, even fewer the right shade of her eyes, but the red of her hair had been consistent.

Even that was a deterrence, though, a misrepresentation of the color her strands now shone. It had been dyed a dull blonde, and cut short, jagged at its ends after she'd chopped it off. The pepper tree leaves he'd brought her had proven useful.

"The bloodthirsty will always need blood," he answered simply. "It need not matter if it comes from the righteous."

Gwenivere said nothing. She stared from the cliffs of their

camp as she watched the blackness stir. Even from where they stood, they could hear the cries of torment as the funeral march came to a halt.

Her father's *auroras* had begun to drift.

"It was them," she said, her voice rasped. Days had gone by of her cries and weeping, but not a tear fell now as she gazed out beyond them. "It was the Treaty of Five. Not a single one of them now remains in Xenith to pay him mourning. After moons of their incessant presence, all have ventured back to their homelands."

"Seems too concurrent a time to me."

Garron rubbed at the place where his beard had once been. Not in all his years of service had it ever abandoned his face. His long hair was gone too, shaved off with the small blade in his pocket.

"Concord and Tiador will take this chance, if they can," Gwenivere continued. "The War of Fire may seem a far gone past, but it's still a mocking presence for their people. They won't show mercy now that it's a boy they face."

Despite the distance, Garron thought he could make out the small stance of Aden before Gerard's sling. Natalia Barie stood a few feet back, a black veil shielding her golden-silver locks.

"I will seek justice on them all," Gwenivere whispered. "The peace is broken, and I will not let them dictate who next shall fall."

She stared a moment at her knight before guiding her mare from the cliff's edge and into the forest. Garron let out a heavy breath, then tugged at his reins to follow.

Abaddon Haroldson

With all that has happened, Dorian believes Abaddon Haroldson, now king of Sadie, is innocent. I do not hold those same beliefs. I am glad Xenith and Mesidia have ceased trade with his country.

There are rumors that Abaddon now has the Dagger of Eve, though, and that he's called on its immortality. I pray to the Creator this isn't true. If one Sadiyan prince as a mortal can ally with fiends and kill royals, what can the other do with no fear of death?

From the sketchbook of Elizabeth al'Murtagh

Epilogue

ABADDON

SADIE

Night had come.

Abaddon, son of Harold, son of Rorik, King of Sadie, feared the night. He feared it more than most feared the voices of their enemies. It was haunting. It was cruel.

Sovereignty, Sadie was shadowed as stars shone. Night meant the yellows of the desert became dark. The sky became blue and violet and black. Even the balcony Abaddon stood on seemed grey from the ascending moon.

He watched the colors shift and change from beneath the weight of his crown. Most of the colors faded against the clays of the capital's buildings, but some reflected from the glass domes of the hospitals and temples. If Abaddon weren't standing where he was, he'd see the night reflecting from the domes of his family's palace.

Not his family's. His. It'd been his for weeks.

He looked from the moon to his city, admiring its simplicity. Most of the shops and homes were made of clay, and cleanly cut. Abaddon used to wonder which flat rooftop Dietrich had been sleeping on for the night. It'd been a game he'd played, when he hadn't been able to sleep. No matter where Dietrich was, he would've at least seen the moon, and all the flecks of stars that had glistened brightly behind it.

"I'm sorry no one was there to watch your *auroras* drift, Dietrich," Abaddon whispered. "You were a good man—too good for the life you were given."

"I'm sorry I killed you."

He glanced down at the Dagger of Eve, pulling it from its sheath. It was so simple a thing, the blade straight and sharp, the grip comfortable. If not for the glowing stone in its hilt, it would've been no different than any other *touched* blade. How strange that something so mundane contained so much power.

"I'm sorry," he said again, letting his eyes get lost in the different colors of the stone. "I'm sorry, Brother."

He slid the Dagger back in its sheath and looked away from it. Instinctively he picked out which rooftop he thought Dietrich would dwell on, deciding it was far better he did that than think him dead.

A knock at his door disrupted his musings. He took a deep breath and said farewell to his city, walking back into his chambers and locking the door to his balcony. The knocking continued incessantly. When he opened the door, he found his watchman Culter, along with a young man, standing in his doorway.

"Culter," Abaddon said, nodding to his watchman. The youth behind him was short, with fidgeting fingers and thick-rimmed spectacles.

"Sam?"

"Your-your majesty."

Abaddon took the young man in with amusement, realizing after a second that they likely weren't far apart in age. Yet there they stood, one a stuttering healer boy who worked in the hospital, the other an immortal king. The only thing separating them was an old, tired-looking watchman.

"He has a message for you, milord," Culter said. "But he refuses to allow any of our men to relay the message on his behalf. He claims the message must be delivered directly to you, and that it's only for you to hear."

Behind him, Sam wrapped his arms around himself. There was a parchment in his hands.

"If anyone else does this, you have my permission to lock them in the dungeons," Abaddon said. "For the healer Sam, here, you needn't worry. Tell the men I said so as well. If he claims his message is urgent and in demand of private deliverance, then he shall have it."

Culter gave a quiet, "Yes, milord" before asking if he was dismissed. Abaddon waved him off and gestured Sam in, closing the door behind them.

"What news do you bring me, Sam?" Abaddon asked. "It's late, and while I appreciate the earnestness with which you've delivered your message, I must remind you that you're not in a position to make such demands of my watchmen. Or of your king."

Sam's throat bobbed. He set the parchment down on a table beside him.

Abaddon took it. It had no seal or envelope, just a simple crease down its center.

"Who sent this? There's no seal."

"Yes, your majesty, my apologies. It didn't come with one."

"Who was the messenger, then?"

"Yeltaire Veen."

Abaddon froze. Yeltaire Veen was Dietrich's alias. It was who he pretended to be when he hunted fiends rather than men.

"I see. Thank you, Sam, for your loyalty. Forgive me my hostility—it's difficult for me to know who to trust. You may leave."

Sam nodded, then stuttered a response. Abaddon hardly heard it, instead grabbing for his chamber's door and opening it for Sam to leave. He did so quickly, bowing one last time before slipping out.

Abaddon stood motionless. He waited until he no longer heard Sam's footsteps before looking back at the parchment. Slowly, carefully, he read each word of the message. Then read them again. Then again. Then again.

Fear justice in the light, they started, mocking and warning. They didn't change no matter how many times Abaddon read them. When his sight blurred he rubbed at his eyes, trying to see the words differently, but they always said the same thing. Breathing quickly, heart pounding, he pinched his nose, squeezed his eyes shut, then opened them and read the words one last time.

Fear justice in the light.
Seek refuge in the shadows.
The Assassin Prince lives.

CHARACTER LIST

A compilation of individuals from various kingdoms, taken from the letters of Ambassador Dorian and Prince Abaddon, reports from Dravian Valcor to Pierre Laighless, notes from the High Council of Eve, travel entries from Dietrich Haroldson, and Peace Gathering reservations from Sir Charles of Xenith.

Abaddon Haroldson:
younger prince of Sadie
Aden Verigrad:
prince of Xenith
Alanna Verkev:
daughter-heir of Prianthia
Alexandria Verkev:
royalty of Prianthia
Alkane:
Guardian to the Shield of Eve
Anastasia Verkev:
royalty of Prianthia
Bernard Barie VII:
duke of Mesidia

Brelain:
healer residing in the towns of the Dividing Wall
Bronal:
Evean captain of the *Seagull*
Catherine, al'Murtagh:
mother of al'Murtagh siblings, sister of Pierre Laighless
Charles:
personal knight of Gerard Verigrad
Cid Orloff:
member of the Evean High Council
Culter Sandborne:

head watchman of Sadie

Daensla:
mysterious Sadiyan woman tied to Dietrich Haroldson

Deladrine:
Sadiyan oracle

Dietrich Haroldson:
elder prince of Sadie

Dorian Cliffborne:
ambassador of Mesidia

Dravian Valcor:
head of the Elite

Edifor:
leader select of Yendor

Elizabeth al'Murtagh:
Mesidian royalty, cousin to Roland Laighless

Fiona Collinson:
wealthy woman residing in the towns of the Dividing Wall

Garron Hillborne:
personal knight to Gwenivere Verigrad

Gerard Verigrad:
king of Xenith

Gregory Collinson:
husband of Fiona

Gwenivere Verigrad:
princess of Xenith, Guardian to the Amulet of Eve

Harold Rorikson:
king of Sadie

Hedford:
commandant of Theatia

Joel al'Murtagh:
husband to Catherine, father to the al'Murtagh siblings

Lenore Daer:
queen of Sadie

Marie Hill:
late wife of Garron Hillborne

Markeem the Mute:
third in command of Mesidian Elite

Maximus Hillborne:
personal knight to Aden Verigrad

Merlin:
personal Elite to Roland Laighless

Natalia Barie:
duchess-heir of Mesidia

Navar:
leader of the Redeemers

Nicolai Verkev:
royalty of Prianthia

Nicolas Hillborne:
knight of Xenith

Odin Iceborne:
fourth in command of Mesidian Elite

Pasha Verkev:
assassinated royalty of Prianthia

Peter al'Murtagh:
Mesidian royalty, cousin to Roland Laighless

Pierre Laighless:
king of Mesidia
Ravel:
Evean sailor of the *Seagull*
Rellor Bordinsua:
second in command of
Mesidian Elite
Rokinoff Verkev:
royalty of Prianthia
Roland Laighless:
prince of Mesidia, Guardian
to the Amulet of Eve
Rosalie Laighless:
queen of Mesidia
Rose Verigrad:
late queen of Xenith
Samuel Sandborne:
healer residing in Sovereignty,
Sadie
Savine:
dragon residing in the
mountains Dividing Wall
Seera:
dragon residing in the
mountains Dividing Wall
Sehan Sand:
watchman of Sadie
Vahd'eel:
mysterious Evean man
Vanessa:
baroness of the Arctic
Veladee Verigrad:
cousin to Gwenivere Verigrad
Victor of the Black:
rumored assassin and shape-
shifter of the Redeemers
William al'Murtagh:
Mesidian royalty, cousin to
Roland Laighless
X'odia Daer'dee:
Evean woman, daughter of
Alkane
Yvaine Barie:
duchess of Mesidia
Zain:
boy residing in the towns of
the Dividing Wall
Zelhada Sand:
watchman of Sadie
Zoran:
dragon keeper residing in the
mountains of the Dividing
Wall